The Charm Necklace

Lauren Rosolino

melitta -
may you always find a light in the darkness and beauty in the brokenness.

cheers!

The Charm Necklace

Copyright © 2014 by Lauren Rosolino
www.laurenrosolino.com

This is a work of fiction. Names, characters, places, and incidents either are the product of the author's imagination or are used factiously.

All rights reserved. This book is protected under the copyright laws of the United State of America. Any reproduction or other unauthorized use of the material or artwork herein is prohibited without the express written permission of the author.

Published by Lauren M Rosolino Inc.

Cover photography by Jesse Speelman
Special font Freebooter Script by Apostrophic Labs
Edited by Barbara Bloom of Bloom Ink

First printing: June 2014

Library of Congress Control Number: 2014908970

Publisher's Cataloging-in-Publication
(Provided by Quality Books, Inc.)

Rosolino, Lauren.
    The charm necklace / Lauren Rosolino.
    pages cm
    ISBN-13: 978-1499377552
    ISBN-10: 149937755X

    1. Bereavement--Fiction. 2. Oakland County (Mich.)--Fiction. 3. Psychological fiction. I. Title

PS3618.O845145C43 2014 813'.6
    QBI14-600090

For Andrew,
my trail-blazing, techie partner in life.
Your courage, love, and support have given
me the strength to pursue my dreams.
You're a rule breaker and rebel.
I couldn't love you any more than
I already do.

Contents

Prologue

Part One
 1. Drowning
 2. Beginnings
 3. Give In to Me
 4. Stopped
 5. Gone
 6. The Bottomless Abyss of My Life
 7. Reality
 8. Plunged into the Depths
 9. Let the Pieces Fall
 10. Stand Still
 11. Guilty
 12. Till Death Do Us Part

Part Two
 13. Still Alive
 14. Seasons Change
 15. Leaves
 16. Contentment
 17. Spellbound
 18. Suspended
 19. Interrupted
 20. Home
 21. It Will Destroy You
 22. Stay
 23. Jump
 24. Letting Go

Epilogue

Prologue

Death comes so suddenly, out of nowhere. In the morning, you wake up in the arms of the one you love, that night you go to bed all by yourself. You remain in a state of shock asking yourself questions like *Did that really happen? Is he really dead? He can't possibly be dead, can he?* And you reassure yourself with statements like *He's just away on a business trip,* or *Just another late night at the office, that's all.*

Oh, you'll come up with 1,001 different reasons to justify your loved one's absence. Then you will start to move on to the *What ifs. What if I'd asked him to stop at the store on the way home like I was going to…? He wouldn't have been in that accident and he'd be in bed next to me right now.* Or you'll ask this, as fear seizes your heart, *What if he didn't know how much I really loved him, how deep I felt his love for me?*

During the days of the funeral, there's a surreal, foggy haze that descends on you that makes time slow down. And with so much to do, you can push away the cold, steely reality of death for a while. But at night, when you're lying in bed by yourself, it crashes into you relentlessly, wave after wave.

During this time, you see friends and long-lost relatives you hadn't seen since you were a child, and it hits you that nothing really matters: not those five extra pounds you were trying to lose, the back porch you've been meaning to repaint, that new show you forgot to record, those new designer shoes you've been lusting for. How could any of it matter in the face of death?

You're faced with the feeling that your life, your work, all your accomplishments are obsolete and meaningless when seen in the finality of death. All those things can't save you from it. You build, you work, you strive, and then you die. It's not like you can slow down the clock or bargain with Death for more time.

During the days of the funeral formalities, when you have time away from work and responsibilities, you begin to reflect. You tell yourself that you're going to spend more time with the people who matter most, you're going to start that exercise and diet routine to improve your health, and maybe you're even going to start volunteering more often. This way your life will matter, it will mean something; it won't all be for nothing.

When you can deny your loved one's death no longer, you will reach what is commonly known as the *angry stage*. You'll be mad at everyone and everything simply because they exist and he doesn't. You will throw things, punch the reflection in the mirror, scream, and curse. Oh yes, you will curse; *fuck* will become your new best friend. As for your house, it will be trashed from your tirades and filthy because you haven't cleaned up in weeks.

Next is the *acceptance stage*. This is when you finally get it: he's gone. He's never coming back. And there's not a damned thing you can do about it. You'll now accept that your life has no further meaning, no further purpose. Your life will become reduced to lying in bed all day, slowly succumbing to death as your body grows weak from lack of food and the willpower to go on. You'll only take a shower when you smell so bad that a stick of deodorant and a pocketful of posies will no longer cover up the stench. Your muscles will be sore from grief, your eyes dry from the thousands of tears you've shed. Your family and friends will have called so many times by now, but you'll never get their messages because your phone is buried in a box in the backyard.

At this point, you are a mere speck of dust in the scheme of things. Everyone else will go on living. But oh, not you. Your heart will hurt so bad you'll wrap your arms around your body to keep yourself from falling apart. It will be raw, painful, and ugly.

You'll be a zombie, void of any life, emotion, or thought. Your body will get up and go to work, but your mind will be stuck in some long-lost memory.

Maybe after this point, you'll start to come around. You'll return a friend's invitation to go shopping or maybe you will even pick up the phone and call her because she stopped calling you months ago after a lack of returned phone calls. Maybe you'll start to laugh again. It will feel wheezy, rusty, and off after months of nothing but crying. Your ribs will crack with the effort, but you'll get used to it again. Maybe little by little the life will return to your eyes, and you'll be able to move on.

    Or maybe you'll be like me and have so little left of yourself—with a wound so deep you wonder if it will ever heal—that you're barely hanging on to the edge.

Part One

I was falling fast, sinking. The cold water surrounded me on all sides, pushing in; the pressure was constant and heavy. I had stopped fighting for the surface; I didn't know which way was up, no light lit the way. I began to panic and thrash around. I gasped for air but found no reprieve. My lungs burned, and I knew I was suffocating. But despite the pain and the waves, I found solace in the silence. Then all was still. I drifted peacefully in the current. Oblivion was grace.
—Skylar Medina, February

I

Drowning

February 27, 2012

Sitting in the passenger seat of my dad's ancient white Bronco, I leaned my head against the window. The car smelled like spilled coffee and cleaning chemicals. It smelled like comfort. The defroster roared, rustling the memorial service papers with Michael's name and picture printed on them against the windshield.

Outside it was dreary and messy; the snow came down relentlessly. The clouds were gray and overbearing. They loomed around every open space, filling every crevice with their gloom.

The stone walls of the mausoleums stood as fortresses against the elements throughout the cemetery grounds. It was so miserable and desolate out there; I was pretty sure that even the dead people didn't want to be there.

"Honey, I'm going to go check on things," my dad said, pulling me out of my thoughts.

"Okay" was all I could manage. I didn't even have the energy to turn around and watch him leave.

The planning, the wake, and the mass were all a blur to me. Funerals are uncomfortable to begin with, but add on to that the crushing, overwhelming reality that my fiancé—my life, my future, my everything—was gone was just too much to consciously deal with.

Something about funeral traditions just doesn't sit right with me. The whole process of it is mystifying; people standing around a building, looking at pictures of the deceased, talking fondly of memories they had shared together, and then congregating together to listen to consoling words from an agent of the Lord. Don't get me wrong, I understand the idea of it all, of remembering and honoring those we've lost. It's the whole death thing I have a hard time with. How can someone be here one moment and gone the next?

Whenever someone approached me with their condolences, I tried so very hard to meet their eyes and be a functioning human being for those few moments. Most of the time they stumbled on their words, trying to find the right thing to say.

But here's the problem: there's nothing to say. There's nothing they can say that will make it any better. Nothing to make the searing pain go away. Nothing to bring Michael back.

My dad looked preoccupied as he walked back toward the car. His olive skin—passed down from his Brazilian heritage—was pale, and his rich brown eyes were clouded over. His thick black hair was spotted with gray and combed back neatly. His face was clean-shaven.

I got my height from my dad, but where I was all angles, he was full and substantial. He was handsome, even I was aware of this. He was also warm and kind, though at times inaccessible. Distant. Sequestered in a secret place in his mind.

I could see so much of myself in him: his complexion, his rough laughter, his ability to keep pressing forward even when it felt impossible. There was a gentleness about him, though, that I failed to possess.

My father was a romantic. He believed in true love, in the stars and planets aligning, and in happily ever after. Not the fairy tale version that took place in castles and horse-drawn carriages but the real-life kind: coming home from work to kiss his wife, spending evenings together, making a family and a home together.

I could only guess that his thoughts had something to do with his only daughter losing her Romeo just like he had lost his Juliet. He knew the heartache, the loss, the deep depression that swallowed me whole. I knew he wanted to shield me from it, shelter me, but he couldn't now any more than he could when I was seven and Mom died. And I think that's what hurt him more than anything else.

My mother had been sick; she had wasted away

slowly at first and then very rapidly at the end. We knew she was going to die. It was expected. Not that it made it any easier, but it made it different. Also, I didn't love my mom like I loved Michael. I mean, of course I loved her, so very much, like a child loves and adores her mother, but not with the same intensity, fierceness, and passion as I loved Michael.

When my mother died, I was sad and a little confused, but I wasn't lost because I still had my dad. As a child, I didn't know what losing my mother would mean when I got older, when she wasn't there to help me pick out a prom dress or help me get ready for my first date or help me when I first got my period. I didn't know, so I couldn't grieve for them.

But now, I knew everything that I had lost. I was so acutely aware that I had suddenly lost everything. In a single moment the rug had been ripped out from underneath me like a magician's trick. Everything I had defined myself by—Michael and a life with him—was gone. The tie was severed and I was lost at sea.

I knew that my dad was sad about losing Michael too. He had really grown to love him as a son over the past few years. He enjoyed Michael's laid-back nature and easy laughter. He appreciated when Michael helped him around the house. He trusted Michael to take care of me, to provide for me, to love me.

He had always wanted me to marry well, a doctor or lawyer perhaps, someone who could provide the best of everything for me, so that I could have more than I had growing up. But I never wanted all those shiny things anyway. I liked my life the way it was; there was nothing wrong with money being a little tight sometimes or having to spread out home improvement projects to fit the budget.

After he got over the fact that Michael never went to college and worked in construction, Dad was able to see how Michael and I fit so perfectly together. We were like jagged puzzle pieces, each of our own sharp, asymmetrical edges matching perfectly with the other. Where I was passionate and volatile, Michael was steady and strong. Where I was guarded, he was open and free. Where I was selfish, he was selfless.

We were the same in many aspects though. We both loved being outside and active. We both wanted a family one day, nothing big or grand or cookie-cutter, just something completely ours—messy, real, and full of love. And most of all, we wanted each other so badly it hurt. The fierceness of our love only grew more with each passing day.

And now there would be no more years together. We would never have a family together—. God, that hurt so much to admit. I was sad that Michael would never be a father, that he would never get to hold his newborn child, that he would never get to go to soccer games and cheer on the sidelines, that he would never get to take his kids to Disneyland to meet Mickey Mouse, that he would never walk his daughter down the aisle. It hurt that I would never have that with him.

A flash of red-hot anger seared through my sadness. He did not deserve this. I did not deserve this. I was pissed at…at who? God? The universe? Fate? The universe was unbiased and impersonal, fate was predetermined, but God? God was supposed to be personal, right? God was supposed to be good. God was supposed to be love. God was supposed to be righteous. The thing was, how could I be so mad at something, or someone, I didn't think I believed in?

Sophie, Michael's beautiful teenage sister, was following behind my dad. Sweet Sophie, with the same piercing blue eyes and ash blond hair as Michael. I felt a connection to her the first time I had met her at a family dinner.

Maybe it was her sensitivity or her openness that I admired most about her. Or maybe it was because she was one of those people who, when she looked at you, could see right into your soul. She wasn't afraid to engage with you or make herself vulnerable, even if it made her appear weak or wrong.

Like Michael, Sophie had a caring heart. She gave so much of her time and affection away to others. She had spent most of her summer break helping us around the house when we first moved in. It was thanks to her that the dining room got painted and the downstairs bathroom was fully decorated.

I had always enjoyed being with her, but I especially looked forward to the times she came over for dinner or to watch *Breaking Bad* with me. I loved having her around, listening to her talk about what she was reading in English class or the project she was working on for the student council. I got to be there as she tried on fifteen different dresses before finally settling on the form-fitting dark blue one for homecoming. I was there to help Michael intimidate the hell out of her date, Tommy, and fuss over her hair as they took pictures with their friends in front of the limo. She was the little sister I never had.

When they got to the car, Dad opened my door, leaned over me, and took the keys out of the ignition. I unbuckled my seatbelt and he pulled me to my feet. He felt so strong and unmovable, and next to him I felt how weak and fragile I really was.

My black boots crunched through the top layer of ice and then deeper into the snow. I could feel my dad's hand on my back guiding me. My body was still functioning, my legs carried me forward, and my lungs breathed in and out, but I was stuck inside my head. Always thinking, always remembering, always feeling the darkness of grief.

When I got to the site and saw the gravestone with the casket next to it, I felt as if my soul was being sucked out of me, I couldn't move or even cry. The stone read

Michael Donal Amherst
Loving son and brother
November 12, 1985-February 23, 2012

"It is not length of life, but depth of life."
—Ralph Waldo Emerson

My vision was cloudy, as if in a dream or some vacant memory. This couldn't be real. But it was. Way. Too. Fucking. Real.

I had always loved Michael's strong Irish name. Donal means *worldly mighty* in Irish, which Michael was in every aspect of his life. He didn't just create opportunities and experiences for himself or, at a bar, just happen to collide into the right person who knew someone who knew someone. These happenings flew at him from every direction like he was a magnet, and they never failed to surprise me.

The truth is the omission on Michael's gravestone—that Michael was my beloved, my future husband, my whole world—didn't bother me. What we had was something deeper than words could express. It was our little secret, and no one else had the right to access that. It was *ours*.

"You know why my parents love you?" I remember Michael asking me on a Sunday morning, as we lay tangled in a mess of sheets and blankets. "Because they see that you make me happy. With you, I'm who I'm meant to be. More myself."

I remember when he said that, my heart had melted, and whatever it was I wanted to say to him got choked up in my throat. I couldn't speak. All I could do was look at him, feel him, breathe him in, burning that moment into my memory so deep it could never be lost.

My eyes filled with tears.

The Charm Necklace

"Do you like it?" Dad asked hesitantly as he looked up and scanned the area in front of us. I followed his gaze, and that's when I noticed that we weren't the only ones at the gravesite. Everyone who was at the church was already here. Michael's family, friends, and guys from his work crew all sat in chairs under a tent. Standing farther away I could see some of my co-workers from the police department—Harry and a couple of the detectives. Standing in front of the tent were Michael's best friends, Shane Harris and Logan Parks, and Michael's parents, Rob and Sue. And they were all looking at me.

I swallowed hard. I was overwhelmed by their attention on me. It was like they were waiting with bated breath for me to freaking lose it, and I was going to if they didn't all stop looking at me.

Sue stepped forward and touched my arm. "Skylar…?" she asked.

I looked at her for a moment. I could see that her face was red from crying. She looked so tired and worn. I suddenly felt terrible that I had completely dumped the responsibility of planning the funeral on her. I didn't want to have to make any major decisions. I didn't want to make the wrong decisions.

"Skylar?" she asked again more forcefully.

"Yeah?" I whispered.

"I hope that you like the, uh," she said, nodding to the headstone. "I didn't know what you wanted, since you weren't there when we had to pick it out," she said without judgment.

"It's fine. It's nice," I said. "Really. Thank you for…everything."

She pulled me into a tight hug. "No, thank you for letting me do it." She let her arms drop to her sides, then I followed her and Rob underneath the tent.

Shane offered a weak smile as I walked past him and Logan. Logan just met my eyes with a deep, empty stare. Behind his eyes there was pain. These were Michael's two best friends; they had become mine too.

Inside my coat pocket I clutched my cell phone. A part of me held on to the hope that Michael would just call and tell me this had all been a huge mistake. He was actually on his way home now, he just had to work a longer shift than he originally thought, and he hadn't had time to call and tell me. He'd tell me that everything was going to be all right.

Here's what hurt the most: that in all of this, I just wanted him there to help me through it. It would be manageable if he were here, but he wasn't. This was all because he wasn't here. It was so hard to comprehend. It was cruel.

I leaned into my dad. I couldn't stand up on my own. Sophie held on to my other hand. Their body heat surrounded me, but I found no comfort in it. My heart felt like ice.

Reverend Romarro stepped up to the podium in front of the grave. He cleared his throat and blew his nose into a tissue. "Brothers and sisters in Christ, we meet here today to lay Michael Donal Amherst to rest."

He cleared his throat again. "We don't always understand why these things happen and we might never know. But we do know that through the glory of our Lord, Jesus Christ, life does not end in death. He was crucified, but on the third day he was risen! He tells us in John 11:25, 'I am the resurrection and the life. He who believes in me will live, even though he dies; and whoever lives and believes in me will never die.'

"So although we are saddened by Michael's passing, we must remember and rejoice in the fact that he is with our Lord, Jesus Christ, in paradise. Our loss is his gain. Remember this. Take heart in this. Jesus also tells us in John 16:33, 'I have told you all this so that you may have peace in me. Here on earth you will have many trials and sorrows. But take heart, because I have overcome the world.'

"Let us pray. Heavenly Father, we thank you...."

My mind drifted to Michael and the life we had started to build together, little by little, piece by piece. I thought about the day we first met during my sophomore year of college, our first date, the first time we made love, moving in together, all those days we spent in bed lying in each other's arms hidden away from the world. I thought about the proposal.

It happened two years ago. At the time we were living

in an apartment, still trying to figure out how to manage the bills and the responsibilities that came with being adults.

It had been just like any other day. I came home from work and we were in the kitchen making dinner. It was nothing special—spaghetti with meatballs, garlic bread.

I was standing by the stove, drinking my glass of wine, telling Michael about my day, getting worked up about a minor detail I had overlooked on a fraudulent insurance claim. He was watching me, smiling. The next thing I knew he was kneeling in front of me with a small velvet box in his hands.

I started laughing and covered my mouth with my free hand. "What is this?" I asked.

"Sky," he started to say, but he was smiling so hard he couldn't get the words out. "Skylar, my life hasn't been the same since you came into it. I can't live another day of my life without knowing that you will be in it forever as my wife. I love you, baby. Marry me?"

He opened the box and showed me the simple round diamond on a white gold band. It was the most beautiful thing I had ever seen in my life.

I knelt down in front of him. "Yes," I whispered. "Forever, yes."

He took the ring out of the box and slid it onto my left ring finger. I hugged him, wrapping arms around his neck. His arms were so secure. I'd never felt safer or more loved.

I pulled back to look at him and I searched his eyes. Then our lips met in a kiss so unbreakable and passionate—we never got around to eating dinner that night.

I was pulled back to reality by the ending of the prayer. "These things we ask in the name of the King of kings and Lord of lords, in Jesus Christ our Savior who is coming again."

And everyone said, "Amen."

Reverend Romarro continued, "May the peace be with you, my brothers and sisters. Go in the Lord's grace."

I thought about the words Reverend Romarro had spoken just moments ago. Did I hope that Michael was somewhere better, somewhere more peaceful, where pain and loneliness didn't exist? Yes, obviously. Did I believe that place was heaven and that some father-like figure with a great white beard was up there somewhere in the sky? No, not really.

Was I mad? Furious. Was I mad at the driver responsible for Michael's death? Beyond words. But was I mad at God? To be honest, I didn't think I believed in God. And if I did, did I believe that God was interested enough to intervene in our petty human matters? Why would God even care? And what would being mad at God or talking to God do? Nothing, as far as I was concerned. Yet that anger toward Him was undeniably there.

The fury inside me was dampened by grief, but I could feel a spark in my heart. I knew that the fire would keep building and burning until it ignited me and purified me with rage. I would get there, just not yet.

Then we all watched as the casket was lowered into the ground. I felt detached, like I was having an out-of-body experience where I was watching myself watch Michael's casket being lowered into the ground.

II

Beginnings

Michigan State University
Fall 2006

It was a Thursday night in early October when I first met Michael.

I left my room at nine and went downstairs to meet up with Ava, Molly, and Halle in the lobby of our building. Ava was a reed-thin blonde who, despite her size, could drink like a sailor. Molly was vivacious, bubbly, and an unapologetic flirt. Halle was the life of the party—loud, crazy, and uninhibited.

Before college, I had kept mostly to myself, busy with school, waitressing at the diner down the street, and walking dogs down at the shelter. I didn't have many friends, mostly because I found it hard to care about the same things most of my peers did—the opposite sex, the next party, sporting events, school dances.

Maybe I would never have a best friend in the

contemporary sense of the word, someone I would call at the end of the day, someone to share secrets and inside jokes with, but I valued friendship. I knew that if I couldn't find kindred spirits at one of the largest universities in America, I wouldn't find them anywhere.

And that's how, studying in the lounge room on a Saturday night freshmen year, I met Ava, Molly, and Halle. They were on their way out to a party, saw me by myself, and invited me to go along with them.

Ever since, I had become a de facto member of their group, joining them on weekends to parties, meeting up with them in the cafeteria, and going to the library together for late-night study sessions. I was definitely the most reserved and studious of the group, but I liked how it felt to belong to other people—accepted, cared for, wanted. I loved how normal and easy it was to walk down the hall and plop down on one of their sofa's to complain about an upcoming exam. I liked how I was more carefree and happy when I hung out with them. I loved all our crazy late night adventures and minutes spent rolling on the floor, our abs aching from laughing so hard.

I finally felt like I was growing into my own person, finding out who I really was. And wasn't that was college was all about?

Now, it was dark outside and there was already a chill in the air as we left the dorm. The streets across from campus were abuzz with music, girls squealing laughter, and the audible collective sigh of all the students ready for the early start of the weekend.

As we walked to the party, I wouldn't say I felt sexy, but it was nice to feel comfortable in my own skin. The waistband on my jeans wasn't digging into my stomach and my olive complexion was still smooth and radiant from the summer.

I was the most underdressed, as usual. While most of the other girls wore cute dresses or skirts with heels, I had on a gray V-neck sweater, jeans, and navy blue Chucks. My hair was straightened, for once, and it hung down my back like a long velvet curtain. I lined my dark brown eyes with black eyeliner and mascara, trying to draw attention away from my obviously sharp nose.

Around my neck was the silver charm necklace I always wore. It was a silver circle with an *S* engraved on the front. My mother had given it to me.

She had called me into the living room one afternoon. I remember the time of day because I was still a little queasy from the bus ride home from school, and Dad wasn't home from work yet. Mom lay on her hospital bed in the middle of the room, wrapped in thick faded comforters. The couch and coffee table had been pushed against the wall a few months ago to make room for the bed and all the medical equipment in the makeshift hospital room.

My mother, with her pale white skin and now-stringy brown hair, had said, "I want to be in the center of the house where all the life is. I don't want to miss anything tucked away in the bedroom."

So of course my dad had gone out of his way to accommodate her and make her comfortable. He hung thick, sun-blocking purple curtains so the nurse aide could draw them closed when the light became too much for my mother, and he bought a soothing humidifier to moisturize the air.

On that afternoon, mom's usually bright and beautiful gray eyes were hollow. They sunk into the bones of her face. I was so scared. All I wanted to do was go watch some cartoons in the other room.

"Baby," she whispered, patting the bed next to her. "Come here. I want to give you something."

She slowly pulled out a small black box from under the blankets and, straining with the effort, handed it over to me.

I sat down and removed the top. I pulled out a small silver chain with a round charm on it. I fingered the *S* on the front of it, wondering what she found so special about it.

"Look on the back," she instructed.

And there it was. The one word I would carry around with me like salvation: Strength.

"I'm so proud of what a good girl you've been since I got sick," she said, her voice resigned. She reached up to push my hair back from my face, her hands cold on my skin. "You've got to be strong for Daddy. And for yourself."

I looked down at the word engraved into the metal,

trying to understand but not wanting to. I sniffed, trying to remove the sting in my nose from the coming tears. "But never for me, baby girl," she said, pulling me down into a hug. "You never need to be strong for me."

And even as she was the one wasting away, she held me close to her chest and rocked me as I cried and told her I didn't want her to go.

Everyone had always assumed the *S* stood for my name, but I knew what it really stood for. And it was like our own private pact—a promise to each other that we'd both be okay no matter what happened.

I had never told anyone about the hidden meaning of the charm, not even my dad.

The party was at an imposing brown brick bungalow. There were a few people outside on the porch, and we could see all the people swarming inside. I followed Ava and Molly into the house. Halle was already off and about making herself the center of attention somewhere.

When we walked into the house, the only thing I could hear was noise. The music was so loud I could feel the vibrations from the bass coursing through my body. I could hear shouts from the dining room where a beer-pong tournament was taking place and the incomprehensible mass of voices having conversations throughout the house.

"Can we go outside?" I yelled into Molly's ear.

"Yeah, let's get something to drink first. I'm feeling thirsty tonight." She wriggled her eyebrows at me and laughed.

There were a few people out in the backyard. Some were sitting on the couches in the garage, and there was a group of guys standing around the fire in the middle of the yard.

"Cute guys ahead!" Molly said, making a beeline for the fire pit. Ava and I rolled our eyes and followed.

"Hey there, ladies," one of the guys said to us, as the fire crackled. "Come to join us?"

My bullshit detector was pretty strong after everything that had happened with Seth. I just didn't want to waste any more time on stupid guys, so my guard was instantly raised. But when I saw the way they hung back easily, without that predatory gleam in their eyes, I relaxed my defenses, allowing myself to enjoy their company.

Turns out, they weren't so bad after all. As the night went on, we all stood around the fire with our red Solo cups, talking about this Saturday's football game and laughing as some of the guys proudly shared tales of their walks of shame.

One of the guys caught my attention. He was funny and bantered back and forth with everyone in the group. He was easy. Easy to be around, easy to like.

He was wearing a red plaid button-down shirt and jeans with work boots. He had intense blue eyes and short blond hair under a baseball hat. His smile was what I liked the most—friendly and unassuming.

There wasn't an instant spark when I first met him. It wasn't like time slowed down as our eyes landed on each other, cue the romantic music. We didn't run toward each other in slow motion across a sunlit green meadow. But it was comfortable. It felt good. It felt right.

"You're pretty quiet tonight," he said as he moved next to me.

"I just like to listen." I smiled at him.

"Can I get you another drink?" he asked.

"No, thanks." Usually one drink was good enough for me to feel the buzz but still stay completely in control.

"I'm Mike."

"Skylar," I said, reaching out to shake his calloused hand.

He smirked at me.

"Hmm, I think you look more like a Michael than a Mike," I teased, instantly feeling comfortable around him.

"Michael? Well I suppose you can call me Michael," he said with a sigh.

"What's wrong with Michael?"

"I'll just feel like I'm getting in trouble every time you say my name."

I laughed. "You probably will be."

"True enough. So, Skylar, mind if I call you Sky?"

"Sure." I shrugged.

"What's your story?" He turned to face the fire, the golden glow lit up his face.

"What do you want to know?" I asked.

"Let's start with: Do you go to school here?"

"At MSU? Yeah, don't you?"

"No," he said, shaking his head. "My buddies from high school do. I'm just up here visiting."

"Where do you go to school then?" I asked.

"I don't. I work in construction."

"Oh," I said. "So where do you live?"

"Still back at home with my parents in New Baltimore."

"That's not very far from where I'm from," I said, then clarified, "Shelby Township."

He nodded. "I do a lot of work in that area."

"Do you like working construction?" I asked to keep the conversation going.

"Yeah, love it." There was no sarcasm in his voice.

"So is this, like, a career thing? Or do you plan on going to school eventually?"

"I don't plan to. I like what I do, I make enough money, and besides, I'm not really what they call studious," he laughed. "What about you? What's your major?"

"Criminal justice."

"What do you do with that? Become a cop or something?" He looked me over, and I knew he was thinking I didn't exactly look like law enforcement material.

"Yeah, or you can go into law or work for the government. But I'm not really sure exactly what I want to do with it yet."

Talking to him was as easy as breathing, so I continued.

"Originally I was an animal science major with the intention of going on to veterinary school. But my roommate last year had an Intro to Criminal Justice course, and I picked up her book one day and started reading through it."

"You read through a textbook? For fun?" he asked me, looking at me as if I had just told him I believed aliens had taken me captive and performed medical procedures on me.

I laughed. "It wasn't really like that. I was bored, so I started flipping through it, and I just found it fascinating."

He took another sip of his beer, watching me. I suddenly felt self-conscious and rushed to finish. "I signed up for the class the next semester and ended up switching my major."

"What made you switch?" he asked.

"Honestly?"

"Yeah." He nodded earnestly.

"I felt more passionate about it the first day of class than I ever had for the animal sciences classes I'd taken. It's as methodical as animal science, but it has a more human aspect to it. It's more meaningful. Every day you're actively working toward making an actual difference in people's lives."

He just smiled at me.

"Okay, that and maybe too many episodes of *Criminal Minds*," I laughed.

"What's *Criminal Minds*?"

"You don't know what *Criminal Minds* is? You know with Reid, Hotchner, Garcia? FBI profilers?" My skeptical stare made a wide grin break across his face, and I couldn't help but smile back. "You do know," I accused.

"Yes, yes, of course I do! I've seen it a few times. My sister loves that show. She has a crush on the one guy...."

"Morgan," we said at the same time.

"And so do you, apparently," he teased. "Well I guess if you're into guys with sensitive hearts, big muscles and who catch bad guys for a living."

"Now, who wouldn't be into that?"

"Well naturally, he's just so dreamy," he joked.

I laughed with him. "So you have a sister? Younger? Older?"

"Yes. Sophie. She's eleven. What about you? Any siblings?"

"Nope, only child. Wait—she's eleven and she likes *Criminal Minds*? Isn't she kind of young to be watching that? There's some gross stuff on there."

"Yeah, I know. She's kind of strange like that. *Mature* is the word she uses. Weird kid." He looked at me. "Only child? I remember the wonderful life I had before Sophie was born—endless presents on Christmas, new toys all the time, a nice bike, my own Super Nintendo. It was a good life."

"I guess," I offered.

"What? It wasn't like that for you?"

"No."

"You didn't like being an only child?"

"No, it's not that. It just wasn't always rainbows and butterflies. I mean, there was never really enough money for all that stuff."

Michael just looked at me, waiting for me to go on.

"Um, my mom, she uh…she died when I was seven. Cancer," I said, answering his unasked question. "And then it was just my dad and me. He's a janitor at a high school, and with my mom's medical bills, we were living paycheck to paycheck for a while."

Why was I telling him all these personal things? *Shut up, Skylar. Shut up!*

"I'm sorry," he said, looking straight at me, not down at the ground, not embarrassed or ashamed, but truly sorry. He was so open and honest. It was refreshing.

"No, it's fine. I mean, it sucked and sometimes it's hard without her, but we're okay. I'm okay. You learn that just about the worst thing in the world can happen, and life still goes on."

I wasn't sure if it was the reflection of the fire in his eyes or the darkness of the night around us that made it seem like he was looking at me so intently, but his gaze rooted me to the ground.

He made me feel like I was the only thing in the world that mattered, like everything I had to say captured his complete attention. For the next hour, oblivious to the party around us, we talked about anything and everything: our families, our friends, the new movies that were coming out, our tastes in beer.

I learned that his mom's name was Sue and that she was a secretary at an elementary school. His dad's name was Rob and he was head of New Baltimore's building department. And along with his sister Sophie, they had a German shepherd named Bruce who weighed 85 pounds.

I also learned that he had grown up with his best friends, Shane and Logan. He told me that he had felt left out when they had gone off to college without him last year. "But after seeing their dorm room, I couldn't live with them. Oh my God, no way. I know we're guys and being slobs is our innate duty or something, but seriously," he laughed.

He didn't hold grudges or have baggage. He wasn't weighed down. He was light as air.

"So they're sophomores too?" I asked.

He nodded.

"Has it been hard for you to be home without them there?"

"Kind of. I'm busy working most of the week, so that's not a problem. And I come up here any free weekend I have. I think it's just getting used to not being in school that's weird."

Before I could say anything in reply, he leaned into me, so close I could smell the clean and earthy scent of his cologne, the cotton in his shirt, and the beer on his breath.

"I think you're the most beautiful girl here," he whispered in my ear.

I laughed quietly. "Is that you or the beer talking?"

"Me," he said. "Or maybe a little bit of both," he smiled.

"Well, thanks," I said, smiling and tucking a piece of hair behind my ear, surprising even myself at how much I liked the effect he had on me.

Later that night, as Michael was walking me back to my dorm room, the campus was dark and silent. There was something magical about it—enchanted even.

"Well, this is me," I said nodding to the crumbling, beautiful stone building with cast iron windows and ivy-covered walls. "Thanks for walking me back. I appreciate it."

He stopped and turned toward me. "I like you," he simply said. "There's something different about you."

"I like you too." It was true. It was that simple.

"Can I call you sometime? Maybe next time I'm up here we can see each other or something?"

"Sure," I said with a grin.

"Good night, Sky," he said after numbers were exchanged. "Sleep tight."

"You too, Michael," I smiled as I turned to enter the building. "You too."

As I was drifting off to sleep that night, my thoughts drifted to Michael. I couldn't help but think that he was the kind of person who, once he was in your life, would never leave.

III

Give in to me

It had been a month since I had met Michael, and I'd seen him a few times over the weekends that he was up on campus. I had learned that he had played football in high school, that he loved when his mom made pumpkin pie, and that the first concert he attended was some local band named the Last Rose, among other things.

I also learned that I loved the way his arms wrapped around my waist when he held me close at the end of the night, not wanting to say goodbye. And the way he smelled—like cotton, the earthiness of his cologne, dirt, and concrete—it made me weak in the knees.

It was late on Friday night by the time Michael made it up to East Lansing. And even though it had only been five days since we had last seen each other, I'd been missing him terribly. Fitting him into my life was seamless. I looked

The Charm Necklace

forward to his phone calls before bed and my stomach fluttered whenever I got a text from him.

I held on to Michael's hand as I followed him into the crowded, hot party. I was glad that he was here and glad that the long week of working and studying was finally over.

I had been waiting for this moment all week long—that moment when you realize the night is young, when you anticipate all of its potential.

I was ready to let loose and have a good time. I wanted to feel the warm buzz from alcohol spread over me, and I wanted to feel Michael's hands on me even more. Things between us hadn't progressed any further than steamy make-out sessions outside my dorm.

But tonight he looked irresistibly hot in his gray T-shirt and jeans, and the look in his eyes told me that he wanted me just as badly as I wanted him.

This was nothing like how it was with Seth, my psychotic ex-boyfriend. He was so controlling and stiff. But Michael was free and fit like your favorite pair of blue jeans: comfortable and just right.

At the thought of Seth, the hairs on the back of my neck sprung up. I was sure it just a knee-jerk reaction, a conditioned response, but I couldn't shake the feeling that something was suddenly off about the energy in the room.

Michael led me to the kitchen and paid the keg guy $10 for two cups. I drank slowly and smiled up at him. He stepped closer to me and guided me through the kitchen into the living room.

As soon as we were past the doorway, he grabbed my arm and spun me around so I was facing him. He leaned his chest into me, pushed me against the wall, and covered my mouth with his. My heart exploded and my head started to spin. It felt so good and I wanted more.

"I've missed you, beautiful," he said into my ear, then kissed my neck. "I've been thinking about you all week."

"I've missed you, too," I said, gently pushing away from him so I could look at him. In my peripheral vision, I caught the briefest flash of angled cheekbones and dangerous dark brown eyes. Panic surged through my body, and I whipped my head around, searching faces in the room.

Michael felt my body stiffen and looked at me, concerned. "What's wrong?"

His voice brought me back to him. I let the muscles in my face relax as I searched his usually good-natured face, now pinched together.

I shook my head. "Nothing. I thought I saw something…," I trailed off. "When are the guys going to be here?"

"Any time now."

I was surprised at how easily Shane and Logan had accepted me into their world. I didn't mind that a good majority of the time I spent with Michael, I spent with them also, lounging around, playing video games, or going out. They were sort of a package deal, as strange as that was, because they were all so different.

Shane was tall and goofy with a big smile. He liked to tell dirty jokes and thought the sole purpose of college was to party. He was cute with his dimples and light auburn hair, but his most attractive features were his larger-than-life personality and even bigger heart.

Logan on the other hand, was serious, quiet, and thoughtful. He had dark, long brown hair that fell across his forehead and his face was smooth and clean. He was wicked smart with a double major in English and secondary education.

While Shane was affectionate and cheerful, Logan was careful and sensitive. He walked with an air of humble self-possession and had a hunger for knowledge. And even though he was completely approachable, his blue eyes often had a faraway look in them that made me hesitant to talk to him, not wanting to interrupt his thoughts.

I was about to ask Michael how his week was when a figure broke through the crowd. I knew, more from an innate sense than from the tattoos, the graphic tee, and ripped jeans, that it was Seth. I had been so sure his reign of terror over me had ended, but apparently he wasn't through with me just yet.

"So he's the one you've been screwing around with?" he jeered at me.

I stepped away from the wall, around Michael, and moved toward Seth.

"Seth, go away. Leave us alone." I didn't want to start

a scene. I needed to defuse this situation as fast as I could.

"Ha! You'd like that, wouldn't you? Why should I? So you can go back to fucking around with this asshole?" he said, nodding to Michael.

"Seth, in case you didn't get the message when we broke up, you don't own me anymore. You need to leave." My voice was dangerously low, just above a whisper.

"I need to leave?

"Yes, you need to leave." I stood my ground.

He came closer to me, the tone of his voice bordering on seductive. "Come on, baby. You look so good tonight and it's been so long. Why don't you and I go find someplace to talk? You can do better than him." Seth said with a nod to Michael.

I had to stop myself from laughing. Seth thought he was a better catch that Michael? He must've been drunker than I thought. Or more narcissistic than I remembered.

"That's not going to happen," I said. And then not able to stop myself, "And trust me, you'd be lucky to be half the man that he is."

He grabbed my arm and squeezed tight. "You listen to me, bitch—."

That's when Michael came barreling through and pushed Seth off me. He stood in front of me, blocking me with his body.

Seth laughed. "You think you're tough, boy?" And then he threw the first punch.

Michael's head snapped back from the blow, but his

adrenaline had kicked in and he recovered quickly. He went after Seth and tackled him. They were roughly the same size, and all I could see were fists and elbows.

"Michael!" I yelled.

Then I saw Shane and Logan come running in the room and pull Michael off Seth. Seth sat up, spit out blood, and slowly rose to his feet. His body was shaking with tension.

"You'd better watch yourself, bro," he said, and he walked out, slamming the screen door in his wake.

I walked up next to Michael. He was breathing hard, I could see his chest rising and falling against his T-shirt. He was giving Shane and Logan the few details he knew that led to the fight.

"Are you okay?" Michael turned to look down at me. "Sky, are you okay? Did he hurt you?"

"I—I'm fine. Michael, please, let's just get out of here."

His lip was bleeding and there was the beginning of a shiner on his right eye. I wanted to kill Seth, that son of a bitch. Logan had gone for some ice.

The relief I felt that Michael had been there to protect me made me uneasy. In my experience, trusting people too fast was soon followed by disappointment. My heart told me that he was different, that I could trust him, but my mind was more cautious.

"Do you want to head back to our room?" Shane asked.

"No, I'll take him back to my room," I said. "It's closer and it should be pretty quiet there tonight." I wanted to be alone with Michael, make sure he was all right.

Logan returned with a ratty tea towel filled with ice cubes that Michael dabbed on his lip before he applied it to his eye.

I grabbed Michael's hand and we walked out into the cold November night. He leaned in to kiss my forehead, pulling me closer to him. My heart skipped a beat, but neither one of us said a word.

We walked down the white hallway of my dorm in an almost uncomfortable silence. When we got to my room, I unlocked the door and turned on the light. Each step sounded like an echoing thud in the empty room.

"Where's your roommate?" he asked me.

"At home for the weekend," I said, steering him onto my bed. I reached into a drawer for some aspirin and grabbed some water from the mini-fridge. "Wait here, I'll get some warm water for this wash cloth."

When I walked back into the room, Michael was lying down with his feet dangling off the side of the bed, still holding the ice pack to his eye.

"Here," I said as I sat next to him. I reached forward with the towel and wiped off the blood on his lip.

"Michael, I—I'm so sorry that this happened to you. He's just crazy; I can't even begin to tell you—."

"Who was that?" he asked.

"Seth. My ex-boyfriend. We broke up last year. I

didn't even know he was still around. I thought he graduated."

"Did he hurt you?"

"What? No, I already told you."

"No, before? Did he hurt you before?" he asked.

I felt so ashamed. I dropped my gaze from his eyes. "Yes."

"How bad?" he looked pissed.

"A few times," I cleared my throat. "A few times he hit me, grabbed my arm a little too tight. I tried to end it after the first time, but he's dangerous. He had all his frat brothers covering for him. But his reach can only go so far. When I went home for the summer, he wouldn't come near me because he's afraid of my dad. I didn't answer his calls. I left him a voicemail saying it was over. And that was it.

"But I should have seen the red flags; I should have seen it coming." I was so upset that a bad decision I had made in the past was affecting Michael, that he was hurt because of something I had done before I had even met him.

And the fact that I was so ashamed and upset scared me even more. I was getting too close too fast. Maybe it was because of Seth or maybe it was because of my mom, but I was afraid of falling for Michael. I was afraid of getting hurt again. I was more afraid that this could be something real.

"Sky," Michael said, grabbing my hand, "don't blame yourself. It wasn't your fault. You didn't deserve that kind of abuse."

"Look at me," he said. His eyes were full of passion and anger. Our connection was so powerful it was tangible. I felt so treasured, like it hurt him that he hadn't been there to protect me before. "I will never hurt you, I promise."

And despite every warning shouting in my head, I believed him. I just knew, in every fiber of my being, that I could trust him.

He raised himself onto his elbows and pulled me to him. I kissed him lightly at first, I didn't want to hurt his lip, but then his kisses grew stronger and deeper. He lowered himself back onto the bed, pulling me on top of him.

He was solid and unyielding beneath me. I took his shirt off and his skin felt like it was on fire. His hands were all over me. My heart pounded and my body tingled.

The first time with somebody is always a little awkward: the fumbling around, the occasional head bump, and the frantic search for a condom.

But still, as we moved together, skin on skin, I felt so alive. I never wanted it to end.

Afterward, I pulled the blanket from the bottom of the bed and laid it over us. Michael slid over so I could lie next to him. He fell asleep with his arms wrapped tightly around me. I held on to his hand, stroking his arm with my fingers.

He was hurt and all I wanted to do was hold him and tell him that everything would be okay, which isn't always true, but this time it would be.

I was home for Christmas break, and I couldn't get enough of the comfort and relief I felt at finally being home. Or of the *House* episodes I was bingeing on.

Since I'd been home, I had talked to Michael a few times, but he was busy plowing all the snow we kept getting. And it took all of one driveway for me to know that my stomach could not handle being a passenger to the constant back and forth of the plow. So keeping him company while he worked was out of the question.

We were reduced to small snippets of texting. I would get text replies from him at random times like six in the morning or four in the afternoon when he woke up from a nap.

On Christmas Eve, I was drifting off to sleep in my bed when I heard *thud, tap, tap, thud*. I sat up, confused. *What the hell?* Then I heard it again. *Thud, tap, tap, thud.*

Then I heard my phone buzz with a text.

Michael
Look out your window

I turned around on my bed and looked out the window into the darkness. There was Michael, outside in his army bomber jacket, standing tall with his hands tucked into his pockets. He looked unaffected by the snow whirling around him.

My phone beeped again with another text.

Michael
I need to talk to you

Well I had assumed as much. I threw on a hoodie and some sweatpants and tiptoed down the hallway. I unlocked the front door as silently as possible.

"Michael!" I said. "What are you doing here?"

"Can I come in?"

"Uh, yeah, sorry," I said, moving aside. I took his hand and led him back to my dark bedroom. "Why didn't you tell me you were coming over?"

"Well that wouldn't have been much fun, would it? Would have ruined the whole surprise," he teased.

We sat down on my bed, the springs creaking with the weight. "I wanted to bring you your Christmas present," he said, holding out a small package wrapped in red-and-green paper. It had a bow on top.

I looked him in the eyes and smiled sheepishly. "You didn't have to...," I started to say.

"Sky, shut up and take it!" His eyes lit up. "Open it!"

I took it from his hands and unwrapped it. In a silver box was a beautiful silver circle charm with the letter *M* engraved on it. My heart swelled.

"Now, I don't mean to be presumptuous," he started

to say, "and yes, I did have to look up what *presumptuous* meant—. I just wanted you to have something to remind you of me when we're apart. And it matches the one you already have," he said touching the charm on my neck.

I reached up to my neck and took his hand in mine.

"I love it," I said. "Thank you, Michael, really. It's perfect."

He shifted on the bed next to me, his face was beaming from the cold outside, his blue eyes looked like glaciers in the darkness of my room. The only light was coming from the moon.

"Skylar. I don't really know how to tell you this because I've never told anyone this before, but," he hesitated, leaning closer toward me. My pulse quickened and I felt the heat rise to my face.

He took my face gently in his ice-cold hands, causing me to shiver, and caressed my cheeks with his thumbs. He looked deeply into my eyes without any reservations. "Sky, I have never felt like this before. I don't want you to think that you're just another girl to me because you're not. You're something special. I can't stop thinking about you. No matter how hard I try, I can't get your face out of my mind. I've never needed or wanted anyone so badly." And with that he pulled me close to him and kissed me with an urgency that took my breath away, his lips pressing against mine.

When we broke apart, I took the charm out of the box and added it to my necklace.

When I was done, he put his arms around my chest and pulled me against him. I looked down at the two charms sitting next to each other and said, "It's complete now."

The day after Christmas there was a knock at the door. Through my window I could see Michael's red pickup truck in the driveway.

Christmas had been the uneventful day it always was. Dad and I slept in, opened gifts, and then spent the day cooking and watching Christmas movies. It had been a nice, relaxing day and I liked our holiday tradition, but I had been looking forward to seeing Michael.

"Hi, Mr. Medina. I'm Mike," I heard Michael say from the front door.

"Please call me Jorge," Dad replied.

I ran the brush through my hair one more time, checked the mirror, and then grabbed my wool coat from the back of the chair. I was wearing my usual ensemble—jeans and a black sweater. I walked into the living room where Dad and Michael were standing.

"Hey!" Michael said, smiling at me. He looked so good. I just wanted to run up to him and throw my arms around him. Even though I had just seen him two days ago, it felt like too long.

"Hey," I said back. We all stood there in a circle in

the middle of the room.

"You ready to go?" he asked.

"Sure."

Dad just stood there, a twinkle in his eye, watching the exchange between the two of us.

"Well you two kids have fun. Call me if you need me," he said, sitting down on his La-Z-Boy chair and turning the TV on.

"Bye, Dad," I said, walking to the door.

"Nice meeting you," Michael said as he followed me.

We got into the still-warm truck. Michael started the engine, then put his arm on the back of the seat so that his fingers just touched my shoulder. He looked at me and smiled.

"What?" I smiled back.

"You look cute today," he said.

I felt myself redden and tucked my hair behind my ear. "Thank you, so do you." I leaned across the seat and kissed him. I could taste the mint from his gum on his lips.

"Shall we?" he asked, when I pulled away.

"I have to warn you," I said. "I've never ice-skated before so I don't know how well this is going to work out."

"You've never gone ice-skating before?" he asked as he put the truck in reverse and pulled away from the house.

"Not really, maybe when I was little. So you'll have to help me out." There was a pause. "So what did you think of my dad?"

"Your dad?" he said glancing over at me. "Really nice,

not a whole lot to say, but he didn't give me the third degree if that's what you're asking."

"No, I just didn't really know what to expect from either one of you."

"I hadn't really thought about it at all, actually."

"Yeah, well you're the first guy I've ever actually brought home…," I trailed off.

"Seriously?" he asked, surprised.

"I didn't really date in high school, and you met Seth. You can understand why I never brought him home to meet Dad."

"Oh, you mean that pleasant fellow who gave me a black eye?" he laughed, over it by now.

"Yes, him."

"So you didn't have any high school boyfriends?" he asked.

"Not really, I was busy with school and work and taking care of Dad. I didn't really have time, didn't really care to," I answered. "Why? Were you like a ladies' man or something?"

"Ha-ha. No, not really. I had two—I guess what you could call serious girlfriends. But that's it."

"How long did you date them for?"

"Hmm. Jenn, for about a year during tenth grade, and Sarah, for most of our junior and senior years. Do you really want to get into this?" he asked, looking a little bit uncomfortable.

"It's just interesting. I like learning about you,

Michael Amherst. So, why did you break up?"

"Umm, with Jenn, we just decided to be friends. And with Sarah, well I thought she was the real deal, but she had bigger dreams, apparently." He looked kind of sad as he said it.

"What do you mean?"

"Well, she went off to Duke, and I was happy right where I was, where I still am. Working, living at home, staying here. It wasn't enough for her. *I* wasn't enough for her."

I reached over and touched his hand. "You miss her?"

"Not anymore," he looked at me. "I did for a long time. But then I realized that sometimes certain people have to walk out of your life for better ones to walk in."

"You're not talking about me, are you?" I teased, trying to lighten up the mood.

"I am," he said, seriously, but with a smile on his face.

We were quiet the rest of the ride there. When we got to the outdoor ice rink, we got out and started walking toward the entrance.

Still thinking about the conversation we'd had in the car, I took his hand and said, "You're something better too. You know?"

He leaned down and kissed me. Then grinned devilishly. "Are you ready for this?"

"As ready as I'm going to be!"

I wasn't as horrible at ice-skating as I thought I'd be, but even after I had gotten the hang of it, Michael still wouldn't let go of my hand.

We skated around and around the rink for what felt like a long time, avoiding little kids who had fallen down and trying not to get run over by the punks who thought they were hotshots weaving in and out of the crowd.

It felt so good to be there with Michael. It's never quite the same as it is in the beginning of a relationship—those defining moments when you're getting to know someone, when you can't get enough of each other, when everything feels new and exciting. You don't realize it at the time, but those are magical moments, ones that you can only relive in memories.

"You ready to leave?" Michael asked after a while.

"Sure," I answered. "Can we get some hot chocolate first?"

"Of course." He leaned in and kissed the tip of my nose.

We went into the rental tent and returned our skates. Michael went to the concession stand and soon brought back two hot chocolates.

"You hungry?" he asked. "Want to go grab something to eat?"

"Yes."

"Where do you want to go?"

"I don't know," I laughed. "Isn't it kind of your duty to figure that out?"

"Why? Because I'm a guy?"

"No, because you're the one who asked me out."

"Fair enough. How about...," he deliberated. "Red Robin's?"

"How about Chili's?" I countered.

"What's the difference?" he asked. "Plus, I thought I was the one calling the shots."

"We just let you guys think you do," I joked, nudging him in the ribs with my elbow.

"I should've seen that one coming from a mile away."

I just smiled up at him.

"So Chili's it is, then?" he asked.

"Yup."

We walked toward the car, and he gestured for me to lead. "Your wish is my command."

"You are really going to regret saying that," I teased.

The day passed slowly and perfectly. We caught a late afternoon movie after we went out to eat. We sat in the dark theater, Michael's arm around my shoulders holding me close to him.

It was dark out by the time the movie was over. I wasn't ready to go home, but there was nothing else for us to do. So Michael pulled into a school parking lot by my house and we sat in his truck, letting the warmth from the heater wash over us as we listened to the radio. We didn't talk much. I sat with my body pressed against his, my legs extended out on the seat.

Michael started to kiss my ear and my neck until I twisted around and threw my legs around his lap. Our kisses were long and heavy. His hands ran up and down my body and I clung to his chest, dizzy with desire.

Our jackets were already off and lying on the floor of the truck. Michael's hands kept going up my back underneath my sweater, and I just wanted to feel his bare stomach against mine. I pulled off his hoodie and T-shirt in one fell swoop, and he followed my lead, yanking off my sweater carelessly and hastily.

He pulled me against him tightly, so that every inch of my torso was pressed against his. I straddled his legs and as our kisses grew more hungry and urgent. Between my legs, I could feel how much he wanted me.

My hips started to rock back and forth. I couldn't control it, didn't want to.

Michael groaned and shifted his weight, leaning back. I went with him, not leaving his lips for a beat, and now I was leaning over him. His hands went up my thighs to grab my behind, and one stayed there while the other moved to the waistband of my jeans and unbuttoned them.

I gasped as his fingers moved to the place between my jeans and my underwear and started to move rhythmically.

It wasn't long before I had to move my lips away from his. I threw my arms around his neck, my hands twisting in his hair, as I moved my hips with him and my breathing became choppy.

I felt his lips trail across my chest and his tongue trace the outline of my bra. It sent me over the edge as his one hand squeezed my ass harder and the other picked up its pace. My breathing hitched in my throat as I leaned my head back and then shuddered, collapsing back into him.

Both of his hands moved to my back as he kissed my neck softly, smiling. I slowed my breathing and felt so relaxed against Michael's chest. He pulled the lever on the side of his seat, so that it went backward and we were reclining at a low angle.

He hugged me closer to him and looked up at the ceiling of his truck. My nose and mouth were at his throat and I breathed in the clean scent of his skin. My lips started to kiss his neck, then trailed to his jaw and his mouth. Then back down again, my hands already down his stomach to his jeans.

When I got home that night, thinking about everything that had happened, I questioned whether it was more than just lust. Because as much as I wanted him like *that,* I also just wanted to be with him. I wanted him to be there with me. I wanted him to lie in bed with me and hold me. I wanted nothing more than to fall asleep in his arms, where everything made sense. Nothing else really mattered when I was with him.

IV

Stopped

February 22, 2012

I remember the moment that my world came crashing down.

It was about seven in the morning. I was in the kitchen. I had just poured myself another cup of coffee, and I needed to finish getting ready for work. But first I had to start defrosting some chili for Michael. It was his favorite thing to eat after a long, early morning of plowing snow, and he had already been out since midnight.

As I scurried about, I remembered thinking about our trip to Home Depot that upcoming weekend and all the supplies we needed to buy to start the renovations on our upstairs bathroom. It was a never-ending list, that to-do list. I remember being overwhelmed by home ownership—how with everything you fix, two more things break. The work was never done. *I'm going to drive myself crazy thinking about all the things that need to be done around here*, I laughed to myself.

I remember the smell of coffee, lavender cleaning spray, and defrosting chili.

I took a sip of my coffee as I looked outside. It was still dark, and the light from the kitchen window created a yellow square on the bright white snow.

That's when the phone rang.

"Hello?" I answered.

"Skylar!" Sue said urgently.

There was something in her voice. Something was wrong. Very wrong.

"What is it?"

"Michael's been in an accident. We're at Crittenton. You need to get here. Now."

That something in her voice, I would realize later on, was the bitter fear that he wasn't going to make it, that her baby, her son, was going to die.

Time stopped. I stood frozen. I was glued to floor. I couldn't move. I couldn't breathe. Michael. I needed to get to Michael. He needed me.

"I'm on my way."

I hung up the phone, threw it into my purse as I grabbed it, and headed out the door. My hands were shaking so badly that it took several attempts to get the key into the ignition.

I made it to the hospital as fast as I could. I was thankful that I hadn't killed anyone or gotten pulled over for my reckless driving. So many thoughts were running through my head, and at the same time it was completely clear.

Detached. I was there, I knew I was, but I still felt as if I was watching myself from outside myself. My soul was split in half. I could feel the fear, but at the same time I was numb to it.

I wanted to think through this. *Is he going to be okay? Of course he is. He's strong, a fighter.*

How could this have happened?
Why did this happen to him?
What am I going to do?
Oh my God! Michael!
Michael!
No, no, no.
This isn't real.
This isn't happening.
This is a mistake.
Oh God, no.
Please, no.

When I finally walked into the hospital I saw Rob and Sue with Sophie, all standing in the brightly lit corridor. They were scared; I could see it in their eyes.

"Where is he? What happened? Is he all right?" I asked frantically, running my fingers through my drying hair, trying to tame the curly mess.

Rob answered me slowly and quietly, "We don't know how he is. The doctors are working on him now. The police told us," his voice quivered slightly, but he carried on trying to stay calm, "that some kid was texting and ran a red light. He hit Michael hard on the passenger's side and sent him into oncoming traffic."

"But he was in his truck?" I asked, daring to hope that it was big enough to protect him from serious harm.

"Yes, but…," Rob started to shake with sobs.

"But what?" I whispered.

"There was a lot of ice, so the kid couldn't stop in enough time," he whispered. "We're waiting to hear more detail from the authorities."

I closed my eyes. I felt the tears pour through. I knew then that there was no more denying it: things were not going to be okay.

"Was anyone else hurt?" I asked.

"All we know is that the kid was brought in, but he's not in critical condition," Rob answered mechanically.

We waited. We sat in those ugly, sticky, plastic chairs for what seemed like an eternity. The fluorescent lights from above cast ghostly shadows on our distraught faces. I tapped my leg incessantly. I felt like I wanted to crawl out of my skin, like I wanted to be anywhere but in that room.

CNN was on the television but no one was watching; world wars and the rising price of gas seemed completely irrelevant now. Dad arrived, followed by Shane after I had called them, trembling to get the words out.

We waited some more. We paced. We drank some coffee. We paced some more. No one said a word.

Because if we said those generic, Hallmark card words, "He's going to be all right. Everything will be fine," we would have to face the reality that those words would be just that: empty words without meaning.

Somewhere in the back of my mind, underneath all the fear and worry and anxiety, a small seed of thought began to germinate. After this, this horrifying nightmare—I shuddered to think of the possible outcomes—is over, I was going to hunt down and *destroy* the person responsible for this. I swore this on the Holy Bible, on the flag of the United States of America, on the latest edition of *People Magazine* that was lying nearby.

But I couldn't think about that right now. I had other things to worry about. Like Michael making it through this alive and okay and warm. Not cold, I thought, shuddering. Not cold.

Finally, a doctor came out through the double swinging doors. He was dressed in green scrubs and a white doctor's coat with a stethoscope hanging from his neck. He was older, with crow's feet hugging his eyes from—what I assumed—many years of long shifts, countless surgeries, and of too many occasions such as these where he had to be the bearer of bad news. His head was completely covered with thick silver hair that was slightly ruffled. Behind the lenses of the clear frameless glasses, his eyes were kind and compassionate.

Before he could say a word, we had all stood and were surrounding him. We all looked at him, wanting so badly to hear what he had to say, but at the same time too scared to ask. I had a million questions racing through my mind: *Is he okay? What happened? Where is he? Can we go see him?* But when I opened my mouth nothing came out.

"You're all here for Michael, Michael Amherst?" he asked.

We nodded.

"I'm Robert Amherst, Michael's father, and this is my wife Susan. This is Skylar, Michael's fiancé," he said, nodding to me.

The doctor took a deep breath. He paused and looked at each one of us. My heartbeat went from a gallop to a full-on sprint.

"Michael is in critical condition. He was unconscious when he was brought in, and we put him in an induced coma until we can assess the seriousness of the brain swelling. Both his legs were broken, and three ribs on his left side were broken. We have set all his bones. He also had some internal bleeding we were able to stop. He's not breathing on his own right now; he's hooked up to a ventilator. My main concern right now is damage to his brain."

"What do you mean?" I asked.

"Well, the brain is a very complex structure and every brain injury is different. There's a very real chance that if he does make it, he won't be the same as he was before."

"Like cognitively impaired?" Sophie asked.

"That's one possibility. But there are also a lot of

emotional ramifications and changes that could happen. We'll cross that bridge when we get there," he said calmly. "Our best neurologists and neurosurgeons are carefully reviewing everything right now to decide what the best course of treatment will be."

"Is he going to live?" my dad finally asked the question we were all afraid of.

"As I said, he's in critical condition," the doctor paused.

"Just give it to us straight, sir." Dad spoke again.

"There's a very real chance that he might not make it...."

Deep breath in, then out. Deep breath in, then out. Hold on. Hold on. Keep your grip, Skylar.

The doctor kept talking, "I have to warn you that he doesn't look good. He's badly bruised and swollen, but you can see him. No more than two people at a time in the ICU."

Before anyone could move I heard my dad ask from behind me, "How's the kid?"

Who the hell cares? I thought.

"He had some minor injuries. He will have to stay overnight, but he'll be just fine."

Of course he will be. He gets to live with a few scrapes and bruises, while Michael....

I didn't argue when Sue and Rob wanted to go in first because I knew that I wanted to be alone when I was with him. I wanted to take my time, touching him, talking to him, praying for him.

After twenty minutes of pacing the waiting room, a nurse came in and led us to a more private waiting room for ICU patients.

I forced myself to sit down on the edge of the more comfortable couch. Leaning forward, I put my elbows on my knees and my head in my hands.

When Rob and Sue came back out, I stood up and my knees shook under the weight of my body.

"Room 821," Rob said. They both looked drained and dried out, like they had no more tears to cry.

When I stood up to give Sue a hug, I towered over her short frame. I wrapped my arms around her round shoulders and leaned my head down on top of her cropped blond hair. Her breath was slow as she tried to hold back fresh tears.

I had always been on friendly terms with Sue, but right now, here in this moment, with my arms around her plump figure, she felt like a mother to me. So nurturing and comforting.

"You take care of my baby, okay?" she commanded more than asked.

I pulled away and nodded, then pushed past the glass doors and headed down the hallway to Michael's room.

It was bright and eerily quiet except for the sounds of the machines and the beep, beep, beep of the heart monitor.

An iron fist squeezed my heart when I saw Michael.

There were bruises all over his face and body. His face was swollen and there were so many bandages he was almost unrecognizable.

He was hurt so badly and there wasn't a damn thing I could do about it.

I wanted to run to him and hug him and hold him in my arms and tell him everything was going to be all right. But I couldn't move from the doorway. I was paralyzed.

I couldn't deny it any longer. Michael was seriously hurt and there was a very real possibility that he was never going to come home.

I lifted my right foot to step forward, and it felt like I was pulling against the entire force of gravity. When I was finally able to make it to his bedside, I touched his hand lightly. Then his face. I ran my fingers softly over his bandages, his lips, his scruff. He looked so out of place here in this clean white room, wearing a hospital gown. Michael was a construction worker. He belonged next to machines and tools and building supplies. Not this room. Not this hospital. Not this delicate, fragile situation.

He was capable, consistent, steadfast. He could beat this, he was a fighter, he didn't give up so easily.

The steady, low beep of the heart monitor became my only comfort as I sat beside Michael in the chair next to his bed. I was so scared for him, for me, for us.

I looked at him. I saw the white plastic hospital band on Michael's right wrist, the IV bag hanging from the rack labeled PENTOBARBITAL 500 mg, and the plastic tubes wrapped around his face that kept him breathing. Here he was, lying no more than two feet away from me, and yet I couldn't move any closer to him. I was afraid to touch him again.

I tried to comprehend that he was very much within death's grasp; that in moments he could be gone and that this might be my last change to feel his warmth underneath my palm.

So I stood up and moved closer. Then I sat on the bed and lay down next to him, pressing my body next to his just like I had for the past several years. Tears immediately started forcing their way through my eyelids as fierce sobs rocked through me. And I let them come. I let the tears streak my face with black mascara, the salt tinge my lips, and the tears soak into the blanket covering Michael.

Somewhere deep inside me I wished for a fairy-tale miracle. I wished my tears could heal him and restore him back to full health. But this wasn't Middle Earth or some other mythical land, and I didn't possess any magical healing powers.

After every single tear, desperate plea, and prayer had left me, I whispered to him. "Michael, I don't know why this happened, and even knowing how this happened doesn't make it any easier. It's not fair. You don't deserve this.

"But, if you can hear me, I want you to know that I love you so much. I want you to come home so that we can pretend this never happened. You can do this Michael. I know you can. Please Michael, don't leave me here all alone. Please…please, without you…," I paused, choked on my thoughts. *Without him, what? What would I become? Who would I be? How could I even exist?*

I let all my thoughts fade away and looked at Michael. I studied his face, his hands, aware of how his body felt next to mine. I relaxed into how solid and sturdy he was.

The next thing I knew, Sophie was leaning over me and shaking me. "Sky? Sky? Wake up."

"Huh?"

"The nurse needs to change Mike's IV. You need to move."

"Oh, sorry," I said and pulled myself off Michael.

I walked back out to the waiting room with Sophie, wiping my face and smoothing down my hair.

"Where's everyone at?" I asked.

"My parents went to the cafeteria to get some lunch, and Shane left to go back to work," Sophie answered.

"Oh," I paused. *How was it only lunchtime?* "Has anyone told Logan?"

"Yeah, Shane called him. He's at work right now, but he said he was going to try to make it later."

I nodded, idly wondering if Logan had his two-year-old daughter Madison that night and if he was going to be able to find someone to watch her. I hoped he could because having Shane and Logan around meant that

Michael was around; by some twisted logic, one could not exist without the other two. They were like a security blanket, a comfort, and anchor in this horrible, horrible situation.

"Sophie, why don't you go join your parents? I'm going to take Sky for a walk," I heard Dad say as he rose out of the chair.

"Yeah, I could use something to eat. Maybe later we can go back to your house and pick up some stuff for Michael and let Scout out?" Sophie asked gently.

"Yeah, okay." I managed, completely bewildered by her ability to think about our big yellow mutt back at home with everything going on at the hospital. Sophie was capable of so much compassion and empathy, yet still able to distance herself enough to not let it destroy her. Where she had gotten her composure from I wasn't sure, but I was thankful for it. Michael tended to get worked up and overreact when he was upset.

I was tired, so tired. What had been only hours felt more like months. My eyes were sore and my head hurt.

"Sweetheart, let's go outside for a second."

"Dad, it's freezing out there."

"The fresh air will do you good."

I wanted to roll my eyes at him, but even that took too much effort. But I followed him through the hallways, down the corridors, and out the door.

The air was cold and stabbed my lungs as I breathed in. It felt surprisingly good.

It wasn't snowing, but it was gray and bleak outside. It was typical Michigan weather and it was fucking depressing.

"Sky?"

"Yeah?"

"How are you doing, honey?" My dad was a little rough around the edges, but if you knew him like I did, you knew that he was just a big teddy bear. His face was rough, but not unkind, and his voice was deep and smooth.

"As good as I could be, considering…." I didn't feel like talking, but if I did I would have told him that I was terrified, confused, exhausted, furious, lost, and feeling so many other emotions that I didn't even know if there were words to describe them. "I feel like this is a really, really bad dream that I just want to wake up from, but I can't run fast enough to get out of it."

He pulled me closer to him and hugged me tightly.

"Dad, what happens now? What if he doesn't get better? What if this is the end? What do I do? I don't even know anymore," I cried.

"Well, if I know Michael as well as I think I do, I'm sure that something like this won't keep him down for long. That boy has too much living to do before anything can take him out."

I wanted to believe him, I really did. I wanted to surrender to that fantasy and let it envelope me. But the possibility that the fantasy could be shattered kept me from giving in to it. It would just be too devastating.

The day passed in shifts as we all took turns staying by Michael's side, praying for him to recover. By six, the doctors had no new information for us; the brain swelling was still the same. Sue, Rob, and Sophie left for the night, exhausted from the extremely taxing day. They all gave me long hugs and promised to be back first thing in the morning.

"Are you sure you don't want me to stay?" Sophie asked.

"No, really. I'll be all right," I responded on autopilot. I was ready for everybody to leave. I was ready to be alone with Michael.

I went to his room, sat in the chair next to the bed, and closed my eyes. I was woken by a nudge on the arm. When I looked up I saw Shane with his effortless smile, holding out a coffee for me.

"Tall, nonfat vanilla latte, right?" he asked, worry etched around his eyes.

"Yes. Oh, thank you! I really needed this," I sighed. "Why did you come back?"

"I just got off work a little bit ago. I thought I'd check in."

"Thanks, Shane. I appreciate it." Shane was like a brother to me. His presence brought me comfort, and in less dire circumstances, comic relief.

"Yeah, no problem," he said settling down in the chair next to me. "Talked to Logan earlier, said he couldn't get anyone to watch Madison, and since toddlers aren't allowed in this area of the hospital…," he trailed off.

"Yeah, I understand. I'm sure he'll get here when he can."

I felt so disoriented. Time in hospitals passed more slowly than it did in the outside world. It was easy to forget that people had jobs and demanding schedules when all that seemed to exist was the reassuring compression of the ventilator and the rounds made by the nurses.

I was overwhelmed by the uncertainty of the situation. There was no set of instructions for something like this.

My feelings must have been written all over my face because Shane turned to me and said, "Skylar, it's going to be okay. He's going to be okay. You know he is. If nothing else, his love for you will bring him back."

How true I wished that was. If my love for him alone was enough to bring him back, he would have been able to come home with me that night.

The nurse on duty kept trying to get Shane and me to leave, I almost laughed out loud the first time she mentioned it, but we wouldn't budge.

I kept nodding off but was always awoken by something: nurses' hushed whispers or the squeak of a moving chair. I never let go of Michael's hand. It was very *Titanic*. Michael would have thought it was funny. He would've quoted to me verbatim, "You must do me this honor…promise me you will survive, that you will never give up, no matter what happens, no matter how hopeless, promise me now, and never let go of that promise…never let go." It was almost poetic how some lines from a movie could be applied to real life.

Then I must have dozed off for good because I was dreaming. I was running down a dark street with one light post at the end. I was running past houses, all with different colored doors, but if I turned to look at them they disappeared. I was moving at a steady pace, my feet hitting the cement with a rhythmic beat. I was getting closer, closer, closer…almost to the light. The beeping stopped abruptly, and my feet were planted. I couldn't move. A long, droning blare was growing louder and louder, the light becoming brighter and brighter until it knocked me off my feet.

"I need help in here, STAT," I heard a stern and worried voice yell. "Code Blue. Code Blue."

My eyes flew open. Nurses were standing over Michael. There was a pin-straight horizontal line on the heart monitor and coming from it was the long, droning blare I heard in my dream.

"One-two-three."

The deathly thud of hands on Michael's chest.

"One-two-three."

I scanned the room. There were several nurses and doctors. And there were tubes, lots of plastic tubes. There was medicine being injected into Michael's IV. Hands pushing down on his chest again. Commotion and chaos.

But still there was a straight line. I pleaded for the

line to move. *Move!* I thought. *Goddamn it, Michael, come on.*

"God, please don't let this happen," I begged. I offered my life, the sacrifice of twenty-five goats, all the money in my savings account, if God would just make that line move again.

Thud, thud, thud.

A voice, "All right, folks. I'm calling it. On the twenty-third of February 2012 at 2:37 a.m., patient Michael Donal Amherst is pronounced dead due to failed attempt to resuscitate from cardiac arrest."

Dead.

The room started to spin. Time stopped as I walked toward Michael. The doctor and nurses stepped back and bowed their heads in respect, pity, shame, or a combination of all three. I saw his still chest, his parted lips, his dead eyes.

The blood in my body seemed to stop in its tracks, my lungs gasped for air but failed, my legs collapsed under my body weight, and I fell onto the bed.

That was the moment that not only the love my life died but also the largest part of myself: 2:37 a.m. Just like that. It was over.

I felt hands grab under my arms and pull me up. I fought like hell. I kicked and screamed as Shane pulled me out of the room and into the hallway. I turned on him and punched and cried and screamed. And he held on until all the fight had left me.

That night, if one were to look down the hallway in the ICU, one would have seen two figures crumpled down on the floor against the wall, holding on to each other for dear life: a young woman wracked by terrifying, primal sobs and a young man silently letting tears run down his face.

V

Gone

February 27, 2012

There were a lot of things in this world that I could handle. I handled the death of my mother when I was only seven years old. I carried the weight of my broken father throughout my teenage years as he struggled to pick himself back up. As part of the support staff for the Special Investigations Unit of Oakland County, I saw too many of the horrific things that human beings were capable of doing to each other, things that no one should ever see. I could handle these things because I had Michael right beside me holding me up.

But losing Michael—that was the one thing I couldn't handle. I was only twenty-six. We were just starting our lives together. We were about to be married, about to be husband and wife. We were about to start a family.

Why did this happen? Why did this happen to Michael? Why did this happen to me?

The day following the accident we learned that after Michael had been hit on the passenger side, he had swerved to the left to avoid oncoming traffic and had smashed into a light pole on the driver's side. His truck was completely twisted and crumpled, except for the plow at the front of the truck that was, ironically, unscathed. After seeing the photos of the accident, it was a wonder that he had survived the impact at all.

After everyone said their last words and paid their last respects at the gravesite, they made their way back to their cars. Sue and Rob left. Sophie followed shortly thereafter. Then Dad gave me a tight squeeze and a kiss on the forehead.

"Take all the time you need," he said. "I'll wait for you in the car."

I stepped forward and looked down at the casket in the cement vault as they lowered the lid down. I heard as the lid was sealed upon the vault. It was the cold, absolute sound of death.

I watched as the rose I then threw landed on the vault, which held his casket, which held his body. His body, which only four days ago had been so warm and welcoming, was now cold in the ground.

I crumbled to my knees and folded into myself, trying to contain the grief that was all-consuming and raged hot like a wildfire. My breathing was ragged and desperate.

"I love you, Michael. I miss you. Please, come back to me, please," I pleaded. My makeup had worn off, and I'm sure my face looked swollen and blotchy, my nose red and raw from all the tissue I had used.

I felt like I was holding on to a live wire as my face contorted and my body shook violently. Agonizing groans escaped my lips. I looked up at the sky, praying that if there was a god up there, he would see me and feel my heart breaking, and if he was feeling generous, to smite me down with a big, fat lightning bolt.

I wasn't afraid of Death. I would have welcomed it.

When I got back to the street, Dad's car was the only one left, and Sophie was sitting patiently in the back seat. I opened the door and slid in next to Dad in the front.

"I only want to go for a few minutes. I really don't know how much more 'people time' I can handle today," I said, talking about the reception Rob and Sue were holding at their house.

"Ten, fifteen minutes tops," Dad assured me.

I flipped through the stations trying to find something to silence the screaming inside my head, but there was nothing on. I slammed the radio off and we drove in silence.

I could tell that Dad and Sophie were worried, but I wasn't about to pretend that I was okay. My mind was filled with thoughts of Michael, with his strong embrace and his heart-melting smile. He was all I wanted. He was the only person I couldn't have.

We pulled into the driveway of Rob and Sue's expansive subdivision home in New Baltimore, the one Michael had grown up in. The lights from the inside shown brightly, leading the guests in. I could see people mingling about inside. I dreaded the look on their faces and the pity in their eyes that was sure to come as soon as I walked through the door.

"Come on, let's go," Dad said. "Ten minutes and we can leave."

Sophie got out of the car and opened my door. She held out her hand and smiled. She was an angel in the midst of hell.

We walked through the front door. Dad went first, acting like a shield, followed by Sophie, and I brought up the rear.

I kept my head down and let my hair cover my eyes as I walked into the foyer, which, fortunately for me, was cut off from the rest of the house.

Sue was adamant that her new white carpet not get dirty, so we took off our boots and put them in the pile along with everyone else's. Slush covered the tiled foyer floor and soaked our feet as we made our way into the house.

I followed Dad into the kitchen. I swept the room with my eyes but never lingered too long on one spot or one person. A few people looked up at me and tried to catch my gaze, but I wouldn't let them.

There were a lot of people here that I knew—Michael's family and closest friends—and some that I didn't. It wasn't that I didn't want to see these people and talk to them, I just didn't have it in me to have a conversation with anyone. My body was tired, and the feeling of wanting to be anywhere but here was so strong that even North Korea was starting to sound appealing.

I walked through the house and said a quiet "Hello" to a few people. It was my feeble attempt at making an appearance. I made sure never to stop long enough for anyone to start talking. It was always the same thing: "I'm so sorry," "If there's anything you need, just let us know," "I'm here if you need to talk," "I can't even imagine…," or "I'm praying for you."

What was worse than the talking, though, were the questions: "How are you doing?" "Do you need anything?" "Are you okay?"

Let me answer them for you. First of all, I know you're sorry. I'm sorry too. I do need something, or rather someone, and there's no way to get him back. Thanks, but no thanks, I do not want to talk. No, you're right you can't even begin to imagine what I'm going through. And please, there's no need to pray for me, it won't do any good anyway. Thanks.

And how am I doing? I'm existing, but barely. My lungs are expanding and contracting, my heart is beating, and my brain is working, so that must mean I'm physically alive, but my soul is dead. It's gone.

I was almost done making my rounds when I turned the corner back into the foyer, and ran into Shane and Logan.

Shane came toward me and picked me up in a bear hug.

"Come here, you!" he said.

I smiled a little, and he saw it as he put me down.

"Was that a smile I just saw?"

I didn't have a response to that.

Logan was still looking at me. He looked so…so sad. His eyes were rimmed with red and his brown hair was disheveled. His shirt was rumpled and untucked, which was so unlike Logan—so normally put-together—that I didn't even know what to say. He managed a smile and nodded, speaking first.

"Hey, Sky," he said, his voice rough and hoarse.

"Hey," I said back quietly.

I looked back at Shane, his halfhearted smile faltering.

"Well, um, there's lots of food in the kitchen. Help yourself. I'm going home." And with that I turned and walked away.

"Sky?" I heard someone say. I stopped and turned around.

"Take care of yourself," Logan said, taking a quick long stride and pulling me in for a tight hug.

I nodded, then went to find Dad to tell him I'd be waiting for him in the car.

After Dad dropped me off at home in Rochester, about a half-hour away from Rob and Sue's house, I greeted Scout and knelt down to hug him. Dad had tried to convince me to stay the night at his house. But I refused.

"Then let me stay at your place tonight. You shouldn't be alone."

"I want to be alone," I had told him wearily. "I need to be."

I think the resignation in my voice held back any resistance he had because he didn't push me any further on the issue.

It was a relief to finally be alone in my own home, but Dad's words still echoed in my mind. After he had kissed me goodbye, he had said, "You're going to get through this, sweetie. I know you don't want to. But you're going to. You're strong. Always have been. Always will be."

What the hell was I supposed to do with that? I thought as I climbed the stairs to our bedroom.

Our room was bright and inviting. The walls were a light olive green with an arched white ceiling. The one window, by the metal-framed bed, let in lots of light.

My favorite part of the room, our bed, was big with soft yellow pillows and blankets. It was old and worn and cozy. I couldn't look at the bed without thinking about Michael, without thinking about lying in his arms at night with the stars peeking in through the window or the way the bed groaned beneath us when made love.

I loved our room. It was ours. It was home.

I went to the armoire and pulled out Michael's favorite shirt. It was a cotton Levi's T-shirt. He always wore it around the house on weekends or days off. I slid back to sit on the edge of our bed, pulling the shirt close. It smelled deeply of Michael—the scent of fabric softener, his woodsy body wash, a hint of concrete and dust.

I lay down and the tears came again, and I didn't fight them. For reasons I couldn't begin to understand, these tears held the sweet relief I hadn't found earlier.

The crying spells never failed to impress me with their endurance and their perseverance. I sobbed and screamed out loud. I hit the pillow and kicked the shoes that were lying on the floor.

After I had depleted my tear bank, exhaustion swept over me. I pulled the soft, blankets around me and fell asleep with the smell of Michael surrounding me.

When I woke up, it was dusk outside. I rolled over on the bed and one of our framed engagement pictures on the nightstand caught my eye. In it, Michael is wearing this blue-and-white striped button-up collared shirt that I loved so much, with khakis. I'm wearing a simple white sundress with brown leather flip-flops.

God, he was handsome, I thought, with his gorgeous blue eyes and a smile that could light up any room. We were so opposite, it was almost comical. He had light skin and mine was a dark olive tone. He had light blond hair, and I had long dark curly hair. He was well built and tall. I was tall too, but I looked so skinny and angular next to him. My sharp features looked strangely severe compared to his round face. It was almost as if these differences had become a chemistry and attraction of their own. Alone we were okay, but together, we were even better. He understood me like no one else.

"You were my whole world, Michael," I whispered aloud. "You are *still* my whole world."

I could have probably stayed there, staring at that picture all night, but I heard Scout whimper and scratch at the door downstairs. So I went to let him out.

As I stood on the back porch, I watched Scout run around. I tried to focus on him sniffing the ground and moving in a zigzag line across the yard. I could try to forget for a minute, but even if I did, everything still felt wrong and out of place.

I called Scout inside and walked into the kitchen to feed him. Our kitchen is small but functional. When we first moved in, there had been a ghastly fluorescent light that Michael had replaced with dimmer lights. I had loved them so much. They made the kitchen feel cheerful and not so institutional. But now they were nothing more than lights; lights that Michael had installed.

Our house was cute but small. It was definitely a work in progress. When we first moved in a few months ago, we repainted everything. That made a huge difference, but we were still in the process of making the place ours.

Michael had so many things planned for this house. *Plans that would never happen now*, I thought.

I opened the fridge and saw that someone, maybe Dad or Sophie, had brought some of the food from Rob and Sue's over. I opened the containers and saw cheesy potatoes, some ham, spaghetti, green beans, and some dinner rolls. I made myself a plate and heated it up in the microwave. My bare feet were cold against the hardwood floors, and I tugged at my long gray sweater, trying to wrap it closer to my body.

I stood in the dim kitchen and picked at the food. I didn't have an appetite, but I could feel that my body was hungry. I ate a few bites, grabbed the dinner roll, and then put the plate on the floor for Scout to eat the rest.

Feeling my way along the walls, I stumbled into the living room and turned on the television. I settled for ABC Family, hoping that the scripted happiness and normalness on the screen would permeate through the TV and into my dark quiet home. I pulled the purple blanket from the basket and flopped down onto the couch.

I don't know how long I watched TV before I fell asleep. I usually hate sleeping with the TV on, but that night I needed its noise to fill the house and surround me.

The night passed with deadweight unconsciousness, the kind of sleep that makes you forget the horrible reality you live in.

When I opened my eyes, Scout was sitting in front of the couch staring at me. I felt confused and disoriented. As

I got up to let him outside, I was hit with the realization that the past few days hadn't just been a dream. Michael was really gone.

My stomach twisted and I slid to the kitchen floor. From there it was an easy leap to shaking, crying, and kicking at the cabinet doors. Michael wasn't here anymore. And if he wasn't here, then what did I have to live for? There was no point for me to go on. Life just didn't make sense without him.

I let Scout back in, and I went upstairs to bed, curling into a ball.

Scout came and rolled up next to me. He understood the pain. He missed Michael too. He knew I didn't want to talk. He knew I just wanted a friend to lean on—a comfortable, warm, and furry friend. Dogs are intuitive like that.

I didn't make it back out of bed until later that night. There were messages on my phone from Sue, Sophie, and Dad. I deleted all the messages without listening to them and then turned my phone off.

All I wanted was to fade away into nothingness. I wanted to drift off into a sweet dream where I could be with Michael again—holding him, kissing him, touching him, talking to him.

"It's all going to be okay," he would say to me.

VI

The bottomless abyss of my life

The day of the funeral was nothing compared to the overwhelming pain that battered me in the days afterward. Every day came and went, each day fading slowly into the next. Fatigue was my constant companion, my muscles were sore and weak. My chest felt bruised from the panic attacks that paralyzed me. Xanax was the only thing I could depend on for relief.

Dad told me there would be a day when I woke up and remembered Michael wasn't there, and I wouldn't roll over to steal a kiss from him. That day hasn't come yet.

My daily routine went something like this: wake up around one in the afternoon, make my way downstairs to watch as many mind-numbing television shows as I possibly could until Jimmy Fallon came on. The nights became this daunting time that I dreaded. Often I just wandered throughout the house like a ghost. Sometimes I took Scout out for a walk or went to the grocery store because only those who weren't a part of the waking world did their shopping at three in the morning. Then when the sun would start to come up, I would climb upstairs and into bed, only to repeat the same thing again the next day.

Over the past week, Sophie had stopped by once after school, staying to watch a few episodes of *CSI: Miami* with me.

"It's weird that you watch this show," she said, taking a bite of pizza. "I always thought people who worked in law enforcement hated cop dramas."

"I like to watch them figure it out," I said with a shrug. "They get a lot wrong, but at least they catch the bad guys by the end of the episode."

I could feel her eyes on me, carefully studying me. "You need to eat, Sky," she said, handing me another slice. "I ordered a large for a reason."

I took another small bite, my jaw and throat working mechanically. It tasted like cardboard to me, and I felt no better after eating it.

Dad and Shane had also stopped by on other days, both bringing me more food that I didn't want to eat. Dad cleaned up around the house and did some laundry for me, then joined me on the couch to watch reruns of *Friends* and *King of Queens*. His body shook the couch when he laughed and just feeling him next to me, solid and real, made the tears not as bitter that night.

Shane had arrived with two Jimmy John subs and wasted no time in putting on the MSU basketball game. By halftime, I had only eaten a few bites of the sandwich. Memories of Michael, of MSU, of going together to the Breslin Center became too much.

I stood up from the couch and without looking at Shane I said, "Thanks for the food and everything. I need to go to bed. Feel free to stay and watch, just lock the door on your way out."

One night, the restlessness took on a whole new level and I fidgeted endlessly. Trailing my fingers down the wall of the dark hallway, I knocked over a framed picture of Michael, Shane, and Logan at an MSU football game.

It fell to the floor with a clatter, but the glass didn't break. I stooped slowly to pick it up with cold, stiff fingers. I studied their happy smiles and the way Shane had his arms around Michael and Logan's shoulders.

I traveled back into my memory. I hadn't been with them for that particular game, State was playing Central, I think, but I could piece together the energy and excitement that would have filled the campus and all of East Lansing. I could smell the barbecues cooking hot dogs, the sound of laughter, the refreshing taste of ice-cold beer, the warmth of the afternoon sun on my skin. That was a time of pure contentment. Everything I had ever wanted was right there in front of me.

I ran my finger over the image of Michael in his jeans and gray State T-shirt, a green baseball cap on his head. I could see the scruff on his face and his blue eyes piercing into mine. I could almost feel the way his presence filled the frame. As if he were actually, physically in there, and all I had to do was let him out.

But as I looked at him, I realized there was a black speck on his face. *That shouldn't be there.* I felt my face contort in anger and frustration.

I took my rugged, chewed-on fingernail to the glass to remove the black speck, but it didn't move. I scratched at it again. When it was still there, I started scratching at it frantically, my nail making a scratching noise against the glass. It needed to come off. Right. That. Moment.

I scratched and scratched and scratched until my fingernail was bloody from trying. When the red blood started to trickle onto the glass, I couldn't contain the fury inside me and threw the picture down the hallway. It hit the front door and smashed on impact. Glass and pieces of wood covered the floor.

I walked over and picked up the picture. The black speck was still there. As gently as I could, I tried to remove the black speck from the picture. But I must have cut myself on another small piece of glass because Michael's face ended up scratched and smeared with blood.

I set the picture down on the stairs behind me, taking great care to lay it down. Then I turned and looked at the picture frames on the wall with hate in my heart. I had once loved those frames, had even paid a lot of money for them, but now I hated them. They mocked my dream of having a happy life. They taunted me for believing that good things could last.

I wanted them down and destroyed. I wanted Michael free from their prison of glass. I wanted to be able to touch him, run my finger over the planes of his body, wanted to be able to smell him through the paper.

Stomping over to them, I grabbed one frame off the wall and whipped it at the door. It hit with a satisfying crack. So I did it again. And again. Until the eight frames were now nothing more than broken wood and glass.

Slipping on Michael's work boots, I crunched over the glass. As I bent to start picking the pictures up, I realized my fingers were still covered with blood. Quickly, I wiped them off on my sweatpants, not caring that the stain would probably never come out. I then painstakingly shifted the pictures out of the mess and took them over to the coffee table in the living room.

I laid them out in a neat row so that I could see them from the couch. Most of these pictures were from my college days. All of them were of Michael, me, and our friends, young and hopeful. How naïve we had been.

Walking purposefully into the kitchen, I searched the freezer until I found a bottle of Stoli crammed in the back. It was half-empty, but it was better than nothing.

Taking it back into the living room, I untwisted the cap and let it fall on the coffee table as I passed it. I sat down on the couch and looked at the pictures staring back at me.

Then I put the bottle to my lips and let the clean clear liquor sanitize me, wanting at the same time to remember and forget.

From downstairs, I heard a sharp knock on the door. *Go away*, I wanted to say. *Leave me alone. I just can't do this anymore.*

By then, I'd lost track of how many calls I'd missed, of how many food containers were stuffed into my fridge with heating instructions on them, of how many days it had been since I'd showered or eaten.

I waited for whoever was at the door to give up and go away, but the knocking continued.

Scout ran downstairs and I heard him bark as if to say, *Come here. I know them. Answer the door.* When I didn't move, he ran up to my bedside and sat down on the floor. He looked at me and cocked his head to one side. His innocent brown eyes penetrated deep into what used to be my heart. It was a desperate plea: *Please do this for me*, I could almost hear him say.

I lifted myself out of bed, my bones cracking from disuse. There was a deep impression from where my body had lain for the past few weeks. I moved slowly, like an old lady with hip dysplasia.

From the top of the stairs, I could see that it was Dad and Sophie. The two of them had grown closer since Michael's death; they had formed a rescue team to save me, to pull me out of the depths.

Everything inside me wanted to turn around, retreat back to my room, and barricade myself in there until I was long forgotten. But I knew that wasn't going to happen. They weren't going to give up on me so easily, curse them. So I walked downstairs and opened the front door.

I saw Dad's mouth drop slightly when he got a real look at me, but he recovered quickly and smiled. "We thought we'd bring you some Chinese food—your favorite."

"I'm not hungry," I said flatly. I honestly couldn't remember the last time I had eaten more than a few bites of something, but I still had no appetite.

"Sweetheart, come on. Let us in so we can make you a nice cup of hot tea. We can eat, talk, maybe watch TV or something?"

Got to give the old man credit for trying.

Without saying anything, I opened the door, gesturing for them to enter. Scout barked happily and wagged his tail rapidly, desperate for attention.

They tried not to notice the broken glass littering the floor, but I saw the horror and confusion on their faces. Too bad I didn't care.

I followed them through the hallway and into the

dining room. I sat down and watched as they got the plates, cups, and silverware from the kitchen and set the table. I listened as they made small talk between themselves.

"How's school going?" I heard Dad ask Sophie.

"Fine. I think I'm going to go out for track or tennis this year," Sophie replied. "I'm just not sure if I really have a chance because I haven't done it before, and everyone else has been on the team for years."

They walked into the dining room.

"Sky, did you hear what I just said?" Sophie asked.

"Kind of," I said, looking out the window.

"I was telling your dad how I might join a sports team this spring," she said. I could tell they were making a serious attempt at keeping things light, trying to make it seem like everything was okay and *normal*.

"Oh, cool," I said. I took a sip of the tea Dad set down and looked at the pile of fried rice with beef on the plate in front of me. Thick steam curled up from it, carrying the potent smell to my nose. It made me feel sick just looking at it. I moved it around with my fork as Sophie and Dad continued the conversation without me.

Sophie talked about her classes, her friends, how she was regretting taking AP Calc her senior year, which colleges she applied to. Mundane, normal, boring, everyday things.

And as she talked about her plans for summer and then college, my rage built up inside me. How could she be talking about her plans for the future? How could she move forward? Was there something wrong with me that I couldn't? Would I ever get out of the past?

"So Mom wants me to stay here in Michigan, of course. But I'm not sure that's what I want to do. I'm thinking maybe New York or—."

The anger and panic built up inside me until I couldn't take it any longer.

"Stop!" I yelled, slamming my fist down on the table, causing the plates to jump. "Just stop. I can't listen to this anymore. I don't fucking care. I don't care about where you're going for college or what you're wearing to prom." I stood up, grabbing fistfuls of my hair, blocking my ears.

Sophie and Dad looked at me with stunned expressions on their faces.

"Skylar, you need to try to—," Dad started to say, but I cut him off.

"Try to what, move on? Try to come to terms with the fact that he's *never* coming back?" I screamed. "Try to accept that I might be stuck here in this place for the rest of my life?"

Tears filled my eyes. "You don't get it, okay? You don't understand what it's like to wake up from a nightmare every single goddamn day just to realize that it's not a nightmare, it's reality. And I know you wish I could be happy for you," I hissed at Sophie, "that you still have your whole life ahead of you, but I can't be. I'm sorry."

"I miss him too, you know," she said softly, looking down at her plate.

I raised my hand and swung, smacking my plate clean off the table. It hit the wall with a clash. My voice rose again, my fists clenched by my sides. "Not like I do! Or you wouldn't be thinking about things like tennis and prom. So don't come over here and expect me to be all happy and interested and excited. Because I can't be. I won't be. It hasn't even been a month yet."

"That's enough, Skylar!" Dad said harshly, his voice rising.

I stared at him for a moment before I turned around and went up the stairs, slamming the door shut behind me.

Well, that was a complete fucking fail.

I could hear them cleaning up downstairs and their incomprehensible conversation. I paced the room and pulled my hair back with my hands. Adrenaline surged through my body. I was unhinged.

I saw, there in the corner of the room, Michael's electric guitar. The one he never played. The one that sat unused, collecting dust and holding coats.

I was so angry at him for leaving me, however irrational that was. I was angry at being in this situation. I was angry that I was alive and he wasn't. I was angry I was alone.

I grabbed that damn guitar by the neck and threw it across the room. It hit the ground with a deep, resounding thud, and the strings made a sick twangy vibration.

I stood across the room, breathing deeply for a second, trying to catch my breath.

The Charm Necklace

Why the hell did I just do that? That was Michael's!

Jesus, I was losing it. I needed to get a grip.

There was a knock at my door.

I walked over and cracked it slightly, so that only half my face was showing. It was Dad.

"Everything all right up here?" he asked slowly.

"Yup," I answered quickly. He tried to see around me, but I wouldn't budge.

"Do you need any help cleaning up whatever you just broke in there?"

"Nope."

"Okay then. Sweetie, listen…," he paused. "I do understand. You know I do. Just please promise me you will take care of yourself."

"Is Sophie okay?" I asked.

"She's a little shaken. I mean, I don't think she's ever seen you like this before. I don't think she's ever seen you yell before, let alone at her, but she'll be fine."

I stepped out of the room to give him a hug. "Tell her I'm sorry, okay?"

"I will."

"Seeing her is just…. She looks just like him."

"I know."

"I want to be happy for her. I do. I just don't know how to be. And now," I said, wiping my eyes, "she's got all these new plans. In a few months she'll be going off to college, and she gets to have a brand new start."

Would I ever have one of those again?

I sobbed silently into Dad's chest, not wanting Sophie to hear me. Little did I know that she had been standing at the bottom of the stairs the entire time.

Dad rubbed my back and whispered, "Shh, shh, shh," not to get me to be quiet or to calm me down, but to comfort me, to let me know he was there.

When I had settled down and could breathe again, Dad said, "Go take a nice hot bath. Relax. Quiet your mind, your heart, for just a little bit."

I nodded. "Thanks, Daddy."

"Love you, sweetheart," he said, kissing the top of my head.

"I love you too."

I turned around to walk back into my room and into the bathroom. As I did, I heard the stairs squeak beneath Dad's feet.

I started the bath, the old pipes wheezing and rattling behind the tiles, and undressed. I could faintly hear Sophie talking to Scout and then I heard the front door shut behind them as she and Dad left. Suddenly I felt so alone again.

I looked in the mirror for the first time in a week. The dark bags under my eyes only highlighted how red they were. My face was gaunt, making my cheekbones stick out at weird angles. My olive skin looked ghostly pale. Grief had aged me five years in a few weeks' time. No wonder they looked terrified when they saw me earlier today. I looked horrible. I looked sick.

Waiting for the water to cool, I looked around the bathroom. I hated this bathroom. It was outdated with its cherry pink tiles, rose wallpaper, and chandelier that looked like it belonged in the '60s.

This was the next project on our to-do list. *Our* to-do list: mine and Michael's. The thought of all these tasks suddenly becoming my sole responsibility overwhelmed me. And without Michael's income, I didn't know how I was going to be able to live here much longer, let alone do renovations. All these thoughts hit me hard in the stomach, and it was unbearable to endure for another second longer.

I stood up and searched for what had now become my holy grail—that blessed little orange prescription bottle filled with Xanax. I popped one in my mouth and waited for the drug to kick in: the slowing down, the relaxation, the medicine-induced oblivion.

I stepped into the water, sat down, and closed my eyes.

These days my thoughts could be turned off like a light switch that was out of my control. Sadness, anger, and frustration were quickly replaced by a state of numbness, confusion, and disbelief.

When I got out of the tub, I towel-dried my hair and threw on my robe. The silence was too loud, but when I turned on music the noise was too quiet. Nothing seemed to make sense anymore.

A few nights later, I took some sleeping pills to help me fall asleep at a normal time. As I lay in bed, feeling warm and hazy from the drugs, I thought about Michael.

"Do you remember that one night when you came to my window over Christmas break?" I asked him. "I never told you this, but that was the most romantic thing anyone's ever done for me. You took my breath away."

I paused. "I remember this one party we went to, after we had been dating for a year or so. You were standing across the room from me and I was sitting on the couch by Shane and Logan. I was listening to them joke around, but I was looking right at you. And then you looked at me and smiled. From across the room, I felt our connection. I remember thinking to myself how lucky I was that you were mine.

"And now, you're not. Now you're gone," I said as my eyes grew heavy.

The first thing I noticed was that it was bright in the room. And then I realized that Michael was here. He was here and he felt so real. He moved his arm around me. I touched his face softly and felt the light stubble on his chin. I ran my fingers through his sunlit hair. I could smell him—the sweet combination of oil, dust, his earthy cologne, and fabric softener. I felt his tight muscles pull me closer. The huge hole in my heart was filled. I was complete again. It gave me a peace I hadn't felt in such a long time.

"Michael," my voice rasped.

"It's okay, baby. I'm here. I'm here," his soft voice assured me. He closed his eyes in sleepiness. I could feel his warmth and the rise and fall of his chest as he breathed.

Suddenly, his warmth faded to icy coldness.

"Michael," I called. "Michael," louder this time.

The room turned pitch black. Then the darkness became illuminated by the numbers 2:37—they covered the walls, the floor, the ceiling. I turned to face Michael. It wasn't him anymore but rather a lifeless corpse with the numbers carved on the forehead, the chest, all down the arms and legs.

A blood-curdling scream escaped my throat. I jolted upright in the bed, covered in sweat.

It was a dream. It was only a dream. I was relieved at first. Then terror seized my heart. *NO*, I thought. *No, no, no. It was so real. Michael, Michael, come back.*

The hole was back, causing me to clutch my chest in physical agony. I grabbed my hair and screamed. I didn't know how much more of this I could take.

I felt like I was going to die of emotional overload. People have died of grief, of broken hearts, right? Right now, I felt like Death would be a welcome friend.

I had already resigned myself to the fact that I would never really feel again, that I'd never walk down the street holding my lover's hand again, that I'd never get excited for anniversaries, holidays, or birthdays. Those emotions and events were now just reminders of what used to be and what would never be.

The screaming continued until I had nothing left in me to give, but I was restless. I needed to move, to take control. I needed to run.

I jumped out of bed, searching for my running clothes, and threw them on. I grabbed Scout's leash from the hook by the front door.

As I ran down the dark street, all I could hear was the wind blowing past my ears and my heart pounding in my chest. It was freezing outside, but I continued running: down my street, down Main Street through downtown, and continuing down the road.

Push on. Run, run. One more step, one more step.

I could hear Scout's heavy breathing next to me and the galloping rhythm of his paws hitting the ground.

Sweat dripped down into my eyes and I could feel the metallic bump of the charms against my chest as I ran. With each step, I gained strength and freedom from my fears.

I didn't even know where I was going until I got there. I knocked at the door. It took a long minute, but then a light flicked on.

"Skylar?" I heard a voice ask before I felt my body hit the hard ground.

"Skylar. Skylar?" I heard the voice again, as someone shook me. My eyes fluttered open. The light above me filled the room with a piercing whiteness, and it caused a sharp sting of pain in my temples. A blurred figure stood over me.

"Skylar?" the voice called again. A male voice. "Are you okay?"

"Huh? What?" I asked, trying to sit up but a strong hand pinned me down. But I wasn't afraid, I was just confused. *Where was I? How did I get here?*

I felt a hot tongue lick my face. I'd know that breath anywhere. *Scout.*

The figure started to become more defined as my eyes adjusted: brown hair, gray-blue eyes, clean-shaven face, and high cheekbones.

Relief swept over me.

"Logan?" I croaked.

"Skylar? Hey! Thank God, you're awake," Logan paused; the tight ridges that had formed between his eyebrows softening and fading. "You scared the hell out of me! I didn't know what was wrong with you."

"What happened?" I asked.

"I was just sitting here, grading papers, then I heard someone banging on the door. When I opened it, you fainted. You nearly cracked your head open in the process."

"Oh," I said, embarrassed, rubbing my head. "I didn't wake Madison up, did I?"

"No, she's with Brooke tonight."

"Oh, okay." I sat up, realizing I was on his couch.

"So are you going to tell me what happened?" He sat down on the chair across from the couch.

That's when I began to tell him about everything that had happened the past few days: the picture frames, the visit from Sophie and Dad, my freak-out, the dream. The impulse to run had been so demanding that I had no choice in the matter. It was mandatory, a survival mechanism.

"I just feel so lost without him," I said. "I just keep spiraling down deeper and deeper."

He just listened, nodding his head.

"I feel like I'm going completely mental. I can't keep things straight anymore. I'm out of control," I said, collapsing my head into my hands.

"I see him everywhere," I confessed to Logan. "I walk down the hallway, and he's standing in the bathroom shaving. I walk into the kitchen, and he's pouring me a cup of coffee, smiling at me like nothing's happened. The other day I went to the store," I paused, then continued quickly, trying to hold back new tears that were starting to form, "and I saw a guy with blond hair and the same body type as Michael. I would have bet my life that he was Michael. I was so sure. I followed him around the entire store. I even called out his name a few times to see if he would react. He never did, of course."

"So what happened? With that guy?" Logan asked.

I laughed quietly. "I followed him out to the parking lot and he gave me this look, like he was wondering if I'd escaped from the local psychiatric hospital. And when I saw him, face-to-face, I knew that it wasn't really Michael, my Michael. My little delusion crumbled to the ground and I burst into tears. I spent the rest of the day in bed. I never even got the groceries I went to the store for."

Logan's eyes glistened. His expression brought my attention back to the fact that I was not the only one affected by Michael's death. A fact that I forgot all the time, so secluded in my self-appointed exile and self-absorption.

He was quiet for a minute. "I miss him too."

I nodded.

"I find myself thinking a lot about college lately," he said, a smile spreading across his face. "How many weekends did the four of us spend cooped up in the apartment, watching movies or playing video games?"

"Hey, to be fair, we did leave the apartment every now and then," I said, pulling the blanket closer around me.

"Yeah, to get food or go to the arcade," he said, grinning.

"We went to a few parties," I countered.

Logan shot me a dubious look. "We sat in the apartment and drank beer. It was just the four of us, not exactly a party."

"No, that's not true! Sometimes you and Shane brought friends or a girl over. And Ava, Halle, and Molly joined us occasionally!"

"Fair enough," he said, shaking his head in assent.

In the following seconds of silence, the lighthearted moment twisted and turned into a deep sorrow; an ache spread through my heart. "What I wouldn't do to go back in time and live those moments again," I whispered, looking down as my fingers played with the frayed hems of the blanket. "Just to see his face one more time and hear his laugh. To be in that space where everything felt so easy. You know?

"It's like, if only we had known then how heavy and hard everything would turn out to be, we could've stayed there a little while longer."

Logan looked down at his hands folded together across his knees. "But we will always have that," he said. "Those memories of those times—no one can take any of that away from us."

Managing a nod, I swallowed hard, trying to hold back a sob.

"You know he adored you. You turned his world upside down in the best way possible.... You were his everything, Skylar. What you guys had was really special."

"We were lucky."

"Yeah, you were. And you'll always have that too."

I shook my head. "No one understands how much of my life was made up of him. I don't think I even knew how much my life revolved around him. Nothing makes sense anymore. I don't know who I am without him."

"Skylar," Logan said, looking me directly in the eye, "we just have to do our best with what we've got. You'll be okay, I know it doesn't seem like it now. But you will make it through this. You'll figure out who you are."

"Will I?" I asked.

"Yes, you will."

I didn't want to listen to him, but the depth of his

words held a truth I desperately needed to hear. "How do you know?" I asked sincerely.

"Because I am getting back to okay again, slowly but surely. He was your whole world, Sky, I know that. But he was my best friend, my brother."

"I'm sorry I haven't been here for you," I whispered.

"Stop. You have no reason to apologize. We're all just trying to figure out how to move on."

I was quiet for a minute. My eyes drifted around the room. I saw Logan's leather messenger bag sitting on the floor next to his desk in the dining room, most likely filled with lesson plans and papers from his high school English students.

On the desk there was a laptop and stacks of books—some literature, some textbooks. Hanging on the wall was his bachelor's degree in secondary education and English from Michigan State University and his new master's degree in English from Wayne State University.

In the corner of the room, bins were filled with Madison's toys and books.

Logan cleared his throat and my eyes flicked back to his. "You just need to take it one day at a time, one moment at a time if you need to. That's what I did when my dad died," he said quietly. "It gets easier...*eventually.*"

"You were seventeen, right?"

He nodded.

"That must have been rough.... I don't remember it being this hard when my mom passed away," I admitted. "I guess I was too young to really understand."

He yawned and I noticed how tired he looked. There were dark bags under his eyes.

"Logan, are you okay? You look exhausted."

"Welcome to fatherhood," he said, smiling. "Sleep has become a luxury."

"How is she?" I asked, a new life to distract from a lost one.

"Oh, she's doing pretty well. She is very well-behaved, very smart—."

"Just like her dad," I said.

"Yeah, I guess," he smiled at me. "We went to the indoor water park with my sister and nephews today."

"Oh yeah, did she like it?"

"Had a blast. She kept wanting me to hold her and stand under the big bucket that fills with water and then pours down over the whole jungle gym."

He started to laugh. "She couldn't get enough of that. Laughed the entire time."

I laughed with him, my lungs shaking with the effort. "How old are your nephews?"

"Jonah's four and Tyler's six," he said, his eyes looking at the ceiling as he thought. "Madison adores them. Chases them around and copies everything they do. But they love it."

"Sounds like you have your hands full."

"Yes, I do. This wasn't how I imagined my life would be. But I wouldn't trade her for the world."

"I always wanted a little boy," I said quietly, touching my flat stomach.

"You've still got plenty of time," he said.

Then in a low gentle tone he asked, "Skylar, why'd you come here?"

"I saw how you looked at the funeral," I said, pausing. "And Sophie, my Dad, Shane, they've been great, but I needed to be with a friend who understands exactly what I'm feeling. Someone who is probably just as fucked up about this as I am."

His lips split into a wry grin. "Then you came to the right place."

My eyes met his, and I was suddenly filled with gratitude to have him in my life.

"I've been stuck in that house for a month now. I had to get out of there. I couldn't breathe anymore."

He looked at me, full of empathy. Then his phone rang. "Sorry it's Brooke, I have to take this."

"Yeah, no problem," I said. I watched him get up and walk into the kitchen. I could hear his side of the conversation from the living room.

Brooke and Logan separated when Madison was seven months old. Logan had told us that it was a mutual decision, that they had decided they weren't right for each other, but I had always suspected there was more to the story than that. For one, if ever two people were meant to be together, I was sure it was them. They were that couple who couldn't take their eyes off each other and were always in close proximity, some part of them always had to be touching. And the glow that radiated from the both of them when Brooke was pregnant, it was something else. Even Michael had noticed it.

In the months following the separation, Logan had tried to hide his heartbreak from us, but we could tell he was pretty torn up about losing Brooke. For a while, he stopped going out with us and quit the bowling league we were all in. When we asked him about why he looked so distraught, he made excuses and blamed it on the stress from school and work.

He had us worried for a while, and we would make a point to stop by the townhouse apartment and help out with Madison when we could. But by Madison's first birthday, he was starting to do better and we all relaxed a little bit.

My thoughts started to drift, and I must have dozed off while Logan was gone because I was only slightly aware of him coming back into the living room and his quiet chuckle when he saw me passed out on the couch. He walked across the room, pulled off my shoes, put an extra blanket on top of me, and turned off the light.

But before he turned to walk down the hallway, he brushed away the hair from my face and leaned down to kiss my forehead, his soft lips meeting my skin. "It's all going to be okay, Skylar," he promised and walked away.

The strong, bittersweet aroma of coffee pulled me from

The Charm Necklace

slumber and I sat up. I looked around the room. I was surrounded by tan walls and I was lying on the couch. An ancient TV sat snug in a rich oak entertainment center full of books and countless DVDs. There were colorful plastic toys scattered across the floor.

"Good morning," Logan said, walking into the living room from the kitchen. "How'd you sleep?"

"Good," I said, not willing to let him know how much unexpected comfort I found in his company, in his apartment.

"There's coffee," he said, sitting on the chaise across the room. He picked up the remote and started going through all the channels.

"Don't you have to work today?" I asked.

"It's Sunday."

"Oh," I said. I didn't even know what day it was anymore, and I didn't even care. "Well, I think I should get home."

"You sure? There's no rush," he said.

"Yeah," I said and sat up awkwardly. I started to put my shoes on and Scout moved toward me, getting ready to leave.

"Do you want a ride home?"

"Um, do you mind? What about Scout?"

"It's no problem. Let me just grab my shoes."

I was still waking up as he drove, and we were silent for most of the car ride.

When he pulled up to the house, he turned to me

and said, "I'm meeting up with Shane and some of the guys later tonight downtown. I'm sure everyone would love to see you, if you can make it."

"Um, thanks, Logan. Really," I paused. "But I can't. Not yet."

"Yeah, I understand. Just thought I'd offer. But Skylar," he reached for my arm, "don't be a stranger. You're always welcome."

"Thanks, Logan. For everything. I appreciate it."

He pulled me in for an awkward hug across the console.

"Bye," I said, trying to smile at him.

I couldn't wait to get out of the car and into my house. Guilt hung over me like a cloud. I felt so guilty for taking comfort in someone other than Michael, for feeling okay for even just a second. Even though it had felt so good, a reprieve from the emptiness.

I wondered if I would ever feel okay again. If I would ever not feel guilty if I felt happy or something other than sad. Only time would tell.

The aftermath following a death is not finite. It's infinite. There's not one straight line to the course grieving takes. It spins around in circles, uncontrollably. It backtracks, it dives down, it stops abruptly, and begins again as quickly and as unexpectedly as it ended. It's not neat or clear. It's messy and ambiguous and it doesn't fit in the neat squares and lines of a calendar like everyone wants it to. It's not one-dimensional; the grief comes at you again and again from a different angle each time so you're left not knowing when and how the next assault will take place. Death is completely unfair.

VII

Reality

My bereavement allowance was up and I had to be back to work the following Monday. The night before brought little sleep as my mind fought anticipation with exhaustion. When the shriek of the alarm went off, I was relieved that there was finally an end to what seemed like an endless night.

I was anxious about going back. *Could I handle all the work right now? Would I be able to make it through the day?* I was tired to the bone, but this kind of tired couldn't be cured with a good night's sleep or a vacation at the beach. Only time would tell if this weariness would go away.

I threw the blankets off and headed to the bathroom to get ready. It had been so long since I had gone through this routine, so long since I cared what the reflection in the mirror looked like.

After I had showered, I walked into the bedroom. I turned on the light and opened the closet. I looked at my clothes and when my eyes wandered to Michael's side of the closet, my face crumpled as tears filled my eyes.

Michael should be here right now. He should be stepping into the shower right now. In ten minutes he should be calling for me to get him a towel because he forgot to bring one into the bathroom. He should be waltzing into the bedroom, all smiles, and give me a hug, a kiss, and a pat on the butt. He should be getting dressed. He should be on his way to work. That's what he should be doing, but he's not.

I felt especially exposed today, like I had been stripped down and left only with my vulnerabilities. I wiped away the tears, telling myself that I was not going to break down today. I was going to be strong. I wasn't going to cry. I was going to go to work, do what I had to do, then come home and hide away safe from the world. No feelings, no emotions, just performing my tasks with dull unthinking functionality.

I pulled on a black blazer and gray work pants. Not bothering to dry my hair or do my makeup, I just pulled my hair back into a wet ponytail.

I didn't feel dread as I walked into the police department, just extremely weak, like I wanted to curl up into a ball and stay that way forever. When I walked into the large empty lobby, I pushed the feeling down, determined to ignore it.

I continued walking through the lobby, discreetly dodging the chatty receptionist. I didn't have the energy for small talk.

My desk was located in the corner of the large squad room. The room was the island for misfit desks. They were all mismatched: some oak, some cherry, some cheap ones of fake pressed wood. They were all beaten up and old, covered with papers, files, and empty coffee cups. Computers hummed on each one. There were a few whiteboards pushed against the wall with pictures and timelines written on them. Captain Harry Field, our boss, liked to say our office has *character*. Right, that's what it was.

The back wall had large windows that let in a lot of natural light, but the fluorescent lights buzzed above our heads incessantly nonetheless. I hated the way they always cast a ghostly shadow on people's faces and made the dark circles under everyone's eyes appear even darker.

Being back in this room, surrounded by people who cared about the work they did, people who knew the person I was before everything had happened, fortified me. There was a hardiness here that kept everyone diligently working, even through the most tedious tasks.

Looking over my desk, with its stack of files and blue desk lamp, I remembered what it felt like to be good at something. I was smart, competent, and efficient; I had contributed valuable services and insights here.

The Charm Necklace

I reached up and touched the charms settling around my throat, holding on to them in my fist. I closed my eyes and breathed in deeply. I felt peace and strength hum in my heart. Maybe coming back to work was exactly what I needed after all.

When I opened them, my eyes focused on the two pictures on my desk. One was of me holding Scout when we first adopted him from the animal shelter; the other one was of Michael and me on the beach during spring break a few years ago.

These pictures were memories frozen in time. Seeing Michael in those pictures comforted me, just knowing that he was there in some form gave me courage.

My job was to help the detectives. I was in constant communication with them, looking up any information they might need, analyzing bank accounts, and watching surveillance tapes. It might not sound glamorous, but I loved my job. I loved the feeling of losing myself in numbers and records. I thrived on the systematic, careful analysis.

It wasn't exactly what I was expecting to do with my degree. I had originally planned to be some sort of detective or special agent working in the field, but after an internship here one summer, I knew this was what I needed to do. My place was in the office, not in the field.

I remember Michael feigning disappointment when I interviewed for the job and got it.

"What do you mean you're not going to be some

badass detective, running around chasing bad guys and getting shot at? And here I was bragging about you to everyone, telling them not to mess with me or else my girlfriend was going to arrest them."

He didn't fool me—I knew he was relieved.

Just as I was sitting down, Harry strode over to my desk. "Medina!" he boomed. "You're back!"

Harry was characterized by mainly one thing: he was huge. Not the obese kind of huge but the big-boned kind of huge. He would tower over you, and if you didn't know him that well, he'd intimidate the hell out of you. He had short, thick brown hair, a chubby face, and flushed cheeks. His eyes, although visibly weary from years in the game, had a flame of gentle determination that drew people to him.

"Hi, Harry," I said. I looked up at him from my desk. I hadn't realized how much I missed him, how much I missed my work.

"How are you feeling? You sure you're ready to come back?" he asked quietly, leaning forward so only I could hear him.

I nodded my head up and down, afraid that if I opened my mouth the words would come flowing out before I could stop them. *Was I ready to come back?* I wasn't sure, but what choice did I have? It was either come back to work and try to function like a normal human being or hide out in my house for the rest of my pitiful life.

He watched me closely, inspecting for

inconsistencies. He had been a detective for twenty-odd years, after all.

"All right, then," he said, but he knew. He knew better than I did that I just needed everyone else to go on like nothing had happened, that I needed to get lost in work so that I could be distracted from my pain, I needed things to go back to normal—or at least as normal as they could be. "Well, we've closed the Smith/Martin case. We've still got five open cases right now, and we got a call about a body earlier this morning that I'm probably going to need your assistance on."

"Who's working it?"

"Hill and Nathanson."

I inwardly groaned. They were such asshats, so full of themselves.

"Anything else?"

"Well they're out right now, following some leads, so stand by for their calls. But for now, I was wondering if you'd mind doing some clerical work?"

"Such as?"

"I need you to update the database with the last few cases we've closed." We always kept the hard file, but everything also had to be converted into digital form now.

"Not a problem."

"They're in my office. Come get them when you're ready. You okay with this? You'll be able to handle it?"

"Yes, sir." I thought I could pretty much handle, or at least survive, anything life threw at me by that point.

"Okay, then. Have a good one, Medina. Let me know if you need anything." And with that he walked away, stopping a few desks over to get an update from some of the detectives.

After retrieving the files from Harry's office, I spent the next several hours at my desk transcribing the files into the database. Focusing on the names, dates, and details of the reports was so absorbing that I had no room in my head to think of anything else.

Early in the afternoon I was startled when a large to-go coffee cup was placed down in front of me on my desk. Looking up, I saw the broad grin and sturdy jaw of Tom Nathanson.

"Welcome back, Medina."

"Good to be here, Detective," I replied with a professional clipped tone.

"Vanilla latte, right?"

I nodded, touched by the unexpected friendly gesture. "Yes, thank you. What can I help you with?"

He handed over a file. I opened it, seeing the record and mug shot of Enrique Delgado. He was young, sixteen according to the file. There were no visible tattoos on his face or neck. He had soft brown eyes and the smooth skin of someone without much facial hair. He had one offense of loitering and two of petty larceny. The report cited no known gang affiliation.

"This is our vic," Nathanson said. "Three gunshot wounds to the chest. Body was found this morning in a vacant lot by a group of kids walking to school."

"That's a pleasant way to start the day," I said.

That got a dry laugh out of him. "Tell me about it."

"How long has he been dead?" I asked.

"M.E. says he was killed last night between eleven and midnight."

"So what's the story? This kid doesn't exactly look like a banger."

"Not sure, exactly. The mom says he was a good kid, worked a lot to help out with the bills, you know the story. But he hasn't been in school much lately and two of his friends haven't seen him the past few days."

"You think he got mixed up with the wrong crowd?"

"It's possible. Maybe he was trying to get in with one of the gangs, maybe he already was in one, something went wrong, and they took care of the liability."

I nodded, biting on my lower lip in thought. Sixteen years old—he was just a kid. And now he was dead. "So phone records, social media, bank accounts, employee records, anything else?"

"Start with those and we'll see what they tell us."

"I'll let you know if I find anything," I said as he walked away.

At the end of the day, after scouring through Delgado's phone records and finding several calls to a suspicious number and connections to a girl named Monica Dierks, I shut down my computer and walked quickly out of the room, before anyone could say anything to me.

I found my gray Civic in the parking lot. I got in, started it, locked the doors, and took a deep breath. I had made it through my first day back at work.

I wasn't ready to heal and move on yet. I wasn't ready to care about the needs of others, to socialize and have responsibilities, to be a person again. But at the same time, I was *not* ready to go home to an empty house.

I didn't feel like myself anymore. I had always been guarded, but never in an unfriendly way. I used to smile at people when I saw them, I used to be able to have a conversation, I used to feel passionate about my job, my friends, my life. Now I felt nothing.

It was six fifteen when I walked through my front door, dropping my purse on the floor.

I was beyond fatigue and it was only Monday. In the kitchen, I flipped on the light and poured some food into Scout's bowl. Then I poured myself a glass of wine. I leaned against the counter and took a sip. *So this is my life now?* I wondered. This is pathetic. I am pathetic.

As the wine went to my head and relaxed my body, I could feel the ache in my heart unleash after being tucked away all day. My throat was sore and swollen from the effort of trying to hold back tears, so I just let them go, my shoulders shaking from the force of them. Standing in the kitchen. Alone.

I walked back into the living room and sat down on

the couch. I looked over at Michael's chair, willing him to be there, but he wasn't. At the office, I could pretend he was there in the pictures because that was the only way that he had been there. He had only been to the office once or twice in person, so when I was at work I kept in touch with him by his pictures or the sound of his voice on the other side of the phone.

But here, in our house, I had known him in person. I knew this home by his presence in it. It was a lot harder to pretend I was okay when his absence was so potent.

I turned on the TV and surfed aimlessly through the channels. I came across *MythBusters* on the Discovery Channel and stopped. It was one of Michael's favorite shows.

I suddenly regretted that I never sat down to cuddle and watch it with him. I regretted not spending that valuable, precious time with him. I regretted that I didn't know the names of the hosts. *Why hadn't I done that?* I thought. *What was I doing during those times? Out running? Cleaning the kitchen? Doing laundry? Reading a book? Working late? Why hadn't I just set those things aside for another day, another hour while I spent those sixty treasured minutes with Michael?*

I was unable to tear my eyes away from the screen. I continued watching the show, searching for signs of Michael everywhere.

Two men were setting up some sort of contraption and talking about trigger devices and the next thing I saw was a huge explosion.

"So that's why you like this show so much?" I asked Michael out loud. "Because they just blow things up?"

"Watch this, babe," I heard Michael say, and when I looked over I saw him sitting in his chair. He looked perfectly relaxed, and happy. "They are about to see if a car stereo can set off a rifle!"

My answer two months ago would have been something like, "Seriously? This is more important than the stack of dishes in the sink that needs to be washed?"

Remorse filled my heart; it forced grief out because there was just not enough room in there for the two of them. *Was it really necessary for me to be such a bitch to him?* It wasn't all the time, but it did happen, and I felt horrible about it now. He deserved better. He didn't deserve to take the backlash for my bad day at work. He didn't deserve my stubbornness, my selfishness, my coldness.

No, he wasn't perfect either. He didn't always pick up the dirty clothes he left in the bathroom or load the dishwasher when the sink was overflowing with dishes. And he had an annoying habit of playing with Scout outside in the mud and then tracking it all over the house.

But he loved me unconditionally. He protected me when I was scared, held me when I cried, ignored all my rude comments when I was crabby. He always gave me a kiss good morning and a kiss good night. *No, I didn't deserve him at all.*

I watched as Michael's face lit up with excitement

The Charm Necklace

and his mouth opened wide with laughter. The sound filled my chest and spread throughout my body. It shocked like electricity in my veins. And it was gone just as fast as it had come. And so was Michael.

The closing credits scrolled across the screen. The sudden emptiness was dizzying and burned like acid. It felt like a cruel joke, like the little bit of life I had left had been sucked out of me by a vortex. I closed my mouth, trying to hold in whatever soul was left of me. My eyes were dry. I was speechless.

I turned off the TV and walked blindly up the stairs and into my bed. I crashed into the sweet release of sleep.

The first weekend after going back to work, I woke up on Saturday morning expecting to feel tired and lethargic. But I found myself feeling the need to do something.

I got out of bed, grabbed a sweater, and threw it over my head. I walked downstairs, nearly tripping on all the *stuff* that had accumulated on them. There were flowers from the funeral home that were now dried out and dead, sympathy cards, brochures and paperwork from the funeral home, bills, and endless junk mail.

I went into the kitchen and stared at the mess that used to be the counters and the sink. The few dishes I had used were stacked in the sink. I had thrown the used coffee filters into a pot on the stove. *What the hell had I been thinking?*

My cell phone sat dead on the counter. I plugged it in and turned it on. It beeped continually for the next hour as all the text messages, missed phone calls, and voice mails loaded.

I pulled my hair back, turned on my iPod, and got to work cleaning the house.

Two hours later, the house was clean and most of the laundry was done. I put the laptop, the checkbook, and the stack of mail and bills on the dining room table.

There were so many things that needed to be done, so many decisions that needed to be made. There were some things that I couldn't take care of because I wasn't Michael's next of kin—we had yet to marry. Rob and Sue would have to take care of those things. But I could cancel his insurance, take his name off our joint bank accounts, cancel his phone, and so many other things.

And then there was the issue of the house. I had no idea how I would be able to afford it on my own, but with our savings and the money that would've gone toward the wedding in June, I had at least a year to figure it out.

It was just the actual figuring out part that I didn't want to do. How would I be able to leave the place that had been ours? But then again, how could I stay?

Beyond my mental capabilities for the day, I ambled into the living room and flopped down on the couch. I looked over the clean and empty house, wanting to believe so badly this wasn't my life.

The remaining days of March slowly evolved into April. I made it to work every single day and was now able to carry on a conversation with Jan, the secretary, Harry, and the detectives.

I had helped Nathanson solve the Delgado case. It turned out Delgado had unknowingly crossed the Los Diablos Rojos gang and initiate Pablo Sanchez had done the hit. Pablo was now in custody awaiting trial.

I could lose myself in my work. I could put on my imaginary crime-solving cape, put aside my emotions, and become someone who wasn't defined by grief.

But there were moments, after hitting the Snooze button in the dark of morning, when depression and despair would swallow me again. I would have to grit my teeth and squeeze my eyes shut to stop the tears from falling. To get up meant that another day had just passed without Michael in it and another one without him was beginning. It meant that the ache in my chest would slowly fade to a warm glow and then to nothing. It meant that I would, somehow, have to move on with my life and move on from Michael's death.

And sometimes, as I lay in the darkness waiting for the alarm to go off, I allowed myself to believe for those few minutes that that didn't have to be true. That I could stay here in this moment forever, remembering Michael, not moving forward, not accepting what happened. I could pretend that he was still right next to me, sleeping.

But illusions can only last so long. So yeah, basically, life still sucked.

VIII

Plunged into the depths

It felt surreal pulling up to Dad's house on Easter afternoon. I thought about growing up here. I thought of happy memories with my mom—that were now overshadowed by the loneliness and barrenness after her death. I thought about how my feelings of inadequacy had changed after Michael had become part of our family. He had brought life back into the house and had shown us what it felt like to be a normal family again. Christmas mornings, when we sat around the tree and opened presents, the house was filled with laughter and joy instead of empty sadness.

In the summers, after Michael and Dad finished working on the house or the car, we would have a barbecue and drink beers together in the evenings. But now, with Michael gone, the lack of life was back like an old enemy I never wanted to see again.

I thought about how for the past seven years, practically my whole adult life, Michael and I had spent Easter Sunday with his family. We would get dressed up and go to church with Rob, Sue, and Sophie. Michael and I, holding hands, would steal glances as Reverend Romarro led the service, and then afterward we would go back to his parents' house for a big dinner. I had loved the feeling of being with him on holidays and sharing those intimate, family moments with him.

When Michael dressed up for holidays and special occasions, I could barely wait for the festivities to be over to get him alone. The way he looked in dress pants and a button-up shirt only made me want him more than I usually did. I laughed remembering the time Sophie almost caught us in Michael's basement bedroom after Easter dinner my senior year of college. We froze when we heard the knock on the door, and I hid under the covers as Michael went to the door and made up some excuse to get Sophie out of there. The excitement of almost getting caught had only made our love making more frenzied and passionate.

All these different memories, from what felt like separate lives, flooded my mind. Memories were like puzzle pieces, but how did you put the pieces together when they were all from different puzzles? When they didn't add up to a whole, coherent picture?

Scout started barking when he saw Dad come out

the front door holding a cup of coffee in his hand.

"Hey, Dad." I called, getting out of the car.

"Hello there, darlin'. Happy Easter!"

"Happy Easter to you too."

"Come on in; I just made a pot of coffee," he said, holding the door open. "I was thinking maybe for dinner we could make roast lamb, mashed potatoes, and green beans. I was even thinking of attempting to make some *folar*."

"The sweet bread?" I asked, perplexed.

"Yeah. I thought that maybe we could start a new tradition this year. Honor a little bit of our heritage."

I was touched by my dad's efforts to make this horrible transition as easy as possible. It almost brought tears to my eyes

I cleared my throat. "That sounds great."

"Listen, honey," he said, as he walked through the living room into the kitchen and sat down at the old linoleum table. I followed him through and went to the coffee pot on the counter. "Not that I don't appreciate you keeping an old man like me company on a holiday, but are you sure you don't want to go to Rob and Sue's? Sue called me yesterday inviting us over. And you know Sophie, she's been bugging me nonstop to get you over there."

I shook my head. Sue had called me last week too, and it wasn't that I didn't miss them. I did. I just wasn't ready for what their presence and that empty spot at the table would bring: an overpowering reminder of who wasn't there among us.

I closed my eyes and exhaled. "I'm sure, Dad."

He must have heard the irritation in my voice because when he spoke it was soft and soothing. "Okay. I understand."

"Will they?" I asked.

"Eventually."

I looked at him, urging him to go on.

"Well for the same reasons that you don't want to see them, they want to see you."

Oh. "I guess I hadn't thought of that."

"Have you talked to them at all?"

"Only once when Sue called last week. The only person I've seen or talked to lately is Logan."

"You saw Logan?" he asked, surprised.

"Yeah, it was only once. One night I just had to get out of the house, and I ended up at his place." I wanted to tell him how nice and comforting it had been, but I couldn't bring myself to do it.

"Oh," he said. "It's good to have friends, isn't it? But Sky, look, Rob and Sue and Sophie, they just miss you," he hesitated then continued, "If you can, you know, try and give them a call. They would probably like to hear from you."

"Okay," I said, not making any promises.

There was a pause in the conversation as Dad yelled at Scout to get out of the garbage.

"Skylar, how are you *really* doing?" he asked.

"Honestly?" I tried to collect my thoughts as I leaned against the counter.

It felt as if my feet were glued to the ground, encased in cement blocks. And everyone else was moving on, going on with their lives. They were able to worry about simple things like the price of gas or which laundry detergent to use or where they were going to go on vacation this year. But I couldn't move. I was stuck.

The strain of living felt like an invisible, ever-changing barrier I was always trying to break free from. Things like getting out of bed and having conversations felt damn near impossible sometimes.

But what I said was, "Some days are better than others. There are days when I just feel nothing, and then there are days when everything just feels really dark."

I struggled to keep a straight face as my voice broke, "The kind of darkness that squeezes all the air out of the room and presses down on you. But being back at work is helping. I'm exhausted all the time, but at least it keeps my mind occupied. I don't really have time to dwell on my issues when there's so much work to get done."

I walked over and sat down at the table. "I miss him so much."

Dad reached across the table and put his hand on mine. "Me too, sweetheart. It's hard and I don't think the pain ever really goes away, it just dulls. Your life will never go back to what it was. There will have to be a new normal. From here on out, your life will be separated into *Before* and *After*."

"That sounds like the most horrible way to view life that I've ever heard of," I said bluntly.

"It's the truth, though."

"Sometimes I feel as though people will forever see me as this grieving widow. Well, not a *widow* because we weren't married, but you know. And then other times, I feel as though everyone is expecting me to just get better all of a sudden. To be back to how I was. To be back to normal—whatever the hell that is." I put my head in my hands. "I just feel like no one understands."

"No one will ever really understand, no matter how pure and good their intentions, because it wasn't their relationship. You were connected to Michael in a way that no one else ever was.

"Even I can't fully understand, and I lost your mother. I miss her like crazy. There are days when I feel like it was just yesterday that she was here. And there's not a day that goes by that I don't think about her. But that was *our* relationship. Do you see? You lost her too, as a mother, but not the same way that I lost her. It's different for everyone. And every death."

He continued. "It's hard to move on because you feel like you're stuck in the past, like you're afraid to move forward, because if you do it's like you're forgetting Michael or leaving him behind. But you're not. He will always be with you. Just like your mother has never left your heart."

The Charm Necklace

He sighed and his eyes fell on the charms hanging around my neck for a moment before he glanced away. I watched him as he looked out the window; his broad, flat nose, his dark black hair weaved with gray, the rich color of his skin.

In his eyes I saw the depth of his courage. No, he hadn't always been the perfect father, but he had done the best he could, given the circumstances, and I never doubted for a second his love for me.

Dad was living his life the only way he knew how. He had never expressed any interest in dating or remarrying again, but he had allowed himself to care deeply for others even at the risk of getting hurt again. He enjoyed watching his football games and found comfort in the routine of his work. When he laughed or smiled, it was real, not put on like a mask.

On the more bleak and hopeless days, I wondered why I bothered at all. It seemed that no matter what I did, I couldn't change the fate that suffering was my birthright. I just kept holding on because that was what I did.

But looking at my dad, I knew there were things worth holding on for. My dad was reason enough, but there was also Sophie. And Scout. My work. There was the companionship of my co-workers and the deep respect I had for my boss and my friends. There were little things too, like the burn of achy muscles from running, the feel of warm wind on my skin, the comfort of sweatpants, the rhythm of a good song, beer, and fried ice cream.

But really, deep down, I knew there were things I still wanted to do. More than anything, I knew I wanted to be a mother. I wasn't sure if it was ever going to happen now, but the desire was still there.

Thinking about what my dad had just said, I let his words seep into me and tried to determine what they meant for me and my life.

"How long?" I asked after a few minutes, crossing my arms over my chest. "How long did it take for you to go back to normal? Not like normal-normal, but to able to go through your day without tearing up or passing out from exhaustion. How long was it until you laughed again? Or looked at another woman with interest? How long?" I pleaded.

"Two years," his voice was laced with pain. "It took me two years before I smiled on a holiday or anniversary, before I could really laugh again and mean it when I said I was fine. Your mom was with me the whole time, giving me the strength I needed, but it was two years before she was finally able to let go of me, knowing that I would be okay so that she could go in peace. But of course, it's different for everyone," his voice was hoarse.

It was quiet for a moment.

"Do you think I'm going to be okay? Am I going to make it?" I asked sincerely.

"Yes, sweetheart, you will. You'll make it," his voice was warm and deep. He reached for my hand across the kitchen table and squeezed tight. In that moment, I felt his love reach out to me and surround me. I rested in it.

The remainder of the day passed easily and slowly like a nap on a sunny afternoon. After we had emptied the coffee pot, we started dinner. We cooked next to each other quietly, only talking to ask one another how the potatoes tasted or to pass the salt.

When dinner was done, we fixed our plates and sat down in the living room to watch whatever sports game was on. As the fans cheered and the commentators continued their endless chatter, I chewed my food slowly, feeling the muscles in my face pop with the movement. The spot next to me felt like a void that was pulling me in—palpable and pulsating. When Michael left it was as if he took all the light with him. Everything just felt dim without him. Broken. Incomplete.

I closed my eyes, imagining that Michael was here next to me. Imagining that his warm, solid body was pressed up next to mine, with his hand resting reassuringly on my knee. I imagined the banter that would pass between Michael and Dad as they watched the game. I imagined the easy laughter and fullness that would fill this room if only he were here.

What was left of me was not a whole lot, not my former self. Because Michael and I were connected, joined, fused together, it was hard to make the distinction between him and me. We affected each other so much and so deeply it was hard to tell where one soul ended and the other started. The seams that fastened us together were twisted and indistinct, folding into each other, entwined like lovers' bodies. So when you took one away, ripped it at the seams, you took whole fragments of the other half, leaving the edges jagged and uneven.

"Skylar?" Dad asked tentatively.

"Hmm?" I asked, opening my eyes and looking over at him in his chair.

"You all right?"

I nodded and gave a small smile.

I wrapped myself in the green fleece blanket like a cocoon and spread out on the couch. I closed my eyes and drifted in and out of sleep for the rest of the afternoon.

I wasn't all right. Nowhere close to it. But somehow on this relaxed day, in this cozy familiar room, those edges started to round and heal.

On Tuesday, Harry called me into his office. "Skylar, can I talk to you privately?" he asked me through the phone. I could see him in his office across the room from my desk, waving me over.

"Sure thing. Be right there." And without even knowing the reason why, that now-constant tight ball in my stomach contracted before loosening up into something cold and liquid that spread throughout my body. I tried to reason with myself as I put one foot in front of the other. I told myself that this was about my less-than-stellar performance since I got back. *I've been too distracted, unfocused. That has to be it.* But I couldn't shake the feeling that I was walking into the lion's den with nothing but my bare hands.

When I walked in Harry was nervously shuffling some papers around his desk. It was so unlike him to be fluttering about like that. "Close the door, please," he said.

As I did, the white plastic blinds smacked against the glass several times before they lost their momentum. I glanced out through the windows of his office into the squad room, watching as "uniforms" and detectives hustled across the room.

After I couldn't stall for another second, I sat down in front of his desk. My heart sped up, and I could feel the icy-hot sensation of a cold sweat break out across my forehead and back.

Jesus, it was like being called down to the fucking principal's office when you weren't quite sure what you did wrong, but you knew you were in trouble. Only this was real life.

Finally he looked up, his hazel eyes meeting mine. He ran a finger through his hair.

He cleared his throat. "So how are you doing?"

"I'm fine, Harry," I said cautiously. "Is there something I can do for you?"

"For me? No, no, not at all." He shifted in his seat. "Listen, the reason I brought you in here…. Well, it's a sensitive subject. A personal one. For you."

"For me?" The cold running throughout my body hardened and solidified.

"Yes."

"Harry, just say it already."

"Okay, look, Skylar. It's about Michael's...it's about the kid who was driving the car that hit Michael."

The floor beneath me vanished. The room started to spin. My vision tunneled on Harry.

"Skylar? Skylar?" I heard him saying louder and louder.

"Yes?" I squeaked. I tried to focus on his lips as he talked.

"Are you okay?"

"Yes."

"Can I continue?"

I nodded, bracing myself for what he would say next, for the next onslaught.

"You understand this isn't something I should be telling you, right? But I thought you had the right to know. Heck, I'd want to know."

I nodded again, unable to form words. The floor felt wobbly and unsteady.

"And I'm sorry I didn't tell you sooner. I just didn't have the clearance to do so, and then I thought, screw it, because you deserve to know."

"Know what?"

"This information won't leave this room,

understood? You are not to do anything," he emphasized again, "*anything* with it."

"Don't do anything with what you are about to tell me," I parroted back to him.

"So listen. The kid's name is Tony Cusato. He's seventeen, a senior in high school," he said, showing me the file with the kid's picture. He had long black hair that fell into his eyes, but other than that there was nothing remarkable about him. He was a normal kid. His eyes didn't even look soulless or empty like I had imagined them to be in my dreams, when I saw him slamming into Michael's truck, laughing manically.

My mind started to malfunction, the gears refusing to click together. Harry must've seen the look on my face because he said, "Expected to see the spawn of Satan?"

"Something like that."

"Everyone does."

"What's going to happen to him?"

He took in a deep breath, hesitating. "He was arraigned the day after the accident. He was released on his own recognizance until his sentence hearing—."

"He what?"

Harry's eyes held steady on mine, now sure and committed to what needed to be said. "This is his first offense, and it's a misdemeanor. He's a minor. He has ties to his family and the community and has no means to flee," he said, going down the laundry list. "The most he can be tried for in Michigan is a moving violation—."

"I don't understand."

"A moving violation. It's basically covers any illegal activities that occur while a car is in motion."

You know those Saturday morning cartoons when the character gets so angry that his whole body turns red and steam comes out of his ears? I suddenly knew *exactly* how that felt.

"You're telling me," I said with slow deliberation, "that the guy, who killed my fiancé, the man I was *supposed* to marry in just a few months, *might* get charged with a moving violation and *maybe* go to jail for less than a year, if that?"

"Yes, but—."

"He KILLED Michael. That's called murder."

"There's no motive, no premeditation, and no intent."

"Then it's called manslaughter."

"Listen, Skylar, I agree with you 100 percent. But in Michigan, killing someone while texting and driving is considered a moving violation, not manslaughter. Not yet, anyway."

I couldn't begin to comprehend this. Harry kept talking somewhere in the background, "I just wanted to let you know because his sentencing is coming up at the end of the month. And since it's his first offense, and he has no traffic tickets, etcetera, he will probably not end up serving any jail time at all, probably just get some community service and probation, unfortunately."

"When?" I asked. "When is the sentencing?"

"April 24 at ten."

"This is un-fucking-believable," I yelled. Rage. All I felt was rage.

As I got up and walked away, the picture in the file burned into my memory, I heard Harry stand up at his desk and yell out the door, "Skylar, don't do anything stupid."

"Define stupid," I said over my shoulder.

"Whatever it is you're about to do," he muttered.

I shouldn't be doing this, I thought as I walked out of Harry's office and out to my car. Somewhere deep in the logical part of my brain, I knew this was a bad idea. I knew that I could get in a lot of trouble.

It didn't matter.

I just needed to see him. The need was all consuming, and I didn't understand it. It wasn't as if seeing him or yelling at him was going to bring Michael back. Nothing could undo what had happened. But still….

I thought maybe, if I could understand, find some answers, then—then what? It would make it all better? I wouldn't feel so horrible? That Michael's death would make sense?

Sometimes there's just no rhyme or reason as to why things happen. They just do. And we're left to deal with the resulting devastation.

Twenty minutes later, I was pulling into the subdivision Tony Cusato lived in with his parents. It was an older neighborhood in Shelby Township, with ranch houses spaced a good distance apart on shady hills. There were no fences separating the yards, and the neighborhood itself seemed kind of sleepy—breezy, even.

I searched the house numbers frantically for his address: 34672. I passed 34650. I sped up until I found 34668, then 34670, and then, finally, 34672. I zeroed in on the details of the house as if they would help me understand. It was a beige brick ranch with white shutters. Simple but clearly dated. All the curtains were drawn.

How was it possible that the person who killed Michael lived in a place like this? An ordinary, regular house?

I pulled into the empty driveway, in front of the white garage. I turned off the engine but left the keys in the ignition of my car. I sat, drumming my fingers on the steering wheel, waiting for the rage either to subside or build enough to launch me out of the car. I felt feverish. Restless. Unsettled.

The clock read ten minutes to noon.

I tried to steady my breathing, to corral my thoughts into something coherent. I shifted in my seat, and as I did, I caught sight of a teal '96 Grand Am sitting next to the curb in front of the house. The mismatched hood was gray.

The hood that had been replaced after the accident.

The accident that had killed Michael.

And suddenly my blood was boiling and I couldn't see straight. All I saw was red. All I felt was an overpowering need for destruction.

I propelled myself out of the car, throwing myself into the momentum, slamming the door shut behind me. Following the curve of my Honda to the back the car, my hands oddly steady, I opened the trunk and grabbed the first thing I saw—a crowbar.

It felt heavy in my hands, substantial and hard, as I marched to the car. I raised it over my head and swung, hitting the back window, shattering it. But I felt no sense of satisfaction, of revenge, and that denial of release only pissed me off more.

I swung again, fueled by madness, working my way down the passenger side of the car. The door, the window, the side view mirror. Desperately searching for vindication.

Adrenaline surged through my blood. I felt the hot rage bubbling at my core, spreading to the surface, bursting across my chest. It continued down the ligaments and muscles of my arms and out through the blows of metal on metal, glass, and rubber.

Tears and snot ran down my face, but I was oblivious. My nerves and emotions were livewires, raw and sensitive, so concentrated that I felt numb to everything except for the burning in my muscles.

I was now at the hood, screaming with each blow, as I swung down and hit it again and again and again.

"What the hell?" I heard a voice say from behind me. "What are you doing?"

"What does it look like I'm fucking doing?" I

screamed, still hitting the car, running out of energy.

"Destroying my car?"

Mid-swing I stopped, my muscles tightening to stop the motion. I turned slowly to face the voice, the crowbar still held out in front of me.

"It's you." The words came out in a harsh whisper.

And now that the moment was here, I couldn't say anything, couldn't move. I just stared at him—the cause of my misery, the focus of my rage. I noticed the way his brows furrowed in confusion underneath his long, dark hair covering his face; the way he stood—tall, his hips angled forward, his arms long by his sides—not a defensive stance, but a careless one; his eyes looked haunted and dark.

How could he have been the person responsible for Michael's death? How could he look so innocent? How could the person who took away the one thing I loved most in this world, look so young? So scared?

There were dark bags under his eyes, the skin on his face looked taut and pale. The thought occurred to me, like a passing freight train, that the small, frail way he looked was as familiar to me as my own reflection in the mirror.

He clenched his fists and I could sense an agitation running through him as his eyes darted from the extended crowbar to the car, but it wasn't aimed at me. It was almost like he was trying to hold himself back from ripping the weapon out of my hands so he could take a few swings at it himself.

There were no tears in my eyes now. Only the

frenzied, impassioned look of someone searching for answers.

"Are you sorry?" I asked suddenly. I was staring at him intensely. Just a few feet separated us. If only I could take that step, swing, then take his neck in my hands and squeeze. Squeeze until there was no more air left, till his lips were blue, until the thick blood from his head wound covered my hands.

"Sorry?" he asked.

"What was the text?" I asked, my voice rising, threatening to break. "What did you have to say that was so goddamn important that it killed my...my Michael." God, I hated the word fiancé so much. I hated that I couldn't call him my husband. And I blamed it all on this rangy fearful creature standing in front of me. "Was it worth it?"

His face ghosted over and his eyes filled with tears.

"You're his wife?" He asked.

"We were engaged," I clarified, the edge in my voice could carve diamonds. "We were supposed to be married in June."

He put his head in his hands and his shoulders started to shake. "I'm so...I'm so sorry," I heard him sob. "I didn't mean to."

Was it possible that he was as much a victim as Michael? That his life would never be the same either? *How do you move forward when the weight of death lay on your shoulders?* I asked myself. But no, he made the decision to text while driving. Michael didn't get a choice. I didn't get a choice.

"Are you really?" I mocked.

"You don't even know," he whispered, his head snapping up to look at me, his gaze meeting mine. "How much I wish I could take back that text and everything that happened. I would take it all back if I could." For some reason this just pissed me off even more. He could never be sorry enough for what he ripped away from me. "I would take his place in a second if I could."

"Well you can't, can you?" I screamed, the anger building up again to a peak. "I didn't deserve this. Michael didn't deserve this. Do you even know who you killed? Do you even realize the full consequences of your actions? You did this. You took him away from me."

His voice was quiet. "I know."

"You killed him!" I yelled.

Tears ran down his face as he just looked at me. A door opened and shut next door, somewhere down the street a dog barked, cars passed by on the road. Everything around us moved, but between us, all was still. Frozen.

"I know," he whispered, as I turned back around again and swung, putting a shimmering crack in the passenger front window. Then I swung again and again, determined to break the whole damn thing.

I was still swinging the crowbar over my head when the shrill drone of sirens sounded a few blocks over.

IX

Let the pieces fall

What the fuck did I do? was all I could keep thinking as I sat in the small holding cell, rubbing my fingertips to remove the ink that wasn't there. Since everything had gone digital, fingerprinting no longer marked you with ink stains, but my fingers might as well have been coated in black for how dirty I felt. I didn't feel vindicated, I just felt stupid. Embarrassed. If it wasn't official already, it was now: I had lost control.

After I had been processed at the station, I was told I would have to wait until damages could be assessed. We'd go from there.

I had nothing to do but think. I resisted at first, trying to block out the noise inside my head by absorbing the quiet of the holding room. But when I couldn't distract myself any longer, I gave in. Leaning my head back against the concrete blocks, I went over the arrest.

When the cop car pulled up behind me, I heard the kid whisper firmly, "Drop it."

And for some reason I listened and let the crowbar drop to the cement with a sick, metallic clang.

Becoming more lucid with each flash of the red-and-blue lights, I raised my hands above my head in surrender and took a step back from the car and the crowbar.

I heard the car door open behind me and I looked over at the kid, who kept his eyes on me. And I swear to God, despite the broken glass and dented metal, we shared something in that moment. Maybe not forgiveness or an alliance. But maybe a little bit of understanding.

Abruptly I was pushed forward into the damaged car, my cheek slamming down hard on the roof and my eyes shut reflexively. That would definitely bruise.

My arms were twisted behind my back and handcuffs were slapped on to my wrists. Whoever the officer was, I could tell she was shorter than I was as she pried my legs apart into a wide stance with her feet.

When I opened my eyes, I could see a young male officer talking to Tony Cusato, with a small note pad opened in his hand.

As she was frisking me, the female officer asked me, "Ma'am, what's your name?"

"Skylar Medina," I responded automatically.

"Ms. Medina, what were you doing here?" she asked.

I shook my head, refusing to answer.

"Anyone hurt over there, Doug?" she asked her partner.

"Not physically at least. She didn't touch him."

From behind me, she called out to the kid, "What happened here, son?"

There was no response.

"He's not talking," Doug said.

She sighed. "All right, Skylar Medina, you are under arrest for the willful and malicious destruction of property. You have the right to remain silent…."

An elderly lady walked onto the lawn next to the kid and put her hand on his shoulder, as I was read my rights. "You all right, dear?" I heard her ask him.

He nodded, not taking his eyes off me the entire time.

Officer Doug had moved on to the neighbor, who had no problem telling them exactly what had happened.

"She just came over here and started hitting the car. Going all crazy-like—."

"And you're the one who called it in?"

"Yes, sir. She was on a rampage. I didn't know what she was going to do; she could've hurt someone. Gone after Tony or something."

"Absolutely, ma'am. You did the right thing. Now if I could get your name and contact information…."

"Let's move to the car," the female officer directed me, pulling back on my hands and pushing me forward.

I didn't fight her, but as she led me to the backseat of

the car, the kid moved toward me, reaching out his hand toward me. "I will never forgive myself for what I did," he said quietly. "Whatever you feel toward me, it's nothing compared to how I feel about myself."

"That's doubtful."

"I pled guilty," he called after me.

"Good," I said flatly. "Because you are."

The officer opened the door for me, and I could see in the window's reflection that she was indeed short with broad shoulders and a strong build. Her blond hair was pulled up in a ponytail and bangs covered her forehead.

I got into the backseat awkwardly and watched as she shut the door and climbed into the front passenger seat to call in on the radio. I wasn't listening though, just staring ahead at the car, at Tony Cusato, at the mess that had become my life.

How did I get here?

The driver's door opened, and I watched through the black metal grate as Officer Doug moved deftly in. He pushed some buttons on the computer screen, buckled up, and turned to his partner. Talking to her as if I wasn't even there.

"It turns out Mr. Cusato was involved in a car accident back in February that took the life of Ms. Medina's fiancé."

"Ah," she said. "Well, everyone has their limits."

A booming voice pulled me back to the holding cell.

"Where is she?" My stomach sank. The arrest was

The Charm Necklace

nothing compared to what was going to happen next.

Footsteps carried their way toward the holding room and through the bars I could see Harry walk in.

"Medina, what the hell?" he asked tiredly, putting one hand on his hip.

There was nothing I could do but shrug.

"I told you not to do anything stupid. I told you that you were not to do anything with the information I gave to you." He moved his free hand to his forehead and rubbed it. "I shouldn't have even said anything to you. If I hadn't said anything, we wouldn't be in this mess. Do you understand the consequences you're going to have to deal with now?" He paced the room and ranted on.

"This is going to be on your record now. Criminal and professional. Somehow in your rampage you managed to miss the windshield, which is a goddamned miracle. Because if you hadn't, the damage would have gone over a thousand dollars, in which case you'd be charged with a felony."

At that my head snapped up.

"But because it was under a thousand, it's a misdemeanor. So you're going to have to be arraigned and have a hearing. You're most likely looking at a hefty fine, probation, and Tony Cusato or his family will ask for a restraining order, I'm sure. You could serve up to a year in jail, but because you have no prior convictions and considering the extenuating circumstances, I'm hopeful it won't come to that. There's also a possibility he could sue for emotional damages."

I stared at Harry in disbelief. "He took away the one person I loved most and *he's* going to sue *me* for emotional damages?" I scoffed.

Harry raised his shoulders slowly in a shrug, a look of sympathy crossing his face. Then he said, in that soft-firm voice usually reserved for fathers, "Skylar, you have got to start taking responsibility for yourself."

After a beat, when I refused to meet his eyes, refused to admit I was the guilty party in this scenario, he squared his shoulders and said, "You're off for the rest of the week, without pay. I don't want to see you at the office until next Monday. And then, we'll discuss your demotion."

"Demotion?"

"Consequences, Medina! You work at a police department. It goes without saying that there will be a penalty for your *illegal* actions. Especially when you used inside, confidential knowledge to commit the crime.

"Let me spell it out for you," he said, flattening one hand out in front of him to strike it with the other each time he made a point. "You will no longer have the privilege of working on cases or assisting the detectives. You'll sit at the front desk and play secretary. You'll answer phones and fill out forms. And you should be happy it's nothing worse than that.

"Your arraignment is scheduled for tomorrow. The union lawyer will be there to represent you. And I'm serious, Medina, get your shit figured out. You do something stupid like this again, it'll be out of my hands and you'll be done."

I nodded, head hung in shame. "Thank you, sir."

"Monday," he said in confirmation as he left.

Fines, probation, jail time? I groaned. And on top of that, I would be taking a pay cut that I couldn't afford, especially now with legal fees.

Not ten minutes later, a uniform walked in and brought the corded phone over to me from the desk.

"Press 9 to make an outgoing call," he informed me unnecessarily.

"Thanks," I mumbled, picking up the receiver and pressing the buttons without even thinking. The phone rang once, twice, three times. Then a click as someone picked up.

"Hello?"

I sighed. "Dad," I said. "I need you to come get me...."

By Friday night, I found myself standing outside the big double doors to Grady's Pub in my signature black boots, skinny jeans, and plain black T-shirt underneath my gray wool coat.

I hugged my arms around myself, freezing. I breathed in the cool night air and closed my eyes. I listened to the traffic pass by, the faint thrum of people from inside the bar, the beat of my heart pounding inside my chest.

Earlier in the day, Shane had insisted I come out with everyone. And as much as I didn't want to see anyone after the week I'd just had, I could use the excuse to drink myself into oblivion.

Despite a few days off work, my arraignment and this whole mess were making it impossible for me to figure anything out. Each action, thought, and feeling just made everything more blurry when I needed it to be crystal clear.

I felt weighed down, like I was sinking in wet sand. Clawing to get out, only to be sucked back in. I took another deep breath and walked inside.

The pub was a local hangout for the young and old alike. It had this worn-in, welcoming quality about it. No gloss. No pretense. Just come as you are, pull up a seat, and have a beer.

The lights were low and there was something about the atmosphere in here that made the dimness seem like a dense heavy fog, as if you could never see too far in front of you. The many TVs shone brightly and reflected off the large mirrors on the walls.

There was a big wooden bar set in the middle of the room, fully stocked with liquor and several different tap handles displaying the season's on-tap selection. Booths and tables, all wooden and roomy, filled the bar.

It reminded me of a bar scene from a Christmas movie. The leading characters are home from the big city, and they meet up with their long-lost friends in the local

The Charm Necklace

pub. They're playing music on the jukebox, laughing with the bartender, and casting a warm nostalgic glow as they swap stories from times long gone.

That was Grady's.

And I could lose myself in a place like this.

I could forget for a night what a terrible, cold place the world really was. I might even be able to convince myself that life's not as bad as it seems.

I had arrived early on purpose. The others wouldn't be here for another hour or so. The place was relatively busy for a Friday night, but there was no one sitting at the far end of the bar, so I zigzagged my way through the tables to take a seat.

"What can I get for you?" The blond bartender asked.

"I'll take a Jameson. Neat."

She poured the whiskey and I paid with cash, not trusting myself to open a tab.

The whiskey burned in the best way possible. I felt so tired, and I just wanted to forget everything for a night, but my mind wouldn't stop turning as I sipped my drink and then another.

I stared off into space. I was lost, drifting in the ebb and flow of the conversations around me. My head was becoming full and fuzzy, my thoughts were slowing down to a snail's pace.

From my seat I saw a busboy in the back of the restaurant drop a glass. I watched, in what seemed like slow motion, as the glass tumbled and shattered on the floor. I felt such envy for the complete brokenness of the glass. It would be such a sweet relief if I could fall completely apart like that, into pieces. When a glass falls, it breaks, it's over. But it wasn't like that for me. Somehow I was still together in one piece. No matter how strained the sinews holding me together were, they were weakened but not broken.

I had no choice but to keep going.

"Exorcising demons?" A smooth voice asked to my right. I turned slowly, my face breaking into a wry grin when I saw who it was. "Something like that."

"What the hell happened to your face?" Logan asked, when he saw the black-and-blue bruise covering my cheek, my eye red and bloodshot above it. In a knee-jerk reaction, he reached his hand up to gingerly touch the side of my face, but he pulled back at the last instant.

"I joined a street gang."

Ignoring my sarcasm he asked, "Are you all right?"

"You should see the other guy," I retorted, avoiding his question.

Knowing he wasn't going to get any straight answers from me at the moment, he nodded his head in the direction of the table and said, "Come join us." I glanced over his shoulder to see our group sitting at one of the high-top tables. All the seats were filled except two.

I grabbed my drink and stood clumsily. Keeping my eyes on the back of Logan's navy blue coat and black cords the entire time, I was thankful for the alcohol swimming through my veins. It made this whole encounter that much easier to deal with.

"Skylar! Over here," Shane said, patting the seat next to him.

At the table sat a ragtag group of people, all of them friends of ours, assembled over the years.

On the other side of Shane sat "bad boy" guitarist Dean, his inked-up drummer James, and Sydney, James surprisingly sweet and modest girlfriend. Sydney and I had become decent friends in the past year or so when Michael and I would join her in the front row for Dean and James' shows. I nodded at everyone in greeting.

Lastly there was Collin with his arm draped around a girl I had never seen before.

"Skylar, meet Jamie," Collin said, looking adoringly at the brown-eyed brunette sitting next to him.

She reached her hand across the seat that separated us. "Nice to meet you," she smiled at me.

I reached over and shook her hand. "You too," I said quietly. *Did she know about Michael?* I wondered. *Had they filled her in on the gory details before I got here? Given her an off-limits conversation list?*

I looked down at the menu, and I could feel the heat of all their eyes on me. Watching me. Studying me. It was unnerving, but I tried my best to ignore it. Just then the waitress came over, placing a beer in front of me.

"Coors good?" Shane asked. "I ordered it for you."

"It's perfect. Thanks," I said to both him and the

waitress.

"It's been too long," he said, his eyes crinkling with sadness. He looked over at me, scrutinizing me. Shane had a humility and gentleness about him. He was generally unfazed by the world and its troubles, but he cared with a depth that most people were rarely able to reach.

"It has," I agreed.

"I'm glad you decided to come out tonight," he said, nudging me with his elbow, trying to shake off the melancholy. "You look good, you rock star."

I rolled my eyes at him. "You're a horrible liar."

"I would never lie to you," he said in mock offense.

Shane had always been the resident jokester and comedian, but I could feel that maybe he was trying a little harder than usual to maintain his positive energy. Because I saw that telltale twitch of his lips and the furrow of his brow that meant he was thinking about Michael. I knew that he might've let himself hope, just for a second, that Michael would come bounding through the door and sit down at the table with us. That he'd still be here. Alive. But the disappointment that followed a moment like that would be a bitter one.

"Does that line work on all the girls?" I teased.

"Usually not," he laughed.

Then he looked over at Logan sitting next to me. "Dude, what's with the glasses?" he teased. "Those lame-ass cardigans you wear aren't nerdy enough?"

"I lost my contacts, smartass." Logan said, throwing a

chip at Shane.

"I don't know what you're talking about, I think he's devilishly handsome with them on," Dean joked, wriggling his eyebrows suggestively at Logan from across the table.

"I agree," I said, assessing him.

"Why thank you," he said, adjusting the black frames on his face.

The banter continued back and forth. They talked about the band's upcoming shows, work, the latest movies. I was only half-listening, but enjoyed the effortlessness of it. I envied the *lightness* of it.

The food came and went. More rounds were bought. An hour or so in, I was on my second beer and *definitely* feeling it. This was going to be one of those nights where I walked right over the edge of my alcohol limits without a glance back or a tap on the breaks. Pedal to the metal, baby.

If I was sober, I knew that I would feel strange being here, with everyone—going on like normal, like nothing life-changing had happened. My life over the past few months had become a series of emotions: anger, sorrow, numbness, loneliness. Each one following the other like ducks in a row. But sometimes, they came in pairs or all at once. It was what I had become used to it, almost to a point of comfort because at least it was *something* I could rely on. But I found, listening to everyone talk about their regularly-scheduled lives, that I could let myself remember what it felt like to be okay again, if only for a minute or two. It caught me off guard, but it was not unwelcome.

"Skylar?" Logan said next to me. "Sky?"

"Hmm?" I said turning to him.

"You all right?" He nudged me. His closeness feeling unexpectedly good.

"Yeah, fine. Just distracted."

"Are you having fun?" he asked.

"I haven't had enough to drink yet for that," I said, turning off my stool and walking to the bar. I ordered a shot of Jameson from the older bartender.

I tipped it back, felt the fire on my lips. "Give me another one."

"You sure about that, sweetheart?" she asked in her raspy voice.

"Never been more sure in my life." I smiled shortly at her.

She poured me another. "Keep 'em coming," I said, pointing to my table, as I took this one back with me.

Logan looked at me uneasily.

Shane smiled at me. "Yeah! That's my girl," he said, raising his hand for a high-five. My hand met his with a satisfying *smack*.

"Ow! Damn, girl. Control yourself."

I couldn't help but giggle just a little bit.

There should've been a neon sign above my head that read "Drunk Hot Mess," with an arrow pointing down at me.

One hour turned into two and then into three. The pub was packed by now, people congregating around the bar because there weren't any open bar stools or tables left.

The table was littered with empty beer bottles and shot glasses. Even in our drunkenness we had managed to stay away from the topic of Michael until Shane slipped.

"Man," he said slowly. "Wouldn't it be like, the greatest thing ever, if Mike were here?"

Everyone at the table stopped talking. Dean, who had a bottle halfway to his lips, paused for several seconds before lowering it back down to the table.

That's when everyone's cautionary gaze shifted from Shane to me. That cold, iron grasp was at my throat again, and my stomach felt like a ton of lead had just been dropped into it.

And that's when I managed a smile and said, "Yes. Yes, it would be."

Shane pulled me into a sideways hug next to him, and for a moment nobody said anything. Then Logan got up to kneel on his barstool.

"I'd like to propose a toast," he said loudly.

"A toast!" the guys cheered in approval.

He was slurring his words and they came slowly. "These past few months since Mike died have been so hard. So fucking hard—."

James said loudly, "That's what she said!"

Then Shane yelled, "Shut the fuck up and let the man talk!"

"Anyway," Logan continued, "Mike was my best friend. He was everybody's friend. There's not a day that goes by that he isn't missed, that one of us here doesn't think about him. He was so loved by everyone here. But there's something that I've been thinking about lately. And that is…that in the face of death, in the face of how fragile life is, there may not be a whole lot that we can do, but we can drink—."

"Hell, yeah!" the guys cheered.

"And dance, and laugh, and cry. We can be scared without being defeated. We can hope. We can fight. But most important," he paused, and I wasn't sure if it was for dramatic effect or to remember what he wanted to say, "we can dare to live. To my good friend, Skylar." He raised his glass.

Everyone at the table raised their glasses and echoed back, "To Skylar!"

I just sat there staring up at him with tears in my eyes.

When people leave your life—either through death, divorce, or of their own choosing—they can't take the memories, scars, or imprints that they've left on you. At some point, they helped mold you, form you, left a mark on you, left you somehow changed. People can't come into each other's lives without leaving an impression. That's just not the way it works. And that's when I realized that Michael was here and always would be. Because he lived inside of each and every one of us.

"Thank you," I stammered, before standing up abruptly, knocking the barstool out of my way and running toward the door.

"Skylar, wait! Stop," I heard Logan call after me.

I pushed open the door into the night. The darkness was encompassing. I stood there breathing in deeply, crying. The release felt so good it made me laugh, a loud cackling laugh intermittent with hiccups and sobs.

"Skylar, wait!" Logan yelled out the door, but I was standing right there. "Oh. Skylar, look, I'm so sorry. Was that too much? It's just something I've been thinking about, and I wanted to do something for Michael and for you," he rambled on drunkenly. "Why are you laughing?"

I stood there looking at him, leaning over to clutch my side. "It was beautiful," I said.

"I'm sorry if I embarrassed you—. Wait, what?" he looked at me confused. "Then why did you…?" He looked back and forth between me and the door.

"I just needed to breathe," I said. "I'm kind of an anxious, emotional wreck these days."

"Then why are you laughing?" He asked with a dubious look on his face.

"I don't know. I—I just got so overwhelmed. I came out here and I started crying, and you know, I haven't cried like that—out in public, in front of other people—in a while, and it just felt so damn good, you know? To just let it go. Let the pieces fall."

"You look insane right now," he said, a smile spreading across his face. He started to laugh too. It started as a small, unsure nervous laugh, and it built and built up to a deep belly laugh that shook his whole body.

It was just the two of us laughing. We leaned into each other, and our laughter died down. It was quiet and cold, and I started to sober up. What had seemed so free and harmless ten minutes ago suddenly felt so heavy and real. Sobs started to shake through me, and I could feel the tears streaming down my face again, in thick full streams.

"Shh, it's going to be all right," Logan said, pulling me into his chest and wrapping his arms around me. "It's going to be all right."

I continued to cry as he patted my hair and rubbed my back. It was such a father-like gesture it made me want to cry even more. Logan had changed so much in the past year—maybe not changed so much as grown. Grown into a good man, a great father.

"There's something I have to tell you," I choked, trying to control the sobs.

"Take your time," he reassured me.

I stepped away from him and put my arms up on his shoulders. I hoped this would help me stop crying and get myself under control.

I took a deep breath and wiped my nose and face on my sleeve.

"So the thing is, I got arrested," I said, letting the hammer fall.

"You what?"

"I saw the kid who—who hit Michael."

"What do you mean, you—," he stopped, his face

turning serious in a blink of an eye. "What did you do, Skylar?"

"My boss told me that in Michigan, if you kill someone while texting and driving it isn't even considered manslaughter," I hurried to get the words out of my mouth before I started crying again. "Just a moving violation. The kid was arraigned and released on his own recognizance. He pled guilty and his sentencing is at the end of the month."

"What kind of jail time is he looking at?"

"The max he can get is a year. But honestly, he will probably get off with probation and community service. They might slap a $100 fine on him, and they'll suspend his license. But that's about it. The son of a bitch."

Logan nodded, taking this all in. "So you saw him? Where?"

"I went to his house."

"And you thought that was a good idea, because…?"

"I had to see him. I had to make sure that he knew what he had done. And then I was there, sitting in his driveway, and I saw his car. The car he killed Michael with. So I took a crowbar to it."

"You took a crowbar to it?" he asked slowly, trying to process it all.

"Yeah, he came out of the house. We had a friendly little chat and then his neighbor must have called the cops because they showed up and I got arrested. And demoted too, so that's going to be fun."

"So what does that mean? What's going to happen to

you?"

"At my arraignment I pled not guilty. My nice union attorney has to meet with the prosecutor to make a plea-bargain. He said he's confident he can get me off with probation and fines. And I will most likely have to take anger management classes."

"Wow."

"Yup. And the kid can sue me for emotional damages, if he so chooses." A beat. "Welcome to the shit show that is my life," I said, spreading my hands in a curtsey.

Logan was silent for a second, mulling this over. "What was he like?" he asked in a whisper, so quiet I could barely hear him.

"That's the thing," I said quietly "he's just a kid. Seventeen years old, still in high school. And I just can't wrap my head around the fact that he was the one who took Michael away from us. That it is all his fault. He was so sorry, that's all I can remember him saying to me. But I'm just so unbelievably angry at him. I didn't know it was possible to be this angry."

"He said he pled guilty?" Logan asked.

"Yes, that's what he said."

"And what did you tell him?"

"Good, because he is."

He just looked at me with heavy eyes. "I am way too drunk for this right now."

X

Stand still

My beeping cell phone woke me up the next morning. I cracked one eye open, and the bright morning light sent sharp shooting pains through my skull. I groaned and searched blindly for my phone. I felt all over the bed, finally finding it tucked between the covers. By then the beeping had stopped.

It took me ten minutes to muster the strength to open my eyes again. My mouth felt dry, and my body felt like it had been thrown around inside a giant washing machine. Everything hurt: my head, my eyes, my stomach, my muscles. Everything.

It was the hangover from hell.

I had two text messages on my phone. One from Shane and one from Logan.

Shane
How you feeling this morning, champ? ;)

I typed in a quick reply.

Me
Not so good. I hate you right now.
And alcohol

Shane
You did that yourself. I only bought you the
first beer. You have no one to blame
but yourself!

Me
Yes, I do. And I blame you

Shane
:) Drink some water and pop an Advil
and stop being such a baby.
You used to be able to handle hangovers
much better in college

Me
Yeah, well we're not in college anymore.
I'm getting old

Shane
Pshh

I wanted to be so mad at him, hate him for inviting me out and letting me drink so much. But how could I be mad when last night was exactly what I had needed? When last night I was able to experience such a…release. I guess I'd let him off the hook this time.

Me
Thanks for last night

Shane
No problemo

Then I looked at Logan's message.

Logan
Just checking in, making sure u r still alive

Me
Barely

I laid my head back on the soft pillow, closed my eyes, and let the hangover drown out all my thoughts and responsibilities.

Later that day, as I was folding laundry, I thought about Michael. I thought about how he always folded the clothes wrong. And how he would always make fun of me when I got mad at him about it. I tried to fold all the clothes lazily and haphazardly like he used to do but then had to redo them all as soon as I had finished.

I thought about how Michael made me feel significant, even though I'm really not. I was never anybody special or important. I'm serious and withdrawn, my stubbornness and anxiety have a way of coming off as bitchy; I act out when I'm frustrated and angry and possibly a million other bad things, but he loved me anyway. I was special to him. I meant something to him.

Because of him I was able to come out of my shell. Because of him I was able to trust and love. After my mom died and I saw what became of my dad, I told myself that love wasn't worth the heartache and the pain. I tried to close myself off to other people, keep my head down, and get through life unnoticed. Until he noticed me. And that's when everything changed.

Michael was open and carefree. Where I had to have structure and schedules, he thrived on spontaneity and randomness. He had presence. He filled a room with his laughter anywhere he went.

I admired him so much, not just as someone I loved, but as a human being. He helped me become the person I wanted to be. He tore down all my walls, crashed right through them, and pulled me through the rubble.

I feel so lost without him, so abandoned. I should have known from the beginning that the only person I've ever truly let into my heart would somehow leave me.

How on earth would I ever move on from this? After experiencing this love and losing it, was that it? Was I done? Has my quota been met? Why would I even consider trying again?

When I visualized my situation, I saw myself standing on top of a heap of debris, like Ground Zero after the towers fell. I can hear the rescue helicopters overhead, feel their propellers whip my hair all around me, and I see them move their searchlights, but they never find me. Because my arms are too heavy. I don't have the energy to move them from my sides, can't fight the exquisite weight of it all to call out for help. How would it even be possible to be rescued from this mess?

In the midst of towels and thoughts, my phone beeped with another text message. I reached down for it and my stomach did a flip when I read Sophie's name.

It had been a little over a month since I had seen Sophie, since I had lashed out at her like a psychopath. I was still angry at the world, but now I could start to feel the pinpricks of embarrassment poking through at the edges of my consciousness.

I had never apologized to her directly.

God, I'm such a bitch.

Sophie
Hey!

Sophie
Your dad filled my parents in on what happened

Fuck. My. Life.
Tentatively I typed back....

Me
Yeah?

I waited for her response, watching the small bubble at the bottom of the conversation that let me know she was typing, but then it disappeared.

I wondered how Sophie and Rob and Sue felt about the kid. Were they as angry as I was? Most likely. How could they not be?

Five minutes later, my phone chirped.

Sophie
Want to go see a movie tonight?

That was unexpected, but maybe this would be my chance to apologize, to explain.

Me
Sure. What did you have in mind?

Sophie
Oh, you know, chick flick. The usual. I forgot the name of it. Just meet me at the theater at 7

Me
Sounds good. See you then

I pulled into the enormous, crowded parking lot at 6:55. People where bustling in and out of the theater. I put the car in park, took a deep breath to steady myself, and then walked slowly to the glass doors of the building.

When I entered, I saw Sophie immediately in the spacious domed lobby and she waved to me from the ticket booth. She looked happy to see me, excited even. Her bright blue eyes glittered underneath the lights and her blond hair had grown past her shoulders. Her skin was so clear and radiant. She didn't look mad at all. I let myself feel a little bit of relief, but steeled myself for whatever was to come.

She gave me a huge hug when I got to her. She was a few inches shorter than I was, and when she hugged me, her arms pinned mine to my sides.

"Hi Sophie!" I said. "You can let go now," I laughed. There were brief moments, like these, when the grief took a back seat, when it wasn't so crushing.

"Sorry, sorry," she said, pulling back. "It's just been so long, it feels like. I missed you so much." Her eyes lit up and she gestured animatedly. "I got the tickets," she said, holding them up.

"You didn't have to do that," I protested.

"Yeah, well, I did. The show doesn't start for thirty minutes. Should give us enough time to get popcorn and get decent seats."

"Sure," I nodded, following her to the usher who ripped our tickets in half and said, "Theater Nine, second on your left."

"Thanks!" Sophie said.

I thought about what I wanted to say to her. I wanted to apologize to her. Tell her I was sorry for my temper tantrum, for not talking to her since that day, for not contacting her family as soon as I found out about Tony Cusato and his sentencing date.

What would Michael think about this? He would probably laugh at me for worrying so much. He would probably tell me not to worry about it because Sophie didn't hold on to things like that. He would tell me to have fun and enjoy myself.

Remember to ask how school's going.

Remember that she's her own person.

"Do you want to split a popcorn?" Sophie's question brought me back to the present. "Combo #2 has a large popcorn with two medium drinks."

"Uh, yeah, sure. That's fine."

We were fifth in line, and while I was altogether too tired to fully appreciate the awkwardness that had come between us, I could feel it intruding in the gaps in our conversation.

"So, how—how have you been?" she asked hesitantly.

"I've been all right," I replied. "Been better. You?"

"Same, I guess." She bit down on her lip. "Everything feels so heavy."

Changing the subject I asked, "Have you chosen which college you're going to go to?"

She glanced over at me with a grin on her face. "Fordham," she said proudly.

I grinned back at her. "You had to pick the farthest one. Are you trying to give your mother a heart attack?"

"Just a stroke," she teased. "I think I need to get out of Michigan for a while. Get a new start. You know?"

"Yeah, I get that," I said softly.

"I did apply to some schools here too, of course. U of M, State, and Oakland. Just to appease Mom," she laughed.

As we moved into the theater and settled into our seats, Sophie plopped the popcorn bucket on her lap. In between mouthfuls, she bent over and whispered, "Mike would have taken you to see this." She gestured to all the couples in the theater.

Sophie had never been one for tact. She had always been straight to the point, a no-bullshit kind of girl, and she was about as subtle as a gun.

"I know," I said remembering. "He was good like that, wasn't he?"

"The best."

"So your parents know all about the, uh, situation

I've landed myself in?" I asked, wanting to get this conversation out of the way.

"Yeah…," she trailed off.

"So what do they think about it?"

"I think that it's upsetting to them, you know? They know you're hurting a lot, and it breaks my mom's heart that it drove you to do something like that. I don't think they understand it, but they're not mad at you."

"And," she whispered conspiratorially. "I'm pretty sure my dad was actually impressed. Don't tell Mom that though."

I sighed. "Listen, I get it if they don't understand. I don't fully understand it myself."

"You'll keep me updated on what happens with your charges and sentencing, right?"

"Sure," I nodded. "Do your parents know about Tony Cusato's hearing?"

"Yeah, they got a notification from the court or something," she said. "They haven't really talked about it, but I don't think they are going to sue him or anything."

"Why not?" I asked, a hot sensation running over my skin instantaneously.

"I think they're tired," she stated. "I think that they don't want this to go on any longer than it already has. I don't think they have it in them to go through all the motions to sue him—you know, getting a lawyer, going to court, etc."

I just nodded, trying to understand.

Sophie continued, "Listen, do I want that SOB to rot in hell for the rest of eternity? Yeah, probably. But my parents, I think, just want to move on. Plus, I kind of feel like maybe he will already be paying the consequence of his actions for the rest of his life. Being responsible for killing someone isn't something you just get over."

I turned this over in my mind, staring at the seat in front of me.

Sophie was good in a way I could only aspire to be. I used to worry that the world would break her heart because she trusted too quickly and loved too easily, but looking at her now, she was a lot stronger than I thought.

"Do you want to press charges?" she asked honestly.

"I don't know. I'm just so angry at him. And the possibility that he won't even go to jail for what he did. I just—I just can't wrap my mind around it."

"Aren't you tired of being so angry all the time?"

If it were any other person asking me that question, I would have chopped his or her freaking head off. But it was Sophie, so I said, "Not yet."

Then the lights dimmed, the movie started, and we stopped talking. I was stuck, sitting there, stewing in my anger. Pushing away the image of those sad, haunted eyes again and again.

An hour into the movie that I was only halfway paying attention to, I felt Sophie's head fall onto my shoulder, and I knew that she was out.

Then, alone in that dark theater, I cried. I cried for

the characters in the movie. I cried out of anger that our legal system would let someone get away with killing another human being. I cried out of sadness that Michael wasn't here with me. And I cried for Sophie.

I cried for her because she would never get her big brother back. I cried for her because her teenage years would forever be scarred with sadness and death and grief.

And I cried for us. Because as much as neither one of us wanted to admit it, back there in that hospital when Michael died, our bond of sisterhood had been severed. We would never be able to get it back, no matter how hard we tried. I cried because things would never be the same between us. She would move away to college, and slowly over time I would only see her on holidays or school breaks and eventually, not at all. And that kind of slow loss is a whole other kind of heartbreak, one that was more subtle but just as painful.

But when she woke up, I would pretend it wasn't like that, I would pretend things hadn't changed until she was able to realize it herself.

After the movie was over and the lights came up, we walked out of the theater and into the lit parking lot.

"Did you have a good nap?" I joked.

"God, I can't believe I fell asleep! I've been looking forward to that movie for ages."

"Maybe you should drink some coffee next time?" I suggested.

"No kidding. I've just been working on a lot of AP projects lately."

"Of course you have," I teased.

When we came to her car, I stopped. "Sophie," I paused, getting her attention, willing her to understand the gravity of my apology. "Look, I am so sorry about how I acted the last time I saw you—."

She bit her lip and looked away from me.

"Just let me try to explain," I pleaded. "Losing Michael so suddenly changed me. I wasn't myself. I wasn't capable of thinking about anything other than my own black hole. How could I possibly care about your future when all of a sudden mine was gone?" My voice broke.

Then I continued. "It was selfish of me and I'm sorry."

I never wanted to hurt her. She was like my little sister, my family. She meant the world to me.

Sophie reached across the space between us and held my hand, her eyes meeting mine. "I was hurt when it happened, but it was too soon for you. I get it.

"Mike was my big brother, my only brother. My whole childhood was following him around and annoying him.

"I remember when he decided not to go to college and my parents fought him on it. I stood by him because I believed in him. And then when he met you, I'd never seen him happier.

"His death…," she drew in a deep, steadying breath

and tears filled her eyes, "was so hard for me. How could my big brother be gone? He was the one who let me sleep in his bed when I had a nightmare, the one who taught me how to catch a football, the one who harassed any boy who had any interest in me. He was the one who always looked out for me. And then he was gone? Just like that? I didn't get it. But then, it started to sink in, really sink in.

"And slowly I started to realize that all the denial in the world wasn't going to bring him back. Nothing was going to bring him back, and that meant that I needed to get back to my life. I could honor him by focusing on school and putting energy into planning my future. That's how I could keep Mike inside my heart. He always teased me for being such a nerd, but he wanted me to go to college and make something of myself.

"And that's why I thought that talking about it with you could help you too, help you be close to him. So that's why I was confused when you got so upset."

I watched her carefully as I wiped the tears away from my eyes. "I'm so sorry," I said again, pulling her into a hug.

"It's okay." She smiled up at me and wiped at her face with her sleeve. "I just want you to know that I'm here for you, and I'm sorry for upsetting you."

I looked at her. "He would be so proud of you."

Then lightening the mood some, "And you look good too, Soph," I said. "Seriously, like a walking advertisement for American Eagle or something," I laughed. "But then again, so was Michael. Maybe it runs in the family."

"No, he was definitely more of an American Eagle-Abercrombie & Fitch crossbreed."

"Yeah, you're right," I said. "He had more of that rugged look to him." I smiled remembering his facial scruff and rough hands. "I really appreciate you asking me out tonight."

"Well," she shifted her weight on her feet, "I kind of had an ulterior motive when I asked you."

"Oh?"

She handed me an envelope.

"What's this?" I asked.

"You'll see when you open it. But you have to wait until later, when you get home."

"All right?" I questioned.

"Just trust me," she said, pulling me into a hug.

As soon as I was through the door, I ripped open the envelope. It was a letter from Sophie to me. I sat down on the stairs and started to read. It was written the day I got arrested.

April 10, 2012

Dear Skylar,

Do you ever wonder why we put Dear at the beginning of a letter? I find that very weird, don't you?

Anyway, it's Easter break and I'm home alone. And with only Bruce to distract me, my thoughts wander to Mike. I wish he were here right now. I wish so much that right now we were getting ready for your wedding, having the final fittings and confirming appointments or whatever it is you do in the last few weeks before a wedding. Probably make the seating arrangements? It all seems so trivial now that he's gone, doesn't it? Don't you wish that he were still here so that we could care about stupid things like that?

Mom took me dress shopping for prom yesterday. She always tries to stay so positive and not show me how sad she really is. But I knew she was thinking about Mike, which made me think of him and how he won't be there to see me take pictures for prom or see me graduate from high school. He won't be there to help me move into my dorm room or be at my wedding. And I can't help but cry when I think that, so after a while I try to forget, but it doesn't always work. I try to be fearless like Mike was. He was never scared of anything. And for him, I will try not to be scared.

I want you to know that I miss you a lot. I don't know if there's anything I could have said or done to make it better for you, and if there was, I'm sorry that I didn't. I just didn't know what to do or say. I know this has been really hard for you. I'm sorry for that too. Not pity-sorry, but really truly sorry that you have to feel this bad.

I want you to know that forever and always you will be my sister. I don't know what's going to happen in the future. I don't know how things are going to be between you and my parents. But I just want you to know that I love you and that I'm always here for you. I really don't want us to grow apart.

I guess I'm not really sure what to say, except that I believe in hope and the future. I want you to believe again too. I want you to know that there is more out there waiting for you. I know you feel like there's not, that Mike was your whole life—and maybe he was—but he can't be anymore.

I've always looked up to you, admired you. And I've always loved spending time with you. Hopefully, we can hang out more often this summer when I'm not so busy with school.

Don't give up, Skylar. And know that it's okay not to be so mad all the time. It gets tiring after a while.

Love always, your sister and friend,
Sophie

>I read the letter once, then twice, and then again.
>"Thank you, Sophie," I said aloud.
>Maybe I would be able to feel alive again. Maybe not today, or tomorrow, but one day. I would be able to live again, love again, hope again. Just knowing that was a possibility lifted a large weight off my shoulders.

XI

Guilty

April 24, 2012

Court was scheduled to begin at ten. When the radio on my alarm clock went off at eight, I had already been lying awake, red-eyed, for two hours. I switched the radio off and rolled back into my spot, lying face up with my hands pressed against my stomach. I tried to concentrate on how my stomach rose and fell with each breath, tried to relax my muscles and calm my nerves, but all I felt was dread.

This whole day, this whole fucking situation was just dreadful.

I wanted to be anywhere else but here. In fact, I didn't even want to be anywhere else, I just wanted to disappear so that I didn't even have to think about what would take place in the courthouse.

Rob had called me over the weekend to let me know

they were publicly forgiving Tony Cusato and were going to ask the court not to sentence any jail time. I couldn't even respond when Rob told me that. I just hung up the phone. Because what was there to say?

The conflicting emotions banging around inside my chest were unbearable. I wanted to rip myself open so I didn't have to feel so much anymore.

I was angry with Rob and Sue for deciding to check out of the fight. I was angry at Tony Cusato for causing this whole fucking mess in the first place. I was angry at Michael for dying, for not being strong enough to live. I was ashamed at myself for even thinking that. I was angry for not fighting back harder. I was a pathetic excuse of a fiancée, of a human being.

I stumbled out of bed to my closet. What did one wear on a day like this? What did you wear to your own death sentence? Because that's exactly what it felt like. I felt that those short, echoing steps into that courtroom today would be the sound of my death march. The little piece that was left of me after Michael died would be exterminated when the person responsible for his death got a "Get Out of Jail, Free" card, please collect $200 as you pass Go. The judge, the lawyers, Rob and Sue, Tony Cusato—they were my firing squad. Each one of their words would take me down further. I would die in that courtroom today. I already knew it.

In the end, I settled for a white silk blouse, black dress pants, and black heels. I felt shaky and hot as I showered and got ready. I couldn't get ready fast enough, but I wanted the clock to slow down. I rushed as I put my makeup on, hastily applying eyeliner and mascara. I let the animosity inside me grow as I blow-dried my hair.

I couldn't eat a damn thing even if I wanted to; my stomach was tight and twisted. Even coffee was a bad idea—the caffeine would just set my nerve endings on fire and make my muscles jittery.

We had arranged the day before to have Dad pick me up. I had reluctantly agreed that I probably shouldn't drive on the off chance I saw Tony Cusato in the parking lot and tried to run him over.

No, I wouldn't run him over. I wouldn't *just* run him over. I would throw the gears in reverse and do it over and over again until he became one with the asphalt.

I felt a grim sense of satisfaction at the image.

From the kitchen I heard a car door shut. I grabbed my purse from the hook on the wall and flew out the door before Dad could make it to the porch.

"I was just coming to get you," he said, smiling at me.

"Let's just go," I stormed past him to the car, slamming the door closed behind me.

He paused before turning around and walking back to the car.

He opened the door and bent over, holding the roof for balance, and peered in. "We don't have to go today, Skylar. Michael would—"

I cut him off, "Yes, I do." I looked at him intently.

He didn't say anything, just got in the car and drove out onto Main Street.

I loved downtown Rochester. It was small and quaint. I looked out my window as we passed the restaurants, stores, and galleries.

At Christmastime the whole town was lit up. Every single storefront on Main Street had strips of lights from top to bottom. It was magical. Mesmerizing. Kind of our trademark.

Now it felt cold. Uninviting. I felt apart from it, unattached. Everything that had held meaning before, now just felt empty.

At the last light, I looked over at my dad. He had on his new black suit, bought for my no-longer-happening nuptials, with a red-and-gray tie.

"You look professional," I commented.

He looked over at me, not quite sure what to make of the remark. "You look nice," was all he said, returning his eyes to the road.

Neither one of us said anything else as we drove down the road and then pulled into the parking lot of the large new courthouse. The roof covering the entrance was a piece of thick curved sandstone held up by six tall columns. Three flagpoles stood proudly in front of the glass entrance.

Dad parked and turned off the car. We both sat for just a second, preparing for what would come next.

"Let's do this," Dad said.

Both car doors shut at the same time, and our feet

stepped in sync as we walked into the expansive marble lobby.

Rob, Sue, and Sophie were standing next to a man I assumed was a lawyer. I couldn't quite place the emotion on their faces. Rob looked sad and apprehensive. Sue looked anxious, refusing to meet anyone's eyes, first looking up at the ceiling then down at her feet. Sophie looked troubled, but I wasn't sure if it was by the actual sentencing or if she was trying to work out how to keep the peace and calm between us all.

The assistant prosecutor assigned to the case was Skip McDowell. He was young, ambitious, charming, and a damn good lawyer from what I heard around the station. His wavy brown hair was combed back, away from his face. His sharp, navy blue suit made his blue eyes appear stark and clear. Overall, he gave off an alluring, authoritative presence. He was someone you wanted on your side.

"Everyone here?" he asked cheerfully. I couldn't figure out why he looked so pleased. What was there to be happy about? Maybe he was one of those perpetually optimistic people, or maybe it was part of his pretrial game face to show his opponents he was not threatened but instead relaxed like this was some kind of friendly tennis match.

"Shall we?" he asked, gesturing for us to enter the courtroom. We all walked in. "Feel free to take a seat in the front row on the right side." Skip walked forward through the waist-high wooden gate to take his place at the prosecution's desk.

Dad went in first and I followed after him. Sophie and her parents took a seat next to us. The walls were white, but the room was overpowered by all the wooden paneling.

Court would start in fifteen minutes. I watched the small hand of the clock tick forward incessantly. On either side of me, I heard Dad and Sophie engaging in small talk, but nothing they had to say was interesting enough to hold my attention.

I heard the door to the court open. I glanced back and saw Harry walk in and take a seat three rows behind us. He nodded at me, and I nodded back in acknowledgement.

"Isn't that your boss?" Dad leaned in and asked.

"Yeah."

"What's he doing here?"

"In order for me to be in the same room as Tony Cusato, he had to agree to supervise me."

The door opened again, and a stern looking woman with a helmet-like short gray bob walked in. Tony Cusato's lawyer, I presumed. Because behind her was a tall, skinny teenage boy with pale skin and gray eyes. His dark hair had grown even longer and was almost to his shoulders.

I felt my stomach clench and my face flush.

I saw Harry staring at me, willing me to behave, but I just stared death rays at Tony Cusato as he walked down the aisle behind his lawyer.

He met my eyes and his step faltered for a second. He

looked frightened and fidgety.

In that moment I felt vindictive and cruel. Like I could stab him and then laugh right in his face.

As he took his seat, I continued to stare at him, watching him, committing him to memory so that in all those daydreams in which I killed him, I could get all the details just right. The way his hair would fall in his eyes, the way his mouth would look when he let out a guttural scream, the way his body would jerk in one particular fantasy in which I tasered him to death.

Hate. Rage. All-consuming. But also there, somehow, pity.

I quickly shook off the feeling. I couldn't think about being sympathetic right now. I couldn't feel even the least bit sorry for him. I had to stand up for Michael, especially because it felt like no one else was.

"He looks like hell," Sophie said to no one in particular.

Skip turned around to face us. "We all set?" he asked. "Court's about to start."

Then the bailiff entered from a door at the front of the courtroom and announced, "All rise," as the judge entered, swiftly and purposefully, through the door behind him. His robes swished as he took his seat at the bench. The bailiff continued, "Oakland County 52-3 District Court is now in session, the Honorable Judge Barlow Walker presiding. Please be seated."

The clerk, a small middle-aged woman, stood from

her desk next to the Judge's bench and cleared her throat. In an uninterested voice she stated, "Oakland County District Court Docket Number 2012-341948-DS, the State of Michigan versus Anthony Cusato now comes for hearing."

"Good morning, ladies and gentlemen," Judge Walker said in a friendly tone. He was older, probably in his early sixties. He had gray hair and clean, slightly wrinkled pale skin. "In the case of the State of Michigan versus Anthony Cusato, I have heard the defendant's guilty plea, have questioned the defendant, and have found him to be knowing and intelligent in entering a guilty plea and to waiving his rights to a jury trial. Would the defendant please rise and state your name and age for the record."

He stood up shakily. "Anthony Cusato, your Honor. I am seventeen years old."

"You understand that since you've entered a guilty plea, it cannot be taken back?"

"I do, your Honor."

"And do you still understand that by entering a guilty plea you are waiving your right to a jury trial, the right to cross-examine your accusers, and the privilege against self-incrimination?"

"Yes, your Honor."

"Were you forced by any party or individual to make this plea?"

"No, your Honor."

"Thank you, please be seated."

"Since guilt has been admitted, we are here today to determine sentencing. We will hear today from the defendant, if he so chooses to make a statement, the prosecution, and any third parties who would like to speak on record. So let us start. Prosecution, are you ready to begin?"

"Yes, your Honor," said Skip McDowell, standing, buttoning his suit jacket in the way that lawyers do. "The prosecution would like to call Robert and Susan Amherst to make a statement to the court."

The court fell silent as Rob and Sue stood from their seats. Sophie grabbed my hand and squeezed.

Sue held a tissue to her eyes as she wiped away tears and sniffled. I felt numb as Rob cleared his throat and read from the creased white paper he held in his hands.

"My name is Robert Amherst and this is my wife Susan. We are the parents of Michael Amherst, who died from cardiac arrest on February 23, 2012, following a motor vehicle accident that occurred on February 22, 2012, in Shelby Township, Michigan. Michael's truck was struck by a car driven by the defendant, Anthony Cusato, who was texting at the time of the crash," Rob's voice caught in his throat and his voice wavered. "Michael was twenty-six years old when he died. He was our first-born and only son. You would be hard-pressed to find someone who cared more about family and friends than Michael did. He was loyal to a fault. He was a hard worker, loved working with his hands and doing physical labor. He was to be married to his girlfriend of six years this June," he paused.

I felt the eyes of everyone in the court on me, pitying me. And I could see how that would be a normal response to the sight before them—this fragile, broken person who had lost everything. But instead of being justified or comforted, I was livid. Their pity and sympathy only enraged me more. I hated that everything about Michael *was*. He *was* loyal, he *was* a hard worker, he *was* an older brother. Now he was all past tense. Never to be talked about in the present or future tense again. Never to be doing or being or existing again. It pissed me off.

It wasn't supposed to happen like this. It wouldn't have happened like this if that goddamn kid had just put his fucking phone away for ten fucking minutes so he could look at the fucking road.

The tears that fell down my face were those of anger and madness. I looked up from my lap.

Rob continued, "My family and I are heartbroken and devastated by the loss of our son, our brother, our partner, and our friend. But it is our wish at this time that the defendant not be sentenced to any jail time. We feel that by admitting guilt and taking responsibility for his actions, he has accepted his punishment.

"We do not want any more lives to be ruined by what happened on that day. We lost our beautiful boy and along with him, his future, and everything he would have become. We mourn for everything we have lost; yet it is our hope that we will all be able to move forward from this tragedy in peace. Thank you."

The judge, the clerk, and Skip McDowell all looked back on the five of us solemnly with disbelief.

Tony Cusato, sitting on the left side of the room, the defendant's side, sat quietly with tears running down his face. Behind him, his mother, a small birdlike woman, sat rocking back and forth in bursts of emotion crying, "Oh, thank you. Thank you!"

Next to her sat a stoic, unmovable looking man. I assumed it was Tony Cusato's father, but from the cold look he shot his son, you would think they were strangers. He sat up straight in a dark suit jacket, and when Mrs. Cusato finally sat back in her seat, he put his arm over her shoulders protectively. Then he leaned closer to whisper into her ear.

Meanwhile, I was seething. I was so mad at all of them, at everything. I had known what they were going to do, and while I could have asked to make my own statement or talked to the lawyer about suing for pain and suffering, I didn't want to overstep Michael's parents or disrespect them. I was also tired of fighting this battle.

If Rob and Sue wanted to move on, fine. If they felt that Tony Cusato shouldn't receive any jail time for killing their son, fine. I wouldn't get in their way. I would let them honor their son the best way they knew how. And I would honor Michael by honoring them.

McDowell cleared his throat, "Your Honor, that is all we have for now."

The judge nodded to Rob and Sue to let them know he had understood, then to McDowell. "Thank you. At this time I will turn things over to the defense. Would the defendant like to make a statement?"

"Yes, your Honor, my client would like to make a quick statement," the defense lawyer, Mrs. Lacey, said smoothly. She leaned over and whispered into her client's ear, then eased back in her seat to watch her client.

Tony Cusato stood up, smoothing his khaki pants as he did so. He lifted his prepared index cards off the table in front of him and said nervously, "My name is Anthony Cusato, and I am pleading guilty as charged because I am the one who was texting while driving. My actions resulted in the death of Michael Amherst. I would like his family and the court to know how sorry I am for what I have done. I know there is nothing I could say that could convey how truly remorseful and horrified I am about what I have done. I want them to know that I take full responsibility and full blame for my reckless actions. What I have done will stay with me for the rest of my life. I will never forget what I have done, and I promise I will never text while driving again. Thank you." When he sat down, the chair made a loud screeching noise.

"Thank you, Mr. Cusato," the judge said. "At this time I would like to hear from counsel about their recommendations for sentencing. Mr. McDowell?"

Skip McDowell stood up again. "Your Honor, on behalf of the State of Michigan, I ask that you sentence the defendant, Anthony Cusato, to the maximum sentence of one year and the maximum fine of $100."

"Mrs. Lacey?" he asked, turning his attention to Tony Cusato's attorney.

She stood up and spoke, "Your Honor, on behalf of my client, who has admitted guilt and taken responsibility for his actions, I ask that you sentence Anthony Cusato to twelve months' probation and sixty hours of community service. He is clearly remorseful and has committed to never texting while driving again."

"Thank you, Mrs. Lacey and Mr. McDowell. The court is in recess for fifteen minutes while I make my decision."

I turned to my dad. "I have to go to the bathroom." I didn't wait to hear his response or even look at Rob or Sue's face as I passed them and walked out of the courtroom.

I pushed open the bathroom door forcefully and went to the row of sinks. I looked at myself in the mirror. My hair and clothes were perfectly in place, or at least they hadn't moved from where I had arranged them this morning, but my face looked disheveled and patchy. I tried to wipe away the black mascara smeared on my face, but the rubbing left it red and raw.

Sophie walked in. Though she still looked troubled, she somehow looked untouched by the events that had just taken place. Her eyes were clear, not rimmed with red, and her makeup was all still in place. She had blush on that made her cheeks glow, and her hair was soft and shiny.

When she saw me looking at her in the mirror, she paused. Then she tentatively walked forward, standing next to me at the sinks.

"You okay?" she asked softly.

"No." I mean, obviously.

"Want to talk about it?"

"Not really."

"Okay" was all she said before entering a stall and closing the door behind her.

It was just me and Sophie in the bathroom. I started pacing in front of the three stalls. Back and forth, back and forth, my heels clicking on the tile. Then the words just rushed out of me, swift and jumbled, "I just don't understand. I mean, listen, I'm trying not to be rude or mean to your parents, but I don't understand why they would say that. And sixty hours of community service for killing someone? Are you serious?"

I pushed my hair out of my face and continued pacing, flapping my hands in front of me as I walked trying to shake off an ominous, sinking feeling.

"Breathe, Skylar," I heard her say from the stall as she flushed the toilet.

"How can I during a time like this?"

"I already told you. They want to move on."

"Yeah, yeah, I get it, okay? Except I don't because I don't feel like I'm moving on or that I want to move on. And I for one, would like to get some justice around here."

"Is that what Michael would have wanted?" she

asked.

I stopped in my tracks. "Are you really pulling the Michael card right now?" I asked, exasperated. "No, and I don't care about what Michael would have wanted. This is about what I want for him." I stormed out of the bathroom.

"Okay then," Sophie whispered as the bathroom door swung behind me.

Five minutes later the bailiff stood and announced again, "Please rise," from the front corner of the room.

Judge Walker reemerged and took his seat. "Please be seated." He opened the manila folder and organized the papers on his desk. He looked across the courtroom. "Will the defendant please rise for sentencing."

Tony Cusato stood from behind the table; he pressed the palms of his hands, undoubtedly slick with sweat, against the surface to steady himself.

"After careful deliberation, I have come to a decision. While I feel that the current maximum punishment for texting and driving that results in a death is poorly inadequate, it is not my job to change the laws but to uphold them. I recognize that what happened was nothing short of a horrible tragedy, but it was also an accident. I have no doubt in my mind that the defendant, Anthony Cusato, had no intention of harm when he decided to text while driving. But nevertheless his actions must have consequences," he paused, looking down at his papers.

"Because the defendant is a minor and has no previous record, he is hereby sentenced to one year of probation, the maximum fine of $100—"

Of fucking course. Even though I knew it had been coming, my shoulders started to shake with the silent sobs. All I could do was close my eyes and listen.

"—and one year of community service in the form of volunteering with an anti-texting campaign.

"This issue is something I feel strongly about, and I feel that spreading awareness and the story of your accident is of greater service to the public than locking you up for a year. Michael Amherst's death could have been completely prevented. We need to make it a top priority to prevent any more of these unnecessary deaths, and the only way to do that is through spreading awareness of the consequences of texting while driving. Additionally, the defendant's driver's license will be suspended for one year."

Tony Cusato collapsed into his chair, looking relieved. I couldn't say that I blamed him; he didn't look like he'd last a night even in juvi, let alone jail. His mother cried into her tissue and his father clapped one of his hands down on his son's shoulders.

I felt drained. Sophie squeezed my hand in hers, and Dad patted my leg.

"I would like to thank counsel and court personnel for the respect you have given to all parties involved and above all, to the law. You are hereby excused, and court is adjourned," he said lightly banging the solid oak gavel.

I was just so fucking done with this.

I stood up abruptly, grabbed my jacket and purse, and as I passed Rob and Sue, I said, "Congratulations. Hope you're happy."

They weren't prepared for my reaction and their mouths just hung open as they watched me leave the courtroom. I don't think I'd ever given them attitude, not once, in the six years I had known them. Guess they didn't know me that well after all.

Dad insisted on taking me out to eat afterwards.

"I'm not hungry," I said slowly, making sure he understood how much I really did not want to go. "Just take me home."

"We're going out."

"No, I'm not."

He looked over at me as we reached the car. "You're going. Stop being so stubborn."

"I'm not being stubborn. I'm upset and I want to go home."

"I know you're upset. I'm upset," he said, pointing to his chest. "And I want to go have a drink and some lunch with my daughter. Now I know you think you live in some bubble and that no one else feels the same way as you do, but we do. I do. We're all upset by this whole situation. And you being such a *bruxa* to Rob, Sue, and Sophie did not help matters."

"Seriously?" I asked.

"You need to apologize."

"Whatever," I said getting in the car and slamming the door shut.

"Stop acting like a two-year-old."

"Stop being so patronizing."

"It's called tough love, baby," he said.

Although we barely said two words to each other over lunch, it was comforting to have him there, good to know that at least someone wasn't afraid to call me out, didn't walk on eggshells around me.

I ordered chicken fingers but only took a few bites. The two margaritas I had though, made me feel a whole lot better about the day's events.

"How's your new position at work going?"

"Peachy," I said with venom. "The one thing I actually looked forward to, and I no longer get to do it. Instead of doing meaningful work, I now get to answer phone calls and help people fill out forms all day."

"It's still important work. Someone has to do it."

"Yeah, I just wish that someone wasn't me."

"Did your boss say how long you have to stay there?"

"Until my sentencing at the very least."

"When will that be?" Dad asked.

I shrugged. "Probably not till this summer. My lawyer said it takes at least ninety days for them to process everything. Then he will meet with the prosecution to discuss a plea bargain."

Dad nodded thoughtfully. "Are you worried? You

could go to jail."

"Honestly, I just don't even care anymore." That was a lie. I was terrified of going to jail, but it wasn't exactly like my life on the outside was all that great either.

"I'm sure it will be fine," he said, more to himself than to me.

After Dad dropped me off, I spent the rest of the day on the couch, obsessively watching *Law & Order* on whatever channel I could find it. If I couldn't get justice for Michael, then I guess I'd have to settle for watching fictional characters on TV get theirs.

XII

Until death do us part

June 23, 2012

Place me like a seal over your heart,
Like a seal on your arm;
For love is as strong as death,
Its jealousy unyielding as the grave.
It burns like blazing fire,
Like a mighty flame.
Many waters cannot quench love;
Rivers cannot sweep it away.
Song of Songs 8:6-7

The church bells rang clearly, announcing to the world that the moment I had waited so long for was finally here. I was adorned in ivory: the fitted bodice accentuated my slim waist. The entire top layer of my dress was a beautiful lace with a delicate flower pattern.

The straps extending from the sweetheart neckline were pushed back on my arms, exposing my bare shoulders. My hair was pulled back halfway and long dark curls fell down my back like a midnight waterfall. Teardrop diamonds dangled from my ears. The dress ended with a modest billowing train. I was a vision from another time, one of mystery, adventure, and romance.

Mendelssohn's "Wedding March" sang from the organ; the sharp, sweet notes accentuated the air. The double oak doors opened, and the guests stood and turned, their eyes lit with excitement and joy.

The chandeliers cast a soft, warm glow as I strode down the aisle, my arm looped through my dad's. Like the parting of the Red Sea, dark cherry pews lined each side of the sanctuary and made a passageway to the altar. Beautiful stained glass windows lined the walls. At the front of the sanctuary behind the altar, two tall gray pillars joined together in a curve at the ceiling, framing a large crucifix on the wall.

I wasn't crying, but I could feel my smile bursting from my face. Everything and everyone disappeared when I saw him. I didn't see Reverend Romarro waiting at the end of the aisle or Sue and Rob to my left. I didn't see Logan, Shane, or any of the other groomsmen beside him. I didn't see Sophie smiling at me, waiting for me to complete the procession. I could barely feel the long stems of the white calla lilies I held in my hand. I couldn't hear the crowd whispering. It was all inconsequential compared to Michael at the end of the aisle. He had a beaming smile that matched my own and looked so incredibly handsome in his black tuxedo. And in that second, I knew that everything was right where it was meant to be.

Suddenly time jumped and I was lying on a recliner, my feet propped up. The blinds were shut, enclosing the room in a mute darkness. A small amount of light peeped through the cracks and lit the room.

There was a monitor to my left. My belly was exposed, my *fat* belly. No, not fat—round. Michael was sitting beside me, holding my hand in anticipation.

Cool thick gel was smeared on my swollen belly. The nurse pressed the white plastic wand of the ultrasound to my skin and guided it across the surface. There was a crackling noise, like static, that came from the black monitor. And there it was.

A small, faint heartbeat that grew stronger as the equipment picked up its location. A rush of emotions released in my heart. I could feel tears slide down my face and a callused hand wiped them away.

"That's *our* baby," he whispered. "It's incredible." He pointed on the screen to the small creature curled up into a ball.

I touched my stomach and nodded.

The nurse pointed to the screen. "This is the head. You'll notice it's quite a bit larger than the rest of the body," she laughed a little.

"And here are the feet and the hands."

"When can we find out the sex?" I asked.

"Do you want to know right now? I can tell you."

The light started to grow brighter and brighter

through the cracks of the blinds. It washed out the room in whiteness. Then I saw green, yellow, blue, and red. The green became more defined underneath my feet as a million blades of grass, the blue sky, the yellow and red tarp of a wooden jungle gym roof.

The blissful sound of children's laughter turned from a faint echo into distinguishable sound. It made me *so* happy. I looked down and saw them: three dirt-covered faces with sticky hands reaching up for more Kool-Aid.

They were absolutely adorable. A boy of about six, Jeremy, had Michael's blue eyes, blond hair, but my olive complexion. One of his front teeth was missing and it made me laugh. I saw him tenderly wipe his youngest sister's knee after she had fallen down, and then he kissed it all better. He was definitely Michael's son.

And there were two girls. Kailey, *my* four-year-old daughter with long black hair, strikingly beautiful with her fair skin and piercing blue eyes. Her purple tutu and silver crown clearly gave away her status in this hierarchy as The Princess.

And the smallest was Allison, a three-year-old still stuck in the terrible twos. Her shrieks from her temper tantrum hit notes so high they were unknown to mankind. She was all me: caramel skin, brown eyes, and dark hair. The only hint of Michael was in her button nose.

I looked over these messy, loud, rambunctious children and my heart exploded in a love-burst. A profound truth hit me: they were *mine*. They'd had my heart all along, even before I met them, even before they were conceived. And I had fallen. Hard.

Their bright faces became fuzzy as the scene changed again. Losing them hurt so badly that it caused physical pain. Then, before us, a grown Allison, who looked so much like me it was scary, walked toward us. She was wearing a black, polyester gown and cap with a tassel on it. She had a bright open smile on her face. A college graduate. The last of our babies leaving the nest. And now it was just us again, me and Michael, now with more gray hair and wrinkles than we cared to admit, standing hand in hand like we had through all the life we had lived together.

And despite the harrowing emptiness of our home and hearts, there was a bittersweet taste of the beginning of a new chapter.

I woke with a start, the tears once again in full force. I sat up, pulling my legs into my chest, and let my head fall as my body shook with sobs. *How many tears would I have to cry before the hurt went away?*

The realization that it was just a dream was crippling, devastating—like I had been simultaneously punched in the chest and the stomach. The pain was raw and unreal. How can losing something you never had hurt so fucking much?

The dream—it was everything I'd ever wanted. I felt that I hadn't asked for much out of life. I deserved that happiness, that life.

But it never worked out that way, did it.

That dream was everything that should have been. The deep ache in my heart throbbed; the healing wound ripped right open again. I missed him. I missed them. I missed *us*.

This is not how it was supposed to be.

Michael had an unfinished life.

That was the moment when I remembered what today was. I remembered what the date on the calendar said. June twenty-third, supposedly the happiest day of my life. Bullshit. Fuck you, "happily ever after."

I could feel heat radiating from the hidden nook in my closet where my dress was sitting on a hanger. I was pulled toward it. I dug through the sweaters, pants, and shoes until I found it.

I yanked off the plastic cover and threw it on the floor. I hung the dress on the dusty valence and sat on the edge of the bed, staring at it.

Today, just like the beginning of my dream, I should have been getting ready to walk down the aisle. I should have had nervous butterflies as I got my hair and makeup done. Dad should have been misty-eyed as he walked me down the aisle. Michael should have been with his groomsmen getting ready at some hotel somewhere. I should have, there should have, he should have....

I stood up with shaking legs and reached out to touch the intricate, delicate lace. It was beautiful. It deserved a chance to be worn and shown off.

Slowly, I took the dress off the hanger and laid it out

on the bed.

I slid out of my pajamas, they looked like rags compared to this masterpiece, and slipped into the ivory dress. I looked in the mirror.

My face was taut and sallow. There were dark bags under my eyes, my skin had dried out from crying and neglect, and my chin was broken out. This wasn't how a bride was supposed to look. She was supposed to look radiant, beautiful, captivating, and breathtaking. Her smile would make her groom's heart melt, and she would fit effortlessly into his arms as if they were two pieces of a jigsaw puzzle.

She didn't look like I did now.

I drew my eyes away from my reflection in the mirror.

Then, caught in a feverish delusion, I danced around the room. I held my arms out to relax them on my groom's shoulders. He put his imaginary hand on the small of my back and pulled me closer. We were in a giant ballroom, draped in golden curtains and rich tapestry. The floor was cleared, the onlookers marveled at our extravagant steps, and we spun and swirled effortlessly, my dress flowed around us. A prince and his princess.

Something caught my eye in the corner of my room, snapping me out of my castle in the sky. It was Michael's red flannel shirt. It was so comfortable and broken in after years of wear and tear. I walked over to the closet and picked it up. I slid my arms through the sleeves.

I pulled the cloth closer to me, my hands drawing into fists around the material. It was so soft. I could faintly smell Michael's cologne on it. I pulled the collar closer to my nose, breathing in the scent that was so familiar and yet so dreamlike.

So many memories contained in one smell it was impossible to remember them all. But maybe it wasn't the memories that the scent triggered so much as a series of feelings. I felt safe, secure, and loved when I smelled this scent. I felt whole, complete, and happy.

I couldn't be in that room, that house, for another second. I put on a pair of flip-flops and ran downstairs. I pushed the door out of my way and it swung back with impressive force. Scout followed after me and jumped in the car. And we drove.

We drove to the church where Michael and I were supposed to be exchanging vows in a few hours' time. We drove to the reception site where our guests should have been dancing, drinking, and laughing. We drove to the hotel where we were supposed to spend our first official night as a married couple together. We drove.

We drove to a McDonald's around dinnertime. I got a two-cheeseburger meal and gave one of the burgers to Scout. We drove to the liquor store where I bought a fifth of Jameson and put it in the trunk. And then we drove some more.

There was a place, not far from Michael's parents' house, where he used to take me before we started living together. During the summertime, we would meet up with Shane and Logan and some other people from their high school and have bonfires out there at night. Other times it was just the two of us. I especially loved to go out there when it was raining—when it was hot, muggy, and wet. It was wonderful.

Our hidden retreat was off one of the main roads, once it turned into a dirt road and tapered off. We'd pull over to the side of the road by this old wire fence. The pathway was hard to see from the road; strangers wouldn't be able to find it unless they knew what they were looking for.

I pulled over and stepped out of the car. The evening summer sun was warm on my back as I watched the dust settle around my tires. I let Scout out and grabbed the liquor from the trunk.

The road was dead; no other cars passed us as I pushed back the rusted gate and we walked through it.

The dirt path was surrounded by overgrowth. After a winding mile the trail opened into a good-sized field surrounded by trees and brush. Scout went out into the field to check the perimeter.

I looked around the clearing. It was obvious that the location had been bestowed upon the next generation because there were logs and chairs set up around a fire pit; empty beer cans were scattered about.

I gathered the skirt of my dress so I could sit on the log. The dress already had tears in the fabric and the hemline was getting dirty, but it was my wedding day and I'd be damned to be wearing anything else.

I unwrapped the Jameson and twisted off the cap. I tilted my head back and I felt the whiskey burn my throat. It sent fire through my veins instantly.

I watched Scout move back and forth across the field, happy to finally get out of the house and get some exercise. I felt kind of bad now that I thought about how inattentive I had been to him the past few months.

So this is my wedding day. I let out a cruel hollow laugh, the kind that echoes around in your mind.

I thought back to the dream I had earlier. I thought about how Sue had to call and cancel all the wedding plans and reservations because I just couldn't bring myself to do it. I was so grateful to her for doing that.

I looked down at my engagement ring. Something about having it on my finger consoled me. It reminded me of Michael, of his love for me, of his promise that we would be together forever, that he wanted me to be his wife. I would be his and he would be mine.

"Michael," I whispered as I fingered the white gold band, the diamond catching the sun. My voice grew stronger, "I'm so confused. I miss you, and at any moment it feels like you're just going to come back as if none of this ever happened. It will all have been a nightmare. But I know that's not going to happen." Anguish broke up my words.

"Today was supposed to be our wedding day, the

gateway to the rest of our lives." I took another swig of whiskey.

"I want to feel again, Michael. I want to live again. But I'm so afraid. How can I go on without you?"

I paused for a minute and took another sip. I heard Scout bark in the background. *What was there left to say?*

"I keep hurting people. People that I love. And I can't stop thinking about all the ways I hurt you. You deserved so much better." I choked out the words.

"You didn't hurt him, Skylar," I jumped at the sound of a man's voice behind me. I turned around. "You couldn't if you wanted to. He loved you too much."

"Logan?" I said in disbelief as I shielded my eyes from the glare. Scout barked again excitedly and ran across the field toward us.

"I thought I'd find you here," he said, coming closer. "Everyone's been trying to find you all day. Sue, your dad, Sophie. When you didn't pick up your phone, they stopped by your house, but when you weren't there they started to freak out a little."

Logan was wearing gray shorts with a black T-shirt and leather flip-flops. He looked concerned but relieved. When I saw him appraising my wedding dress and Michael's shirt, he quickly looked away and didn't say anything.

"Oh. I didn't realize people would be looking for me," I said, looking away from him. "I left my phone at home. I didn't even realize until after I had left. Where is everyone now?"

Scout had made his way over to us by now. He went up to Logan and barked for attention.

"Hey, buddy," Logan said, kneeling down to pet Scout's ears. "I think they went back to Sue and Rob's."

"Wait, how did you get involved in this?" I asked.

He laughed. "I think Sophie called every single person in your phone book. I was just dropping Madison off at Brooke's place when she called. I had a feeling you'd be here. So I told them I would check a few places and get back to them if I found you, which I did, so...," he said, taking his phone out of his pocket. "I'm going to call them real fast." He started dialing the numbers.

"Please don't tell them where we are," I pleaded. "I really just can't see anyone right now."

He nodded in understanding. I could hear someone on the other end of the phone.

"Thank you," I mouthed.

"Hey, I found her," he said.

More on the other end....

"She's fine, she's okay. She just doesn't want to talk to anyone...."

More voices....

"I really can't tell you that. Hey! Don't shoot the messenger. Yes, okay, yes, yes. I'll stay with her. I'll get her home safe tonight. Don't worry. Yes, yes, okay. Bye."

"Sue?" I guessed.

"Nope, Sophie. She's actually worse than her mother,

I think."

"Thanks again, Logan," I said. "But you really don't have to stay. I think I'll be all right."

He sat down beside me. "No one should be alone on their wedding day," was all he said.

I didn't say anything in response, but I was glad he was there. I hadn't realized how alone I had felt until he showed up.

"It's nice out here," he said.

"Yeah, it is," I smiled.

He was quiet.

"You know that bible verse, the one that talks about faith, hope, and love and how the greatest of the three is love?" I asked him.

He nodded.

"Well I guess I can't really argue that love is the greatest, but you can still have love in your life and not want to live. Hope, now that's something that you can't live without.

"Because look, I have the love of my family, my friends, even my dog," I said, reaching down to pet Scout. "And I have Michael's love. I still have that, right? Even though he's not here?"

"Of course," Logan said.

"So I have all this love in my life and it still feels so hopeless, so…so meaningless." I paused. After a moment I said, "I'm afraid. I don't want to lose him."

"You have to let go to be able to move on with your

life, otherwise you'll stay stuck where you are," he explained.

I kicked at the ground.

"Mike will always be in your heart," Logan said. "He will always be a part of you. He was such a big factor in how you grew into the person you are today, in how you think, and in the decisions you make.

"But unlike you, he doesn't get to move forward. You have to acknowledge that. You aren't going to stay stagnant. You weren't meant to."

"So what do I do?"

"You feel it. You dig in and you really feel it, the pain. You grieve. You grieve for a life that was cut too short, you grieve for him, you grieve for the life you thought you were going to have with him. And then when it's time, you stop holding on so tight and you move on with your life."

"But when do you know it's time?" I asked.

"For me, it's when thinking about your time together brings more happiness than sadness. And when the time comes, you'll be ready."

"I don't think I'm there yet," I said. "But I feel like I'm getting there. Maybe. Eventually. One day."

And in the warmth of the summer sun, I felt like my heart was starting to thaw a degree or two.

"Was that what it was like with you and Brooke?" I asked. "I know she didn't die or anything, but did you have to grieve the breakup?"

"Yeah, but I don't think it was nearly as hard as what

you're going through. I mean, I had to acknowledge that this person I loved, that I wanted to spend the rest of my life with and raise my child with, just didn't love me anymore. That she didn't want the same things that I did anymore. And it took me a few months. But I dealt with it, and I let go of that dream."

"Do you have a new one?"

"No, not really. Not yet, anyway. I guess now I'm just content with being open to new things. People tell you that life doesn't ever go the way you plan, but you never really believe it until it happens to you. You think that you have some control over your life, that if you work hard enough or give enough that you get to write the script, but that's not always true," he paused and I waited for him to continue.

"You can't always control what happens to you, but you can control how you react to things."

"You make it sound like it's easy or something," I said.

"It's not easy. Not at all. But given the two choices—depression or hope, I'd take hope any day of the week. Because like you said, you can't live without hope. Otherwise, how do you keep going?"

"You don't," I said shrugging. "Can I tell you something?"

"Sure."

"I'm tired. Tired of feeling so sad and lonely and miserable all the fucking time. But I feel like I'm not allowed to not feel this way. I feel like if I don't feel this way then it means I don't love Michael, or that I never did."

"First of all, that's crazy. We both know that's not true. You love Mike. You always will. And secondly, Mike would not have wanted this for you and you know that. He would want you, when you're ready, to start to pick up the pieces again and move on. He would want you to feel good again."

"You think?" I asked.

"I know. Hey," he said, grinning at me, "I think right now we should honor Michael by treating ourselves to a little something special."

He dug in his pocket and pulled out a small bag. His smile grew. There was a joint in it.

"Yes, tonight is the perfect night," he said. "Madison is at her mother's and it's your wedding day, after all."

"I suppose it is."

He pulled out the lighter that was in the Ziploc bag. It was an old Zippo featuring a Vietnam War soldier with a large peace sign printed over him.

"To Michael," Logan said, raising the joint in the air. Then he put it to his lips, lit it, and took a long drag.

"To Michael," I said as I took the joint from him and took a hit.

The smoke burned my lungs. I started to feel the molecules bubble up into my brain, and I got excited. I knew that in a few more minutes, not a whole lot would matter anymore. Everything would feel okay, if only for a little while.

"I can't remember the last time I smoked," I said.

"Me neither. I've been holding on to this guy for a while, waiting for the perfect opportunity. I'm glad I found it."

After we had each taken a few hits, we lay down on the ground side by side. It was dark and the bugs started to bite, but I was too high to care.

"Is it hard?" I asked, lying on the ground next to him.

"Is what hard?" He asked, looking over at me.

"Being a dad?"

"Like you couldn't even imagine," he said. "You're responsible for this little person, this human being. Not only for her physical well-being but for her soul and spirit. It's incredibly daunting."

I turned on my side to face him. "But you seem to be doing a really good job, like you were meant to do it or something."

"She changed my life. Things that were such a big deal before don't even matter now. All of a sudden, it's not just about you. You have to keep living for this person. Because you're all she's got right now."

"I had a dream about mine and Michael's kids last night," I admitted.

"Tell me about them."

"There were three of them. Jeremy, Kailey, and Allison. When I saw them in my dream, I felt so—so connected to them. I mean, obviously, they were a part of me, they came from me, and I was so happy when they laughed. It felt like things were exactly how they were supposed to be. And now it breaks my heart that they will never be anything more than a dream, a figment of my imagination."

Logan didn't say anything. He just put his arm under my shoulders and pulled me closer to him in a sideways hug. It felt good to have physical, human contact again, even if it wasn't Michael.

I looked over at him and watched him look up at the night sky. "Thank you, Logan," was all I said.

Later we both stood up and walked back to the cars with Scout. The moon lit the way and you could hear Scout's heavy breathing over the sound of the crickets.

When we reached the cars, we said goodbye and left.

The house was dark and quiet when Scout and I got home. I flipped on the lights as I walked upstairs and into the bedroom.

I decided what I needed was a nice hot shower to rinse the dirt and sweat off my body. I turned the knobs and let the water warm up before stripping off my dress and getting in. I stood there for minutes, letting the hot water glide over my body.

I started to feel overwhelmed. All the hope of renewal quickly unraveled in the shower.

I felt incredibly guilty. Like those Warner Bros.

cartoons in which the larger-than-life anvil always drops on Wile E. Coyote. I betrayed Michael by going to Logan's that one day. I betrayed him again by letting Logan comfort me tonight.

Even though I knew it was nothing more than friendly companionship, a tie to Michael, had I betrayed Michael by spending my wedding day with someone other than him? Had I done anything wrong?

Regardless of the truth, my feelings weighed down on me the rest of the night. I couldn't stop blaming myself for making such a stupid mistake.

Guilt collided with anger. Why can't I be happy? Why should I feel guilty for visiting an old friend? Or for feeling okay for just a little bit? I deserved that much for the hell I'd been through didn't I?

Part Two

XIII

Still alive

On a Saturday afternoon in July, with nowhere to be and no one to see, I ventured into the backyard. I started pulling at the weeds in the cracks of the driveway, which started out as mindless nit picking, but then led to a therapy session of weeding all the gardens lining the house. Time did not exist as I pulled and dug, and the pile of weeds in the driveway grew.

My thoughts drifted to the conversation I had with Sue earlier that week. I hadn't talked to her since the sentencing hearing, and when I saw her name flash on the caller ID, my stomach tensed and I suddenly felt light-headed. My hands shook as I pressed the button and brought the phone to my ear.

"Hello?" I asked.

"We haven't heard from you in a while. We were

getting worried you'd never speak to us again," she said gently.

"I just didn't have anything to say," I said quietly, holding on tightly to the edge of the kitchen counter. Enough time had passed for my anger towards them to subside.

"We're sorry for upsetting you. We didn't realize how strongly you felt about it," she paused, her voice going up an octave. "I was the one who lost my son, but I can't help thinking what if Michael had been in the other car? What if it had been Michael who was texting and killed someone else's baby? What would I want for him? I'd want forgiveness. So that's what we did. It could have happened to anyone. We meant what we said, we didn't want any more lives to be ruined."

Her words crashed against my impenetrable walls. "Sue, I hear what you're saying. I know I acted rudely, and I'm sorry about that. But I guess I just don't understand how you're not angry? How you could just let him walk away scot-free?"

She paused for a moment. "It's not that we weren't mad or still aren't mad about what happened. It's more of purposefully letting it go and trying to move on. We believe that's what Michael would've wanted us to do."

She continued. "You know, we miss him so much. I'd do anything to have him back, but we have Sophie to think about. We want to make things as okay as possible for her."

It wasn't that I didn't understand where they were coming from. I did. Both Sophie and her parents reasons for wanting to move forward made sense. The thing was, they all had things to look forward to, things to live for. I didn't.

I didn't have a child to take care of or the possibility of starting over somewhere new. I didn't want to go back to school or switch careers. The life I had with Michael was my future, was everything I'd ever wanted.

"My dad says that every death affects each person differently. I guess that I'm still trying to figure that out," I said.

"We all are, honey," Sue said. "I know this must be so difficult for you. But you feel how you feel, and it's okay for you to be mad at us or disagree with us. That's what families do, right?"

"Yeah," I said. That they would still consider me family after everything—I couldn't express how much that meant to me, but I could try. "Thank you for everything, Sue. Thank you for letting me be a part of your family, and for Michael, and for your kindness these past few months. It really means the world to me."

"Oh, honey. We love you, you know that right?"

I nodded and placed my hand on my chest, even though I knew she couldn't see me. My mouth felt dry and unable to form words, but I was finally able to manage, "I know."

The sweat dripping in my eyes brought me back to the present. It was hot outside, and I wiped the sweat off my forehead with my arm. I studied my yard. The grass still needed to be cut and could really use some fertilizer, but it was too hot for that now. It would have to wait until it cooled off in the fall.

For now, the bushes lining the back of the yard and the back porch were in need of a trim. They waved around wildly in the wind.

The shade of the garage was a welcome respite from the heat of the afternoon sun. I stared at the wall of tools, searching for the hedger. I saw an ax, a shovel, a rake, even a saw, but no hedger. A second assortment of tools lay to one side in a sloppy heap. I started to dig through them, sorting them as I went, when I felt the sharp edge of a blade cut into the soft skin under my upper arm.

"Fuck," I yelled, pulling my arm carefully out of the mess of tools. "Fuck. Fuck. Fuck."

I saw the blood run red, and tears pricked at my eyes, for once not from emotional pain but from physical pain from a visible wound. I watched as the blood flowed brightly out of the cut. That's when I realized that I was still really alive.

I wasn't ready to give up just yet. I still had some fight left in me.

XIV

Seasons change

The change couldn't really be documented, it just happened. From that moment in the garage, in the middle of summer, I had decided that I wanted to live again. I knew it wouldn't be easy. Just now had the good days started to outnumber the bad. The haze of grief still lingered over me, less like a fog and more like a cloud. Overcast.

Most days I didn't feel so defeated and heavy. But I still experienced those random, sudden moments of sadness that stabbed like an ice-hot knife in my stomach. I would have to stop and catch my breath when they happened, slowly easing the blade out.

"Don't ignore it," Dad had said. "Let yourself cry. Listen to yourself. Trust yourself. If you need a break, take it."

In the last month of summer, I received my official plea-bargain deal from my lawyer. I pled guilty. In return, I only received one year of probation, during which time I had to stay away from Tony Cusato, which wasn't really a problem. What was a problem was the $2,500 restitution fee the court was making me pay and the fifteen weeks of anger management classes I had to attend.

So far I had already attended three weekly group sessions. For an hour on Saturday mornings, I would sit on a couch in a therapist's office and listen to my eight angry comrades talk about their inappropriate and angry responses to various situations and explain why they reacted the way they did.

The counselor David Kennah, a fit middle-aged man with graying day-old facial hair and gentle eyes, would talk through alternative ways to deal with highly reactive situations and how to recognize when our anger was getting out of control.

On the first Saturday, after we had gone around the circle and introduced ourselves, the first thing David said was, "I'm sure you're all aware of the ramifications when your anger gets out of control. The first thing you have to do is acknowledge that you have a problem with your anger. Then acknowledge that you have control over it."

I couldn't deny that I had a problem. Obviously, or I wouldn't be here. But I couldn't help but feel justified in my anger. Why would I want to get rid of it? My fiancé had been killed. Of course I was pissed.

At this point, I had shared nothing more than my name and why I was there, but it wasn't an altogether waste of a weekend morning. It certainly had its entertaining moments, and I had even made a new friend.

In a room full of middle-aged balding men, Samara Gem piqued my interest instantly with her brightly dyed red hair and larger-than-life laugh. She looked relaxed, yet tough, in her faded jeans and tan corduroy jacket. Her ears were lined with silver studs and small hoops.

There was something so real about her. Maybe it was the way the corners of her mouth were touched with smoking lines or her perpetually weary hazel eyes. Maybe it was that she laughed at my sarcastic remarks or wasn't afraid of confrontation. Most likely, it was the way she carried herself with the hardened resolution that comes from a lifetime of making bad decisions.

When it was her turn to share why she was there, she charged forward. "Maybe I could've saved my marriage, or hell, even prevented it if I hadn't been so angry at everyone, including myself. I'm here because I'm making changes in my life, making myself better. Even thinking of going back to school, getting out of the hospitality business."

I knew then that I wanted to get to know her. I just didn't know how to approach her.

She made it easy though. Right after the first session ended, she came up to me and asked me if I wanted to grab a bite to eat.

Over the course of lunch, I filled her in on the vague

details of my life, keeping it to a minimum because I kept wanting to know more about her. I learned that she was in her early thirties, divorced, no kids, and worked at the MGM Grand Casino in Detroit as an assistant stewarding manager in the kitchen.

Three weeks in, going out to eat after every session had become our thing. At our last lunch I told her how Sue and Sophie had come over the last weekend of August to go through some of Michael's stuff before Sophie left for college.

It had been a strange feeling, going through his things. Michael's smell had started to fade from his clothes, which had taken on the hint of mustiness and stagnation.

I felt like I was in limbo or something, atoning for untold sins. I didn't want to see his clothes every single day when I opened my closet to get dressed for work, but I wasn't sure if I was ready to get rid of them either. His clothes, a reminder of his absence, had moved past the point of being a comfort and had become a burden now. They were weighing me down.

As we sorted and folded and boxed, Sophie said, "I mean, seriously, look at these clothes. When's the last time he went shopping? High school?"

Sue chuckled softly. "Sophie, you know your brother. He wore his clothes till they were literally falling apart," she smiled at me.

Michael never really paid much attention to what he wore. After we had been dating for a few years, I was the one who did most of his shopping, and before then, it had been Sue. He didn't care about clothes or name brands, and it was one of the first things that drew me to him. To me, it meant that he was focused on the more important things in life: his work, his relationships, having a good time.

"Seriously, you can't even *buy* jeans this distressed," Sophie said, holding up a pair of faded jeans strewn with holes and tears.

I sighed and took the jeans from Sophie. I stood there holding them, staring at them in my outstretched arms. My eyes misted over and a subtle sadness filled the room.

"I just wish he was still here to wear these stupid jeans," I whispered.

Sue stepped toward me, over the piles of clothes and boxes, and put her arm around me. "We all do," she said, rubbing my arm.

Sophie stood in the closet, facing us. "But these things, they aren't Mike. I don't know if they ever really were," she paused for a moment then gestured at all his things. "And I bet he's up there in heaven somewhere, looking down at you thinking what a weirdo you are for keeping all his junk when you could have cleared this out months ago and made more room for new clothes."

"Maybe," I had said. I wasn't sure which statement I was responding to. Maybe he was in heaven. Maybe he did think that I was a weirdo. No, scratch that. I knew he thought I was a weirdo.

But I didn't know for sure about the heaven part.

How could I? It was all a guessing game. As much as I had told myself that heaven was just a nice, fluffy place people made up to make themselves feel better about losing loved ones—all that "They're in a better place now" bullshit, there was still a part of me that wanted to believe it. There was something so comforting and reassuring about the idea that he was safe and sound in some paradise, that I would see him again someday. I wanted to surrender to the delusion so badly, but I felt like a fool for believing it.

"You're still wearing it," Sue said, gesturing to the ring on my finger.

"I don't know how to take it off," I said.

"Maybe you could make it into some kind of necklace. Take the diamond out and get it made into a pendant or something. Keep the actual ring tucked away in a drawer or something," she suggested.

I thought about it. "I like that idea," I said, a grin spreading across my face as I looked down at it. "That's a really, really good idea. I should do that."

She smiled at me kindly. She didn't say anything, but I think she was moved by how much I had liked her suggestion.

As we were sorting and folding and boxing, Sue asked me what I was going to do with the house.

"What do you mean?" I asked, not wanting to confront the question that had been creeping up through my subconscious on a daily basis for the past two months. I was just fine with dodging the question until it went away.

Sue cleared her throat and her eyes shifted across the room, clearly uncomfortable. "I just meant that, um," she bit down on her lower lip, "you can't really afford to stay here by yourself, can you?"

I continued stuffing the Goodwill box with clothes, not meeting her eyes. "No," I said softly, "I can't."

"You know Rob and I would be more than happy to help you out—."

"No," I cut her off, picking the box up and moving it toward the door. "Thank you for the offer, but no. I'll figure it out. Eventually."

My hands on my hips, I stood at the door and let out a deep sigh.

"I'm going to take these boxes downstairs," I said, hitching my thumb over my shoulder.

I heaved the box up and out of the room, breathing a sigh of relief at leaving the close quarters of my bedroom and all the questions that had to be answered.

I had four more months to figure out what I needed to do about the house. Four more months, that was plenty of time. I stacked the box by the front door and returned to the bedroom to finish packing.

After several more hours, each of us had two or three boxes worth of Michael's stuff we wanted to keep. In Sue's boxes there were a few of Michael's T-shirts, his birth certificate and social security card, his grandfather's watch, and random objects and projects from his childhood.

Sophie's box held all his yearbooks, one of his

hoodies, a few of his baseball hats, and Michael's DVD collection.

In my boxes I kept a few of his favorite shirts, that pair of ripped jeans, his work boots, his shaving kit, his favorite pair of pajama pants. I kept his cologne, his belt, his wallet, his keys, and his dead cellphone—all quintessential Michael.

There were still things lying about the house that were his: his Xbox, video games, his tool kit, his computer, and some of his sports equipment. So far I had found a pair of ice skates, basketballs, a football, and a hockey stick. There were still pictures of us on the wall of the upstairs hallway. Pictures of us from college, at concerts we'd attended, and places we'd been too. In all of them we looked young, bright-eyed, and hopeful. And so in love. These things scattered around the house would keep him here, in bits and pieces, as a reminder, not as an overwhelming absence.

There was a dull ache in my heart whenever I looked at the people we used to be. In one picture, we're standing in front of Niagara Falls, our hair damp, both of us wrapped in blue plastic ponchos. We looked so happy it was stupid. My arms were wrapped around Michael's waist. If only I had known then to hold on tighter, for just a few more moments, so that the feel of his body would never leave my skin, forever be embedded there.

Everything else of Michael's was either tossed—his toothbrush for example—or donated to charity, like the rest of his clothes. It was not a light task, and the day did not escape without a few tears.

"So how'd it feel?" Samara asked.

"It was on a completely other level. Neither harder nor easier than I thought it was going to be," I responded. How could I describe the feeling of sorting through the earthly possessions of the person I loved most in this world? These were the last material things reminding me that he was here. Keep? Toss? Donate? It was a position no one should be in. I wouldn't wish it on my worst enemy.

"Well, did you feel better with his stuff gone?"

I looked at her for a second, almost afraid to admit what a relief it had been to carry the boxes out of the house.

"I was surprised," I said. "The house didn't feel as empty as I thought it would. Just neater, cleaner. And when the Goodwill truck pulled away, I wasn't even that sad."

In fact, I was stoical. I was free.

Now we were in the early days of September, and the days were slowly getting shorter. The air was clean and warm; the leaves still green on the trees.

Around my neck, along with my *M* and *S* charms, now hung a diamond pendant. Taking off the ring for the first time had been terrifying; I kept checking my finger for

The Charm Necklace

the ring constantly the night I left it with the jeweler. But by the time I picked up the diamond and had it around my neck with the other two charms, my finger felt light and unburdened, and my chest filled with pride. I had done it.

It was hard for me to believe that it was my first autumn without Michael. It would be my first Halloween and trip to the apple orchard without Michael in, what? Seven years?

This year I would rake the leaves by myself. I would put up the Halloween decorations and hand out candy by myself. Later on, I would put up the Christmas lights and tree by myself. Maybe Dad would help me. But Michael wouldn't be there. It wouldn't be the same. I wondered how long it would take me to get used to being alone.

I guess this is what Dad had meant by *After*. I had now accepted this, however unwillingly, like a kid who has found out that Santa Claus isn't real—disappointed, nostalgic, and inescapably never turning back.

Last night Logan had called, frantically trying to find someone to watch Madison on the nights he had a graduate-level English composition class.

"I know it's last minute, but I promise, it'll only be temporary. I'm working on finding someone permanent," he had begged. "A late cancellation created a last-minute opening for my usual sitter to study abroad for a semester in Spain. My mom is an hour away in Novi, and my sister is too busy with the boys and work to watch her."

"Sure, I'll do it," I said without hesitation.

"Are you sure?" he breathed in relief.

"Yes, I'm sure," I laughed. "I'll see you Tuesday."

When I showed up at his apartment after work, Madison was sitting on the living room floor playing with her barnyard animal blocks. "Moo," one blared, when she placed the cow in the right spot. She clapped her hands excitedly and squealed.

She was a beautiful little girl. As I watched her, I saw she had Brooke and Logan's brown hair and Brooke's warm brown eyes. Her cheeks were rosy, her skin smooth and soft. A clean slate. Unblemished. Untarnished.

She was openly affectionate with Logan, clinging to him and hugging his neck and giving him kisses whenever she was near him. But she was wary with strangers, a little bit withdrawn and not quite ready to trust.

"Daddy, the cow!" she exclaimed in a high, innocent voice. "It goes 'moo.'"

"Good job, sweetheart," he said distractedly, as he collected his things from the desk and put them in his leather messenger bag. He was in a zip-up sweater with dark work pants and black Converse sneakers. His long dark bangs were pushed over to one side of his forehead. "What about the piggy?"

She looked hard at the animals on the floor around her. "Ah!" she said after a moment. "Found it." She placed it in the slot and the toy made an oink-oink sound.

"Okay, sorry, I'm running a little bit late," Logan said, flustered. He was organizing the folders in his bag.

"We ate a little bit ago. I wasn't sure if you were going to pick up dinner or what, so I made you a plate. I put it in the fridge. It's nothing special, just some Hamburger Helper."

I grinned at him.

"Don't say anything," he said with a mock-accusatory tone. "I am not ashamed to say my cooking skills don't extend beyond boxed meals and sandwiches. I didn't get to the dishes, but don't worry about them. I'll get to them when I get home."

I glanced over to the kitchen. Various dishes were scattered over the laminate counter and in the sink.

He started in a rush again. "Bedtime is eight thirty. I usually start winding her down, getting her PJs on, and brushing her teeth at about a quarter to eight. Then we read a few short books until she gets tired. Don't worry, she's one of those weird kids who likes to go to bed. She will probably start falling asleep while you're reading. Just leave her night-light on and the door cracked open."

I stared at him, perplexed, trying to remember everything he had just said. I was more than anxious that he was about to leave me alone with his three-year-old daughter.

I glanced over at Madison. She was watching us now, understanding dawning on her face that her dad was about to leave her with me.

"Daddy, no! No go. No leave," she cried, running across the room to him. He picked her up in a tight hug.

"We talked about this, remember?" he asked softly, rubbing her back. "Daddy has to go to class, remember? We talked about how much fun this was going to be that you would get to hang out with Skylar? You remember Skylar. She's one of daddy's really good friends. You two are going to have so much fun."

She looked at me apprehensively, like she was just humoring her dad, but didn't really believe him.

Still holding on to her, he said to me, "You two can do whatever you want. There's a park down the road, or you can go for a walk, or play with some toys. Her favorite shows are saved on Netflix, but try not to let her watch too much. I use that as a last resort."

"Anything else?"

"Umm," he said, thinking. "Oh, yes. Try to avoid liquids an hour or so before bedtime. We've been having a little bit of a bed-wetting issue," he whispered. "But if she gets thirsty, just give her a sip of water. She can have a small snack before bed if she's hungry, and her pull-ups are in her closet."

He shifted his attention to Madison. "Okay, baby girl. I've got to go."

She started to whine and tugged at his neck tighter. "No!"

"Yes. Now be a good girl. Why don't you show Skylar your new stuffed animal? What is it again?"

She lifted her head from his shoulder and looked at me. "It's a kitty."

"A kitty? Can I see it?" I asked, really pushing myself here. The very small amount of information I knew about three-year-olds came from a quick Google search I did before leaving work.

But if I was being honest with myself, I wasn't getting on too great with adults right now. I think my pissy disposition made them uncomfortable. Maybe hanging out with a toddler was more my speed. Less complicated. Simple. Untangled.

Madison nodded.

"Yeah?" I said nodding, reaching out my hands for her.

Logan leaned in toward me, attempting to get her into my arms.

She was reluctant at first, but then gave in and let me hold her. She was warm and delicate. I had the sudden urge to squeeze her close to me.

"Okay, see you," Logan whispered, while Maddie was distracted. He came close and gave her a quick peck on the cheek, his face noticeably close to mine. "Um," he stuttered. "Okay, girls, have fun."

Then he was gone.

I looked down at the beautiful brown-eyed girl in my arms. I could do this, right? I was an intelligent human being. I could figure this out, right? Right?

"So, how about that kitty cat?" I asked. "Where is she at?"

Madison wiggled out of my arms. "Come here," she

said grabbing at my hand. "What's your name?"

"Skylar."

"Like the sky?"

"Yes."

"Kay," she said, pulling me down the hallway into her bedroom. It was pink and yellow with white furniture; sweet and innocent. I felt like I could stay in here forever.

Madison went over to her bed and picked up a small gray-striped stuffed cat. "Her name is Amber. She has blue eyes and lots of whiskers," she said, stroking the cat's head.

"Who thought of that name?"

"Mommy."

"It's a very pretty name."

"Cats purr," she said abruptly.

"Yeah?" I asked, rhetorically. I thought it was strange how I somehow adjusted myself, my words, the way I presented myself, the way I acted around her. It wasn't a conscious change. It just happened as if it were preprogrammed into my brain.

"Yeah, and dogs bark. Woof," she said.

"And frogs?"

"Ribbit, ribbit!"

"And?"

"Hop," she said, jumping up and down.

"Yes," I laughed. "What color are frogs?"

"Yellow!" She said excitedly, getting ahead of herself.

"Some of them are," I said. "But most of them are green, like the grass, so they can hide in it."

She looked down, petting the stuffed cat on the head.

"How about we go for a walk? Go to the park?" I asked.

"Yeah! Amber come too?"

"Sure. Come on. Let's go get the stroller ready."

I walked back into the living room and found the stroller jammed into the front closet. I struggled to extricate it from the coats and shoes and bags. Apartments were not the most kid-friendly places to live with all the accessories they needed.

It took me a few frustrating minutes to figure out how the stroller opened and locked into place. This was all foreign to me. I felt like I had tripped and fallen down the rabbit hole headfirst. Skylar in Wonderland.

I wondered if I would have been better at this if my mom were still alive or if I had younger siblings to help take care of.

"Rock and roll, dude," she said, climbing into the stroller, wearing hot pink sunglasses. I pressed lightly on her back as I held on to the stroller, making sure she didn't fall backwards.

"Rock and roll," I agreed, pushing the stroller out the door into the evening sun.

Later that night, after Madison had fallen asleep to *If You Give a Mouse a Cookie,* I was in the kitchen washing the dishes and wiping down the counters when Logan walked in.

"Hey," he said tiredly. He sat his bag down on his desk and leaned against the kitchen doorway.

"Hi," I said, looking back to see him through the doorway. "How'd it go?"

He sighed. "Good. How was the monster?"

I smiled. "She was just fine."

"Did she go down easy?"

"Yes, out like a light halfway through the second book."

"Good. No problems then?"

"No. Why? Were you expecting there to be?"

"No, but you never know. She can get so moody sometimes. Out of nowhere." He stepped into the kitchen and saw me cleaning. "You don't have to do that."

"I don't mind," I said. "I almost fell asleep in Maddie's bed with her. I had to get up and do something or else I would've crashed on the couch."

"You could've."

I just shrugged. Falling asleep on his couch again would be too familiar, too comfortable.

"Did you eat?" he asked, walking over and opening the fridge.

"Oh, no. I forgot," suddenly realizing how famished I felt.

"I'll heat this up for you," he said. "I know how she can work up an appetite."

I finished wiping down the counters and stood against the counter, facing Logan. "Oh my God. I had no idea. It seems like she doesn't stop moving."

He laughed. "It doesn't get any easier."

"Thanks for the pep talk."

"Sorry, don't want to scare you off," he paused. "But seriously, thank you so much for watching her. I had no one else I could trust." He handed me the plate of Hamburger Helper and a fork.

"Thanks," I said, sitting on one of the stools at the breakfast bar. "Watching her isn't a problem; it's not as if I have anything exciting going on in my life," I added. "But if you don't mind me asking, why doesn't she just go to Brooke's on the nights you have class?"

"She's back in school too, at the College for Creative Studies down in Detroit. So she's usually in class during the day, and she works at the hair salon most evenings."

"Oh," I said. "What's she studying?"

"Graphic design."

"Ah," I nodded, thinking. "So when does she see Madison?"

"Weekends, mostly."

"Does it bother you that she's so busy?"

He shrugged, grabbing a beer. "Do you want one?"

"Am I off the clock now?" I joked.

"Yes."

"Then yes," I said. He came over and sat next to me, setting down the beers on the counter.

He started back on Brooke again. "She always wanted to go back to school and have a more fulfilling career than cutting hair. So if that's her dream…," he trailed off, then added, "I just want her to be happy."

"Has Madison been with you a lot lately?" I asked.

"Yup," he took a long drink from his beer.

"So on top of your day job as a high school English teacher and being a full-time parent, you're taking a college class? You already have your master's."

He grinned, peeling the label on the bottle. "I do. But for that degree my area of focus was on comparative literature. This is a composition class."

"I still don't get it."

"I'm thinking about applying for a Ph.D. program one day, and I'm trying to figure out which area to concentrate in: composition and rhetoric, linguistics, or literary theory."

"So this class you're taking right now doesn't really count toward anything? You're just doing it for fun?"

"That's one way to put it."

I laughed. "You're such a nerd."

"Basically," he said. "Here, let me take that."

He picked up my plate and rinsed it off in the sink, placing it in the dishwasher. "I'm going to try to find someone else to watch Maddie as soon as I can. Do you mind, though, if I ask you to watch her again on Thursday?"

"Not at all. In fact, don't even bother looking for anyone else. I'll watch her. Permanently."

"You sure?" he asked tentatively. "I don't want to

impose."

"I'm sure," I said nodding. "Just one condition."

"What's that?" he looked over at me curiously.

"Well since I'm gone at work all day and Scout is home alone, I don't really want to leave him alone all evening too."

"So you mean not only do you want to watch my daughter free of charge, twice a week," he emphasized, "but you also want to bring over a real, live animal for her to play with?"

I shrugged, trying not to smile.

"How could I say no to that?"

Over for the next several weeks, Madison and I spent every Tuesday and Thursday night together. I knew she was having a hard time adjusting to not seeing either parent or her old sitter as much as she was used to, but we adjusted together. And having Scout there, with his golden brown eyes and tawny soft fur only added to Maddie's delight and her openness toward me.

We fell into an easy way of being with each other, talking to each other, answering each other's questions. It was a relief to spend my time with someone who wasn't demanding or needing a constant flow of conversation.

She would ask me things like: What's an engine?

And I would say: It's the big metal thing in cars that make them work.

Once while we were taking a walk, I asked her, "What's your favorite season?"

She responded, "What's a season?"

"It's a period of time—three months," I told her, explaining the different seasons.

"Which one is it now?"

"Fall."

"That's my favorite," she exclaimed, clapping her hands.

"Mine too," I laughed, feeling overwhelmingly happy.

One night as she was getting ready for bed, Madison stood on her step stool in front of the sink trying to reach the faucet, but she could barely see over the top of the counter. Her hair was wet and her skin was clean from her bath.

I sprayed the sweet-smelling detangler into her hair and gently worked the knots out of her long hair.

"Do you like me?" she asked.

I looked up at her, over her shoulder. "Of course I do. Why wouldn't I?"

She ignored my question. "You like my daddy?"

"Yes, he's one of my friends. From before you were even born."

"What 'bout my mommy?"

"Yes, I like her too."

She was quiet for a minute.

"Do you miss your mommy?" I asked.

She nodded.

I turned her around so she was facing me and hugged her. "I know, sweetie. You'll see her soon."

She suddenly let go of me and scrambled out of the bathroom. "Go read *Horton*."

Her mood swings were worse than mine, in and out, swift and sudden. It was dizzying to keep up with them.

I called after her, "Wait! You have to brush your teeth first!"

Oddly, she returned without an argument. After she had brushed her teeth and I had propped up the pillows, we sat snuggled in bed. I read to her, slowly turning the pages so we could look at all the images. I pressed my cheek against the top of her head. Her wet hair smelled like a pear-and-strawberry smoothie, all sweetness. I kept reading the story, but all I could think about was her fruity smell and how warm and small she felt next to me. I thought about how she fit so perfectly in the curve of my hip, and how good it felt that the hole in my heart was starting to fill back up.

Madison interrupted infrequently, but when she did, she asked questions like "What's that?" or "Why's he green?"

When I explained she nodded her head in thought. It amazed me how much she picked up and understood.

I watched as she fought off sleep but then slowly succumbed. I felt the rise and fall of her chest rhythmically slow down and grow deeper. I watched her sleep, wondering what she was dreaming about. Her mom? Her dad? Horton and the Whos? Maybe even me, I dared to believe. But who knew what happened in the dreamland of three-year-olds.

After waiting a few minutes to make sure she was sound asleep, I slowly twisted myself out of the bed and quickly put her blue stuffed teddy bear in my spot next to her. Her eyelids fluttered and she moved her mouth, but she didn't wake up.

I turned off her bedside lamp, bent down to gently push back the hair out of her face, and kissed her on her forehead, lingering a moment to smell that sweet, sticky, soft smell.

I turned around and there was Logan standing in the doorway, smiling.

I jumped. "Jesus, Logan," I whispered, walking toward him and pulling the door closed to a crack behind us. "You scared the shit out of me."

"You're good with her," he said, nodding toward Maddie's door.

"It's easy being with her," I said, walking down the hallway into the living room to get my stuff together.

"Are you hungry? Do you want something to eat?" he asked following me into the living room.

"No thanks," I said. "We walked to the ice cream stand earlier."

"Let me guess. She wanted—"

"Vanilla with sprinkles," we said at the same time.

"Yeah, it was a good night," I paused, looking at him.

"So how are you? How are things?" he asked.

"Oh, you know. They're going."

"How's work?"

"Oh, my job as a front desk secretary? It's thrilling, really. All those files and forms that need to be filled out and filed. And don't get me started on the phone calls. Man, I'm telling you, some really ground-breaking, world-saving stuff right there."

Logan laughed, his shoulders shaking slightly. "It's not forever, is it?"

"God, I hope not. I'm hoping once I'm off probation, they'll let me off for good behavior."

"Speaking of which, how's that all going?"

"Six weeks down, nine more to go of anger management, that is. I still have another eleven months of probation."

"Are the sessions helpful?"

"Uh, not really."

"No? Why not?"

"Because it's easier to be angry," I said harshly, suddenly feeling uncomfortable by the direction of the conversation and the casualness and familiarity of the room.

"I need to get going," I said quickly, picking up my purse and heading for the door before Logan could say anything in response.

"You sure you don't want to stay for a drink? We can

talk or not talk about anything."

"I'm good. Thanks, though."

"All right, we'll see you Thursday?" he asked, stretching his arms over his head.

"Thursday," I confirmed, whistling for Scout to follow me. Before I walked out the door, I turned and looked at him. "Logan?"

"Hmm?" he asked distractedly, looking up from the mail in his hands.

"You should read or something," I suggested.

"Read or something?" he asked.

"Yeah, you used to read all the time. You always had a book on you."

He smiled sadly. "You're right. I should."

"And Dr. Seuss doesn't count," I added, walking out the door.

I rushed out before he could say another word and practically ran to my car. How could I tell him how his little girl was changing my life? My heart? That maybe, he was too. I admired how strong he was for taking charge of his life, for raising Madison on top of a demanding career and taking extra college courses.

How could I tell him that his little girl was able to chip away at the dense wall I had built up around me? How could someone so small understand so much?

It scared the shit out of me. And yet, I was ready for more.

Those days spent with Madison and nights spent

talking with Logan were radiant, warming and lighting up the cold dark corners. The rough edges of my soul were being buffed with every hug, kiss, and laugh. I was starting to feel like my own person again, coming alive again. Like an amputee who lost her arm, I was compensating for the loss.

I thought about how easily Madison loved. It was unhindered, uncomplicated, unencumbered, and undemanding.

I still didn't have all the answers, but I knew that that beautiful baby girl was about to change my life.

XV

Leaves

"Um," I said hesitantly, standing in Logan's living room on a Tuesday night after Madison had gone to bed. "I kind of made Madison a promise."

"What kind of promise?" he asked, looking up from his computer.

"A promise that you guys could come over this Saturday afternoon and help me rake up the leaves. So we can jump in them," I clarified, not wanting him to think I just wanted him to come over to do my yard work for me.

He smiled. "Did you, now?"

"Yeah, look, I'm sorry," I said hurriedly. "It just came out. You know how she is! She asks all innocent and cute. How can you say no? And before I knew it, I was saying that you two could come over this weekend, not even thinking if you had plans or if she was supposed to be with

Brooke."

"This Saturday?" he asked.

"Yeah."

"I think that can be arranged," he grinned, his gray-blue eyes shining.

Saturday morning at group, after everyone had shared their highs and lows of the week, David started the session by saying, "Anger can cause lots of physical problems: heart disease, depression, high blood pressure, just to name a few. I know that in the heat of the moment, it's hard to see the consequences of your anger. But they're very real."

He continued. "So far we've talked about using relaxation and breathing techniques to calm down, using humor, and changing your environment in order to prevent a blowup. This week let's talk about cognitive restructuring."

I wasn't the only one in the room who looked at him with confusion. In my head I sang the lyrics to the Beatles' "Let it Be," using David's own relaxation technique against him.

"It's nothing fancy, so don't look at me like that," he said. "Cognitive restructuring is just thinking about things from a different perspective. And reminding yourself that getting angry doesn't solve anything. Or make you feel better. Just the opposite, in fact."

He had us break into groups and handed us index cards with various scenarios that we had to "cognitively restructure" in a positive way. I worked with Samara and a gas station owner named Tyrese who had a tendency to bite the edges of his Styrofoam coffee cup.

Though not the most exciting exercise in the world, I marveled at how Samara handled any situation thrown at her. She had this way of taking it seriously, yet making light of it at the same time. Her alternative reactions to the scenarios were ridiculous and hilarious, yet accomplished the task of diffusing the anger so David couldn't scold us.

After class Samara and I slid in to our usual booth at the diner. I ordered a BLT with fries and she ordered pancakes and coffee.

"Is your last name really Gem?" I asked.

"That it is, sweetheart," she said, removing her black sunglasses and sweeping her shaggy bangs out of her eyes.

"You weren't an exotic dancer or anything, were you?"

"Hell, no. I have enough issues with men as it is. There's no need for me to go looking for any more trouble." Her laugh was raspy and loud.

I laughed too. It was refreshing to spend time with another woman who I didn't have to pretend around. She was just as crass, unpredictable, and rough as I was. Yet she had the courage to improve herself. She wasn't afraid to admit she was wrong, but she never apologized for who she was. I wished I were half as brave as she was.

"So you were married?" I asked.

"Yup."

"What happened?"

"He couldn't accept me. I couldn't accept him. It's what it all came down to."

"What does that mean?"

"Bryan is a man's kind of man, if you know what I mean. He's a roofer, spends his Saturday nights playing poker and drinking beer with his buddies, expected me to be a certain way.

"And me," she continued, "I work all sorts of crazy hours at the casino. I enjoy my job and independence. I like to go to the bar with my friends and wear suggestive clothing," she winked at me. "I don't do laundry unless I need to, and when I do I leave it in the basket. I barely know how to cook. Long story short, Bryan wanted me to fit his definition of *wife material*, and I didn't."

"I thought I was wife material," I said. "Not really sure about that anymore."

"Aw, honey. You definitely are. You might try to look like a hard-ass with your black boots and eyeliner, but you've got that maternal instinct. I can smell it a mile away. You take care of people. I, on the other hand, was never really good at taking care of anyone but myself."

"So why'd you get married?"

"Because I loved him."

After lunch, I sat on the porch steps watching Scout sniff out the small square of grass that was the entire front yard.

The season was starting to get its first touch of chill, and I pulled my cream-colored boyfriend cardigan around me tighter. I looked down at my baggy rolled-up jeans and beat-up red Keds. I thought about Michael and how he should be here, how nice it would be to have him here. I thought about how good he would look in his worn-out jeans and gray flannel shirt, how he would smile at me with that mischievous grin of his, how his muscles would extend and contract as he raked up the colorful leaves.

It was then that Logan pulled into the driveway in his old blue Focus.

"Hey," he said, getting out of the car, wearing his usual slim-fitting black jeans and gray zip-up sweatshirt.

"Hi," I said, getting up off the steps.

He walked around to the back passenger side and opened the door to get Madison out of her car seat. I saw her little pink-sneakered feet moving underneath the car as she ran around the car toward me.

"Sky!" she squealed, her long hair falling into her eyes. She had on brown leggings and a red hooded sweatshirt.

"Maddie!" I exclaimed as I picked her up. I swung my body back and forth so that she had to hold on tighter. I never thought a hug could feel so wonderful.

"Whose house are you at?" I asked.

"Yours?"

"Yes! Are you ready to rake some leaves?"

"YEAH!" she screamed.

"Okay, ouch, that was my ear," I laughed, setting her down on her feet.

"Do you have any idea what you've gotten us into?" Logan asked, standing next to me with his arms folded over his chest, watching Madison chase Scout around the front yard.

"I have a feeling I'm about to find out."

Madison laughed and screamed as Scout turned around and started chasing her. We both watched, entertained.

"Ready to get started?" I asked him.

"Ready if you are."

"Follow me," I said, walking down the driveway toward the garage. "I have a few rakes in the garage. And I picked up those orange garbage bags that look like pumpkins."

"Madison will love those," he said, smiling at me. I couldn't help but smile back.

So on that late autumn afternoon, we raked and raked until there were large piles of red, brown, and yellow leaves in the front yard.

Logan held on to Madison's feet, I grabbed her hands, and we swung her into the biggest pile of leaves we could make. She squealed and laughed so hard she even snorted a few times.

She was struggling to get out of the leaves when Scout

came barreling through, trying to find her in the mess of leaves. It was his own search-and-rescue mission.

Madison loved to gather lots of leaves and throw them up in the air over our heads. And for those brief moments, while the leaves were suspended in the air, we would all be lost together in the enchanting rain of color.

"It's leaf snow!" cried Maddie.

The three of us lay together on top of one of the leaf piles, catching our breath from running around and laughing. The air was crisp and cool. It felt good on my skin, flushed from exertion. My senses were overwhelmed with the smell of leaves, trees, dirt, and moss. The earth smelled divine.

"Isn't there something about fall that makes you feel good?" I asked.

"I know exactly what you mean," Logan said. "Like everything is settling in."

After we caught our breath, we started to pack the leaves into the orange pumpkin bags, much to Madison's dismay.

"But look at how cool they look," Logan said, trying to cheer her up.

"But now they're all GONE!" she frowned, stomping her feet.

"They're not gone, they're just inside there."

"Nooo!" she started to wail and tremble, the beginning of a temper tantrum threatening to break through as Logan put the bags together by the front of the house.

"Maddie. Maddie, listen to me," I said taking her hand, crouching down. "Look, they're a family now. A pumpkin family."

"They are?" she huffed through tears.

"Yup," I nodded reassuringly.

"Like us?" she asked.

"Like us, what?" I asked back.

"Together, like us, a family."

Logan's eyes met mine. I waited for him to say something.

"Um, yeah. Kind of, sweetheart. Because you see, families are made in all different ways—," he started to say, rubbing the back of his neck.

"Mommies and daddies," she interjected.

"Yes, except that your mommy and daddy aren't together anymore. So that means that you get two families."

"Two?" she asked excitedly.

"Yup," he said, trying to explain gently and clearly at the same time. Regret and heaviness crossed his face. "You have your mommy's family—."

"With Marc?"

"Yes, with Marc," he said, trying unsuccessfully to hide the hurt look on his face. Then he whispered to me, "Brooke's boyfriend."

"Oh," I said quietly in the background, feeling sadder and sadder for Logan as he talked, wanting to jump in and somehow fill the void from losing Brooke.

Logan continued, "And you have daddy's side. With me, grandma, auntie Cassie, uncle Brett, and your cousins."

"And Skylar," Madison added assuredly.

I smiled, unsure of what to say. He looked at me apprehensively. He was about to say something, explain to Madison that no, I wasn't a part of their family, when I jumped in and said, "Yes, me too," wanting it to be true so badly.

"Are dogs part of families too?" she asked.

"Of course!" I said.

"So Scout's part of our family too?"

"Sure," I said, feeling happy and light. Until I saw the look on Logan's face that said I had crossed a line somewhere, had gone too far. I was overcome with dread. I didn't want to jeopardize the one good thing I had going.

But before I could say anything else, a white Prius pulled into the driveway. It was Brooke, a beautiful petite brunette with a pixie cut and freckles sprinkled over her tiny nose.

"Mommmyyy!" Madison screamed as she untangled herself from the pumpkin bags and ran toward the car.

"Hi, baby," her clear voice sang out the car window. She pushed her sunglasses on top of her head and got out of the car. She was wearing a cute mustard-yellow dress with dark wedged boots.

Brooke was an artist. She was eclectic, unique, charming, and cute all rolled into one. Sometimes with the graceful way she moved and the vintage dresses she wore, I thought she looked like a fairy straight out of a storybook.

Brooke was holding Madison now, giving her Eskimo kisses, making Madison giggle. "You want to go get a snack? Maybe an ice cream snack?"

"Yes! I'm *very* hungry, Momma."

Brooke kissed her forehead. "Of course you are! Look at all the work you did."

"Yeah, the pumpkin family," she said pointing to the group of orange plastic bags.

"Yeah?" Brooke asked quizzically looking at Logan. He just shrugged. She peered over at me, giving me a guarded look.

"Okay, give me a kiss, sweetheart," Logan said, leaning in to peck Madison on the lips. "I'll see you in a few days."

"Do you want to say goodbye to Skylar?" Brooke asked.

"Bye, Skylar!" Madison waved from her mother's arms, not wanting to let go.

"See you later, alligator," I said lightly, trying not to show my disappointment from not getting a hug goodbye.

I sat back down on the porch stairs, giving Brooke and Logan a minute. I could see Madison watching from the backseat, her face clouded with confusion as Logan and Brooke's discussion got a little heated.

Watching them talk with two feet of space and tension separating them, it was so clear to me that they were perfect for each other, but somehow Brooke didn't seem to think so.

Logan stood in the driveway and watched as Brooke backed out of the driveway. He walked slowly as he moved to sit next to me on the front steps. His brows were furrowed, creasing lines between them, and he had a distant look in his eyes.

We were quiet for a minute.

He sighed.

"Logan, look, I'm sorry if I said too much to Maddie earlier."

He looked over at me tiredly.

"About being a family," I continued. "I just, I don't know, it just feels really good being with you two. Like I belong, and I haven't felt something like that since—," I stopped short. "I love spending time with Madison. I want her to know that she can count on me, that I'm not going anywhere."

He looked out across the lawn, thinking to himself.

"I'm not mad at you," he said slowly.

"Then what?" I asked softly. "What is it, Logan? Is it about Brooke and Marc?"

"It just wasn't supposed to be like this, you know?"

"You're telling me," I muttered under my breath.

"It's hard to see her with someone else."

He paused, trying to gather the strength to say out loud what had hurt him so much.

"When Brooke got pregnant, we were only twenty-three and hadn't been together that long. But we were so in love," he reminisced.

"Everything in me shifted. I was scared of how the baby would change our lives, but I realized that having a family was all I wanted. Maybe it wasn't what I wanted before, or maybe it was something I secretly wanted all along. I don't know." He shook his head.

"And I thought we were going to make it. I really did. I love—loved," he corrected himself, "her so much. I poured everything I had into our family. But it wasn't enough." He paused. "I wanted to make her happy, but I couldn't. Don't get me wrong, Brooke loves Madison so much, but I think things with us got too heavy too fast, and it was too much for her in the end. So she left, and from where I'm standing, it looks like she is restarting, getting the life she always wanted. With someone else."

I sat there next to him, taking this all in. I didn't speak, didn't want to say the wrong thing. I knew what it felt like to be abandoned like that. Being left hurt like hell, like something you've never felt before. I wanted to comfort Logan, lean my head against his shoulder to let him know that I was there for him, that I understood. But I didn't.

Instead I said, "It sucks, doesn't it? Love's a bitch."

He chuckled. "You could say that."

"I know you don't want to hear any of the cliché bullshit because I know I sure didn't, and still don't. But you want my honest opinion?"

"Sure."

"It was her loss. And I don't know what the hell she

was thinking, but you are a good person; you have a good heart. And maybe you don't think there's a person out there who's better than Brooke, but there is and you will find her. Someone who's worthy of you. Maybe you'll find her tomorrow, maybe in ten years. I don't know. But you will find her. And she will love every part of you."

"You really think that?" he said, his head tucked into his chest, his elbows resting on his bent knees. "You think I'm worth that kind of love?"

"I know it," I said, bumping my shoulder against his. Because I did. I knew that Logan deserved to be loved like that. He deserved to have someone who'd love him for all the goodness and strength in him.

"Even being a single dad? And not being anywhere near where I thought I'd be by now?" he asked jokingly. But behind his self-depreciating façade, his words were laced with defeat.

"Logan, don't be stupid. You are so much more than you think you are," I shook my head at him. "And besides, I remember a certain someone saying that our lives never turn out the way we think they will. But that we still get to choose hope, even when we don't feel like we deserve it."

He gave me that look—the one that said he didn't believe me but would let me think he did—with his lopsided grin. "Must've been a very wise man who said that."

"That's debatable," I teased. "Some days he can be very stubborn and moody."

He tried to hide his smile, then after a minute, grew serious again. "How do you learn to trust someone again after you've been jilted? How do you know the next person won't leave you?"

"I don't know," I said shaking my head. "I guess we'll have to learn that one together. Because I don't know how to trust again either."

"Thanks," he said, putting his arm around my shoulders.

"For what?"

"For being such a good friend."

"Ditto. These past few months, you've been there for me when I needed it most. I don't know how I would've gotten through them without you." I leaned into him. "I'm just so glad that you're one of my best friends, that you're still in my life even though Michael isn't."

"Same here," he said, and then changing the subject, "How do you feel about ordering some pizza and watching a movie?" he asked.

"Sounds perfect," I said.

We went inside and I ordered the pizza while Logan searched through On Demand for a decent movie to watch. "What are you in the mood for?" he yelled from the living room.

"Something funny or action-y?" I suggested, coming down the hallway.

In the living room, Logan was leaning into the couch with his head resting back on a pillow.

"Twenty minutes for the pizza," I said. "Here," I offered, handing him a Coke.

"Ah, thanks. Okay, our options are *National Treasure*, *The Bourne Identity*, or *The Fast and the Furious*."

"Oh, good choices. What are you in the mood for?"

"Call me a total nerd, but I'm feeling kind of *National Treasure* right now."

"Why am I not surprised?" I teased. "Well, *The Fast and the Furious* is one of my all-time favorites, but Michael and I have watched it so many…," I trailed off. "*National Treasure* sounds good."

"Nicholas Cage it is," he said, pressing the Play button on the remote.

We watched the movie, losing ourselves in the story line, and ate the whole pizza, not even bothering to use plates or yell at Scout when he stole a piece from the open box. By the time the movie ended, we had both fallen asleep, each on one side of the couch, our legs side-by-side.

I stirred first, moving my legs and flipping onto my back, waking Logan. He sat up slowly. "What time is it?" he asked sleepily, his hair flattened against his head on one side.

It was dark outside and dark in the room, the only light coming from the TV.

I looked at my phone, sitting on the coffee table in front of us. "Seven thirty."

"Damn. That was a really good nap, though."

I nodded, feeling more rested than I had in months.

"What do you have planned for the rest of the night? A hot date?" he grinned.

"You're so funny," I mocked. "But nothing, really. You?"

"Nothing. Wide open," he paused. "We should do something."

"Like what?"

"I don't know, go out to the bar or something. How is it that two twenty-six-year-olds don't have any clue as to what do on a Saturday night? Are we really that lame?"

"Yes. Obviously," I sighed.

Logan threw the pillow at me.

We sat there thinking. "We could go downtown. We could go to Callaghan's. Just walk there so we don't have to drive to Grady's," I suggested. "And call Shane and see what he's up to."

He grinned at me. "Yeah, that sounds good. How about I go home and take a quick shower, you can get ready, and I'll meet you back here in an hour?"

"Sounds good," I said, feeling unexplainably pleased about how the day was turning out.

Logan groaned from across the couch.

"What?"

"That means I have to get up. And I'm so comfortable."

"Crybaby," I said. And then I quickly slid my legs under him and flipped him off the couch, laughing.

"Ugh, you are so going to pay for that," he said into

the floor, not moving to get up.

"Yeah, yeah. Blah, blah, blah," I said, getting up off the couch. "I'm going to go take a shower."

"Good, you smell," he teased.

"You're just grumpy because now you've got to get up."

"You better go run upstairs and lock the door before I move," he threatened.

"Oohh, I'm so scared," I mocked.

And then he placed his palms flat on the ground and started to push himself up.

"Okay, I'm going. See you in a few," I said, running up the stairs, not looking back.

A little over an hour later, Logan walked back into the house. "You ready?" he yelled up the stairs.

"Yeah, hold on. I'm coming," I said, zipping up my jeans and throwing on my black-heeled boots. I looked in the mirror one more time, raking my hands through my straightened hair while double-checking for smudges from my eyeliner.

When I walked downstairs in my jeans and red tank top, I heard a low wolf whistle.

"I see you called Shane," I said.

"How could you tell?" Logan asked. "Was it his elephant-like steps or his distinctive two-toned expression of admiration?"

"What do you think? Who else would whistle at his

best friend's girl?"

"Hey! I resent that!" Shane said.

"I'm teasing," I said, walking up to him and hugging him.

"But seriously, you look good, Sky," he said.

"Thanks," I said, grabbing my purse and jacket off the coat rack.

Logan stood against the front door in jeans, a gray plaid shirt, and his black leather sneakers. "No crying this time," he said to me.

"I promise," I said to him. "And now *you* have to promise *me*, that you will have the time of your life tonight."

"I promise," he said, touching his hand to his heart.

I heard the downstairs bathroom sink running, and turning to figure out why, saw the door swing open. A strikingly beautiful blonde in a green silk dress and a year-round tan walked out of the bathroom.

Her green eyes popped when she saw us all staring at her.

"Skylar, there's someone I want you to meet," Shane said, gesturing for the blonde to come over to him. "This is my girlfriend Joanna."

I raised my eyebrows at the declaration, amused. Shane *never* had girlfriends, only flings.

"Joanna, this is Skylar."

"Nice to meet you," she said in a melodic voice, reaching out her hand for mine. "You can call me Jo if you'd like."

I took her hand. "You too," I said, unsure of what to make of her and the situation.

My gaze slid over to Logan who silently mouthed: Be nice. But I could tell he was trying to hide his amusement.

I shot him a look that said: What are you talking about? I'm always nice.

"You guys ready?" Logan asked, breaking our silent communication.

"Let's do this," Shane said, pumped.

The four of us walked out the door and down the street. Logan and I walked side by side behind Shane and Joanna, watching them flirt and hold hands.

Shane was always openly affectionate and flirtatious with every girl he met. It was something we always teased him about. It was funny because he was such a ladies' man, and the ladies, well they sure did love him. But at the same time he was such a kind-hearted, lovable person. You would be hard-pressed to find someone more genuine and sincere than Shane. His former lady friends, all short-term flings, could only look back on their time spent with Shane with fondness because he had never promised them anything more than a good time.

"This is different," I whispered, gesturing in front of us.

"You think so?" Logan asked, looking at me, then at Shane and Joanna.

"Yeah. I don't know, he seems more serious about

her."

"Well, this should be interesting," was all Logan said.

At the bar we talked easily, a feeling still kind of foreign to me. So different from the last time I was out with them and had felt so isolated and hollow. Back then everything seemed so fuzzy, like I had headphones on and couldn't quite hear what everyone was saying. Now it was clear, there was no interrupting static.

We listened as Joanna told us all about how she and Shane had met, about her family, and about her job. "I'm a veterinary technician," she said, sipping her margarita.

"Oh, where do you work?" I asked.

"At an office in Sterling Heights. I have an apartment over there, but I also volunteer with the Michigan Humane Society to assist vets on neutering and spaying stray dogs and cats, as well as pets of low-income families. It's really important that the stray community be taken care of. There's an epidemic going on in Detroit right now. Did you know it's estimated that there are more than 50,000 strays in the city?"

"Wow," Logan managed to say, probably as taken aback by her as I was. "I didn't know it was such a problem."

I knew the beer I was drinking probably helped, but I was seriously impressed by her.

"And," she continued, "you should always encourage people to adopt from shelters and not buy from breeders. The horror stories I could tell you...," she drifted off, taking another sip of her drink.

"Maybe another time," I suggested.

"Of course, sorry for my rant. Let's just have fun tonight!"

By the time we had finished our third round, I was feeling buzzed, and the music was flowing throughout the bar. The beat was contagious.

"Let's dance!" Joanna exclaimed. She was one of those girls who always looked flawless. Her skin was radiant and her still-fresh lip gloss caught whatever light there was. I, on the other hand, felt sloppy. My eyeliner was probably smudged and my straight hair had most likely started to curl; not that I cared enough to check in the mirror.

Shane smiled and took her hand, leading her out to the dance floor in front of the band.

Now that we were by ourselves, I turned to Logan. "I guess I shouldn't be so quick to judge," I said.

He turned to look at me.

"Joanna," I clarified.

"I know, what was all that about?"

"I don't know, but I actually kind of like her. Shane deserves to have someone whose heart is as big as his."

Logan nodded, sipping his beer. "I'm surprised you actually like someone."

"Shut up. So I have issues getting along with others sometimes. I'll add it to the long list of things I need to work on."

"I'm kidding, Sky."

I knew he wasn't being serious, but it seemed like a good opportunity to change gears, so I let my defenses down. "There's something I need to tell you."

"What's that?" he asked.

"I can't afford my house anymore. And I have no idea what I'm going to do."

"Shit," he said. "Well, what are your options?"

"I don't know," I said, running my hand through my hair. "I can sell it and move out or get a roommate or two."

"Where would you move to?"

"I can't really afford any apartments in the area on my own, and besides, there'd be no fenced-in yard; I would always have to take the dog out. So that wouldn't really work. The only other option is to move in with my dad. Don't get me wrong, I love him and everything, but moving back home after being on my own for so many years would be...," I shuddered, "less than desirable."

"So roommates it is, then?" he asked.

"Logan, I just don't know if I can stay in that house anymore. It will always be mine and Michael's."

"How about renting a room in a house that has a fence?"

I nodded, thinking about it. "But I'm not sure I'm ready to leave either."

Logan grinned at me and squinted his eyes. "How about this," he said, taking my hand. "Tonight, we're going to dance and not think about it. And I promise you, I'll help you make a decision later."

I smiled. "Okay," I said as he pulled me toward the dance floor.

And we danced. Us, platonically, with Shane and Joanna next to us dancing close and seductively. It made me laugh, and I didn't care to hide it. Logan laughed too.

In the colored lights that beamed out from the small stage into the darkness of the bar, we jumped, thrashed, and threw our hands in the air. Sometimes we would hold on to each other close as we swayed back and forth, mostly because we were stumbling and didn't want to fall down, but also because it was nice to feel someone close.

For that set, for those forty minutes, nothing else existed except us, our skin, and the beat of the music. Death didn't exist there. Or loneliness. Or abandonment. Or resentment. Or self-loathing. Only intoxication and lightness lived in that space.

And we laughed—at our shortcomings and failures. We laughed because we were alive and free and enraptured with the music and the alcohol and each other. We laughed because we could. And there is no amount of words that can describe just how good that really feels.

XVI

Contentment

"Maddie, you have to pump your feet back and forth," I called from behind her, pushing her on the swing.

She just giggled, holding on tightly to the plastic seat of the baby swing.

"Oh, I know, you think it's just so great. Why should you learn to swing by yourself when you have me to push you, huh?" I said, trying to reach in and tickle her for those few fleeting moments when she was within my reach.

"I want to swing with you!" Maddie said loudly.

"What do you say?"

"Please!"

I carried her over to the bigger swings and sat her down on my lap. "Ready?" I asked, planting a kiss on her cheek.

"Ready!"

"Okay, this is how you start," I said, pushing back to straighten my legs, then pushed off the ground. My feet pushed off the ground several more times before we were high enough that they didn't touch.

"Now this is where you pump your legs. Back and forth. Back and forth." I moved my body with the effort, holding on to her tightly.

She screamed excitedly as we climbed higher and higher. From the heights, we could see more clearly the sea of colorful leaves that burned golden and red in the trees surrounding the park. We watched as the other kids chased each other around the park, screaming and laughing.

Before spending time with Maddie, I hadn't felt contentment in ages. But if this is what it felt like, this whole, exhilarating feeling as the wind rushed through my hair and Maddie squeezed me closer to her, then I never wanted to leave this place again.

Saturday after group, Samara and I debriefed at the diner.

"Guess where I'm going tomorrow?" I asked her.

"Oh, let me think," she hummed. "Mars!"

I gave her a pointed look. "The apple orchard with Logan and Madison."

I thought back to Thursday night when Logan had

walked into his apartment. He had on a navy blue cowl-neck sweater that heightened the blue in his eyes.

After the usual exchange of information about the events of the day and Madison, I had asked him, "Any plans for the weekend?"

"Oh, that's right. I forgot to ask you—," he said, wincing.

"Ask me what?"

"I'm sorry. I was supposed to ask you like a week ago. Shane and Joanna asked me if we wanted to go to the apple orchard this weekend. With Madison."

"They asked if *we* wanted to go?" I asked, perplexed that we were coupled together like that. I was caught off guard by how much I liked it, being included and grouped together casually like that. "Why didn't Shane call and ask me himself?"

"I don't know. He probably figured it was less work just to ask me."

"Oh," I said, sinking with disappointment.

"So?"

"So what?" I asked.

"Do you want to go? Sunday?"

"Oh, yeah. Of course. I'd love to."

Logan smiled. "Good. I didn't really want to go without you."

Samara tapped her long acrylic fingernails against the table. "Well, you two are getting awfully close these days." She smirked.

"We're just friends," I said, failing to hide the excitement in my voice. "But enough about me, why are you so dressed up today?"

She looked nice in a denim skirt, knee-high black boots, and a black blouse with wide sleeves. I looked down at my blue hoodie, jeans, and beat up combat boots.

"I'm glad you asked," she said, sitting up taller. "I have a meeting with a career counselor this afternoon. David hooked me up with her."

"Really?" I asked. "That's exciting."

"I know, right? Finally feel like I'm making progress."

"What do you think she's going to suggest?"

"I have no idea! Hopefully things I haven't even thought of. I'm open to almost anything at this point even though I like my job."

"Even if you have to go back to school?"

"Especially if I have to go back to school. I barely got my high school diploma. And now I'm ready to work for it and actually learn something," she laughed.

I took a bite of my hamburger, wondering why she *barely* got her diploma. Instead I asked, "What about your family?"

"What about them?"

"What do they do?"

"My older brother Jason is a hotshot lawyer. He lives on the west side of the state. He's got himself a nice family, a gorgeous wife, and two boys. Nice house, nice car, nice life."

"You ever see him?"

"On holidays usually," she said with a shrug. "We were never really that close."

"Why not?" I asked. She was such a mystery to me. I knew why I was so messed up, but I wanted to know what made her the way she was. I wanted to know if there was something different about her that made her so willing to make the much-needed changes in her life.

"What's with the twenty questions? You doing a case study on me or something?"

"No, just curious."

She took a sip of her coffee, leaving dark pink lipstick stains on the rim of the cup.

"Jason is ten years older than me, and he wasn't around much even before he left for college. Not that I blame him. Mom's a drunk, and Dad was a truck driver. He was never really around either, but at least he sent money to Mom and me. It was what kept a roof over our heads and food on the table."

She paused. "They're not in my life anymore. But I don't hate them or blame them. Everyone has their demons, you know?"

Did I ever.

"Where are your parents now?" I asked.

"Mom passed away five years ago, and Dad lives Downriver. He's retired, but I couldn't tell you what he does all day."

"Sorry to hear about your mom."

"Don't be," she said, taking some cash out from her wallet. "It is what it is."

Logan pulled into the driveway at ten on Sunday morning and honked his horn. It was chilly and overcast outside, and I pulled my scarf around my neck.

"Mind if we stop by the bagel shop for breakfast?" Logan asked as I slid into the passenger seat.

"Hey, Maddie!" I said, reaching behind me to tickle her shoeless feet. "Where are your shoes at, Silly?"

"Took them off!" she said indignantly.

I turned back to answer Logan, "Sounds good. I could use some coffee."

I noticed then that he was wearing a red thermal long-sleeved shirt.

"What?" he asked.

"I don't think I've ever seen you wear a red shirt before."

"Madison picked it out for me."

"Ah," I said. "Any chance you're hiding some denim overalls and a John Deere hat in here?" I asked glancing around the car, biting down on my lip to keep the laughter from spilling out.

"You're teasing me!"

I gasped. "I would do no such thing. Would I,

Maddie?"

"Yes, you would."

"Hey!" I said turning around in my seat. "You're supposed to be on my side."

She just giggled. "No, Daddy's side."

"Fine," I sighed, turning to Logan. "It looks good on you. Don't worry."

"I wasn't," he said, but a slight blush crept up his cheeks. I wasn't expecting the little charge the blush triggered in me.

"So I thought we were all driving together?" I asked Logan.

"We were supposed to, but Shane called me last night and said they were going to drive separately because they're going to Joanna's parents after."

"He's meeting her parents?" I asked, surprised. "Sound's serious."

The hour drive to the apple orchard was pleasantly noisy. Music played from the radio as Madison chatted away in the backseat. Before we left the parking lot of the bagel shop, as I was getting Madison situated with her chocolate milk, Logan had cut up my bagel and put the cream cheese on it for me. When he handed it to me, I looked at him, perplexed.

"It's just a habit," he said shyly, his lips pulling up on one corner.

"Thank you." It felt nice to have someone take care of

me, even in the smallest of ways.

When Madison fell silent in the backseat, Logan asked, "So what'd you do last night?"

I frowned, thinking. "Not much. I was pretty tired from the week. I just got some takeout and caught up on some shows. You?"

"Basically the same. Brooke was supposed to have Maddie, but she ended up having to stay at the salon. So Maddie and I watched *Monsters, Inc.* for the ten-thousandth time. When she went to bed, I graded papers. I assure you," he joked, "it was as thrilling as it sounds."

He also told me about what he was teaching in his classes right now and talked about some of his students. Then he asked, "So did you figure out what you're going to do? About the house?"

I cleared my throat feeling a twinge of anxiety. "I posted an ad online earlier this week for a roommate."

"So you're not ready to leave after all?"

"It was more that I didn't want to move back in with my dad," I laughed. "I'm kind of nervous though."

"Why?"

"I haven't lived with anyone besides Michael for the past four years," I admitted. "It's going to be weird to live with someone else."

Logan nodded. "But maybe it'll be nice to have someone else in the house."

It was nice to talk about normal things, like jobs and roommates. But then, reflexively, frantically, I searched inside myself for that tight-knitted bundle of anger, reassuring myself that it was still there, that I was still connected to it, that it was still real.

I looked out the window at the passing cornfields and open space. I thought about how much Logan and I had in common now. We both had been dealt devastating blows in the past year that had drastically changed the directions of our lives. We both had to reevaluate what we wanted and where we were going. We were both wounded, and still a bit tentative, but recovering.

Neither one of us was in a rush to move on to the next thing. By the same token, we didn't want to stay stuck where we were. It was this constant give and take between wanting to move forward and fearing to do so.

I was just glad to have someone around who understood how that felt.

"Wouldn't it be nice to live out here?" I asked absentmindedly, still staring out the window. "Somewhere where you can breathe."

"In a big old farmhouse or something?"

I turned toward him in surprise. "Logan Parks! You continue to amaze me with your complexity."

"What on earth are you talking about?"

"I would never have pegged you for a country boy, not even after seven years of knowing you. I always pictured you as this super cool hipster urbanite."

He shrugged dismissively. "What can I say? I'm a bundle of contradictions."

"How poetic," I teased, rolling my eyes at him. "If I ever lived away from the city, I'd want a lot of land—something that's mine, you know? Something no one could touch or take away."

"Yeah, unfortunately, with my salary the house would have to be practically falling down for me to afford it."

I laughed. "You're not kidding. It's a nice dream though, isn't it? Buying a big country house and fixing it up exactly how you want it. Something to pass down to your grandkids after you're gone."

"Yes, it is," he said softly.

An easy silence fell over the car as we drove the remaining few minutes to the apple orchard. I dreamed of a life out here, a life shared with someone I loved.

The dirt road crunched beneath our tires as we turned into the gravel parking lot. People milled about everywhere.

As soon as I stepped out the car, my senses were assaulted with that distinct apple orchard smell. It was the smell of hay bales piled up high for the kids to climb on. The smell of manure from the petting zoo. The smell of cinnamon and sugar from the freshly fried donuts. The diesel smell of the tractor that pulled the wagon to take groups back to the orchard fields. The smell of apples, fresh air, leaves, and grass.

I breathed it in deeply, closing my eyes. "Smells good, doesn't it?"

"It smells gross," Maddie said with attitude.

I turned to her quickly, with a surprised look on my face, my lips forming an *O*. "You did not just say that."

"Oh, yes I did," she said shaking her head and waving her hand.

I tried to stifle a laugh. "Okay, I don't know where you learned that from, but we can't be friends anymore if you don't like how the apple orchard smells."

"Yeah, yeah," she said, waving her hands flippantly at me.

Logan just looked at me with a smirk on his face. "What?" he asked, raising his shoulders. "I'm not getting involved in this one."

We walked through the parking lot to the main entrance, Maddie holding on to both of our hands. Logan looked down at his watch. "We made pretty good time. There's a play area we can take Maddie to until Shane and Joanna get here."

"Well knowing Shane, he's probably running late anyway," I said.

"He's reliable that way."

Madison dragged us as she ran towards the play area, stopping briefly so that we could take pictures of our faces on the wooden stand that had funny bodies painted on it. Madison had her face pictured on a cow's body. She thought it was hilarious and wanted to see the picture over and over again.

As we waited for Shane and Joanna, I spun Madison around in circles. I contracted my muscles and pulled my elbows to my sides, keeping my grip on her tight as her small feet lifted off the ground. My feet stepped rhythmically on the ground as I spun in place, the soft grass beneath my feet pressing down.

As we spun faster, the cider mill blurred together in a kaleidoscope of color.

Madison squealed in delight as her feet dangled in the air and her hair whipped around her face.

After what was probably only a minute or two, I slowed down and we both fell softly to the ground.

"Phew!" I said. "I am really dizzy right now."

"Me too," Maddie said. She tried to stand but couldn't get her bearings and fell back down on top of me.

Logan laughed. "Take it easy, Tiger."

"Daddy, I can't see."

"Give it a minute," he reassured her.

I looked up at the blue-and-gray sky, my vision wavering on the edges, slowly returning to normal. Then I saw Maddie's face block my view. I felt her sticky warm palms on either side of my face as she pulled closer.

"Can you see me?" She asked innocently, her forehead touching mine.

"You're kind of hard to miss right now."

She laughed and then pushed herself to her feet, taking off in the direction of the wooden jungle gym.

"I think I see Shane," Logan said, putting his hand out for me to take. He pulled me to my feet and then chased after Madison. I brushed the grass off my clothes.

The Charm Necklace

"Hey!" A booming voice yelled. When I turned, I saw Shane, tall and commanding, striding toward us with Joanna next to him. She had on jeans, a nice sweater, and big dangling earrings.

When Shane reached us, he picked me up in a bear hug.

"Shane, for God's sake, I'm twenty-six years old. Put me down."

"Nope," he said, shaking me like a child.

I started to wiggle out from his grasp and punched him in the stomach.

"Ow, Dude!" he said, bending over, clutching at his stomach. Then he straightened up, smiling. "Just kidding. You hit like a girl."

"Would you like to see what it feels like when I don't punch like a girl?" I threatened.

"No, thanks," he said backing away, hands up in surrender.

I turned my attention to Joanna. "Hi," I said.

"Hey! How're you doing, sweetie?" she asked sincerely.

Trying to process the fact that she just called me sweetie, and the fact that coming from her it didn't actually bother me, I managed to stutter out, "I-I'm fine. You?"

"I'm good—," she was cut off by Madison.

"Shane!" Maddie yelled, running up to him with Logan trailing behind her.

"Munchkin!" he cried back, picking her up and

throwing her over his head.

"That makes me nervous," Logan whispered into my ear when he got next to me.

"You and me both."

Shane was tickling her now, and she was laughing so hard she couldn't breathe. "Ha-ha-ha! I've got you now, you little monster." He flipped her over so that he was holding onto her back. He raised her shirt and blew raspberry kisses onto her bare belly.

"Stop it! Stop! No berries. No berries," she yelped, trying to catch her breath.

I couldn't stop laughing. I loved watching how easily she was amused. How easily she laughed. I never wanted her to lose that innocence, never wanted her to forget what it felt like to be so loved and protected.

"Daddy!" she cried out, reaching for Logan. Logan went over to Shane and plucked Maddie from Shane's arms. She whispered something in Logan's ear.

"Yes, I know. He is crazy," Logan confirmed.

"I heard that!" Shane said. "You better run!"

Maddie cried out a high-pitch laugh as Logan took off running with her in his arms, Shane chasing close behind.

Joanna and I followed after them. "I was so happy you all could come out with us today. It's so much more fun with a group," she said.

"Well thanks for inviting us," I said. "If you hadn't, I probably wouldn't have made it out here this year."

Her eyes softened with understanding. "I look forward to coming out here all year long."

"Me too," I said with a smile.

Later in the afternoon, after we had seen the animals at the petting zoo, picked apples, and gone through the corn maze, Logan and I searched for an empty picnic table while Shane and Joanna went to get the cider and donuts.

"Don't forget to ask for cups." Logan reminded them.

"What do you think I am, a dumbbell?" Shane asked, turning around to face us as he walked backwards, his arms spread out to his sides.

"Well, sort of," Logan teased, under his breath.

Shane waved him off, turning back to put his arm around Joanna.

Throughout the day, I had noticed how Shane would drape his arm around her shoulders, and how she would snuggle up next to him. I didn't want to, and I wouldn't have admitted it to anyone, but I felt a stab of jealousy. I wished that Michael were here to embrace me the way he used to. I wished I'd realized what a good thing I'd had before he was gone. As we walked I grew pensive thinking about Michael. Remembering his smile, his laugh.

I wanted that again, but I didn't think I wanted it with anyone other than Michael. What did that leave me with? As I thought about it, I felt something shifting inside of me, something coming unplugged, but I couldn't place my finger on what it was.

"I have to say that it's pretty nice to have you helping me out with Madison. I appreciate it more than you know," Logan said, as we sat down at an empty table.

"It's no problem." I paused for a moment to watch Madison climb on the picnic table. "She has this way of taking my mind off things."

"Things?"

I shrugged not saying anything.

"Like Michael things?"

"Yeah," I said, nodding slowly, looking down at the ground.

"Have you talked to Rob or Sue or Sophie?" he asked, pulling Madison down from the top of the table and setting her on the ground, not taking his eyes off me. He was so attuned to Madison that he knew what she was going to do without even looking at her. It was impressive. I wondered if I would be like that as a mother.

"Sophie's emailed me a few times, updating me about New York and Fordham. But I haven't talked to Sue since we went through Michael's things," I paused. "I don't know the protocol for this sort of thing. I mean, if we'd had kids it would be different, you know? I would make it a priority that they saw their grandparents. But that's not the case. And honestly, seeing them is hard. I feel like it makes things worse. At first it was just because they reminded me that Michael was gone. But now...," I trailed off.

"Now you feel like they would hold you back?"

"Maybe," I shrugged. "I know it's a horrible thing to

say, but I feel like keeping them in my life makes it harder for me to move forward. I wish it wasn't like that. I will always love them and care about them," I added softly.

Some would call it self-destructive, cutting the people you love out of your life before they could hurt you. I call it self-defense. Losing them would hurt, but I thought I could extricate myself from their lives, and them from mine, like pulling off a bandage: quickly, immediately, and efficiently. Relationships weren't quite as sterile as bandages though. You couldn't pull away without taking pieces with you or leaving some behind.

Logan looked at me thoughtfully, his eyes full of caring and affection. "I understand," he nodded slowly. "But maybe you should tell them that."

I looked at him in horror, shaking my head adamantly. "No, I don't want to hurt their feelings."

"Don't you think cutting them off completely from your life without explanation hurts them just as much?"

I froze. I hadn't thought of that. "I suppose." Then after a moment, "Have you been talking to them?"

"Here and there. Not as much as I'd like, though. Sue calls me from time to time. And Sophie texted me the other day about a Chaucer paper she was working on."

"Do you talk about me?" I asked nervously.

"I told them how you were helping me out, watching Madison twice a week. They think it's really good for you. They care about you a lot, Skylar. They're still worried about you."

I nodded as tears filled my eyes. I crossed my arms stubbornly, willing my eyes to hold back the tears. But they were filled to the brim and I couldn't stop the small slow tears from falling down my cheek. I wiped them away quickly, averting my gaze from Logan and Madison.

"Sky," he said, reaching out to touch my arm gently, "I didn't mean to upset you."

"No, you're right," I said, my voice quivering. "There's just nothing easy about this. Just as I think I'm getting somewhere, something pulls me back down, or another obstacle appears." I wiped away new tears with the sleeve of my sweater. "I'll try to talk to them."

Out of the corner of my eye I saw Madison climbing back onto the tabletop.

Before Logan could respond to me, Madison lost her balance and fell off the table with a heart-stopping scream. She hit the ground hard on her hands and knees.

Blood started to come out of the cuts on her hands and she cried loudly. Logan picked her up, cradling her into his chest. "Shh. It's all right. Shh," he said, rocking her. "Let me see."

"No, it'll hurt," she said, still sobbing.

"I promise, I won't touch it."

I peered over Logan's shoulder as he set Madison down on the bench and kneeled down to examine the wounds. They weren't that deep, just little gashes with dirt and some small rocks lodged into them.

He gently poured some water over her hands,

dislodging the debris. She tried to yank her hands away, but he gripped her firmly so that she couldn't move. She whimpered.

"He has to clean it out so it doesn't get infected," I explained to her. "Does the water hurt?"

She shook her head up and down adamantly.

"It doesn't hurt," Logan said, concentrating on cleaning out the scrape. When he was done, he pulled three SpongeBob Band-Aid's out of his wallet.

"Always prepared," he grinned at Madison and me. Like a pro, he quickly unpeeled the wrappers and placed the bandages on the cuts.

"See, all better. But that's what happens when you play on top of tables," he said, cleaning off her face with his shirt.

Shane and Joanna returned to the table with a white paper bag, grease seeping through in spots, and a gallon of apple cider.

"What happened?" Joanna asked, concern on her face.

"She took a little bit of a fall," Logan said, bent over awkwardly to hug Madison to his leg as she hid from everyone, embarrassed. "She's fine now."

"Well, who wants some donuts?" Shane asked excitedly. "I think I know a certain little girl who would like some."

Madison looked out shyly from behind Logan's leg.

Shane took a donut and put it down on a napkin on

the table. Joanna poured a small cup of cider and put it down next to the donut.

Madison smiled and climbed up onto the bench. "Thanks," she said.

"Dig in, everyone," Shane said, biting into a donut.

I sat back down on the bench next to Madison. Logan sat on the other side of her, munching on a sugar-and-cinnamon donut. He glanced down at Madison. "You like the donuts? Aren't they good?"

"Mmm, so good, Daddy," she said, licking her lips.

"You're a goofball," he smiled down at her.

There was something about watching the two of them together, something that made me so happy and full of good feelings. Watching the love they had for each other—this pure, untainted, unconditional affection—it touched something deep inside of me.

I was so proud of Logan. I felt pulled to him. I just wanted to be near him.

"Before we go, there's one last place we have to see," Logan said to the table.

"Where's that?" Shane asked, digging in the bag for his third donut.

"The pumpkin patch."

"Dude, you realize it's a total rip-off here, right? They cost like twice as much here as they do at the grocery store."

"Where's the fun in buying pumpkins at the grocery store? No, my daughter is going to go to the overpriced pumpkin patch and pick her own pumpkin," Logan said strongly.

"All right, all right," Shane conceded.

"Isn't that right?" Logan asked Maddie over Shane, nudging her. "Only the best for my little girl."

"Yes!" she said, laughing. "But I'm not little."

"Yes, you are. And you're going to stay that way forever, right?" Logan joked.

"Nope!" she said, shaking her head and climbing down from the bench.

As we walked toward the pumpkin patch, Maddie ran up next to me and grabbed my hand.

"Sky, I walk with you."

"Okay," I said, smiling down at her. If only she knew how that small gesture melted my heart.

It took ten minutes to walk through the crowd to get to the pumpkin patch. Madison barely lasted a minute before I had to pick her up and carry her the rest of the way, her head resting on my shoulder.

"Someone's tired," Logan said as he walked next to me. When we stopped in the pumpkin patch, he stood in front of me, rubbing her back. "Sweetheart, we need to get some pumpkins. Then we can go home and take a nap," he reassured her quietly.

In that moment, I knew what we looked like to the casual observer: a small, new blossoming family. They would see the way Madison clung to me, the love radiating out from Logan, the way we leaned in toward each other, the way we could communicate without saying a word. I don't think I could even admit to myself how desperately I wanted the illusion to be true.

Madison reached for Logan. "I was thinking," Logan said, "We can get a small one for you, and a big one for Daddy, and maybe one for Sky too?" He looked over at me questioningly.

I met his eyes.

He continued, "I was thinking that maybe, if you wanted to, you could come over on a night that I'm actually home, and we could carve them all together? Make some pumpkin seeds?"

"You really want me there?" I asked uncertainly. I was caught between wanting so badly to be with them and fearing I was getting too close, feeling guilty of sharing a favorite tradition with someone other than Michael.

"Yes, I want you there," he said. "Skylar, when are you going to get it through your head that we want you around? You're our family."

"Yeah, our family!" Madison echoed.

I just smiled back at them and let the feeling of belonging wash over me, ground me.

Maddie was getting fussy, so we quickly picked out three pumpkins, pausing to take a handful of snapshots with our phones. I took several of Maddie and Logan walking through the thick green vines, making their selections. There was another of Maddie sitting on top of a huge orange pumpkin with Logan kneeling behind it, holding her up, both of them with smiles spread across their faces. In the picture Maddie has her hands outstretched toward the sky as if she were embracing a world full of possibilities.

Shane took one of Logan, Maddie, and me. In it, Maddie is pointing to a small pumpkin, and Logan and I are smiling at her. When I would later see that picture, I would recall the feeling of pure happiness and belonging and affection. Maybe even the faintest hint of something else.

After we paid for the pumpkins and said our goodbyes to Shane and Joanna in the parking lot, we loaded a tired and grumpy Maddie into her car seat and started for home.

The car felt warm compared to the crispness of the air outside, and a mellow indie band played through the speakers from Logan's iPod. I felt tired in the best way possible. I settled into the seat and looked over at Logan as he drove.

It struck me then, how handsome Logan was. The way his brown hair fell into his eyes and hung down by his ears. The way his grayish-blue eyes lit up when he was with his daughter. The way his body had grown thicker and more muscular since his college days. His shoulders now broad and unmoving. His legs long and lean. He was strong, but not in the way that Michael had been. Where Michael was summer—warm and light and sunny, Logan was winter—serious, dark, and heavy, yet beautiful. So beautiful.

"Want to do something for dinner?" Logan asked me quietly, looking over at me.

"What did you have in mind?" I said, averting my gaze before he could realize I was staring at him.

"We could grill up some chicken?" He suggested.

I wanted to tell him how his idea filled up my heart, how the thought of getting to spend the rest of the day with them made me ineffably happy. This day—doing ordinary things with Logan and Maddie like a "family"—just felt so *right*.

"I'd like that," I said.

After a few minutes he looked over at me and said, "Sky?"

"Hmm?" I asked sleepily.

"I'm really happy you came today."

"Me too," I smiled at him. Thinking about how the day had turned into one of those unforgettable, remember-all-your-life days. The kind that was so full of life and love that you thought you might burst from it all. It was the kind of day that left you feeling sad and a little bit empty when it was over because you didn't know when you'd feel that complete and saturated with joy again.

As I leaned back into the seat, feeling drowsy and peaceful, my arm went limp on the armrest next to Logan's. I closed my eyes and started to drift off to sleep, but not before I felt Logan's soft hand take mine, his fingers snaking through mine. I felt a strange mixture of excitement and comfort.

I squeezed his hand lightly, letting him know that I didn't mind. In fact, if I was being completely honest with myself, I didn't want him to let go.

XVII

I must've looked as irritated as I felt when I walked into group on Saturday morning.

"What's got your panties in a bunch, Medina?" Samara asked.

I set my stuff down on the couch and joined her at the coffee station. "I need to find a roommate or I'm going to lose my house."

"A roommate, huh?" she asked, stirring in a packet of sugar.

I nodded. "I've met with three prospects already and none of them have worked out. I don't know what I'm going to do."

"How soon are you looking to have them move in?"

"As soon as possible, I guess."

"I might have someone for you," she said.

"Who?"

"Well, me," she said playfully.

"You?" I asked, surprised and confused.

"Just so happens my lease is up soon. And I've been looking for a new place to stay. So what do you say?" Her eyes were lit up and she had a smile on her face.

"That depends. You like dogs?" I asked slowly.

"Sure."

"You got $500 a month?"

"Sure do."

"Plan on bringing home any strange men?"

"Not in the habit of it. I find it easier to use 'em and lose 'em if I'm the one who gets to leave in the morning."

"Clearly you don't have any intimacy issues either," I said under my breath.

"Hey, I never said I was Gandhi."

"Alright," I sighed. "Two weeks good for you?" I asked with a grin, cool relief spreading throughout my body.

"Should work."

"And no smoking in the house."

"Oh, be still my heart," she mocked.

"You have to hold it like this," I said to Maddie the following Tuesday, showing her how to hold a crayon.

"You have to move your hand up, so that your pointer finger—," I wiggled mine in front of her nose, "is bent on the top and your thumb is on the side, like this."

We were sitting on the floor in Logan's living room, leaning over the wooden coffee table. I turned the page in the Sesame Street coloring book to a picture of Big Bird. "Here, you try. Get the yellow crayon and color him in."

"No! Purple."

"But he's not purple, he's yellow," I argued fruitlessly.

"I want to color him purple," she said, defiantly grabbing the purple crayon.

"Okay. Whatever you want."

She pressed the crayon down hard on the paper and started to color in Big Bird, lines and scribbles going everywhere uncontrollably.

"Don't press down so hard, Maddie, you're going to break the crayon. Here, let me help," I said, placing my hand on top of hers, covering her tiny fingers with my long ones. I slowly guided her, showing her how to control her wrist as she pivoted the crayon back and forth across the page.

After a minute, she grew irritated with my help and threw her hand back to dislodge mine. "I don't want your help!"

"Madison, that wasn't nice," I said, my voice rising. "If you didn't want my help, you just had to say so." I fought to make my voice softer.

I went into the dining room and sat down at the

kitchen table, putting space between us. I was annoyed, but she acted so much like me—stubborn and determined—that once the irritation wore off, I had to stop myself from laughing.

It was seven thirty, nearly time for Madison to take a bath and start getting ready for bed. *This battle is going to be fun*, I thought to myself, mentally preparing for the temper tantrum that was sure to come when I told her it was time to stop coloring and to clean up.

"You've got ten more minutes, Maddie," I warned her gently.

She ignored me studiously, concentrating furiously on her task.

"Did you hear me?"

"Uh-huh."

"Then what did I say?"

She shrugged. "I don't know," her voice high and soft around the edges, not fully enunciating the words.

I walked over to her and placed my hand gently over her hand, stopping her. She looked up at me indignantly, her brows pulling together in a scowl. "I said you have ten more minutes, okay?" I said slowly, controlling my irritation.

She just nodded her head.

"Good," I said, turning to sit back down at the dining room table. I laid my head on the table, wishing for a glass of wine or some whiskey. Sometimes life could get *very* frustrating when you spent a lot of your free time with a three-year-old.

Although Maddie could be a complete pain in the ass, my frustration started to melt away when she got into the bath without a fight; and it disappeared altogether by the time she was dried off and tucked in her small bed. As I sat next to her reading, she fought off sleep. When her small delicate eyelids fluttered to a close, I was absolutely, undeniably in love again.

I couldn't help but think of my mom when I was with Maddie. My mind flashed through the handful of memories I remembered with Mom: our beige tub, her red lipstick, her long curly hair. The way she would wake up late on weekend mornings—her hair a mess and her legs bare under a nightgown—and gracefully amble down the hallway to join me and Dad on the couch for cartoons and cereal.

The memories were starting to fray at the edges, but I kept hold of them, never grasping too tight for fear they might squeeze through my fingers.

It had taken me years to realize that the driving force behind my need to be a mother so badly was to have another chance at the family that had been taken away from me; not once, but twice now. Right here in this moment though, as I looked down at Madison, with her parted lips and soft skin, I knew that, for now, she was enough.

I don't think she would ever know just how thankful I was for her presence in my life. Caring for her required so much energy and attention to detail that when I was with her, she was the only thing I thought about. She tapped into my heart and drew me out of the dark places inside myself.

When I carefully lifted myself out of the bed, tiptoed out of the bedroom, and then not-so-quietly tripped over Scout, it was a quarter to nine. I felt weary and exhausted from Madison, from work, from life, but I was hesitant to sit down on the couch and relax. I knew that Logan wouldn't mind if I drifted off, but there was something too intimate about him coming home to find me asleep out on the couch.

But isn't that what you wanted? I asked myself. *To be, somehow, part of this little family, to belong?* Families are intimate and exposed and come home to find loved ones sleeping on the couch all the time.

The inner battle, the tug of war between what I wanted and what I feared, continued as I went into the kitchen to clean up. Despite Logan's protests, cleaning up had become part of my nighttime ritual. There was something comforting about the dim lights in the kitchen as I scrubbed rhythmically while Maddie slept in her bed at the end of the hallway. It was the feeling of being at home, of nurturing, of creating a safe haven from the outside world. I wanted Logan to be able to come home from his long day and sit back and relax without having to worry about anything else. The burdens placed upon his shoulders already seemed Atlas-like in nature, heavy and unyielding. Anything I could do to lessen that load, I wanted to do for him.

When I walked into the dining room, I accidentally bumped into Logan's desk and knocked one of his books to the floor. It landed facedown and opened. It was a paperback copy of *The Great Gatsby*, the one with the blue face on the cover hovering over the glowing, golden city.

I picked it up carefully so that it was still on the page it had opened to and saw a highlighted section.

I heard the door open and close as Logan sneaked in.

"My eleventh graders are reading it next semester," he said, setting his bag down and taking the book from my hands. "'There was something gorgeous about him, some heightened sensitivity to the promises of life,'" he read. "'An extraordinary gift for hope, a romantic readiness such as I have never found in any other person and which it is not likely I shall ever find again.'" Logan closed the book, his fingers tracing the white book spine.

"Reminds me of Michael," he said.

"It's beautiful," I whispered.

"It's heartbreaking," he countered, angling his body around mine to put the book back in its spot on the desk. "Beautiful but tragic. Jay Gatsby fights his whole life to be someone, something he's not for the woman he loves. And then once he finally has it all, he dies and she leaves."

"But that wasn't Michael," I said, sitting down on the desktop. "Not the last part anyway. He never chased after a life he didn't have. He never wanted anything more than what he had."

"And he got the one he loved in the end, didn't he?" Logan asked grinning, a hint of sadness touching his features. He folded his arms across his chest and leaned back against the wall.

"He did," I nodded.

The dining room was dim, the only light coming from the kitchen and the table lamp across the space in the living room. Logan's blue eyes peered through the dusky light.

The room was charged with emotion. I wasn't sure whether it was from the night I just had with Madison, from talking about Michael, or from something else—something unsaid between Logan and me. I could feel the sensations—grief, guilt, reluctance—building in my chest as tears stung my eyes.

Logan came closer and put his arms around me. I buried my face in his chest. His brown T-shirt was thin and I could feel his warm skin beneath it. I felt my body shake against his. He continued to hold me and said, "I know. I miss him too. That's part of the reason why I wanted to teach this book this year. So I could hold on to him longer, somehow."

I nodded my head and then spoke slowly, trying to steady my voice. "What if he's all alone?"

"I don't think he is," Logan said softly, rubbing my back comfortingly.

"You believe he's in...," I trailed off, pulling away from him.

"In heaven?" he asked, moving back to lean against the desk, but still staying close.

I nodded, wiping my face off.

"Yeah, I mean I don't know if it's the idea of heaven as we understand it, but I don't think he's alone. Isn't that kind of the point of the afterlife? To be with all the people who have gone before you. To be with God."

"Do you believe in God?" I asked, searching for guidance, an answer, someone to tell me what to believe in.

He paused, thinking for a moment. "I think it's complicated," he said. "But I do believe that there's something—some power that's bigger than us. And I'd like to believe that we're more than what we are here on earth. That we're eternal. That we have souls. That we're a part of some big, cosmic plan or something."

"I'd like to believe that too."

"What's stopping you?"

I shrugged. "What if it's not true and I spend all this time believing in something that's not real? What if I spend the rest of my life hoping to see Michael again and then I die and don't?"

"You're right. We don't know what's going to happen. For all we know, we die and that's it. But I think there's something in us that has to believe there's more. It doesn't matter if it's true or not because the belief is real."

I stared off into space thinking. "You're not alone either, Sky," he said.

I blinked, breaking my stare, then looked up at him.

His eyes were kind but firm and full of conviction. "You have so many people in your life who love you and have your back. You have your dad, Sue and Sophie, Shane, you have me, and I know Madison loves you to pieces. You're not alone. You never were."

The next morning at work, Harry came up to the front desk. I was on the phone.

"You're looking for Children's Village?" I said into the receiver. "I have the number right here for you. Are you ready?"

Harry leaned against the wall waiting for me to get off the phone. He thumbed through a stack of papers in his hands.

I gave the number and hung up the phone. "I don't even understand why they call here in the first place. The numbers for the different departments are all listed online. It's not exactly rocket science."

"I see you're enjoying yourself up here, Medina."

"Oh, it's riveting," I sighed. "What's up, Boss? Come to give me another death sentence?"

"Nope, you're fully capable of doing that all by yourself."

I looked at him crossly, narrowing my eyes. "So to what do I owe the pleasure?"

"A fellow can't just come hang out with you and enjoy your witty bantering skills?"

"Um, no."

He laughed and pushed away from the wall, placing the stack of papers on the counter in front of me.

"What are these?" I asked, shuffling through the papers. They were bank statements, phone statements, and DMV records. I leaned in closer, my heart raced. "Are these what I think they are?" I asked softly.

"We could use your help."

"Am I looking for anything in particular?"

"Suspicious sums of money coming and going, repeated phone numbers, and check to see if work on the vehicle matches any payment history."

"So the usual," I said.

"Yup. And despite how much you hate it up here, you've handled yourself remarkably well these past few months," he said, patting my shoulder.

"Don't patronize me!" I shrugged him off, hiding my grin.

"And here I thought you were getting soft, Medina."

He started to walk away. "Get me something by four o'clock."

"Yessir."

That night I rushed home to meet Logan and Madison for Halloween. We were going trick-or-treating in my neighborhood because, unlike Logan's apartment complex, my neighbors went all-out with the decorations, and the streets were filled with kids.

As I walked into my house, I passed the three jack-o'-lanterns that we had carved together a few days earlier. Logan and Madison had come over on Sunday evening, and we drank hot apple cider as we laid out old newspapers on the dining room table to carve the pumpkins.

After Logan had rolled her sleeves up, Madison squealed with disgust and delight as she stuck her hand into the cold and gooey guts of the pumpkin. We showed her how to separate the seeds and scrape out the inside of the pumpkin. Of course by then she had lost all interest and had wandered off to the living room to join Scout on the couch, her fingers buried in his thick coat, absorbed by the witches and broomsticks on TV.

That left Logan and me to finish off our own large pumpkins and Maddie's small one, but we didn't mind. I put a witch on mine, and Logan decided on a vampire. We laughed and talked underneath the glow of the dining room light as the world outside grew dark. Logan called Maddie back to the table and helped her carve a cat into her small pumpkin. My house was starting to feel like a home again, with life and laughter filling the rooms.

Later, I remembered looking into the living room and seeing Logan sitting there with Madison, watching the movie. I remembered the way he smiled and pointed to the screen, explaining to her who the ghouls and monsters were. I remembered the way I felt a rush of emotion fill my body, the way I felt so suddenly lucky and happy.

I smiled thinking back on that night. But it scared me, how much I hoped this feeling wouldn't go away. Because if it did, if they did, I didn't think I'd be able to recover.

It wasn't long after I got home and changed into some jeans and a sweatshirt that Logan and Madison walked through the front door. Scout jumped up and down, excited to see his friends.

Logan walked into the kitchen wearing black pants with a white button-up shirt and red tie underneath a black vest. While that wasn't completely out of character, the black cloak he had over his shoulders was.

"Whoa!" I exclaimed, raising my eyebrows.

"You like?" he said, spreading his lips to reveal sharp fangs.

"Holy crap, those look so real," I leaned in to get a closer look. "Where'd you get those?"

"Well clearly, Skylar, I am a vampire," he said, his voice filled with mock scorn, taking his cloak in his hand to cover half his face Dracula-style. "So they're mine."

"Right," I said, humoring him.

"Brooke should be here any second now. Madison wants her to do her makeup."

Down the hall, I could see Madison sitting by the front door petting Scout.

"Maddie, are you excited to go trick-or-treating?" I asked.

"Yeah!" she said, getting up and walking toward the kitchen.

"What are you dressing up as tonight?" I asked, picking her up for a hug.

"A FAIRY!" she yelled excitedly.

"Sorry, I didn't quite hear you, a what?" I joked.

Logan smiled from across the kitchen.

"A fairy!"

I felt her small fingers play with the charms on my necklace.

"Pretty," she said.

"Thank you," I said, pointing out the charm with the *S* on it. "My mommy gave me this one when I was little."

"She did?" Maddie marveled.

I nodded.

There was a knock on the door. "I'll get it," Logan offered as I lowered Madison back down on the ground.

"Opening up her doors now, are you?" Brooke asked with an undercurrent of hostility running through her voice.

Behind her I could see Marc. He was tall, easily six feet, and I could clearly see his dark cropped hair and hard angular face over Brooke's head. He had a wide jaw and green eyes. I could see from here that he was built. His shoulders were wide and hulking. Immense biceps, forearms, and chest muscles filled out his shirt, outlining all the contours of his massive build. The beginning of a black tribal tattoo stuck out of his collar and crept up the side of his neck.

"Mommy!" Madison cried, running down the hallway to Brooke.

Logan moved out of the way as Brooke and Marc stepped in and Brooke picked up Madison, talking to her in a soft soothing voice.

I envied Brooke's small, compact form and her tinkling bell-like laughter. But I knew that she was capricious. I could see now that Brooke was all about Brooke.

I saw the way that Logan looked at her. Behind the wall he had built between them, there was a shadow of the fire and love that had once kindled there. He still looked hurt when he looked at her, but there was no passion there anymore, no allegiance. Only the shared connection of Madison. He would always love her in a way, I knew. She was the mother of his daughter after all, but I could see then, in the clipped, constrained way he talked to her that he wanted nothing more to do with her. She was a disease to him, like a beautiful, dangerous fire. He was always careful not to get too close.

Brooke saw me watching them from the doorway of the kitchen. "Hi, Skylar," she said, forcing herself to be cheerful. She smiled at me, but it didn't reach her eyes, which were tight and lined.

"Hey, Brooke. Marc," I greeted them, as Marc nodded in acknowledgement. "Happy Halloween."

"Thanks for having us over," Brooke said to me

quickly. "Where can we get ready at?"

"Bathrooms on your left," I said, watching as Logan handed Brooke the costume. Brooke and Madison crowded into the small half-bath, forcing Marc to stand in the hallway.

Logan and I went back into the kitchen to wait. "Since when is she into professional wrestlers?" I half-joked to Logan in whispers.

He just looked over at me with a small, sad smile on his lips. "He's actually a personal trainer," he said.

The look on his face revealed all his insecurities and perceived shortcomings. I could see him comparing himself to Marc.

It hurt like crazy to see him sell himself so short. If only he could see how beautiful and wonderful and brilliant he really was.

I wanted to say something to him, to reassure him, but I couldn't think of the right words to say. So I just placed my hand on his arm.

Logan flinched when I touched him and I drew my hand back quickly. He turned away from me.

I ran my fingers through my hair, trying to figure out what I had done wrong. But before I could come to a conclusion, Madison burst into the kitchen. Her face was made up with purple and pink swirls. Her costume was a purple flowing dress with layers of green fabric underneath it. She wore a light purple sweatshirt and sweatpants underneath the dress to keep her warm. On her head was a crown made of flowers, and she carried a ribbon-strewn silver wand in her hand. On her back were green-and-purple glittering wings.

"You look so pretty, sweetheart," Logan said to Maddie as Marc snapped a picture.

"Thanks, Daddy." She twirled the skirt of her dress around. She was loving all the attention she was getting tonight.

I glanced at the clock on the stove. It was six. "I think it's time," I said.

As we walked down the sidewalk, darkness and the sound of children's excitement filled the air. The streetlights overhead turned on and illuminated circular pockets of the street.

"How long do you think she'll last?" Brooke asked Logan.

"Hmm, I'd say an hour tops. We'll see how much candy she has by then."

"You just want it for yourself," Brooke accused lightly.

"So do you."

"I'll admit I'm not above stealing candy from my three-year-old," she laughed, the tinkling sound drifting off in the wind.

Brooke and Marc, who was pulling the plastic wagon Madison was sitting in, led the way. From where I stood next to Logan, I could feel that there was something unpleasant between Brooke and me. She was cautious and hesitant toward me, not overly unkind or rude, but guarded. There was something she didn't like about me. I couldn't remember ever being super close with her in the past, but I thought it was something more than that. Maybe she didn't like me being around Maddie because of my run-in with the law. Or maybe she didn't like me being around Logan. The thought flew at me suddenly, and I was unprepared for how it made me feel.

If Brooke didn't like how close Logan and I had grown, was maybe even a little bit jealous, did that mean there was something to be jealous of? Was there something more between Logan and me than a long-standing friendship and a shared loss? I would be lying to myself if I said there wasn't. Logan made me feel alive and *real* again. I loved to see his lopsided smile, and my heart raced whenever we got close to pass Maddie between us. I thought back to the car ride home from the apple orchard, how Logan's hand had been soft and warm as he held mine.

I shook my head to dislodge the imagery. Guilt rushed in to take its place. No, it couldn't possibly be. I couldn't have feelings for Logan because I loved Michael. Those two feelings couldn't coexist, could they?

"Who do you want to take you up to this house?" Brooke leaned down to ask Maddie.

"You!" she said, pointing her small finger at Brooke.

"I'd love too," Brooke beamed, sweeping her out of the wagon. "Make sure you've got your candy bag." It was a white plastic bag with Disney princesses on it.

Brooke glanced over at Logan. "You bought her that bag?" she asked incredulously.

He shrugged, his hands in his pockets. "She really wanted it."

"I thought we said we weren't going to push the princess and damsel-in-distress stereotypes," Brooke said sharply, keeping her tone down but picking a fight at the same time. Her moods changed so quickly, from airy and aloof to bitchy and confrontational, it could give you whiplash. *So maybe that's where Madison gets it from*, I thought.

"Jesus, Brooke, I wasn't pushing it on her. She wanted it, I got it for her. I wasn't going to sit there in the store and have a debate on gender roles with a three-year-old. I want her to be strong and independent just as much as you do."

Marc and I stood to the side awkwardly, watching the heated interaction. Concern clouded Maddie's face as she felt the anger between her parents.

"Well, I'm just saying—," Brooke started to say.

"Well, I'm just saying that maybe next time you can take her to go costume shopping."

"Logan," she said dangerously low. "We're not doing this right now."

"You're right," he said, trying to constrain his anger. "Go take her up there." He nodded toward the house, which had white cotton spider webs spread out on the bushes and Styrofoam gravestones in the flowerbeds.

He looked at Maddie and softened his expression. "Do you remember what you say when you get to the door?"

"Trick-o-Treat," she said quietly.

"Close enough. And then what do you say after you get candy?"

"Thank you."

"Yes, now go get some candy!"

She giggled, her anxiety dissipating. "Okay, Mommy. Go!"

Brooke carried her up to the porch, Marc trailing behind them.

"Are you okay?" I asked Logan, turning towards him.

"I'm fine," he said, staring at the house in front of us, but I could see the muscles of his jaw working.

"It's hard to keep up with her," I said quietly. "You're never quite sure which Brooke you're going to get."

"*That* Brooke," he said, nodding toward them, "is the only one I know now. I can barely remember the person I fell in love with." His words were filled with resentment. "I've always known she was selfish, but I guess I never realized how mean and cold she could be."

"I don't understand why she treats you like that. You're the one who takes care of Maddie most of the time. I mean, aren't you the one who makes all her daycare arrangements and doctors' appointments? You're the one there for all the important day-to-day stuff."

"I don't know either," he shrugged. "But sometimes you just have to put up with shit you don't deserve."

"Yeah, but you shouldn't have to—," I cut myself off at the sight of them coming back down the walkway, all smiles.

"What'd you get?" Logan asked curiously.

"M&M's!"

"Ugh. Aim for some Skittles next time," Logan said under his breath.

"What?" Maddie asked loudly.

"Oh, nothing. Let's go see what the next house has," he answered.

When Marc and Brooke took Madison up to the next house, I noticed how Marc hovered over Brooke protectively. How, when she talked to him, he would put his hand around her tiny waist, pulling her closer, and listened to her every word.

Small, delicate fairy-like Brooke with the massive personal trainer/bodybuilder Marc; there were just some things in this world I would never understand.

But love was love. Or maybe it was lust. Either way, we can't always help who we fall for or who we want.

I turned back to Logan. "You're pretty good about not letting Brooke get in the way of your and Maddie's relationship."

I didn't tell him how upsetting it was to see Brooke treat him like that. How it was even more upsetting that he just took it.

"Just because Brooke and I couldn't get our shit together doesn't mean that Maddie should have to miss out on having us both there for her. You know?"

I nodded.

"And even though Brooke can be a colossal bitch and petty and immature, she's still Maddie's' mom. So I have to do everything I can to make sure Maddie doesn't feel the animosity between us. Because she doesn't deserve that."

He paused. "I just want my daughter to be happy."

"Logan, from where I'm standing, that little girl could not be any happier or more well-adjusted than she is. She adores you. You're her hero. Well, at least until she's a teenager, then all bets are off," I teased and I saw a ghost of a smile on his lips.

I wanted to make one last point, "You should see the way you look at her sometimes—I honestly don't know if I've ever seen someone so full of such unconditional love. She is so lucky to have you."

"Thanks, Sky," he said. "Really."

"Anytime."

When I looked up at him, I felt my heart expand, like it was accommodating all the emotion, all the happiness and sadness I felt at that moment. There was something about Logan that was just so *good* for me. The still-jagged edges of my soul didn't scare him away. In fact, he had the same scars as me, the same grief and heartache. He understood me like no one else could. He saw my brokenness, and I saw his, and it was what drew me to him.

I wanted to fix him and, I thought, maybe he could fix me. We could save each other.

And those thoughts scared the hell out of me. But before I knew what was happening, I was up on my tiptoes, leaning in toward Logan, placing my lips on his in a quick, gentle kiss.

I pulled away suddenly, my hand coming to my lips. "Oh my God."

Logan's face registered shock. I couldn't read anything beyond that. He was speechless.

A tidal wave of emotions crashed through me: happiness, regret, embarrassment. *What had I done? Why? Why would I jeopardize our friendship like that? How could I do that to Michael?*

At the same time, how could something so potentially detrimental feel so good? *How could those few seconds move me so much?*

Because I felt different. Changed.

Neither one of us said a word as the trio returned, and we moved on to the next house.

For the rest of the night, I stepped back and fell into the background, needing to process everything that was happening between me and Logan, but also knowing that Madison needed the undivided attention of her parents that night. And I wanted Maddie to have this moment with them.

As Brooke and Marc pulled away with Madison passed out

in the back seat, Logan and I stood on the porch together.

The night was quiet around us; all the trick-or-treaters had gone home, and Logan had changed out of his costume and vampire fangs into his normal jeans and hoodie.

We stood there, the darkness surrounding us like a blanket pulling us closer together. I tried to untangle myself, free myself from the space around us, but it was thick with tension and unspoken words.

There was no point denying there was something between us. Tonight it had cumulated in a kiss, but it was more than that. There was something developing between us, and it had been for a while. I couldn't tell when it started, but I knew that it was there, strong and powerful.

"Sky—," Logan started to say.

"No," I said, cutting him off, putting my hand up. "We don't have to talk about it," I choked on the words. They felt hot and fuzzy in my mouth. My head swam with the uncertainty of what would happen next.

"But I want to talk about it."

I missed the urgency in his voice. I felt cold and alive with exposed nerve endings. I wanted nothing more than for this conversation to be over, to be locked in my house, alone. At the same time, all I wanted was to kiss Logan again, to feel his lips on mine, to press my body against his. I didn't want to hear him say that I'd gone and ruined everything.

"Sky—," he tried again, but I kept talking.

"Just forget it ever happened and we'll never talk—,"

"SKY!" he said louder and more forcefully this time, grabbing both of my arms, forcing me to stop and look up at him.

Taken aback, I stopped talking. "What?" I asked nervously.

His eyes were full of something I hadn't seen in them before. Passion. Intensity. Yearning. He took a step toward me. I was frozen, glued to the ground. I was aware of the way his body leaned into mine, the coolness of his hands on my flushed face.

And then his lips were on mine, urgently searching. He pulled me closer and I wrapped my arms around his waist, letting my hips sink into his.

His kisses grew deeper and harder. I could feel his heart beating, paralleling mine in speed. I felt light and heavy at the same time. Like I could float off the ground, but there was a wonderful pressure holding me down.

Then he was slowing down, pulling away. But I didn't want him to. I didn't want to let go.

He looked down at me, grinning, "I was beginning to think that was never going to happen."

"What?" I stammered, unbelievingly.

"I like you, Sky. I feel better when you're around."

"Really?" I asked, my body racing with anticipation, a smile breaking out across my face.

"Yes, really," he grinned. Then his voice lowered, deepened, "So just shut up and let me kiss you, damn it."

And I did. I looked up at him expectantly and leaned into him again. The way the heat from our bodies mixed with the cold air was almost electric. I let him kiss me deeply, softly. I let him make me feel awake and vital and whole.

XVIII

Suspended

November came in with a cold front, and the start of winter was quickly approaching.

Madison and I had switched from walks and trips to the park to playing in the living room while cartoons played on the TV. Most of the time we occupied ourselves with toys. We colored or played with Legos. Madison especially loved to sort her wooden blocks by color and shape or read books to me, making up her own story as she went along. I looked forward to those slow and peaceful evenings I got to spend with her.

Tonight I was glad to be at Logan's again. It was nearing nine o'clock, and I sat on the couch reading with Scout curled up against my feet. As I was turning the page of my book, I heard the locks on the front door click, and Logan walked in with a gust of cold air following him, blowing his dark hair in front of his face.

"Hey," he said warmly, shutting the door behind him. He took off his navy wool coat and hung it up in the closet. He was wearing his usual uniform of slim dark pants with a gray V-neck sweater.

He looked as tired as I felt. His clear pale skin looked almost translucent from the cold, and small lines crinkled around his eyes when he smiled.

Despite those lines and the whisper of dark circles forming under his eyes, he looked youthful. His skin was smooth and radiant. His blue-gray eyes glowed with excitement. No, it was more than that. They glowed from something deeper, some inner life force.

"Hi," I said, sliding my bookmark into place and closing the book. "How was your day?"

He kicked off his shoes and came over to sit next to me, gently putting his arm around my shoulders. I settled in next to him.

"It was all right," he said yawning. "Long."

"You look exhausted," I said, placing my hand lightly on his thigh. Feeling his body beneath my hand generated a tingling rush. My pulse sped up from an act so simple yet so intimate. Possessive, even. As if to say, *you're mine*.

I felt his breath catch in his throat. He coughed quietly before saying, "Yeah, well I had a hard time falling asleep after that kiss last night."

I grinned, putting my cheek down into his shoulder. "So I'm not the only one, then," I said.

He leaned his forehead against my head, his lips just below my temple. I felt his eyelashes brush my skin as he closed his eyes.

We sat there for a moment, leaning into each other, letting the excitement of being so physically close to each other *thrum* through our bodies. I breathed him in—crispness of the late autumn air, the earthiness of his wool sweater, the realness of his skin.

"So I have this crazy idea…," he trailed off.

"Yes?"

"Well I was thinking that maybe…would you want to go out with me this weekend? Saturday night?"

"On a date?" I clarified.

"All official and everything."

"Do I have to wear a corsage or something?" I teased.

His mouth curved upward in an amused smile. "I said official, not formal."

"Well then, yes," I said. "I'd love to."

He tilted his head to the side, his face an inch away from mine, pausing so that we were suspended in that beautiful tension-filled moment before a kiss. He looked into my eyes and smiled, those soft lines forming around the corners of his eyes.

Then he kissed me softly and slowly. His lips moved rhythmically against mine. He pulled me in closer, enough to let me know that he wanted me, needed me closer, but not enough to make me uncomfortable.

After a pleasantly long time, he pulled away and

sighed. "You're pretty incredible, you know that?"

I attempted a smile, but the corners of my mouth turned down in a small frown. I was remembering a time when someone else had told me that he loved me, that I was everything he'd ever needed. I remembered kissing a blond blue-eyed boy who made me feel hot and dizzy all over.

Logan could tell I was momentarily distracted, reliving a memory. Gently, he took my hand and started talking again. "So I was thinking of doing something a little different. Maybe we can go to Ann Arbor? Go to a cool restaurant. We could check out the Michigan Theater and see what's playing there?" he suggested.

"That sounds perfect," I said.

"Good," he nodded.

The whole ten-minute drive home, passing brightly lit gas stations, I thought about our upcoming date. I was excited and nervous, even though there was nothing formal about Logan or about our relationship. It was completely organic and natural.

But I knew I didn't want to rush this. I wanted to do this right.

It was five o'clock on Saturday night, and I still hadn't

decided what to wear. I looked at the clothes scattered around the room: dresses, tops, and shoes covered every surface.

I shifted through what was left in my closet and moved some of the clothes on the floor absentmindedly with my foot. I didn't remember getting ready for a date ever being this difficult.

"This is ridiculous!" I said aloud, annoyed and exasperated.

Mentally, I started to remind myself why I was going out with Logan in the first place. I thought about our kiss on Halloween night and holding hands in the car. I thought about how he had become a constant in my life after everything I had come to know and expect was taken from me.

I thought about how complex our lives were and how layered our relationship was. But despite the complexity, there was something so simple and wondrous about what was happening between us. He made me feel better. He and Maddie had brought joy and laughter back into my life. When they were around, I didn't feel like the anger was going to consume me. They were like a drug, an antidote for the loneliness and bitterness.

I didn't need to wear some elaborately styled outfit. I needed something classic yet beautiful, not overdone. And I knew just what that was: a body-hugging, V-neck gray knit dress. I slipped on some black tights, my knee-high black medium-heeled boots, and silver hoop earrings.

I looked at myself in the full-length mirror and tilted my head to the side, examining myself critically. The dress still fit pretty well, thankfully. The earrings were the perfect complement to the diamond and silver charms that hung around my neck. With my long dark hair and smoky eyes it actually looked like I knew what I was doing when it came to styling.

As I was finishing in the bathroom, touching up my hair and dabbing clear gloss on my lips, the doorbell rang.

I ran out of the bathroom and hurried down the stairs, pausing at the bottom to catch my breath. I opened the front door and there was Logan. He was standing with his back to the door and swiveled around when the door opened. He froze and looked at me awe-struck for a moment before realizing he was still standing outside.

We stood in the warmly lit foyer. "You look…," he paused, staggering his words. "Wow. I just—you look amazing."

I smiled, tucking my hair behind my ear. When I looked at Logan with his still-damp hair that fell across his forehead and his brown sweater, I felt a rush of heat through my body. He looked unbelievably beautiful.

"You don't look too bad yourself," I said.

I stepped toward him, wrapping my arms around his neck and hugging him close. I sank into his arms, relishing how it felt. He relaxed his hold on me so he could kiss me, but my lips were tacky from the lip-gloss. I pulled my face away from his and laughed. "Sorry," I said, wiping the makeup from his lips with my fingers, "I just put that on."

He laughed too, wiping what was left on his lips on the back of his hand. "It's fine. Are you ready to go?"

The drive to Ann Arbor took about an hour, and we sat in a comfortable quiet while the headlights danced on the road in the darkness. There was an exciting energy between us. We were happy to be with each other yet nervous for what the night might bring. It was the feeling of starting something new.

Logan's now-familiar smell—mint gum, wool, the suggestion of ancient paperbacks and the richness of the stories they told—was close and comforting. I wanted to wrap myself in it. I felt safe. Yes, that was the word for it. Safe. And understood. Like nothing could hurt me in this little cocoon.

"So I forgot to tell you," I said, turning to him. "Samara, the woman I've been hanging out with after anger management, is going to be my new roommate."

"Really?" he asked, his eyebrows going up. "When did this happen?"

"Last weekend at group."

"Can you trust her?" he asked.

I thought for a second. "Yeah. I know I don't know her that well, but I trust her."

"So how are you feeling about all of this? Excited?"

"Strangely, yes. You'll have to meet her once she moves in—she's quite the character. But I think this whole

The Charm Necklace

roommate thing might actually be a good thing."

He looked over at me and smiled. "I'm happy for you." A beat. "Does she need help moving in?"

I shook my head. "I think she has some of the guys from her work helping her out."

"Well just let me know if you need anything."

We pulled into the city. After finding a place to park, Logan took my hand in his and led me through the streets, our breath suspended in clouds around us as we walked.

Logan brought us to a small window-fronted restaurant. Peering in I could see it was busy and lively. Patrons huddled in wooden chairs around cloth-draped tables. In the center of the room, I could see a man playing an upright piano. Candles burned on each table, and despite the narrowness of the space, the cream walls and weathered hardwood floors made the space feel open and inviting.

For a second I felt as if I were in a dream, somehow separated from the life and jovialness inside the restaurant.

"It's European," I heard Logan say distantly, pulling me back. "They specialize in Polish, Hungarian, and Austrian dishes. So I hope you're feeling adventurous tonight."

"It's perfect," I said, turning to him. I smiled widely, pushing myself to grab hold of the evening.

Logan opened the door and we were greeted with a distinct smell of what I assumed was Polish food. As we were guided to our table toward the back, the ebb and flow of conversation and the soft piano music surrounded us.

"It's so cozy in here," I said, taking off my coat and sitting down. "Like I've been here before or something."

"It's cool, right?" Logan asked, settling down in his chair.

"How did you find this place?"

"Do you remember the summer program I did at U of M a few years ago?"

"No," I shook my head quizzically.

"Oh, well I did. Anyway, you get bored studying—."

"Wait, what?" I exclaimed, cutting him off. "You, Logan Parks, get bored from studying? I think somewhere right now a dead pretentious poet is rolling over in his grave."

Logan chuckled under his breath. "Yes, even I get bored studying. Anyway, as I was saying," he looked at me pointedly, "you get bored and you start wandering around downtown, checking out new places and restaurants, and this was one of them. I haven't been back here since then. I haven't had a reason to, until now."

"I'm honored," I said, amused.

"The honor is all mine," Logan said, picking up the menu the hostess had dropped off earlier. "How about some wine?"

"Yes, please."

"Red or white?"

"Umm, red?"

The waitress, with dark hair pulled back in a high

bun, approached our table. Wrinkles hugged her quickly made-up green eyes and her white button-up shirt was stretched tightly over her stomach. Even so, she was starkly beautiful. "What can I get you two to drink?" she asked in a deep voice.

"We'll have a bottle of the Masi Modello delle Venezie," Logan said uncertainly, reading off the menu.

"Certainly."

After she'd come back and served the wine, Logan ordered for us. Foods I had never heard of before: potato and cheese pierogies as an appetizer and Krakow chicken and grilled kielbasa for the entrees.

I can't say that I was paying too much attention to the food though. The wine and the music and Logan sitting across from me were all going to my head. I felt light and buoyant. And somehow, in the candlelight, not so broken.

Between sips of wine and bites of the pierogies, Logan filled me in about the summer program he did at U of M.

"It was an eight-credit English program," he said. "I took it during the summer semester between junior and senior year."

"That's so weird," I said, thinking back through the past. "I can't remember you being gone for an entire summer."

He shrugged. "You were busy."

I probably was busy, likely preoccupied with other things—school things, work things, Michael things—but I refrained from saying anything. I didn't think either one of us was purposefully trying to avoid bringing Michael up, but it didn't seem like we were going out of our way to bring him up either.

I wanted to see if I could forge a new path with Logan. Something that wasn't tied up with and defined by Michael. I wanted something that was just ours—mine and Logan's.

I felt a sharp quick stab of guilt in my heart but pushed it away.

Logan was here, he was alive, and he was right in front of me. If he felt the same way that I felt about him, if there was even the faintest hope that he could maybe one day love me, if he could help heal the hurt, then I had to give this a fighting chance.

"But you've already been to Europe!" I said to Logan, as our dinner entrees arrived.

"So? There are lots of places in Europe to see."

"You went to England, right?" I asked.

"Yeah, and Ireland too. For study abroad."

"How long were you there?"

"It was like three weeks total. We got to go to all the nerdy places like The Eagle and Child, where J. R. R. Tolkien, C. S. Lewis, and the Inklings used to hang out at. And of course we stayed in London for a few days and saw Buckingham Palace and Westminster Abbey, the London Eye, all those famous places. And in Ireland we went to Dublin—."

"And drank Guinness," I cut him off.

"Yes, and drank Guinness," he laughed. "The fun part was the time we spent touring the countryside looking at castles, mostly ruins now, and the small villages."

"Sounds amazing," I said.

"Why didn't you ever study abroad?"

"I never really had the desire to," I said shrugging. "And even if I did, I didn't have the money to."

"Isn't there any place you'd like to go?"

"I'd really like to go to Brazil someday. That's where my dad's family is from," I added. "I don't know. I think I'd like to go to Colorado or somewhere out west and stay in a log cabin in the winter. Go snowboarding or skiing."

"That," Logan said, pointing his fork at me as he talked. "*almost* sounds better than Europe."

"Almost?"

"Truth be told, I don't see any international trips happening any time soon. So I think a trip to Aspen or Vail will just have to do."

"You could pretend you're in the Swiss Alps," I suggested. "I can buy you some Toblerone."

Logan laughed. "Remind me to take you up on that."

"Maybe I can even get you to snowboard," I teased. "I know Michael could never get you to try it."

And there he was, popping up in the conversation without me even being aware of it. But Logan wasn't fazed.

"Oh, he did get me to try it. It's just after eating snow seven or eight times in a row, I had no desire to keep trying. He was so frustrated with me."

I laughed. "Well we both know that he wasn't the most patient teacher."

"Everything just came so naturally to him. I swear, he could pick some obscure African tribal game, and by the end of an hour be as good as someone who had been playing his entire life. It just wasn't normal."

"That's Michael for you…," I trailed off, pushing my food around my plate with my fork.

Logan was quiet for a second. I could feel his eyes on me, but I didn't want to look up. "Do you not want to talk about him?"

"No, it's not that," I said, finally daring to meet his gaze. "It's just that…I don't know. I still miss him, but I don't want that to get in the way of this, and I guess I just don't know how to balance those two things out."

"Sky," Logan said, reaching across the table and putting his hand on mine. "You know that I would never ask you to forget him or stop missing him. He will always be a part of you. And I miss him too. Figuring out how to go on without him here, it's hard." He paused. "But we're going to figure it out together."

"You promise?"

"I promise. As a friend, or more than that if that's what you want. I'm here for you, no matter what."

"And Skylar," he added. "I don't necessarily think that those two things, your love for Mike and whatever it is that's going on between us, have to be two separate things. We wouldn't be here right now if it wasn't for Mike. We

The Charm Necklace

shouldn't have to forget that or pretend it isn't true to move forward."

"Doesn't it bother you? My history with him? The fact that right now, I'm supposed to be married to him? That in a way he has some kind of claim on me?"

"Does it bother you that I have a past with Brooke? That I have a child with her?" He countered.

"No, not really."

"So there you go," he shrugged. "Listen, I understand that you have spent the last several years loving Mike. You had your future planned out with him, just like I did with Brooke.

"But here we are." He paused for a moment. "I don't expect you to be anyone other than who you are."

"How did you get to be so amazing?" I asked solemnly. Then switching gears, lightening my tone. "Are you secretly a Buddhist? Did you visit the Tibetan monks on one of those study abroad trips?"

"Yes, but unfortunately, the whole vow of silence thing just wasn't working for me," he joked. Then his face grew serious and he set his shoulders squarely. "I don't want to take his place, Sky. But I'd like to see where this might go."

"Me too," I said, not taking my eyes from his.

His lips turned up in a small smile.

The waitress, approaching us with perfect timing, set our main courses down breaking the intensity of our conversation.

As we ate, I watched Logan as he talked about the college course he was taking and the final paper he was working on. I had no idea what he was talking about, but I was mesmerized as his blue eyes gleamed in the candlelight and his thin lips moved as he talked. I studied the way his hands moved up and down the thin stem of the wine glass, the way his eyes would wander around the room. I felt drawn toward everything about him.

I was transfixed. I just wanted to be in the moment with him. I wanted time to freeze, for the world around us to stop.

The entire time I had known him, I had always thought of Logan as being so guarded, withdrawn. And yet I had always been aware of how sensitive he was to what was taking place around him. Previously there had always been something about him that I couldn't quite access. Now that he had let me in to his inner world, I could see how open and mindful he was. How had I not seen it before? I felt like Saul when the scales fell from his eyes. I was no longer blind and I was able to see Logan as he truly was—brilliant, beautiful, generous, strong in his own subdued way, and overflowing with quiet, vibrant life.

"Are you planning on taking another course next semester?" I asked.

"I'd like to. The next linguistics course I'm interested in taking isn't being offered until next fall, but there's this course on the history of books that I'd love to take. It's all about the evolution of reading, writing, and publishing. It also covers some of the defining moments of the written word—."

I couldn't help it, I laughed out loud. "Some things never change."

He grinned. "Hey, don't make fun of me! I enjoy the challenge. After all, I'm a teacher, I should like learning."

"Or you could just embrace the fact that you're a nerd."

"I'd like to think I'm setting a good example for my daughter."

"That's true," I admitted. "Isn't it hard being away from her so much?"

"Yeah, there are times when I feel like I'm missing too much, but taking those courses are important to me. And besides, it's only two nights a week. I'm with her the other evenings, every morning, during all the breaks I have in the school year, and every time she wakes up in the middle of the night," he said with a grin.

The waitress came back around the table. "Are you two interested in any dessert?"

I nodded vigorously, looking over the dessert menu.

"That'll be a yes," Logan said, amusement in his voice.

After we had placed our order and the waitress had left, I asked, "So, how did you get full custody of Madison?"

"Technically, it's not full custody. Brooke and I have always tried to keep it out of the courts and just work it out between ourselves. Originally we tried to do fifty-fifty: a week on and a week off. It started off okay, but it was really getting to Madison. She was irritable, cried all the time. It was miserable. Then last year when Brooke started going back to school, Madison was with me all week by default. The change has been for the better."

"That's a lot on you though."

"It was at first, but now I love it. I wouldn't know what to do if the arrangement were suddenly reversed."

"It must be rough for Brooke to not see her daughter that much. I know Madison takes it pretty hard sometimes."

Anguish flickered across Logan's face and he rubbed the back of his neck. "I know," he said quietly. "To be honest, Brooke always had a harder time with parenting than I did, for whatever reason."

"Maybe she wasn't ready."

"That probably has a lot to do with it, but I wish it didn't hurt Maddie so much."

Now it was my turn to comfort him, and I didn't hesitate. I reached both of my hands out to his and took them in mine. "You are a great father. And I'm not just saying that. When I see you with her, it makes me believe that having a family of my own is a possibility again. That's how good you are."

I hadn't meant for things to get so heavy, but when I looked at Logan, his eyes were glistening.

He cleared his throat, "You don't know how much it

means to hear you say that."

I smiled at him. "Well, it's true."

"That's what you really want? To be a mother?"

I nodded. "More than anything."

"What else do you want, Skylar?"

Because that wasn't a loaded question or anything.

I thought for a moment. "At first, all I wanted was Michael. Then it was vengeance. Now I think I'd just like to feel okay again. Not just in small snippets but really, truly okay. Happy."

I continued, "I've always wanted my own family. So I think I want to love again and to be loved. And I'd like to know how to do all those things without feeling all mixed up inside."

He smiled at me over the table. "You'll get there. If those are the things you really want, you'll get them. It just might take some time."

"Time. That's what everyone keeps saying."

"Hey, look at how far you've come just in the past few months. Eight months ago, you wouldn't have been able to sit across from me at a restaurant and hold a conversation. Now look at you. You're the strongest person I know, Sky. You've got to give yourself some credit."

Before I could respond, our waitress set down the dessert in front of us.

"Here you go, white-chocolate macadamia torte and two forks."

"Thanks," we said at the same time.

We picked up our forks and took a bite, easing the intensity of the conversation. But I didn't forget the words Logan spoke, the way they made me feel full and open.

Logan made me start to believe in myself again, and I was filled with such gratitude and admiration for him.

"Good call on the torte," I said with my mouth full of chocolate. "It's delicious."

He laughed, taking another spoonful. "I told you so."

When we had finished off the torte and the wine, Logan paid the check despite my protests. "This is a date, Skylar," Logan said. "I asked you out. That means I pay."

"Thank you," I smiled, as we put on our coats and ventured into the night.

When we got to the theater a few minutes later, there were only a few stragglers outside—smokers and a man talking on his cellphone.

The Michigan Theater was one of those old grand theaters that lit up like Hollywood in the 1920s, round light bulbs outlining the sign and marquee.

We stood in the golden light and looked at the marquee. The only movie playing, some Sundance film I had never heard of before, had started an hour ago.

"I guess I should've checked the show time beforehand," Logan said, sounding crestfallen.

"It's okay," I said cheerfully.

He looked at me like he wasn't ready for the night to be over yet. I could see the gears turning in his head, thinking of a way to prolong the night.

"I have an idea," I said mischievously.

His face brightened, and a slow smile spread across his face.

Pinball Pete's was slow for a Saturday night; there were only five other people there. All of them were college-aged guys in jeans and hoodies, who eyed us suspiciously when we walked in. It was apparent from the scowls on their faces that they didn't trust 1) outsiders, 2) skin care products, 3) any T-shirt that didn't have an ironic/funny/scientific or mathematical saying on it, 4) girls, 5) girls wearing dresses and heels, 6) guys who dated girls wearing dresses and heels, and 7) anyone besides themselves being in an arcade on a Saturday night.

Logan and I eyed them back as if expecting them to suddenly jump up, surround us, and then bully us out of their clubroom.

We turned away from them, stifling laughter, and walked toward the change machine. The room smelled like old carpet and was filled with the noises and lights coming from the arcade games, which were bright and raucous, clashing with each other.

"Takes you back, doesn't it?" Logan said nostalgically, looking around.

"I feel like I'm an undergrad all over again," I agreed, thinking back to the hours spent at the Pinball Pete's in East Lansing.

"So what first?" he asked, collecting the coins from

the machine, handing me half of them.

"Pac-Man?" I challenged.

"Pac-Man," he agreed.

We walked over to the game consul, each of us taking a seat on the worn leather stools and hooking our feet through the metal frames.

As Logan turned to insert the coins in the orange plastic slot, I grabbed the red plastic joystick, mentally preparing to kick his ass.

"Okay, let's make this interesting," I said. "Loser has to pay for drinks next time we go out."

"How about for the entire next month?" Logan countered.

"Someone's feeling quite confident about his gaming abilities tonight."

"Not just gaming abilities," he joked.

"Oh, wow. You're on, Parks."

"Oh Skylar," Logan said to me. "You have no idea what you just started."

I loved this fun, lighthearted side of Logan. And knowing that he was opening up and being this way with me, made my skin feel pleasantly tingly, like feathers caressing all over.

The game started and for the next half an hour, I dominated, concentrating furiously. But in the end Logan won, and I very ungraciously accepted defeat.

"Oh, whatever," I said, throwing my hands up and walking away. "Stupid game," I mumbled under my breath.

Logan hurried to catch up with me, trying to hide his satisfaction from winning.

"I know you're laughing at me!" I said, wheeling around to face him.

He stopped suddenly, not daring to come any closer. "I'm not! Honest!" he said as a small laugh escaped his lips.

I turned to start walking away, but he grabbed my wrist before I could move any farther. "Okay, I know what will make you feel better," he said.

"What?" I asked defiantly.

"How about we go kill some zombies?" he said, nodding to the game down the row with the two machine guns holstered in the front.

I thought for a moment, my anger subsiding. "Okay," I said grinning.

In the car, with Ann Arbor behind us, we settled in. Logan adjusted the heat and I looked out the window. I recounted the night and how we held hands on the walk back to the car. Even now, I couldn't keep the smile off my face.

"Thank you," I said into the car.

"For what?"

"For making this easy."

He didn't say anything, just stole a quick glance in my direction before returning his eyes to the highway.

"You make it so that I don't have to try so hard. I can just be me," I said, the words coming out of my mouth before I even had time to think about them. There was something about being around Logan that made it easier for me not to have to think or feel so much. Well, I did *feel* things, just not as many sad things. "But you make me want to be better."

I wanted to be better. For him. Because of him.

He was quiet for a second. "I don't ever want you to feel like you have to be something you're not. If you're sad, be sad. If you're happy, be happy. If you don't want to talk, don't talk. If you want to talk, I'll listen.

"Besides, I happen to like dark and mysterious things."

He grinned over at me, passing headlights sweeping over his features. I smirked in return.

"You do have a thing for troubled women with destructive tendencies," I teased.

"Just one of my many vices," he conceded.

"Everyone has their demons," I said, quoting Samara.

I stared out the window, gathering the nerve to ask him the question that had been on my mind for the past few weeks. Afraid to face him, afraid to know his answer, but needing to know. "Earlier, at dinner, you said that you were here for me as a friend, or more, if that's what I wanted. But what do you want?"

He was quiet, and in the reflection on the window I could see the green glow of the clock faintly illuminating the inside of the car. "I want you," he said simply.

Then quietly, "I know you might not be ready, but I am. And I'll wait for you. You know you can trust me, right?"

I nodded slowly. My face flushed with heat, and I felt a feverish wave sweep over me. The car suddenly felt small and confining, like it was suffocating me. I fought the urge to push my hands out in front of me to stop the walls from closing in.

I closed my eyes and leaned my head against the window, letting the cold glass cool my skin. I willed away the claustrophobia and cleared my throat.

"I know," I said thickly. "I always have."

He reached over, taking my hand and squeezing it.

"I'm scared though," I said, still not looking at him, but all too aware of his presence in the car.

"I know. I am too," he admitted.

The music played quietly in the background as he moved his thumb back and forth over mine.

"There's something else I want you to know," he said.

"What's that?" I asked, turning my head toward him and resting it on the seat.

"I love how much you love my daughter," he said, his voice dropping low. "If nothing else comes out of this, you need to know how grateful I am for that."

I couldn't argue with him there. I did love that little girl. But before I could respond, he went on, "When I first asked you to watch her, I never imagined … I mean, it was nice being able to see you more often. In some way, it was kind of like having Mike around again."

He shook his head. "And now…the way you are with

her, the way you are with me. I just didn't think that there was someone out there who could blend so well with us, you know? Someone who wasn't afraid of the responsibilities I have as a dad, or being around a three-year-old, or dealing with Brooke."

My heart shifted, the broken bits began to reassemble into something whole. "Logan, for being one of the smartest people I know, you can be really stupid. Anyone would be lucky to have you and Maddie in their lives. I'm the lucky one here."

"But I come with a lot of baggage," he insisted. "Who wants to be caught up in that when this is the time in life when we should just be setting out with a clean slate and finding our place in the world?"

"Everybody has baggage. I don't even know if there is such a thing as a clean slate anymore. And you want to talk about baggage, look at me," I said, gesturing to myself. "You may have a kid and a semi-crazy ex, but I have a dead fiancé and a criminal record. Sorry, but I think I got you beat."

He smiled that sad smile at me, his lips pulling up on one side.

I shrugged. "That's what makes us who we are."

XIX

Interrupted

It was almost eleven when we pulled into my driveway. We had prolonged the night as much as possible, and yet I could feel with certainty that neither one of us was ready for the night to be over.

"I'll walk you to your door," Logan offered.

I nodded, climbing out from the car and pushing down my nerves, my fears, and my thoughts. The heels of my boots clicked on the pavement and Scout started to bark from the front window. I pulled open the screen door and turned to face Logan. We stood there staring at each other for a moment, wanting to say goodnight, wanting to feel each other.

But Scout apparently had other plans for us because he kept barking.

Disappointment crossed over Logan's face as he

pressed his lips together tightly.

"Come in?" I asked. I could feel my body start to shake and my heart race.

"Sure," he nodded, relief washing over him.

I opened the front door and we stumbled into the darkness. Scout ran to greet us, wagging his tail and jumping up in excitement.

"I need to put him outside. Hold on," I said to Logan, pulling off my boots.

After Scout ran past me and into the yard, I shut the door, but held on to the knob, facing away from Logan. I took a deep breath and closed my eyes.

"Sky?" Logan called softly.

"Hmm?" I responded, turning around to face him. The kitchen lights were off, but some ambient light came through the windows and made the kitchen a game of shadows. I could make out Logan standing against the doorway.

"Everything all right?"

I nodded, seeming unable to find words.

"Come here," he whispered.

Those blue-gray eyes held steady on mine as I walked slowly across the floor to him. I stood in front of him, not a foot away. The energy between us was palpable.

"Can I kiss you?" he asked, his voice deep.

I nodded, leaning into him, my hands going around his trim waist.

He pulled my face closer to his and kissed me. Again

starting off softly and gently, then building, his hands going from my neck to entwine in my hair. My hands trailing up and down his back. I pushed off his jacket, and following my lead, he shrugged my coat off.

Logan's hands explored my back. His fingers felt fiery against the knit of my dress, the only thing separating skin from skin. I pulled him closer to me, cherishing this closeness, this physicalness.

He pulled away from me slowly. His forehead against mine, he closed his eyes and breathed in deeply, trying to slow down his rapidly beating heart. Then his hands were on my face again, gently, and he kissed my lips in a series of small pecks.

"I'm not sure what's supposed to happen from here," he admitted breathily.

"Follow me," I said, grabbing his wrist and leading him upstairs, ignoring the voice in my head telling me this was a bad idea, ignoring the pictures of Michael and me on the walls.

I was an adult. I could do whatever I wanted with whomever I wanted to do it with. So why didn't it feel that way? I shoved the feelings down.

When we got to the bedroom, I turned to face him and wrapped my arms around his neck, burying my face in the space between his chin and chest. I pulled him closer to me and started kissing his neck. We stumbled closer to the bed.

Logan lowered me onto the bed gently, his arms

around my lower back so that I didn't feel the fall. He noticed the piles of clothes on and around the bed. He laughed into my lips, "Have a hard time figuring out what to wear?"

I pulled back and turned my head to look at the mess. "You could say that," I sighed, embarrassed.

He started kissing my neck softly, moving up and down and around my throat to my jawline. "Well," he said in between kisses. "You look good in anything that you wear, but this dress you're wearing right now...," he trailed off. His hands climbed my thighs. I shivered. It felt so amazingly good to have someone touch me and kiss me again after so long.

I tugged Logan's thick sweater over his head along with the T-shirt he wore underneath it.

I pulled Logan on top of me, running my fingers down his arms. His skin was solid against me as he started kissing my neck again.

"I wish you could see yourself the way I see you," he said softly.

"How's that?"

"Beautiful. Passionate," he kissed my lips, "incredibly brave." He inched back and when he looked into my eyes, I swear I could've lost myself in them.

His voice was husky. "Fearless in how you love," he said, trailing his fingers down the side of my face. "Completely captivating."

His voice was filled with such adoration I could

barely handle it.

"Logan," I sighed, feeling hazy and caught up. I held on to his arms to anchor me.

Holding my head in his hands, he kissed me fiercely, and his body shook from the force of it.

I kissed him back and moved my body against his. I felt myself opening up to Logan, wanting more and more of him with every kiss and every touch. But there, at the back of my mind, was Michael.

The black hole that had consumed me after he died no longer had a hold on me. I still missed him so much and thought about him often. *He's gone. He isn't here anymore*, I had to keep reminding myself.

Logan made me happy. He made me feel hopeful again. He made me feel like I deserved to be loved again. He made me want to believe in things again.

I didn't want to think anymore. I just wanted to feel Logan's touch, the pressure of his weight on top of me. But I couldn't stop thinking that maybe this was happening too soon. That this wasn't the time or place.

But I wanted him so badly. I just wanted to feel him, to feel good. I wanted to make him feel good too.

As the ever-waging war raged inside my head, my body moved beneath Logan's as his tongue met with mine.

It had been so long....

Logan shivered again as I ran my hands down his back to his waistband. I ran the tips of my fingers over the elastic of his boxers.

Logan kissed my neck, down to the crevice between my breasts and moved his hands to cup them.

That's when I heard the alarms going off in my head. I needed to stop this *now*. I wanted to do this, just not yet. Not now.

Logan trailed kisses back up my neck.

"Logan," I said shakily, my hands trembling as I pushed them against his chest.

"Hmm?" He continued working around toward my lips.

"I can't," I whispered. "I can't do this."

He froze over me and pulled back. When his eyes met mine, they were cloudy with desire and longing.

"I'm sorry," I said, my voice twisted with anguish and frustration.

"No," he closed his eyes and shook his head. "It's okay. It's fine. You have nothing to be sorry for."

He leaned over me and pressed his lips to my forehead. "Are you okay?"

No, I wasn't, but I wasn't about to tell him that.

Suddenly, I felt something vibrating against my leg. It took me a second to realize it was Logan's phone going off.

He groaned and pushed himself back onto his knees. He dug his phone out of his front pocket and answered the phone gruffly.

"Brooke."

I couldn't hear what she was saying, but I could make out that she was talking very fast. After a few seconds,

Logan's expression changed from irritation to concern.

"What's her temperature?"

I couldn't make out Brooke's response. I sat up on the bed, pulling my dress back into place.

Logan proceeded to ask a series of rapid-fire questions: "How does she look? Has she eaten anything or had anything to drink? How long ago did you give her medicine? Is she uncomfortable?"

Logan was quiet as he listened to Brooke's responses. His eyes met mine and stayed there, held me there. I couldn't have looked away if I wanted to.

My head was foggy from the heat and confusion of the previous moment and my current concern for Maddie. I felt stuck, drugged even, like everything was moving in slow motion and I couldn't get a grip on it.

"Yeah, I agree. Let's take her in. I'll meet you there. I'm leaving now. Bye."

There was a question on my lips, but he beat me to it.

"Maddie has a fever, and the medicine doesn't seem to be helping. I'm going to meet them at the hospital." I couldn't read the look on his face. I could see concern in the way his eyebrows knit together, but his body was stiff as he pulled on his T-shirt and sweater.

I sat on the edge of the bed watching him dress. When he looked back up to me, there was hesitation in his eyes. He bent forward and kissed me gently on the lips.

"I'm sorry. I have to go."

"Don't be. You need to go be with her."

He sighed and turned to walk away. When he was at the door, I said, "I had a great time tonight."

He smiled over his shoulder. "Me too."

"Let me know how she's doing?" I asked.

"Yeah." And then he was out the door.

Words could not describe the relief that rushed over me in that instant. Followed by guilt at feeling relief. Followed by guilt that I had almost had sex with Logan. Followed by anger that I felt guilty. Relief. Guilt. Anger. Then sadness.

Sadness that Logan was gone, that he wasn't Michael, that this is what my life had become.

Fuck, I thought, as I pulled my legs into my chest and curled into a ball. It wasn't long until my pillow was wet from tears. My heart was aching for everything lost and everything gained.

Outside, Scout barked into the night.

XX

Home

The next day, after waking late, I loaded up Scout and headed over to Dad's house for the afternoon.

"What's for lunch?" I asked, pushing open the front door.

"Well hello to you too," Dad yelled from the kitchen. He was standing at the stove stirring a giant pot, in jeans and a worn plaid flannel shirt.

"Oh my goodness. You made chili!" I exclaimed, walking over to him and embracing him.

"I did. It's football Sunday, it's cold out, and my favorite daughter is coming over to visit. I had to make something special."

"Dad, I'm your only daughter."

"That we know of…," he joked.

"Dad!" I said, hitting his arm.

He laughed. "So how's it going? What's new?"

He looked over at me expectantly, not realizing what a loaded question that was. I hadn't talked to him since before Halloween. He knew I had been spending a lot of time with Logan and Maddie, but I hadn't told him about our date last night or how much things had changed between Logan and me.

I sat down at the table, taking off my coat and setting my phone down. I breathed in the smell of the cooking chili, slightly burnt coffee, and wood paneling.

"Oh, you know…," I trailed off.

"No, not really," he said, sitting across from me at the table.

When I didn't offer any conversation, he asked me, "How's work?"

"Boring. I'm dying to get my position back. I swear if I have to answer one more question about filing for restraining orders, I'm going to leap over the desk and restrain them myself."

Dad chuckled. "How's—?"

He was cut off by the sound of my phone vibrating on the table between us.

Logan's name came up on the screen and I quickly grabbed it, pretending my dad didn't see who it was, knowing that he had.

"I've got to take this," I said, heading into the living room.

"Sure," I heard my dad say. I ignored the amusement

in his voice.

"Hello?" I asked shakily.

"Hey, Sky," I heard Logan on the other side of the line.

I was so happy to hear from him, yet I felt the wall coming back up. How was it possible to go from being so comfortable with someone to feeling like you're on opposite sides of the planet in less than twenty-four hours?

"Hi," I said cautiously.

"How are you?" he asked.

"I'm fine. How's Maddie?"

"She's doing okay now. Resting all day, drinking lots of fluids." He was talking quietly and slowly as if he had just woken up.

"How late did you have to stay at the hospital last night?"

"Well I got there about midnight, and we didn't leave until about four this morning."

"You must be exhausted."

"You have no idea. But at least she's feeling better."

"Her fever is going down?" I asked.

"Yeah, she's still on medicine, but it seems to be controlling it now. She's lying on her little pullout sofa now watching *Scooby-Doo*."

"Of course," I interjected, laughing softly despite myself.

He continued, "She's with me today so Brooke can work and take tomorrow off. That way I don't have to miss work."

"Oh. Okay," I said, nodding even though he couldn't see me.

Logan sighed. "Listen, Sky. About last night.... I'm sorry."

"You don't have to apologize," I said hurriedly.

"But I want to. Can you—can you come over so we can talk? Face-to-face?" he asked.

"I can't right now. I'm at my dad's."

"Oh," he said, sounding disheartened. "Maybe later then?"

"Maybe," I said, my stomach twisting into knots.

It was quiet on his end.

"And Logan?"

"Hmm?"

"You should get some rest."

"I'm heading over to the couch as we speak."

"Good. I'll talk to you later, okay?"

"Yup," he said, stifling a yawn. "Bye."

"Bye," I said, after I had already hung up the phone.

I walked back into the kitchen. "Everything all right?" Dad asked.

"Madison had a fever last night and they had to take her to the hospital. But she's doing better now."

"Good, good," he said, setting down a cup of coffee in front of me with the milk and sugar. "Now, where were we?"

"Oh you know, you were just interrogating me. The usual." I stirred some sugar and milk into my coffee.

"Oh, yes. That's right. So how is that all going? Watching Madison?"

"It's going surprisingly well," I paused, waiting for him to react. "I know, I know. Hold on to your hats, boys, I've managed not to endanger Maddie or myself, and I actually like spending time with her. Who would've thought, right?"

"I don't know," he shrugged, smiling. "I would have."

"Oh, stop with the "old wise man" routine," I snapped back playfully.

"Shh," he said, closing his eyes and placing his hands on his temples. "My ancestors are trying to tell me something…," he trailed off mysteriously.

"They are not!" I said, searching the table for something to throw at him—a banana or an old piece of mail, anything—but came up empty-handed. "You're being ridiculous."

"I'm the ridiculous one? You're the one not telling me something." He narrowed his eyes at me.

"I—I don't know what you're talking about," I stammered.

His gaze pierced me, taking away any resolve or hope of privacy I had left.

"I had a date with Logan last night," I mumbled under my breath.

"What was that now?" he said, leaning closer, cupping his hand around his ear.

"I had a date with Logan last night," I said louder this time.

"Ah," he said leaning back in his chair. Not the least bit shocked or surprised.

"Wait, you knew?" I asked, incredulous.

"A father always knows," he intoned meaningfully.

"Oh, I'm sure you do. Who told you?"

He shrugged noncommittally.

I narrowed my eyes at him. "Dad," I threatened.

"Fine, all right," he said, throwing up his hands and forgetting his charade. "Sue."

"Sue?" I asked confused. "Wh—what? How did she know?"

"Logan."

I was in such complete disbelief that I couldn't speak. How had this happened?

"He called her to ask her how she felt about him taking you out on a date."

"Did he take an ad out in the newspaper too? Maybe rent an airplane to write it in the sky?" Anger rose up inside of me. *How could he do this to me? Why would he do this to me?* I wasn't ready for everybody to know about us yet. That would make it real, and I wasn't ready to confront what that would mean. Not yet.

"Don't be mad, Skylar."

"It's a little late for that."

The Charm Necklace

"Always so fiery. I swear, you would've given your mother a run for her money."

"Don't bring mom into this," I snapped.

He took his time, taking a sip of coffee and breathing in deeply. "Skylar, honey. Listen. He called her the other day. Thursday, I think she said, after Halloween. He said you two had been spending a lot of time together because of Madison, and he thought he was starting to have feelings for you. And maybe you, for him, so he wanted to ask the Amherst's if it was okay with them if he pursued this—you," he clarified, keeping his tone pliable and warm. I suppose he was doing it on purpose to calm me down, soothe me. It was working, damn it.

"Why did she call you about it though?"

"She wanted to know if I knew anything about it. Which I didn't, obviously," he said, giving me a look. "And I think she just wanted to talk to somebody else about it."

I felt the anger give way to panic and uncertainty.

"So they know?" I asked. "And you know."

He nodded.

An odd, hot sensation filled me. Shame. "They must be so mad at me! They must hate me." I buried my face in my arms on top of the table.

"No, no, honey. Not at all," Dad said, coming around the table to kneel next to me, rubbing my back.

I sniffled into my arm. "Yes, they do," I protested, sounding like a child. "They hate me, and I'm a horrible human being."

"Skylar," he lowered his voice, letting me know I needed to listen to him seriously. "Sue called me after she talked to Logan. And she was so happy for you two. She couldn't stop going on about how wonderful it was. With Michael gone she couldn't think of anyone better for you than Logan."

This shocked me enough that I lifted my head from the sanctuary of my arms. "She what?"

"She was happy for you two. She told me how Logan asked her if it was okay with them if you two gave this a chance. And she told him that he was a fool if he didn't try. She wants you two to be happy. She wants you both to move on."

"But what about Michael?"

"What about him?"

I shrugged. "I don't know. Isn't she worried that if I start seeing someone else that I'll forget him or something?"

He smiled at me. "Honey, I think he's kind of hard to forget. You'll always have him in your heart. Logan will too. And she knows that. I think that's why she isn't upset about you and Logan. Together, you two will always remember Michael. And in a way, she won't lose him."

"That doesn't make any sense to me."

"It never does," he said, shaking his head and sighing.

"So she, what? She gave him their blessing? Rob feels the same way?"

"Yes, he does. And you don't need their blessing, but yes, they're okay with it."

"Why are they all such good people?" I rubbed my hands over my face, my eyes. "It's annoying."

He laughed, going back to his chair.

I took the coffee cup in my hand and sipped. We sat there for a minute, quietly. *How could Sue and Rob be okay with this? Why did it seem like I was the only one having such a hard time moving on?*

"So you've been spending a lot of time with Logan lately," Dad commented.

"Yeah. Most of it with Maddie, though."

"But still…."

I looked at him. "But still what?"

"You like spending time with him." It was a statement, not a question.

I nodded.

"And how did last night go?"

I smiled, not able to contain it. "Pretty well." All things considered. "Logan has this way of making me feel like I'm my own person again," I said, filling him in on the PG details of my date.

"You deserve it," Dad said. "It takes a lot of strength to move on and rebuild. Finding someone you could potentially, really love shows that you're healing.

"And I'm proud of you," he said. "To even let someone new in to your life—you have a lot more courage than I ever did."

"I don't know," I shrugged, not feeling anything but cowardice. "I just feel like, when Michael died, I was holding on to him as hard as I could. I didn't want to lose him. Didn't want to let go. But now with things with Logan, I feel like that grip is getting looser and looser."

"And you feel guilty about that?"

"Incredibly. I feel like I need Michael's permission or something."

"Don't you think he's already given it to you?"

"How do you figure that?" I asked.

"It's simple, really. He loved you. You knew that, we all knew that. And more than anything else, Michael would want you to be happy. And if Logan makes you happy, I think Michael would want you to be with Logan."

"Isn't it weird that Logan was his best friend? I mean what is this, *Pearl Harbor*?"

"Oh, dear God, Skylar," he shook his head at me. "Are you still mad at Logan?"

"I want to be."

"You know he was only trying to do what was right."

"Yeah, yeah. I know."

"Now how about some chili? The game's about to begin."

As we sat there eating with the game on, I couldn't stop thinking about last night, the last few months, and Sue knowing about Logan and me. I didn't know if I should feel angry or relieved that Sue knew. I didn't know if I should feel happy or sad about Logan. I just didn't know.

"Skylar," I heard Dad saying from a distance. "Sky."

My eyes fluttered open. I had fallen asleep on the couch during the game, and now it was dark outside. I sat up slowly my head spinning. I felt terribly disoriented.

"What time is it?" I said groggily.

"Almost eight."

"Oh, shit." I rubbed my eyes, stood up and stretched. "How long was I asleep?"

"About three hours."

"I didn't even realize I was that tired," I said walking into the kitchen, pulling on my boots. "I've got to go. Sorry I passed out on you," I said, walking over to him.

"No worries. I'm just glad you came over," he said hugging me tightly. "See you soon?"

"Yup."

"And you know there's that invention called the telephone. Use it more often and call me, would ya?"

"Yeah, yeah," I said opening up the door. "You know, Dad, if you're so desperate for gossip about my love life, maybe you should get one of your own."

"Now that's a funny one, Skylar. Really. Cracking up over here," he said dryly.

"Bye!" I said, shutting the door and ushering Scout into the car.

It took twenty minutes to get to Logan's house. I had completely forgotten to call him. I parked in front of his apartment, stared at his front door, and debated what to do. If Madison had fallen asleep in the living room, would a knock wake her up? Should I call or just go up to the door?

Anxiety was creeping in at the thought of seeing Logan's face. *Why was I so nervous?*

I picked up the phone and hit Logan's number. It rang several times before he picked up. "Hey," he said quietly.

"Hey, sorry it's so late in the day. I fell asleep at my dad's house."

"Seems like it's one of those days. You still there?"

"I'm outside," I said.

"You are?" he asked, surprised. I saw the curtains in his window part as he looked out. "You are."

"I am."

"Do you want to come in?"

"I have the dog with me."

"That hasn't seemed to stop you yet," he teased.

"Okay, we'll be right in."

When I walked in, I saw Logan at the end of the hallway, shutting Maddie's door. He came down the hallway in gray sweatpants, his hair rumpled and flat on one side from sleeping on it.

I was not used to seeing Logan dressed so casually. There was something about it that gave him a certain vulnerability, like I just wanted to lie on the couch, curl up next to him, and make him feel secure, pour what strength I had into him.

Before I had been nervous to see him, to have this

conversation. Now all I wanted to do was run over to him and fold myself against him, feel his arms around me as he held me tight. He grinned at me. "We've been sleeping all day, but Maddie just took some more medicine, so I think she'll be out for the night."

I was still standing by the front door and Logan stopped next to the couch. "Are you going to come in?" he asked, turning on the lamp before sitting down. Scout had already trampled down the hallway to lie down outside of Madison's door.

"Yeah, sorry," I said, coming over to sit on the ottoman across from the couch.

We sat there for a moment, staring at each other, my resolve disappearing with every second. But no, we needed to talk. He's the one who wanted to talk, but now he wasn't the only one with something to say.

"What did you want to—," I started.

At the same time, Logan began, "I'm sorry again about—."

We both stopped awkwardly.

"Go ahead," I said.

"I just wanted to apologize for pushing you too far last night. And I guess I just wanted to explain why I didn't ask you to come with me to the hospital," he said, running his fingers through his hair.

"Logan, you don't have to."

"Yes, I do. Last night was something special to me. And I wanted you to come with me, but I didn't want to confuse Madison or get into it with Brooke. I didn't want anyone to ruin the night for me. I just wanted to keep it hidden, and *ours*, for just a little while longer."

"But you told Sue," I accused, my anger flaring again, reacting violently with the excitement of hearing him say exactly what I wanted to hear.

Confusion crossed his face before realization dawned. "How did you...," he started to say before he was cut off by the betrayed look on my face. "Sky," he said reaching out to touch my hand, but I jerked back.

"Why didn't you tell me?" I asked, my fists clenching involuntarily. "Or ask me if I thought it was a good idea to tell them?"

His voice went up reactively to mine. "Because I didn't know how either one of you were going to react. I didn't want you to feel pressured or guilty. And I didn't want them to feel like they had to give their blessing. I didn't know what else to do. I felt like they had the right to know. They're like parents to me, Sky. I didn't want them to find out any other way."

I took a deep breath. "I know," I said, my voice cracking. "I just wasn't expecting everyone to know yet."

I looked away from him, directing my gaze to the corner of the room, trying to hold back my tears. This was all becoming too real, too confusing. But then I heard him say my name, and I couldn't help but meet his eyes. When I looked at Logan, saw the concern and love on his face, the rubber band inside me snapped and a tear fell slowly down my face. I moved my hand to quickly wipe it away, but another one was already following.

Goddamn it, not again, I thought. *This is the second time in less than twenty-four hours.*

"Come here," he said, reaching forward and pulling the ottoman closer to him so that my legs were squeezed between his. And then he leaned forward, gently holding my face with both of his hands as he wiped away the tears.

"I'm tired of this being so hard," I mumbled through sniffles.

"I know, I know," he moved his thumbs over my cheeks.

I whispered, "Logan, I wasn't ready for what almost happened last night."

"That's okay," he smiled, sliding his hands from my face to my hips, leaning his forehead against mine. "We'll take our time."

And in that moment, I felt so incredibly weak. I felt soft and exposed and stretched thin. But I felt Logan next to me and I knew I was protected, guarded. Nothing would hurt me. He wouldn't let it.

He was strong and gentle and he understood.

I wanted to draw from him, let him make me better. I moved my lips to his, my hands to his face. And he kissed me back, drawing me forward onto his lap, our chests pressed tightly against each other.

We kissed. It was the kind of kiss that was desperate and searching and raw and comforting. It was the kind of kiss that wouldn't go any further than that. Just being there with him—my lips on his, my body against his—was enough.

XXI

It will destroy you

I peeked my head into Harry's office. "You wanted to see me?"

"Yeah, come in. Sit down," he said without looking up from the document in front of him. Then he signed the paper quickly and efficiently.

I sat on the edge of my seat and worked my thumbs together in my lap. I looked around the office with awards and newspaper articles hanging on the walls—"Oakland County Homicide Solve Rate at All-time High," "Special Investigations Unit Better Than Ever," "Harry Fields New Police Captain at SIU."

Finally Harry looked up at me. He was thinner and looked more refreshed than I had ever seen him. The color in his face looked healthy, and the lines in his forehead weren't as deep.

"Have you taken up yoga or something?" I asked curiously.

"Me? Yoga?" he started laughing. "No."

"Well whatever you're doing differently, it's working."

"What are you talking about?"

"You look good," I said seriously. Then, changing my tone, "Wait—did you dye your hair? Maybe get some Botox? There's no shame in admitting you've had a little work done."

"And here I thought you were trying to butter me up."

"For what?"

He placed his thick elbows on the desk and looked at me earnestly. "Well that's what I wanted to talk to you about," he paused. "Getting your position back."

"Are you serious?" I asked, my voice going up an octave and a smile breaking across my face.

"Yes, but," he said, drawing it out.

Of course, there was always a *but*.

"Getting your position back is conditional."

"On what?"

"The *successful* completion of your anger management course."

My smile fell. "What do you mean by successful? I've gone to every class."

"What I mean is … in three more weeks I'm going to get a report from your counselor indicating your improvement. He may say you're ready to return to your position, or he may recommend that you need more personalized care."

"Personalized care?" I repeated, clutching the bottom of the seat. "Getting my position back is dependent on David Kennah's opinion?"

"Not entirely. I have the final say."

I took several deep breaths, channeling my frustration into determination. I would do whatever I had to do to get my job back. "Okay," I said quietly. "I understand."

Harry watched me for a long moment, studying my face. "Medina, between you and me, I want you back. Quite honestly I need you back on this side of the ropes. But more important than what I want or you getting your job back is *you*. You owe it to yourself to get healthy. All right?"

"Yes, sir." I nodded.

"Go make me proud," he said, turning to his computer. "And do you mind grabbing me a coffee before you go back to the front lines?"

"Sure thing, Harry," I said, shaking my head at him.

Samara was moving in Saturday afternoon, and I had every intention of getting through group without a lot of excitement.

David, however, had other plans.

It started with the icebreaker. This week we had to name our favorite thing about ourselves.

"I want to say something lame like my hair or my dry sense of humor, but I know David will just make me go again," I mocked lightheartedly when it was my turn. "So I guess it would be my loyalty to the people I love." Wondering even as I said it, if it was true. I'd always been loyal to my Dad, my friends, and Michael while he was alive. Was I being disloyal now by moving on? Where was the line between honorable and dishonorable?

"What about your ability to persevere?" David asked, leaning forward in his chair.

"I don't know if that's what I would call it," I said, meeting his pale blue eyes.

"What do you mean?" he asked, rubbing his hand over his permanent five o'clock shadow.

"Just because I'm still going doesn't mean that I'm truly living," I said with a shrug. "Sometimes it feels like I'm just existing."

"Only sometimes?"

"I guess."

"Hmm," he said, nodding his head. "Well, Skylar, thanks for sharing."

The real kick to the gut came when David started this week's lesson.

"Relationships suffer the most from our anger," David said. "Who is it worth controlling your anger for?

Your family? Friends? Co-workers? Yourself?"

I breathed in deeply as my hands started to shake. I *so* did not want to deal with this right now.

I tried to listen as we went around the circle, but I kept getting distracted by my thoughts. *Who was worth controlling my anger for?*

I knew that my actions and outbursts had affected other people. I knew my anger had consequences, but I had always been willing to pay the price. But what about the people caught in the crosshairs? Why should they have to pay? I hadn't been able to see until that moment how much my anger had cost others.

My dad—watching his only daughter destroy herself, her home, her integrity. Worrying about me, getting the call from jail and having to pick me up, watching as I dealt with the repercussions of pleading guilty to a misdemeanor.

Sue, Rob, and Sophie—pushed out of my life, not allowed to share their grief with the one person who understood it most. Hearing from everyone else but me about what was going on in my life: the issues with the house, the assault on Tony Cusato's car, dating Logan. The cold distance I had put between them since Michael's death because of my inability to think about anyone other than myself.

Harry and the detectives—losing my input in terms of research and assistance and costing them countless hours of additional work, slowing down progress, and jamming up solve rates.

And those were just the front liners.

To me, the anger had always been worth the small amount of pain I inflicted if it kept me connected to Michael.

But what if the price was starting to become too much? What if I couldn't afford it any longer? What if my anger cost me my time with Maddie? My job? My relationship with my dad? What if it cost me Logan?

What if it cost me love? Was it still worth it then?

My vision blurred. I felt the weight of a thousand bricks on my chest and I couldn't breathe.

I couldn't let that happen.

I wouldn't.

Breathe in, one…two…three…four. Breathe out, one…two…three…four. "Everything little thing gonna be all right," I sang in my head.

I was still working through my thoughts when it was my turn to share. "My, umm, my dad," I said. "I don't think he needs to get another phone call from me in a holding cell."

Everyone nodded, but I saw Samara studying me. Her expression was serious and unyielding; her eyes, discerning. I clenched my fists and looked away from her.

Fuck. I just couldn't deal with this right now. It was all too much.

After group ended, David asked me if I could stay after for a minute.

"I'll wait for you outside," Samara said. "I need a smoke."

Everyone else filed out of the room. I had no idea what David wanted to talk to me about, and I really didn't care. I just wanted to get out of there. My head already felt heavy from the weight of all my thoughts and anxieties.

"Why don't you take a seat?" he asked, and when he saw my hesitation, "It will only take a minute."

I sat back down on the edge of the couch and looked at him coolly. He studied me, his eyes boring into mine unapologetically. I already felt like he had sucker-punched me several times today, might as well go for the knockout.

Finally David cleared his throat, and I braced myself. "We haven't heard much from you these past few weeks, and I just wanted to touch base with you. How are things?" He folded his hands on the table in front of us.

"Fine."

He nodded slowly. "I understand Samara is your new roommate?"

"That's right. She's moving in today."

He smiled. "I think that's wonderful, the friendship you two have forged," he said, locking his fingers together. "It's been insightful and inspiring. A counselor can only hope that his clients maintain strong ties to comrades after they complete their therapy. It's important to have people around you who understand."

"Absolutely." *Can we get to the chase already? Holy hell, man.*

"From where I stand, or sit," he joked, "you seem to

have made some progress throughout the last several months, and while I'm not naive enough to think it was this program alone that is responsible for your growth, I'd like to think it certainly helped." He smiled at his own humor.

"Can you tell me what you've learned?" he asked.

"Enough to stop myself from taking another crowbar to someone's car," I deadpanned.

"Fair enough," he conceded. Then his lips formed a hard line, turning serious. "I know it's called anger management, but we do have a lot more to offer than simply teaching you how to manage your anger. We can help you deal with it in a healthy manner so that you can release it. You don't have to live with it, but you have to want to make the change. I can't do it for you."

Ironically the more he talked about dealing with my anger, the angrier I got. I could feel the steam building up inside me.

"Listen, David, I get that it's your job to help me. I do. But I don't need it," I said automatically, defensively.

"I think you do. In fact, I think you might need it more than anyone else here," he paused, waiting for my reaction, but I refused to give him one. Even though it felt like I could physically feel the spike in my cortisol and adrenaline levels preparing me to run away or stand my ground and fight. My vision narrowed, my fingers clenched into fists.

He continued, "And you've got every reason to be

pissed. Probably more than anyone else here. But it's no way to live."

I couldn't take his patronizing tone any longer.

Keeping my voice threatening low, I said, "You're damn right I have every reason to be angry, and I am. And the truth is, I like being angry. I'm comfortable with angry. Because it's something I've known my whole life. I embrace my anger, I revel in it," I sneered. "Because if I can keep it tucked away inside of me, than I won't lose him."

The words fell heavy in the room, and the following silence reverberated with the weight of them.

I flew up from the chair, hastily grabbed my purse, and made a beeline for the door. Already knowing that I was ruining my chances of ever getting my job back, but not able to control myself. I wasn't going to be able to fake my way through it like I thought I could.

I heard David's voice over the sound of my footsteps. "It doesn't work like that," he said, making me stop momentarily in my tracks. "Anger like that, so poisonous and toxic, cannot be contained or compartmentalized. It'll spill over into other areas of your life—your work, your relationships, your thoughts. You won't be able to stop it. It will destroy you."

I didn't let David see the battling emotions, or tears, written clearly across my face as I walked down the hallway and slammed the doors open. Fresh, cold air burned my lungs as I gulped in the oxygen.

"What the hell happened in there?" Samara asked,

leaning against the wall, smoking a cigarette.

I wiped my face and turned to her.

"That's a good look on you," she said, gesturing with her cigarette.

"Is it the runny mascara or the blotchy skin that seals the deal?"

"Oh, definitely the mascara."

I couldn't help but let out a dry laugh.

"You ready?" I asked with a sigh.

"Ready as sin on a Saturday night," she said, crushing out her cigarette.

I rolled my eyes at her. "I'll meet you at the house."

Several hours later, all of Samara's furniture and boxes had been unloaded off three different pick-up trucks and a large minivan and moved into the house.

"Thanks a lot, Tommy," Samara waved to the last of the convoy drivers, a tall, gangly cook from the casino kitchen.

"Ain't no prob, Boss Lady," he drawled. "See you on shift tomorrow."

I stood in the dining room, taking inventory of all her boxes.

"How did you get all of them to do this for you?" I asked of the six young men who helped move her stuff in.

She shrugged. "When you're decent to people, especially the people who work underneath you, it has a way of coming back to you."

I nodded. "So what's first? I already have all the kitchen stuff," I said, looking into some boxes filled with pots and pans. "I don't think there's any more room in there anyway."

"Got any storage space for the extra stuff?" Samara asked.

"Sure, in the basement."

"Fine by me."

It took us twenty minutes to move all the extra boxes downstairs. We then started on the boxes that actually belonged in her room.

"For someone who's hinted at a nomadic lifestyle, you sure have a lot of shit," I said, panting at the top of the stairs.

"Well, I wasn't about to let Bryan keep all my stuff now, was I?"

"I guess not."

Later that evening, we sat on the living room floor, exhausted, working on the large pepperoni pizza we'd had delivered.

"What'd you think about the session today?" Samara asked innocently enough.

I took another sip of my beer, trying to avoid the question. When I looked over, she was staring at me expectantly with a smug look on her face.

"What are you afraid of, girl? Answer the question."

"I don't want to talk about it." My mind was still

reeling. I hadn't quite come to a coherent conclusion yet.

"Okay, well I said in class that I wanted to control my anger because I wanted to get my life in order. But honestly," she said with a low sigh. "I don't want to be alone forever."

I was caught off guard by her sudden admission. "Me neither."

I thought about Madison. I thought about Logan and my dad and Sophie. I thought about Tony Cusato. I thought about my work. I thought about Harry. I thought about Michael.

"The people in my life," I finally said, "they've stood by me through all my bullshit. They deserve better. I get that. But I've held on to my anger for so long that I feel like it's a part of me. It's hard to let it go. I don't know if I can. At the same time, I can't lose another important person in my life. What if I did something stupid, and Logan or Brooke decided they wouldn't let me see Maddie anymore? Or what if I lost my job? Being a front desk secretary is torture enough but losing my career altogether?" I shook my head.

"Well, what's your anger doing for you?" Samara asked.

"I already had enough of David for one day, thank you."

"I'm being serious," she said softly.

And I responded in kind. "It keeps me connected to Michael."

"How? I look at all these pictures of you two on the walls, and I assume your relationship wasn't built on anger or hate?"

"No, of course not. I loved him more than anything."

"So explain to me how holding on to your anger connects you to him? That doesn't make any sense."

Samara paused then picked up where she left off. Her voice was quiet but full of conviction. "You know what I think? I think anger is what makes you feel alive. It's so overpowering that it numbs your pain. Because it's better to feel something than nothing, right?"

I studied the lines of the hardwood floor beneath me, tracing the straight edges with my finger.

I listened as Samara continued, "I've never lost someone like you have, but I know what it feels like to be boxed into a corner. The only way to fight your way out is with rage. Pure unadulterated rage. But once you're out of the corner ... the very thing that broke you free becomes your prison. When I look at you, I see someone who is strong and passionate and has suffered a lot. But I also see someone who refuses to let go of the type of anger that can only lead to self-destruction."

My stomach plummeted and I felt like I was free falling down a deep dark pit to my death. Samara was right.

"So what do I do?"

"Shit if I know," she said, leaning back into the couch.

XXII

Stay

Two weeks had passed since my date with Logan. We had gone out a few more times since then—to the movies, to a casual dinner, we even took Madison bowling. We hadn't explained anything to her yet, since we didn't know what to tell her.

Logan had told Brooke though, and as I suspected she wasn't all that thrilled about it, bringing up a million reasons why it wouldn't work, why I was damaged goods. Logan finally told her that she didn't get a say in it and walked away from her, her mouth hanging open in disbelief.

We were slowly integrating into each other's lives. Now, instead of only seeing Logan on Tuesdays and Thursdays, he would come over on some of the nights he didn't have Madison, and we usually did something together on the weekends. Sometimes it was all three of us; sometimes it was just the two of us. Sometimes we would walk downtown and get coffee; sometimes we would stop by a bar for a drink after work. Once we even went grocery shopping together. And strangely enough, that was the time I liked the most. I enjoyed all the new date stuff too, but it was the routine, everyday events that mattered more to me: driving in the car with Logan, talking to him about his day, walking the dog together.

I was getting to know the side of Logan that he usually kept hidden; he was getting to know the side of me that wasn't just his best friend's girl. He was getting to know me as a person, an individual. I was getting to know that person too.

Living with Samara was turning out to be easier than I thought it would be. I found that I liked having her around, even if it was just knowing she was asleep in the other room. The few evenings we had been home together, we opened up a bottle of wine and sat in front the TV watching *The Voice*, cheering on our favorite teams, and making predictions.

It was comforting to see her to-go containers on the shelf when I opened the fridge, and I appreciated it when she let Scout out during the day.

But what I liked about Samara more than anything else was that she respected boundaries. We hadn't talked much about the heavy-duty conversation we'd had the weekend she moved in, and she hadn't pried further. She knew when to let things be.

At the moment it felt like I was living in two separate worlds—anger management and everything else. In the former I was angry and confused and suddenly lost again. The other world, with Logan and Maddie, was peaceful and loving. In that world, even at work, I was happy to not think about my unresolved feelings and issues. But I knew it wouldn't be long until those two worlds collided. They were already touching on the edges.

The following Tuesday night, I was falling asleep on Logan's couch when he came home from class.

From the living room, I could hear him rummaging around the refrigerator, and he came out holding a beer. Sitting down heavily in the chair, he casually asked me, "So what do you have planned for Thanksgiving?"

"Thanksgiving?" I responded absentmindedly. "Hmm, I don't know. Probably just go to my dad's and hang out with him, watch the football game. How about you?"

"My mom always hosts Thanksgiving for the family. Maddie and I are going over there in the morning so my mom can spend time with her before Brooke gets her in the afternoon. Maddie's staying with Brooke all weekend."

"All weekend?" I said with skepticism.

"Thursday through Sunday," Logan confirmed.

"Is Maddie going to make it that long? When's the last time she's been away from you for four days in a row?"

"She'll be all right," he shrugged.

"Don't sound too excited," I mocked him.

"I'm not saying I won't miss her, but she needs to spend time with her mom."

"And you need time to sleep in and play video games," I teased light-heartedly.

"Well I'm certainly not going to complain about that," he said with a grin on his face.

I laughed at him. "So who all is going to be at your mom's?"

"My sister and her family. Most of my aunts and uncles and cousins."

"Sounds festive."

"You and your dad are more than welcome to come with."

At first I thought he was just being polite, but when he didn't say anything further, just looked at me waiting for a response, I said, "You're serious?"

"Hey, there's no obligation or anything. Just a friendly offer."

"Thanks, but I think I need to keep it low-key this year," I said.

I couldn't shake the knot in my stomach that tightened at the thought of my first Thanksgiving without

Michael. Sue had invited Dad and me over a few weeks ago. Despite her well-intentioned efforts, I just wasn't up for pretending we were still one big happy family. And even though I knew I wouldn't accept Logan's invitation, there was a part of me that wanted to.

Thanksgiving Day passed slowly and quietly. Throughout the morning, Dad and I worked in the kitchen preparing the food—a small turkey, mashed potatoes, corn, gravy, stuffing, and rolls—as we watched the parades, and Scout paced the kitchen, begging for a scrap of food.

The meal was more than enough food for the two of us, but it was nothing compared to the feast I had gotten used to with Michael's family. And when the food was ready and laid out on the table, set for two, the room felt lonely and sparse in comparison.

I was dizzy with trying to figure out how to deal with all the different emotions I was feeling. Moving on was like walking a tightrope—it was a struggle to keep my balance, find my center, and gain control. Each time I'd get closer to Logan, there was something to remind me of losing Michael and bring me down.

Over dinner, Dad and I kept the conversation light: work, the insanity that was Black Friday shopping, whether I had started Christmas shopping yet.

The Charm Necklace

"I talked to Sue and Sophie this morning," I told Dad.

"Oh?" his eyebrows drew up in surprise. "How're they doing?"

"Good," I shrugged. "Sue was busy in the kitchen, as usual. She not so subtly reminded me that we were more than welcome to stop by."

"Hmm," Dad mumbled, taking a bite of turkey.

"And, of course, Sophie begged us to come."

Dad laughed.

"It was good to hear their voices," I said. "You know I'll always care about them. No matter what."

"Well I'm sure they appreciated hearing from you," he paused to take another bite of turkey. "What's that new roommate of yours up to today?"

"She went to her brother's house in Grand Rapids. She's staying the night there."

"Am I ever going to get to meet her? I'm starting to think you made her up."

"I assure you the $500 she paid for this month's rent isn't imaginary," I threw back at him with humor. "Don't worry, I'm sure you'll meet her eventually. Besides, what do you want me to do, invite her over for dinner?"

"Why not?"

"Dad! I'm not dating her," I said exasperated.

"Speaking of which, are you ever going to bring Logan over here?"

"Oh my God," I said with an affectionate eye roll. "If

you don't stop, I'm going to sign you up for eHarmony without you knowing. Then we'll see who *you* bring home to dinner."

"You better not," he grumbled under his breath.

The quiet that fell over the house after dinner, while we watched the football game, was restful. But the cold, lingering hollowness was still with me. As the second quarter started, my thoughts turned to Logan. I wondered what he was doing right now. Was he still at his mom's house? Was he having a good time? Was he thinking about me at all? What was his favorite holiday food?

I vaguely remembered what Logan's mom was like: calm, reserved, and soft-spoken. I knew that she hadn't remarried after Logan's dad died. I wondered if she was happy.

I wondered what his mom's house was like. I pictured it being spacious and inviting like pages out of a Pottery Barn catalog. I pictured Logan sitting at a big dining room table with his family. I pictured how handsome he probably looked dressed up in a sweater with slim-fitting khakis, his long brown hair sweeping across his forehead, his blue eyes watching intently. My heart warmed at the image.

I wanted to be there next to Logan, his arm around my shoulders, me leaning into him. I wanted to hug Maddie to my chest, experience Thanksgiving with them both, belong. But it was hard to belong if you've already given yourself to someone else.

It was six in the evening and already dark as I left my dad's. I told myself I was just going to drive by Logan's, see if he was home. I wasn't going to go in or see him today, wasn't even going to call him.

Yeah, I didn't believe myself either. Why else would I have intentionally left Scout at Dad's house?

Holidays have a way of bringing buried feelings back to the surface. Things you can ignore in your regular day-to-day life become poignant and acute through the lens of important dates and celebrations. The void that Michael's death left called for something to counter this sadness. I needed to feel something bright, something golden and luminous.

And I missed Michael. God, I missed him. But those feelings bled and mixed with the longing I had for Logan so that it was getting hard for me to tease the two apart.

I wished Michael were here, but I wanted to see Logan. I knew that if I could just see Logan, talk to him that I wouldn't feel so lost.

I saw Logan's car parked in his usual spot when I pulled in front of the townhouse. I got out of the car and quickly walked up to the door, but it was locked. Through the curtains the apartment looked dark and I couldn't see anything. I stood there for a minute, dumbly looking at the door, unsure about what to do. But then I remembered that I had a spare key. I fumbled through my keys, found it, and clicked the locks open.

It was quiet when I walked in.

"Logan?" I whispered, shutting the door behind me.

I walked slowly and softly down the hallway to Logan's half-opened door. The orange glow from the streetlamp softly illuminated the room through the open curtains. I could see Logan asleep on the bed, tangled in blankets, his stomach pressed against the mattress. I stood there in the doorway, watching him breathe slowly and deeply. There was something so intimate and so innocent about seeing him lost in dreams, eyes closed in sleep.

I wondered how long he had been napping. He couldn't have gotten home that long ago; he must've been exhausted if he had fallen asleep that quickly.

I scanned Logan's room. For all the time I had spent in his apartment, I had never spent any amount of time in here, never had a reason too. On the nightstand next to the bed there was a lamp, an alarm clock that glowed 6:30, and a stack of books. *Of course there were books*, I thought, smiling.

After a minute, I turned to leave the room and let him sleep when I heard him move, the blanket and sheets rustling slightly.

"Sky?" he whispered, confused. "Is that you?"

"Sorry, I didn't mean to wake you," I said, facing him. "I just wanted to see you."

"I'm glad you came," he said, sitting up against the pillows.

He looked even more handsome now than he had in

my thoughts earlier. His blue eyes were foggy with sleep and his body was relaxed.

I felt that pull towards him again. I sat down next to him on the edge of the bed.

"How was your Thanksgiving?" I asked, reaching forward to put my hand on his.

"It was pretty good," he said grinning. "Though it would've been better if you had been there with us."

"I'm here now," I said, pausing, looking down at our hands. I could feel his eyes on my face. "It was lonely today, just me and Dad. I was expecting it to be…quiet," I said hesitantly, searching for the word. "But I didn't think it would be so depressing."

Logan nodded, entwining his fingers through mine and squeezing.

"The first few holidays are always the hardest," he said softly. "It gets better."

"All day I just couldn't stop thinking about you," I admitted. "I just wanted to be with you."

"Me too."

He leaned forward putting his hand around the back of my neck and pulling me closer to him. He looked into my eyes, and as my heart raced, as time seemed to stop, I knew without a doubt that I was falling in love with him.

He wanted me. And I wanted him.

He closed his eyes and pressed his lips against mine, moving both his hands around my face. I pressed closer into him, my hands gripping his shoulders. We kissed deeply and I lost all track of the heaviness of the day, of the past, of where we were heading. I was lost in the desperation of Logan's kisses, the tenderness of his fingers caressing my cheeks, the warmth filling my body.

My head was swimming and I needed to come up for air. I needed to breathe. I pulled away from Logan, his hands falling away from me.

"Logan, I—I," I stammered, confused. I wanted this so badly, why was I pulling away from him? The one good thing that had happened to me since Michael—.

Michael's name echoed in my head, bouncing around my mind. That's why. I was scared. I was scared of what this would mean, of betraying Michael despite everyone else telling me it was okay, of not being able to give Logan my whole heart.

"I'm not enough," I whispered into the dim room.

"You are," Logan said huskily.

I looked away from him, toward the door.

Sensing the tightness in my muscles, the compulsion to run, Logan grabbed onto my arm, his long fingers overlapping around my wrist. His hand was hot against my skin, burning.

"Stay," he urged, his eyes glittering with intensity. "Don't leave me."

We looked at each other, searching for the words as the tension in the air grew.

Logan moved forward, onto his knees so that he was kneeling above me. He pushed back a strand of hair from my face and gently pulled me up. I felt his fingers under my chin as he lifted my face until our eyes met.

"You know how I feel about you, right?" he asked, resting his free hand lightly on my hip, the other still on my face.

I felt my skin flush with heat.

"You are…," he started to say, then ran his tongue over his lips in concentration. I could see his chest rising and falling as he slowed his breathing. He spoke again slowly, enunciating each word. "You are so fucking *real* to me. You've brought me back, Sky. I don't think you understand how much that means to me. How much *you* mean to me."

I was speechless, my breath caught in my throat. The room started to feel small and hot. I was light-headed with emotion.

"You trust me right?" he asked.

I nodded.

"Then let me in," he implored. "Let me make it better. Let me love you."

"Oh, Logan," I whispered. The war raged inside me. Fear fought with desire. Guilt with anger. Grief with love. In the time that my emotions battled, I said nothing, and I didn't trust the expression on my face. Logan's look of expectancy turned into disappointment and hurt.

In that moment, when I saw Logan's eyes close in the pain of rejection, something inside me snapped and any hesitation I had gave way. I gave in to reckless surrender.

I threw my arms around Logan and pressed my lips to his neck, kissing just under his ear. He drew in a sharp breath, and his hands tightened on my hips. "I want you," I said. "I need you."

"Sky—," he started to say.

I pressed my finger against his lips. "Just kiss me."

He responded, kissing me hungrily. Hands, slowly at first, were touching, feeling, caressing, and then there were too many layers of clothing separating us.

I pulled off Logan's thin T-shirt and he removed my heavy sweater. His skin was smooth against mine and our mouths were touching again, consuming each other, his tongue wrapped in mine.

I groaned into his mouth, his hands in my hair. I trailed my nails down his back and he pulled me back onto him.

His hands reached up the backs of my legs, my butt, my back, and to my bra clasp. I shivered at his touch, needing it. He unhooked the bra and tossed it off, not paying attention to anything but me.

He made me feel beautiful. When he looked at me, he really saw me. He saw through the pain, the walls, the heartache, and he saw that there was someone there on the other side. Someone worth fighting for.

He traced his fingertips over my chest, and I leaned forward so his lips touched my neck, my shoulder, the rise of my breast, finally finding my nipple.

I hugged his head to my chest and I was high.

Effervescent. Infallible. Drunk with passion, desire, and longing.

Then his hands were fumbling with the button on my jeans. I followed his lead and pulled his sweats off. He lowered me onto my back and pulled off my pants. I reached for him, and then he was on top of me, holding me down. He kissed me deeply, his hips pressing into mine.

Logan broke our kiss and I was so lost in the moment that I didn't catch the concerned look on his face. I just kept kissing his jaw, his neck. I ran my hands over his smooth skin, my fingertips memorizing every curve and scar.

When I realized he had stopped, I pulled away from him. "What's wrong?"

"I don't have any…protection," he said, groaning and dropping his head into his chest.

"It's okay," I said, looking up at him, pushing the hair out of his eyes. I felt splendidly vulnerable as he looked down at me. "I never went off the pill."

"Are you sure?" he asked.

"Please," I whispered. "I trust you."

He looked at me for just a second. Reconfirming my permission, I nodded.

The urgency in his movements startled me as he pushed backwards onto his knees, pulling off my underwear, kicking off his boxers.

Then he was moving slowly as he lowered himself back between my legs and gently pushed into me. I gasped in a mixture of excitement and relief.

I was only aware of the closeness of our bodies and his touch. His hands on my thighs, gripping me closer to him. My arms wrapped around his back, my hands in his hair, my lips on his neck, my legs wrapped around his.

And we were there, together, just me and him. No one else existed, nothing else mattered. We were connected in every possible way. The threads of our lives were weaving us together.

Logan moved above me, in me. We rocked together. I felt him move faster, deeper. He laced his fingers through mine and pressed me into the bed. His lips were on mine and he was pouring himself into me. Then I felt him shudder and groan, relax into me, his head tucked into my neck.

We lay there breathing slowly, our bodies hot and shimmery. I kissed the top of his head, his hairline, his temples.

After a moment, Logan moved and lay down next to me. "Are you okay?" he asked, running his hand down the length of my arm.

I nodded slowly. "I just need to use the bathroom real fast," I said. I got up quickly, grabbed Logan's shirt off the floor, and darted into the bathroom, closing the door behind me.

After I had cleaned up, I stood in front of the mirror, drying my hands. I was naked; my long hair disheveled and knotted, my body trembling. I studied my reflection: there was weariness in my dark brown eyes, red blotches on my face from Logan kissing me; my skin felt flushed, but I was smiling. I hadn't felt this *vibrant* in a long time.

Logan knocked softly on the door. "Hey, everything all right?"

I threw on the tee and opened the door. Seeing him there, looking at me expectantly with only his boxers on, his hair a mess and his chest exposed, I couldn't help but smile at him.

"Come here," he said and pulled me into a hug, his arms enveloping me.

It felt so right being in his arms, being with him. It didn't make sense how right it felt.

"Logan?" I whispered.

"Hmm?"

"Let's go back to bed."

He pulled back slightly and kissed my forehead, then took my hand and led me back to his room. We crawled into bed, and he pulled the covers over us. I moved so my back was against his chest, our legs bent together, his arms around me.

He turned on the TV, flipping through the channels until he came to a Christmas movie. "This all right?" he asked.

"Sure."

We settled into each other, watching the movie, secluded and safe.

My eyes were growing heavy and my body warm with

comfort, but before I could completely give in to sleep, I whispered, "Logan?"

"Hmm?"

"What's your favorite Thanksgiving food?"

His lips moved against the back of my head as he spoke. "My mom's baked macaroni and cheese. Why?"

I shrugged, "Just curious."

"What's yours?" he asked.

"Mashed potatoes. Or pie. It's a tie."

Logan squeezed me gently, and I soaked up his body—the shape of his muscles, the wall of his chest behind me. And that's how we stayed all night, completely unaware of the world outside the bedroom.

XXIII

Jump

The next morning I woke up in a haze. Clean white daylight spilled in through the window, and I wasn't in my bed. I sat up slowly, my left shoulder stiff from sleeping on it. The sheets and blankets were tangled around me. The TV was off, and I was alone.

I reached my hand out to feel the spot Logan had slept in. As I ran my fingers over the soft indented fabric, the warmth from his body still lingering there, I thought about the night before.

I thought about the bareness of Thanksgiving day—the festive glow absent from the holiday without Michael there, without his family. Although there had been a simplicity to the day with just Dad and me, there had also been a sharp longing for more—more people, more celebration, more life.

I drew my knees into my chest. Last night Logan had been present, aware, intimately engaged in a way Michael never had been. Michael was a physical creature. He had been attuned to the way our bodies moved together, the feel of skin, the sound of sighs, always direct and in command. It was what I was used to. It was how I learned to love.

Logan was something else entirely. It was like he knew how it *felt*, what it meant, why it mattered. He was soulful and sincere.

The way our bodies had joined together…. I hadn't expected it to be so seamless, so easy and natural.

Michael had been bigger than Logan, solidly built with broad shoulders, and when we were together I remember the feeling of strength and action. Logan was more lean and fluid, his muscles long and ropy under my fingertips. He surrendered himself to me. It was pure intimacy, as if our souls had been wrapped together, touching on some spiritual dimension outside the physical realm.

I had always reacted to Michael, more following his actions than us moving in unison. With Logan, we moved in sync. Give-and-take. Equals.

And in the cold bright light of morning I felt the gravity of what we had done. I had just slept with someone who wasn't Michael. And I was scared at how absolute it felt.

My chest squeezed and contracted, the icy dread of doubt spreading throughout my body. Slowly, like gears turning in a clock, I felt the tsunami of emotion that had been building up finally come crashing down. Muddled, uncontrollable tears seared down my face.

I was angry at the sudden doubt I felt because what had happened with Logan had been beautiful and healing in a way I didn't know love could be. I was angry at the guilt I felt; that I could feel such happiness and bliss from someone other than Michael. Angry because I was so tired of feeling sad. Angry because I never would have been in this situation if it weren't for Tony Cusato and his damn cell phone. I was terrified of the heartbreaking reality that I would have to walk away from the only good thing in my life; because as much as I wanted to, I didn't think it was possible to let go of all my anger, and I wouldn't bring Logan down with me.

And all that anger, consuming and wild, cut me up inside like sharpened blades with crooked, rusted edges.

I jumped out of bed, needing to be anywhere but where I was, and dressed quickly. I wasn't sure where Logan went, but I wanted to leave without him knowing. He couldn't know how much of a mistake this had been. I was already going to hurt him enough.

Tears streaming down my face, I pulled on my jacket and slipped into the hallway. I moved as quietly as I could, but as I passed the kitchen Logan saw me.

"Good morn—," he started to say, but stopped abruptly when he saw my face. He slammed his coffee cup down on the counter and came after me.

My heart throttled in my chest. I willed myself not to meet his gaze, not to turn to look at him. I headed straight to the door, but he was right behind me. When I went to open the door, Logan's hand reached over my shoulder and pressed against the door, blocking me in. I started to panic, but my body wouldn't move.

"No," Logan insisted, his breath hot on my ear, his body trembling waves of fear and disbelief. "Please, don't do this, Skylar."

With my back still to him, I sniffed, wiping my nose on my jacket sleeve. "Do what?" I asked, buying time, trying to avoid hurting his feelings, trying to wade through the overload of emotion surging through my body.

"Don't leave. Don't walk away from me."

"I—I was just going to go pick up Scout," I said, failing at nonchalance. "My Dad's expecting me."

"No, you weren't," he said, his voice high and tight. I heard him swallow, feeling his anxiety.

"Yes, I was."

"Then why are you crying? Why were you trying to sneak past me?"

"I—I...," I stammered, coming up empty-handed.

Logan grabbed the back of my arm and turned me around, my back pressed against the door. I diverted my gaze, not wanting to look at him, afraid that if I did I wouldn't have the strength to leave.

"Look at me," he whispered.

I hesitated. But when I did, his eyes were wild with

fear and panic. He felt me giving up.

"Aren't we worth fighting for?" he asked, his voice steeped in urgency.

I looked into his eyes. I had conflicting desires. I wanted to fight. I wanted to win the fight. But I also wanted to run.

"Kiss me," he all but begged, his voice deep and raw.

I was paralyzed, but Logan grabbed my arms and pulled me into him. He started kissing me desperately, searching for a response.

I was so tempted to give in to him. I wanted to so badly. But I felt those gut-wrenching stabs in my stomach and held on to the pain to give me strength. *I have to do this. For him. He doesn't deserve the pain that a life with me would cause him.*

Reminding myself how lost I was, how I was too far gone for anyone to save, I became resistant and unyielding to Logan's pleas. He tried harder, curving his body into mine, and I stiffened, straightening up. He held my arms, tears starting to fall from his eyes, his body tensing with the buildup of heartbreak.

My heart breaking, again tearing into pieces.

Logan.

Michael.

Anger.

Logan pulled his lips away from mine, and kept his gaze on the ground. "Why are you doing this?"

I didn't know how to answer.

"Why did you come over here last night? Just to be cruel?" his voice grated.

"No!" I protested. "I—I," my voice dropped off. What I had said to him last night—that I wanted him, that I needed him—it hadn't been a lie. But how could I admit that to him and then just walk away?

"What are you running away from?" he demanded. "Give me something, Skylar. Talk to me."

So I went for the low blow. The one thing he would understand.

"Michael—," the name caught in my throat.

Logan's eyes were filled with pain as he exhaled.

"He was my best friend, Skylar. You don't think I haven't felt conflicted about this?" He stepped back from me, pacing, running his hands through his hair.

His voice was low, "I know I can't compare to him. I know that what you guys had was once in a lifetime. What we have must feel like a fraction of what you and Mike had. I know you could never love me as much as you loved him."

"Stop," I pleaded, because it wasn't true, not anymore. New tears spilled out from my eyes. I felt like the room was spinning around us, everything but me and him a blur.

Logan stopped pacing and faced me. His face contorted in anguish. "But it doesn't change how I feel about you. No matter how messy this is, I keep coming back to you."

"Last night was so...right. How? How can it feel so good if I still love Michael? How do we fit together so well?" I cried. I hated that I was questioning everything about my relationship with Michael.

Logan stepped away from me, watching me intensely, not sure how to respond.

I started again abruptly, everything I was afraid of bubbling up, "If I belong to you that means I don't belong to Michael anymore." A beat. "I'm afraid to let him go."

"But you have been, Skylar," he said emphatically, stepping back toward me. "You have been moving on, whether you want to admit it or not." He looked me in the eye. "You will always love him. And so will I," he said, pointing to himself. "That kind of love doesn't just go away.

"But Michael's gone," he said his voice cracking with sadness. "He was. He used to be. He isn't any longer. I wish so much it weren't true. What I wouldn't give so that he could be here with us. But he's not here, he's not coming back," Logan paused for a moment. His words echoed in my mind, tugging at the memory of that day in the field.

"I know," I said, taking a deep breath. Then in a whisper, "But it's not just about him." The truth was finally going to come out. I couldn't run away from it any longer

Relief, disbelief, and uncertainty crossed Logan's features.

"I'm a ticking time bomb, Logan," I said, yearning for him to understand, to somehow fix the situation. "I haven't been able to move past what happened. My anger is going to destroy me, and if I don't leave now, it's going to destroy you too."

My body shook violently and I could feel my face contorting.

Logan reached out to me, but I smacked his hands away.

"No," I said, my voice rough as gravel. "You don't understand."

"Yes, I do," his voice forceful, his eyes blazing. "You're the one who doesn't get it."

I was stunned into silence.

"You've been holding on to all this anger. You think I don't see it, but I do. You're angry because just as you thought you were going to get everything you've ever wanted, it was taken away from you. You're angry because you feel like nothing ever works out the way you want it to. If you think I'm a stranger to that kind of rage, you're wrong."

I roughly wiped away the tears on my face.

"But you're failing to see how far you've come. You say you don't know if you can let go of Mike, but you have been. You say you can't stop being angry, but I can see you changing. I can see it in your smile, hear it in your laugh, even your eyes are more peaceful. You're ready."

His voice was deep and full, "You've already proven to me that you're capable of it. You're capable of loving me. My daughter. You want this as much as I do. I know you do. You belong here, with me, with us. I know it, and you know it too. That's why you came here last night. That's why it felt so right."

Logan placed his hands on either side of my shoulders and looked down at me. "You've got to choose which side is going to win. You can walk out this door right now and give in to all that bitterness and resentment. And that will be your life. You'll be alone and miserable. Or you can choose to let the anger go."

"It's not that easy," I said, feeling defeated. I tucked my chin into my chest.

"No, it's not." Logan placed one of his palms against my cheek, turning my gaze toward him. "But you, you make me feel things I didn't think I was capable of feeling anymore. After everything with Brooke and losing Mike, you make me feel alive again. With you here, I'm not just aimlessly wandering, waiting for something to happen. With you, my life makes sense and has meaning. You hold everything together. Please, Sky. Don't walk away. I need you."

Then he continued in a whisper, "Let me in, Sky. Let me help you."

He looked at me intensely. I could see his longing for me in his eyes. I could see that he meant every word that he said.

"Why?" I asked.

"Because you're worth it, Skylar. You're worth fighting for."

"Why? Why am I worth anything?" I cried.

"Because, goddamn it, I love you. Why can't you see that?" he said, his voice rising.

"Y-y-you do?" I stammered.

"Yeah. I do," he said, his eyes going soft, but his voice holding firm.

I knew these next moments would define the rest of my life. Logan was right. My obsession with Michael's death was no longer all-consuming, and Logan was here, right in front of me. He wanted me. He knew the painful truth about everything, and yet, he was still asking me to let him in. Logan loved *me*. All the broken parts included.

Logan saw an opening and continued passionately, "I want to be with you every day until forever. I want to wake up every morning and have you next to me. I want to call you from the grocery store to see what you need me to pick up. I want to give you everything that was taken away from you. If you want a farmhouse in the country, I'll do whatever I can to make it happen. You want to have a baby? We can make that happen too. You want to get married? Just tell me the time and place. I'll do whatever it takes. But you have to be all in."

My mind raced. Logan's words swirled around in my head. Could I do it? Could it be done? Could I begin again with Logan? Could I let the anger go and not look back?

"Logan," I breathed.

I closed my eyes. I was at my very edge. It was from that precarious place that I considered all the people and events that had led me to this single defining moment. My mom's death, lonely teenage years, Michael, Sophie, the accident, my Dad, Tony Cusato's car, anger management, my job, Madison, the apple orchard, Logan, Shane, laughter, Samara, Logan.

Understanding filled my consciousness and I started to accept what I hadn't been able to accept before now: *the crash that killed Michael was an accident.* Tony Cusato was just a kid who had done the wrong thing at the wrong time. He hadn't meant for the accident to happen. Now and for the rest of his life, Tony Cusato would have to live with the fact that he had killed someone.

In that space of milliseconds, I felt nothing but humanity toward him. That kid didn't deserve what happened any more than I had.

Somewhere from deep inside of me, I heard Michael's voice, the prompt I was looking for. "It's time now, Skylar. Trust him. Take a chance. It's time to let go."

And that's when I fully understood that my anger was never going to bring Michael back. It wasn't going to change anything. It was only going to make me lose everyone I loved. I wouldn't pay the price anymore.

Logan leaned in, wrapping both hands around my neck, lifting my head up toward his. Our foreheads touched, and Logan fingered the charms resting against my chest.

Sky," he said, "you're so much stronger than you think you are."

I had always been convinced that my life was predestined to be filled with bad things and heartache, no matter what I did. But the truth, I realized now, was that I was the only thing standing in the way of my own happiness. Horrible, dark things happened but I had the power not to be enslaved by them. I had the choice to break free of those bonds.

I hadn't deserved all the loss and suffering I'd endured over the course of my life, but I knew I was strong enough now to love again, strong enough to allow myself to be vulnerable. I was strong enough to let go and let Logan in.

Knowing this, without a parachute or bungee cord, I jumped.

Peace filled my heart.

"I love you," I said absolutely, throwing my arms around Logan's neck. "I'm in. I'm all in."

Logan sank into me as if the weight of the world had been lifted off his shoulders.

"I'm so sorry," I whispered into his ear.

"We're going to be okay," he shushed me.

I pulled back to look at him, my sight blurry with tears, smiling, "We are, aren't we?"

Logan led me back to his bed. This time we took our time. Moving slowly and sensually, together as one. Fingertips trailing on soft skin, kisses caressing and soothing. It was like we were healing each other with every kiss, every touch, every smile, every laugh, and every tear.

Hope. Rebuilding. Restoring.

Becoming more and more familiar with Logan's body—his skin beneath my fingers, how he felt, how he tasted, and how forever would feel with him.

XXIV

Letting Go

February 23, 2013

No one said a word as we drove slowly through the winding path to Michael's grave. Logan was in the passenger seat next to Dad. I sat in the back next to Sophie and stared out the window.

I thought about how a year had passed—a year since Michael died, a year since my whole world turned upside down. As much as I didn't want to believe it, each passing day made it more real. So much had changed in the last few months.

On the last day of anger management class, I walked in feeling lighter than I had in a long time. As I sat next to Samara, I didn't feel unsettled as we went around the room and shared our most difficult moments of the course and the lessons we would carry with us. When it was my turn to speak, I folded my hands in my lap and sighed deeply.

"When I was seven, my mom died. I carried my anger like a badge of honor without even realizing it. I decided I was going to be strong and independent. I wasn't going to need anyone."

I shook my head. "At least that was my plan until Michael came along. He was just so good and loved so freely that my anger no longer seemed to define me. I had him. I had my future with him. I was finally going to have the family I never had growing up.

"When Michael died, my anger resurfaced with a vengeance. It consumed me and I let it because what else did I have? At least I knew this demon. I understood it.

"But the thing is that death exists. It's real. Pain is real. Bad things happen and good things come to an end. But that doesn't mean that life is over. Or that those good things aren't worth fighting for.

"So I guess what I'm saying is you have to open yourself up to the vulnerability of getting hurt in order to get to the good stuff. You can't just pretend or hide behind a wall. You have to confront the dark, scary parts of yourself to grow and to live. And you absolutely have to let go of the anger because it stops you from truly loving.

"And I know now that I want love in my life more than anything else." I turned toward David and beamed a smile filled with gratitude.

I owed him so much. David was the one to challenge me and push me to the edge of my anger. It was because of his recommendation that I was able to return to my old job at the beginning of December, working with the detectives.

My first Christmas season without Michael had been bittersweet, but the sting of the blow had been lessened by Logan's patience and Maddie's fascination with Christmas lights and *Rudolph the Red-Nosed Reindeer*.

During the month of December I had leaned on Logan, and he had carried me through. There were times when I would grow quiet, and Logan wouldn't say a word as I momentarily withdrew into myself remembering Michael. But I would always come around, and Logan would squeeze my hand. Then we would continue doing whatever it was we were doing: Christmas shopping, wrapping presents, watching Christmas movies, attending holiday parties.

I brought the majority of my Christmas decorations over to Logan's apartment, and we spent a weekend with Maddie putting up ornaments, lights, wreaths, village houses, and candles. In the end, it looked like the North Pole had come to Michigan. Every time I walked through the door I was filled with joy and comfort, and I really let myself feel it. Because even though there were moments of sadness, there was also a lot of happiness and cheer.

Since neither one of us were home very often, Samara and I decided to put up just a small Christmas tree with white lights. In honor of our new outlook on life, we bought ribbons—red for me, green for her—and inscribed them with things we were thankful for before tying them to the tree.

Mine said things like Scout, Madison, Logan, family, good beer, my roommate, Christmas cookies, my job, peace, hope, and love.

Samara's said things like a Christmas tree, new beginnings, my new brunette hair color, dark pink lipstick, good friends, trust, companionship, vanilla pudding cups, and happiness.

"It looks good," Samara said, sipping on a glass of wine, standing back from the tree.

I stood next to her and surveyed our work. "It's just enough."

"It's the first Christmas tree I've had since I was five years old," she said.

"It's the first tree I've decorated without Michael in six years," I said.

"To new traditions," she said, clinking her glass against mine.

"To new traditions," I echoed.

Brooke had Maddie Christmas Day, so Logan and I opened presents with Maddie on Christmas Eve, delighting in her excitement, paper flying everywhere.

Christmas Day, Logan and I spent the morning in bed, wrapped in each other, watching *Miracle on 34th Street* as snow fell outside.

When I came back to the bed after getting another cup of coffee, Logan held a small wrapped present on his lap.

"What's this?" I stopped next to the bed and set my mug down on the table.

"It's a present," he said, grabbing my hips and situating me between his legs. "For you."

"For me?" I asked, surprised. I settled my back against his chest. "I thought we already exchanged our gifts."

"This one is special," he said, handing it to me.

I opened it carefully, my anticipation growing. I pulled out a small cardboard box and lifted the lid.

I gasped, bringing my hand to my lips.

"Oh, Logan," I said as my eyes misted over.

There were two charms. One was a silver bird with a long blue-and-green tail and fiery wings. The second one, the one that caught my attention, was a silver bar engraved with the one word that had become my mantra, *Hope*.

Logan's arms snaked around my waist, and he pointed to the bird. "It's a phoenix," he said. "It symbolizes resurrection, life, power, rebirth through fire, triumph."

"Rising from the ashes," I whispered, running my fingers over the beautiful red-and-gold wings.

"It's you," he said into my ear, sending shivers down my back. "Turn it over."

On the reverse there was an inscription: *Only the phoenix rises and does not descend. And everything changes. And nothing is truly lost*—Neil Gaiman.

I felt such overpowering love and adoration. I was at a loss for words.

"I wanted you to have something from me," he said,

"something you can always have."

I turned around to face him. "I want to say thank you, but I don't think that's good enough."

I looked into his blue eyes and felt grounded. I was connected to this beautiful, soulful, sincere person.

I leaned to the side and put my hand behind Logan's neck, pulling his lips toward mine. "I don't think you'll ever know how much I love you."

He just grinned and peppered my face with kisses.

The rest of Christmas day was spent with my dad and then with Logan's family. It had been festive and joyous and warm. And it had felt so incredibly good to be around other people again. It felt good to laugh with them, eat with them, be in their company. The whole time Logan was by my side, never too overbearing, giving me space when I needed it, but always there, unwavering.

At his family's party, as we stood off to the side watching all the younger kids open presents, I whispered to him, "I couldn't have done this alone."

Logan just pulled me closer to him and kissed the side of my forehead. "Me neither," he whispered back.

Getting through the holiday season had been difficult, but when it was over I knew that I had overcome a giant hurdle—that I was one step closer to being okay.

As I stood in front of Michael's grave with Logan, Dad, and Sophie sitting on a bench a few yards behind me, I closed my eyes and felt the wind whip my hair around my face. I kneeled down on the icy ground. The grass was stiff beneath me. My hands were steady as I took a letter out of my pocket and unfolded the pages, worn from handling and tear-smeared ink. I took a deep breath and began to read aloud my words to Michael. The warmth from my breath hung in clouds around my head.

> It's been a year since you've been gone, Michael. And it's been one hell of a year, to say the least. There were times when I didn't think I'd be able to make it through.

My voice caught in my throat as it constricted, trying to stop the oncoming sobs.

> There's not a day that goes by that I don't think about you, but the thoughts don't seem to linger as long as they used to. Often now they're happy thoughts—like things I want to share with you, things I wish you were here to see and experience.
>
> I've gotten better. It didn't happen overnight. The change was so slow it was like watching paint dry or mountains erode. At least, that's what it felt like. A little bit changes every day, but you don't notice it until it accumulates, and suddenly the weight doesn't seem so heavy anymore.
>
> I don't know how we ever comprehend death. How we grasp the fact that a person we love is here one second

and gone the next. I don't think we ever do. We just learn to accept it without fully understanding it. We learn that normal doesn't exist anymore, and our picture of life won't look the same as it did before. But if we look hard enough we'll be able to see that it's not all bad. In fact there's a whole lot of good to be found if we're willing to look.

I don't know where you are now, Michael. I don't know if you're in heaven with God. I don't know if there even is such a place or if God exists, but wherever you are, I hope it's somewhere good. I hope you're happy there. I hope that when you look down and see me, you smile and know that I'm okay.

I'm going to be okay without you. I didn't think I'd ever get to the place where I would be. But I am.

Ever since we were together, I never imagined life without you. I built my dreams around you, around us. I was happy with our small world. I wanted you and me, our family. I wanted to share my life with you. I've learned that you can grow to want new things. There will always be a part of me that wonders what our life would have looked like, but now I have to believe in what Logan and I can have together.

He's not you. No one could ever replace you. But I want you to know that I do really love him. I want you to know that you gave me the greatest gift you ever could have without even knowing it. You brought Logan into my life all those years ago. Without him, I don't know where I'd be today. I know, it caught me by surprise too.

Logan and Madison were my anchors. You'd laugh

if you could see how I am with Madison—how easy and natural. Having her need me is grounding. Not just Madison but Logan too. There have been a lot of things that have happened over the past year that I never would have believed could happen. Madison is one of those things. I never knew I could be captivated by a little girl, but there's just something about her that makes me feel good, makes me remember that we can find happiness in the smallest things.

I'm not sure how it's going to be with your family from here on out. Our relationship has been fragmented since you've left, but I still care about them. I probably won't see them as often as I used to, but with Logan, I'm pretty sure they'll always be in my life. I think I'm finally getting to the point where I know how to have them in my life and go forward at the same time; where I can be with them and your absence isn't the main thing on my mind.

I don't want to disappoint Sophie. She's already lost her brother, I don't want her to lose her sister too.

I'm still upset that you were taken away from me, but it's no longer the living-breathing kind of hate that eats away at you. It's the kind of anger that just wishes you could still be here. I can see now that your death was an accident. No one meant for it to happen.

Logan and I are talking about moving in together. I think I'm going to have to sell the house. I don't know if I can have a life there with anyone other than you, and I don't really think I'd want to. I know we had a lot of dreams for that house, and maybe that's why I have to walk away from it.

And Scout's doing well. He's still big and loud and lovable, but I know he misses you. I know he feels your absence just as much as I do.

Michael, you were one of the greatest things that ever happened to me. And losing you was the hardest thing I've ever had to go through. I don't know how I can ever thank you for all the good things you brought into my life—all the love and light and laughter. You changed me, Michael. You changed my heart and how I saw the world. You made me into the person I was meant to be. You showed me what it meant to live and how to embrace everything life has to offer. You showed me the wonderful things that could happen when you put yourself out there and dared to hope for the best.

I don't know how to end this letter. I don't really want to end this letter, but I have to. Even though you may be physically gone, you will always be in my heart. Please know that I'm happy and I'm okay. And know that I will always love you.

"Bye, Michael," I whispered, standing up.

Logan walked over to me, putting his hand in mine. "You okay?" he asked gently.

I nodded. "I will be."

Logan put his arm around my shoulder and pulled me into him.

"I miss you, brother," he said to Michael. "I'll take good care of her. I promise."

I looked over at Logan, his eyes wet with tears, his face pale from the cold.

It was such a strange feeling. This person who balanced Michael out now held me in balance. He made me feel connected to Michael in a way I never could have imagined. It's like we'd come full circle.

I thought about Michael and Logan. And I thought that maybe I was just lucky enough to have two great loves.

The common bond of losing Michael had only made Logan and I stronger. There were no secrets between us. We didn't hide anything or pretend that we each had a past, our own separate histories. And sometimes, the past directly affected the present, but we could deal with it together.

We could because we were uniquely solid. Not solid in the way that Michael and I had been, unmoving and steady and certain. But solid in that the hottest fires make the hardest steel. The interwoven threads that had made up our friendship, our pasts, and our pain had connected us together. And through the flames of death and heartache, the yielding and flexible material had been transformed into an unbreakable iridium metal, resistant to the corrosion of time and heartbreak of everyday life.

As the four of us walked back to the car, our feet crunching on the frozen ground, I grabbed Sophie's hand. While I knew there would be dark days, the future looked pretty bright.

Here's to Hope
Spring 2014

The following spring as the weather grew warmer and the flowers began to bloom, Logan and I found ourselves standing in front of an old 1940s farmhouse after making the thirty-minute drive to the town of Romeo. The white paint was peeling off the wooden shutters and the siding needed to be replaced, but the foundation was solid, and the lot had plenty of space.

"Five bedrooms, four baths. Two levels with a basement," the Realtor read off the sheet of paper in front of her. "It was originally 1,700 square feet but the previous owners added on another 700." She turned the key in the door and pushed it open. "This is it."

We entered the small foyer. There was a hallway directly in front of us, a front room to our left, and a large wooden staircase that led up to the second floor on the right. "The floors are relatively new, but as you can see, they closely resemble the look of the original hardwood."

We followed her down the hallway to the back of the house, which revealed a great room that was defined by the family room to one side and the kitchen and dining area on the other. A large bank of windows showed the expansive backyard, an open field lined with trees.

"As you can tell, the previous owners expanded the space from the original layout," the Realtor commented. "There are some obvious repairs that need to be taken care of, but nothing that can't be done over time."

I looked over at Logan and smiled. You couldn't put a price on the feelings of peace and overwhelming certainty that filled my heart.

"A girl could breathe out here," I said, looking into the yard.

"It's perfect isn't it?" Logan agreed.

I nodded, placing my hand over my stomach protectively. Inside my belly there grew a life, a growing bud, a girl. A precious baby girl.

"What should we name her?" Logan had asked a month ago when we had found out the sex.

I thought back to that day in the field, the conversation Logan and I had nearly two years ago, fiddling with my necklace. "Hope," I said. "Because I want her to always have it."

Joining me at the window, Logan could see the life we would create here. He could see the swing set and the pond. He could picture riding four-wheelers. He could picture the epic bonfires we would have. He could see the leaves turning golden and russet in autumn, surrounding the property. He could see the blanket of snow covering the house in winter. He could hear the sound of crickets echoing in the summer. He could hear the sound of children's laughter and Scout barking. He could feel the joy, the peace. *This* was the life he had always wanted. Everything before had been a stepping-stone to get to this. This was it.

He squeezed my hand and beamed saying, "We'll take it."

Acknowledgements

First and foremost, I want to thank you - yeah, you, the one who took the time to read this book. Besides for my need to get this story down on paper, my readers have been my biggest motivation. It has been my highest hope to create a story that people could escape in and carry something away from. So thank you, fellow lover of words and adventures and stories for taking a chance on me. If you enjoyed the story, I'd love to hear from you (I'm being completely serious, it's not just a nicety, I'm hardly ever proper or polite when I'm supposed to be). Email me at contact@laurenrosolino.com, tweet me @laurenrosolino or contact me on Facebook.com/laurenrosolino.

A big GIGANTIC thank you to all my friends and family who have supported me throughout this *very* long process. My parents - Gary and JoAnn Lopp, and Kathy and Ron Boreo; my in-laws Gary and Renee Rosolino; my favorite sister-in-law and brother-in-law Stephanie and Matt Bremenour; my siblings (especially Brother Man, Steven); and all my extended family on all sides (there are entirely way too many of you to actually name you all, sorry!).

I also want to thank the best set of friends a girl could ask for: Tijana Radinkovic, Samantha Firestone, Ashley Gordanier, Shelby Kieliszewski, Chelsea Heaton, and Katie Spanos for all of your encouragement and support. You ladies understand me without any judgement, and words cannot express how much that really means to me. Thank you for all your help along the way!

A very voluminous shout-out to my editor, Barbara Bloom, for challenging me, pushing me, and helping me take this story to whole new heights. I cannot thank you enough. This story would not be the same without you.

Thank you to my beta readers: Craig Young, Kathy Boreo, Stephanie Bremenour, and Tijana Radinkovic. Apologies for the torture I put you all through. I owe you guys an alcoholic beverage or two!

Thank you to my cover collaborators - the ingenious photographer and longtime friend Jesse Speelman, and my very attractive and photogenic cover models Justina Smith and Caleb Jesse. Also, thank you to my cousin Holly Miller for enduring the cold with us that day.

I also want to thank Michael O'Malley from Vandeveer Garzia, P.C. - Attorneys and Counselors for letting me question him about all things regarding law and legalities.

And of course, the best for last, I want to thank my wonderful husband Andrew for all his encouragement, understanding, and support. It's your irrational, illogical, crazy love for me that made this all a possibility. I love you, honey bunches of oats.

About Lauren

Author of *The Charm Necklace* and writer of stories about finding beauty in brokenness.

Lauren graduated from Wayne State University with her BA in Psychology and lives in Rochester, MI with her techie husband, dog, cat, and bunny. Lauren grew up in the suburbs of Detroit reading Harry Potter, watching Gilmore Girls, listening (and dancing) to a lot of music, and wondering why people do the things they do.

To find out more about Lauren and *The Charm Necklace* check out www.laurenrosolino.com. You can also find her on Facebook, Twitter, and Pintrest.

Want to know what happens with Skylar and Logan? Go to the *Lost Chapters and Unpublished Extras* tab on the Books page of www.laurenrosolino.com to find out!

Made in the USA
Charleston, SC
19 June 2014